SEPTEMBER THOMAS

Of Monsters and Madness

A Three Kingdoms Novel

First edition

ISBN: 978-1-7342545-6-3

Editing by Fiona McLaren
Cover art by Rebecca Frank
Illustration by Natalia Junqueira

This book was professionally typeset on Reedsy.
Find out more at reedsy.com

To the man who taught me patience and perseverance.
Dad.

Preface

Three kingdoms on the brink of destruction.
Three princes facing down ruinous fates.
These are their stories…
And those of the women who guided the way to glory.

Lexicon & Pronunciation Guide

Seasons

Fret (fret) - Frost/Winter (January to March)

Rapt (rapt) - Rain/Spring (April to June)

Sient (sigh-ent) - Sunshine/Summer (July to September)

Etret (eht-ret) - Dying/Winter (October to December)

Additional words

Aether (ee-ther) - The magic that enables hybrids to shift

Aurora (ah-ror-ah) - Kingdom of bear shifters

Eritris (er-ih-tris) - Kingdom of insect-hybrids

Fior (fee-ohr) - Kingdom of wolf shifters

Hael (hay-el) - Hell

Idilea (ih-day-lee-uh) - Kingdom of dragon shifters

Riten (rih-ten) - The god worshiped by the people of Eritris

Zira (zee-rah) - A massive bird comparable to horses

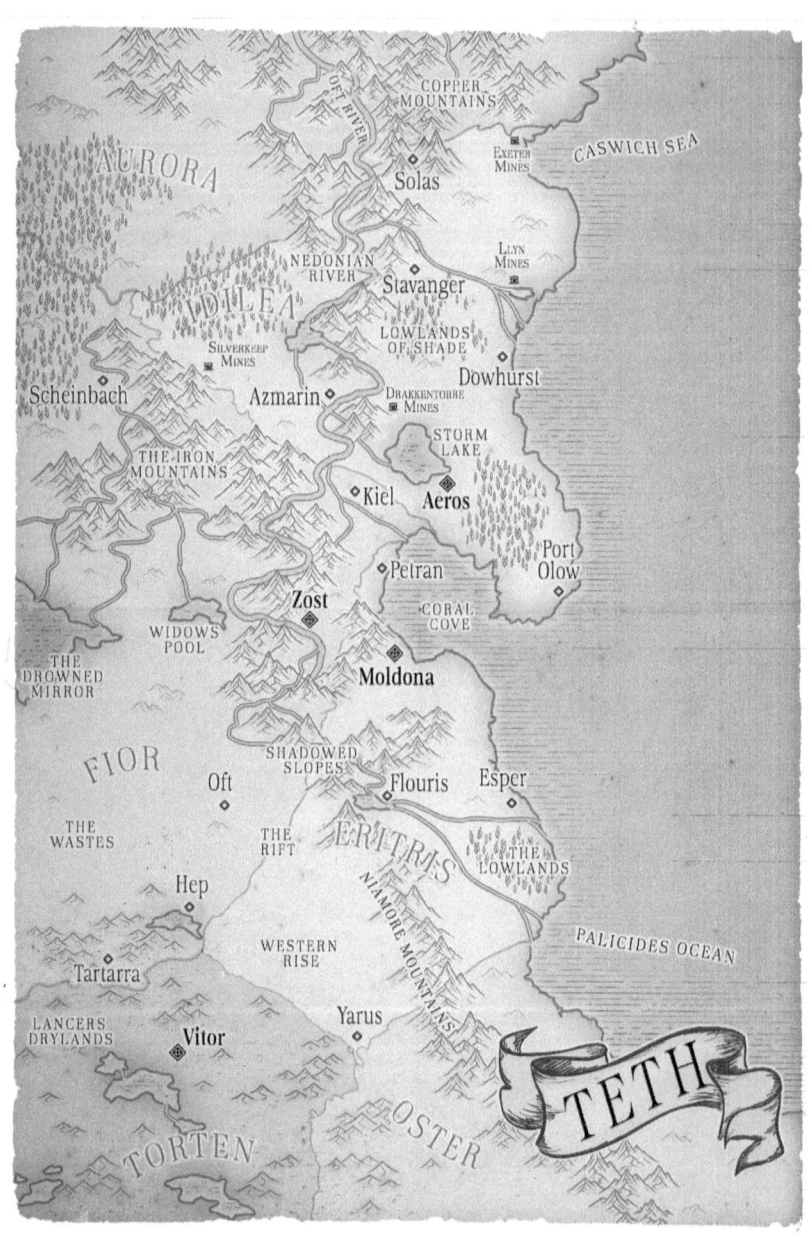

Introduction

"A fight to first death."

I swiped my hands across my thighs, the wraps over my palms gliding smoothly over my pants as the head of the church's voice reverberated around the arena, echoing off the tall walls before being absorbed by the thousands of cheering insect-hybrid spectators.

How had I not known this was what they planned? They never fought to the death in the first round. Never. But this time they went straight for the jugular.

I felt the stare boring into the side of my head, hair, wraps, and all. Of all the ants and roaches and termites and crickets hammering their feet in the stands, clapping their hands and cheering or whistling, I felt that one, hard look strongest of all.

How had I gotten here? Why had I agreed to this?

I squeezed the handle of my jawram beneath my cloak. I hated fighting. It's why I was a thief. Quick in and quicker out. So why had I allowed this to happen to me?

Finally, I turned my head, meeting the furious gaze of the prince who had yet to look away.

Him. This was his fault. He and his ideologies had roped me into this nightmare of bloodshed.

"You may begin."

1

Cursed City

Nim

As long as I ignored the twinge of guilt, my dreams of escaping from this cursed city of my birth would be one step closer to reality.

The man I trailed through the long, winding street of Merchant's Row hid his wealth well. From the wrinkled shirt peeking out from the hem of his leather jacket to his pants stained with salt from the sea to his cracked leather boots, he looked the part of a sailor making a quick stop in the insect-hybrid city of Moldona. But this was my territory, and this was where I stole the coin I needed to survive. Sure, he'd carefully considered the state of his attire and the haphazard bun he'd twisted his hair into, but his hands and nails were far too clean to belong to the average sailor.

I glanced down at my nails, filed so far down the white crescents were barely visible, and the grime worked so deeply into the cuticles that it changed the color of my skin. Familiar. Forgettable.

I very much doubted this man knew the meaning of the second word. Though far from soft, when he'd passed right beside me in the street, I'd noticed his skin was clean, his nails buffed and scrubbed. I could almost smell the lye. His face was similarly free of dirt and muck, his goatee trimmed close, hair free of greasy, salty residue. Signs of a merchant used to bartering with those spouting the upper-crust accents of blueside.

Sure, he probably understood the workings of greenside, we were an uncomplicated people, but his true clientele resided past the copper wall separating the districts and the duchies tucked behind them.

I imagined he'd adopted this façade under the premise of staking out the competition for whatever industry he worked in. Maybe he had some black-market bills to settle, as was the case for many foreign merchants who docked in Moldona. Whatever his reasons for this disguise, they did not matter to me.

This man had money. And he could afford to lose some.

I stepped behind a stall tucked between a pair of massive oak trees where a silkworm operated a complicated-looking loom while hawking colorful tapestries, and I inhaled deeply through my mouth to avoid the putrid odor of vegetables rotting in a bin in the alleyway. The food was so far gone even the dung beetles wouldn't touch it.

Before leaving the dappled shade cast by the trees thickly lining each side of the road, I tugged my maroon hood farther over my brow, obscuring the strips of pale fabric I painstakingly wound around my head and neck, hiding most of my flesh. The female flanking the merchant to his left murmured some quip that made him throw his head back in laughter. The deep sound hummed against my bones.

A male dressed similarly to my mark jogged up and slapped him twice on the back, his other hand pressed to a stitch in his side. Like many of our kind, a long set of translucent hornet's wings punched through holes embroidered in the back of his jacket and rested flat along either side of his spine.

"Find what you're looking for, yet?" the newcomer asked.

"Not yet, but I'm close," my mark replied, dragging a hand across the lower rung of a rustic ladder woven from dead branches and hefty vines that led to the elevated stalls operated by flies and mosquitoes and cicadas. Though accessible from the ground, citizens who preferred flying to walking more frequently perused the wares tucked away in stalls obscured from the ground by thick foliage. The whirring of their wings added to the white noise of the already crowded marketplace, and I forced myself to focus on my mark once more.

My natural eyesight wasn't great; the edges of shapes lost their sharpness a few feet away from my face. However, that's where the vibrations came in. My aether allowed me to process the tumult of messages passed through the air every second of every day, sharpening the world and bringing it into violent focus. Focus far keener than what most could see through their eyes, if not a little void of color.

"Think we can grab a bite soon?" the female asked, pausing to examine a delicately crafted violin displayed on a table outside a cricket's stall. The merchant's eyes lit with the possibility of a sale and rubbed the bows protruding from the flesh of his forearms together, producing a thrum of anticipation. The female ignored his melodic sales chatter and turned away without a second glance. Her own set of hornet's wings fluttered with indignation. "It's almost suppertime, an' thanks ta yer antics, I missed midmeal."

My stomach growled in response, and I clutched at the front of my shirt to quell the sound. How long had it been since my last true meal? Two days? Three? I quelled the burn of envy that seared my chest, reminding myself that three days was nothing. If I wanted, I could spend a few rucks from my stash, but I had far more important things to save for than food.

But Riten help me, I deeply missed regular meals.

My mark cocked a half-grin in the female's direction. "My antics, huh? If I recall correctly, you were the one who insisted on that last round." He trailed off with another laugh, dodging the fist she threw at his side. "Fine, fine. Can't have you hangry. We'll stop at the first alehouse that smells good."

They were certainly headed in the right direction.

My shoulder brushed a black banner hanging from the silkworm's stall as I slipped into the crowd. Mentally, I rolled my eyes. The mandated four weeks of mourning ordered by the crown felt excessive. Sure, the late King Nicholas had negotiated our way out of two wars, but his restrictive trade agreements heavily limited income by most who lived within Eritris' borders, and his ham-fisted local policies had cost us greensiders many of our rights in recent years.

I kicked a leafy bag riddled with mildew closer to the curb. Inside, empty bottles of sticky, lime-colored sap the aphids preferred to drink rattled like dice in a cup. Most greensiders had ditched their black mourning attire days after the king's passing was shouted from the walls. Still, several of the more stalwart merchants clung to tradition in hopes of garnering favor with the crown, making our already drab streets appear even darker than usual.

Keeping an eye on the trio, I crossed the street and dipped around a cluster of hollowed-out trees marking a series of stalls operated by carpenter ants. The depths of my hood masked my smirk while a family of termites squabbled over whose selection of oak and maple was of the best quality.

"This one." The female's voice was barely audible over the din of the crowd. She pointed at the sign for the Honeycomb, an eatery operated by a family of honeybees who specialized in baked goods and honey ales. I dragged my thumb across the bandages crisscrossing the backs of my hands. The group I'd tagged had taste, I'd give them that much. "Their biscuits haunt my dreams."

So, this wasn't their first time stopping on our shores.

No worries, my plans remained the same.

My mark hopped up the first of several waxy steps leading to the door of the hive-shaped business, tossing a grin over his shoulder that relaxed his entire demeanor. What insect aether ran through his veins? Whatever his hybrid form was, he kept it under wraps: no wings, no antennae, no obvious protrusions along his forearms visible through his sleeves. None of the typical tells. If he were a foreigner, he could be human through and through, but something about that idea felt off. The merchant was *too* at ease among my people to belong to the outside world.

Friends in tow, my mark pulled back the gauzy curtain draped across the doorway, and the din inside grew considerably without its muffled barrier. He inhaled deeply and groaned. My aching stomach clenched. "It smells amazing. Rags, grab us a table."

A wide grin split the severe set of the female's face, and the other hornet jostled her forward, hands pressed to her shoulders, tripping over her in his eagerness to order. What it must be like to choose an establishment of class and know I could honestly afford the wares inside, to not feel the prickle of suspicious eyes boring into my hands and back. I shoved said hands into my pockets, stifling the unease bubbling in my gut. When I stole, it was only out of necessity.

I dipped behind a zira munching on sugared oats that smelled faintly sour as my mark hovered at the entrance, scanning the crowd. A burble of thunder rippled from the gray clouds overhead. Their dense bellies were ready to burst, and the merchant stepped inside with a nod to himself, the sheet falling flat behind him.

Of course I'd chosen a group that would make me wait for their coin.

Since I couldn't follow them inside without rousing suspicion, I dragged a discarded crate riddled with splinters and black with mold to the corner of an alley with a perfect view of the entrance and settled on top of it, mentally bracing myself for the long wait ahead. The first droplets of rain splattered my nose, and I shivered, pulling my cloak tighter around my shoulders. What did I care about a little wet if it meant I could make rent in the morning?

2

Spot the Shadow

Sebastian

Eritris was rotting from the inside, a monarchy as broken as the spirits of its people, and as long as I tamped down the panic I felt at returning home and trapping myself within its borders forever, I intended to fix that shattered system. But first, I had to survive the Trials and the nastiness that came with the lethal competition.

With one last look at the shimmering glass windows of blueside and the shadow cast by the mountain behind them, I dropped the flap of the curtain and drew what felt like my first full breath in hours, ignoring the groans of aching muscles running the length of my back. I appreciated the undercurrents of yeast and sweet honeys that filled the café. For as terrible as her taste in male companionship was, Rags rectified her faults with her nose for food.

Grev waved me over from a high table close to the bar, one foot braced on a lower rung of the stool he perched upon, wings draped casually over the low back. His normally pinched expression had relaxed. Beside him, idly twirling one of her many braids around her finger, sat Rags.

I dipped my head and picked my way across the crowded room, noting the worn cushions on the seats, both short and tall, to accommodate the varying heights of clientele. The beeswax scrubbed into the soft wood of the tabletops was fresh, the scent clean. Those crowded around those tables wore plush fabrics in varying shades of mourning black, fingers curled around glasses of mead and plates of fluffy biscuits. Clever sayings were scrawled in bold cursive slashes across the walls; things like, 'Honey, you're the bee's knees," and "to bee or not to bee, that's the question." The phrase over Grev's head read, "It's a bright and sun-honey day," and I lost my inner war with my grin as I dropped into my seat.

"We ordered ya' a plate of hotcakes and sausage. An' a creamed honey biscuit," Rags murmured, still scanning the menu splayed open before her. "The waitress recommended the latter."

I braced my elbows on the table. "Exactly how long did I wait at the door?"

"Too long." Grev accepted the trio of steaming mugs offered by a cricket who appeared at my shoulder, her black antennae twitching against her curly blonde hair. She winked when she caught my eye, tucked her tray under her arm, and skipped off again.

"What's this?" I asked, lifting the mug to my nose. Cinnamon, ginger, and honey swirled up from the dark contents and I tipped it back, appreciating the flavors. There was nothing quite like Eritrian honey anywhere else in the world.

Rags mirrored my groan, cheeks flush with pleasure. "If Eldash had mead like this, I bet we never woulda left." She had a point. All three of us had thoroughly enjoyed our time in the country across the Palicides Ocean and its soft, sandy beaches, abundance of fruit, and year-round warmth. I took another sip. We had visited more than two dozen countries in our seven years away from Eritris, but Eldash left an impression.

"You're crazy," argued Grev. He paused while another waitress dropped off a bowl of biscuits so hot and fresh that steam curled from the bread. "Ochra was the definition of exquisite eating." He moaned around a bite of biscuit. "I would sail back alone on the promise of a bowl full of curry."

Rags snorted. "If ya want to go so badly, it's not like anyone's stopping ya."

I shook my head as the two launched into their typical bickering. The pair had been by my side for the last thirteen years, and I couldn't picture my life without them. My father had assigned them as my guards on my tenth birthday after I flung myself from the window of a ballroom in a sad attempt to fly and broke both my legs when I came crashing down. My wings hadn't fully developed yet, but I hadn't been able to resist the dare cast by my oldest brother. While I was confined to my bed, my middle brother, Micah, kindly reminded me that listening to Vincent never ended well for me.

Regardless, my father determined that if I was willing to fly, I was likely willing to get into other kinds of trouble, so along came my guards. Grev was five years older than me, Rags only four, and both were standouts among those training to join the military. We'd taken to one another like worms to mud once I'd figured out they weren't there to hold me back, but rather to keep me from getting into too much trouble. We hadn't been separated since.

Their presence in my life was perhaps the only thing I appreciated from my father's hands—that and when he'd gifted me my freedom from Eritris' borders.

"Did ya spot the shadow?" Rags asked me, licking butter from her fingers. Her almond-shaped black eyes with specks of white denoting her pupils were fixed on something over my shoulder. Likely the door, keeping watch like always.

I took another long sip and shoved up my sleeves, scratching idly at the soft spikes feathering lengthwise down the backs of my forearms. They hardened into lethally sharp blades when I felt threatened. "Yeah, he's good, I'll give him that. Never closer than half a block, moves with the crowd, blends in with the surroundings well enough." I picked at a knot in the table. "Speaking of, does everything feel, I don't know, *dirtier* to you?"

"Yes," Grev stated at the same time Rags said, "No."

She frowned at her companion, wings flaring out from her shoulders in agitation. "Greenside has always been a mess: too many hybrids an' not enough space. Trust me, unlike the botha ya, I grew up near the docks. I survived the patches on my elbows and knees, the hunger that gnawed so hard yer stomach folded in on itself." She sniffed, plucking at her shirt as if bemoaning its lack of fraying hems. "It's always been dirty, but ya might have not realized it from yer gilded window."

"Check your wings," Grev snapped, a saying veteran air force members scolded recruits with when they fumbled with a formation. "I don't mean *dirty* dirty. More like there's a sheen of filth that wasn't here before."

I leaned away from the table, shame curling like smoke. Rags had a point. Though I enjoyed taking risks and escaping the confines of the castle when I wasn't supposed to, I'd always viewed my trips into the city as an adventure, marveling over all the different kinds of hybrids and trades. When we'd left for the open seas, I'd been a pupa. Now I'd returned as a transformed adult.

"Everyone feels more desperate," Grev continued, "like they've given up hope and are getting by on oxygen alone." He rubbed his arms through his sleeves in discomfort. "The poor just keep getting poorer."

And there it was. The reason we were here, the guiding light that had brought me back to Moldona's shores despite living a luxurious life everywhere and anywhere else. Our country was in desperate need of change, and because of what I'd experienced outside our tight-knit world, I believed I knew how to fix it.

The waitress appeared over Grev's shoulder, balancing a tray loaded with plates against the fuzzy yellow and black hairs ripping over her neck and shoulder. Hastily, we shoved our mugs aside, giving her room to put the food in front of us.

"Don't you hesitate to ask if you need anything else," she said when she finished, popping a sugar cube into her mouth, spinning the tray idly. "I'll be back with refills of your mead in a jiffy."

When Rags had said they'd ordered me a stack of hotcakes, I hadn't expected a pile that nearly touched my chin. To be fair, the way Grev tucked into his bowl of chunky soup and Rags stared wide-eyed at her plate of country-style potatoes slathered in vegetables, bacon, and some sort of red sauce told me they had not anticipated such a hearty meal, either.

"We have enough coin to cover this, right?" I asked, pouring a stream of sticky honey so fresh I could scent the wildflower pollen over my plate. "I washed enough dishes on the ship to last a lifetime."

Grev swallowed a spoonful of onions. "Since you put me in charge of finances, yes."

More like he took control of them by brute force.

"A good call," Rags added, eyes dancing merrily. "Tides know where we'd be if ya kept it all in yer pocket."

"You're both awful insects," I snipped as they laughed, and dove into my plate before they could badger me further. It wasn't my fault dice and cards held the mystical allure that they did. We didn't speak for the remainder of the meal, fully invested in our appreciation of the food.

Only when I put my fork down with a clink on my plate, hand on my stomach, did Grev speak. "So the shadow. You think he's the one?"

My mood soured at the reminder of the reason for our return

and the trip through Merchant's Row: my quest to find a champion. Someone who would fight and possibly die for me in the fast-approaching Trials. For as civilized as Eritris pretended to be, at the core we were bloodthirsty fiends—as the pamphlets pinned up behind the bar reminded me. Here in greenside, they called the competition the Bloodletting, a far more fitting term for the darkness that fell across our lands with the passing of our monarch.

My father passed away from natural causes three weeks ago. Once the missive had arrived, it had taken some bartering and a lot of extra coin to convince the pirate king under whom we sailed to leave early for Moldona. As dictated by seven hundred years of tradition, it was not the eldest child who inherited the throne of Eritris. Rather, a "civilized" battle was fought among the five royal houses to determine who would get the honor of claiming the crown.

Each house picked one family member to inherit the crown should they win, the only exception being the current ruling family, where all princes and princesses could compete if they chose. My family. The old books reminded us that in the beginning, it was the heirs themselves who fought in the bloody competition of claiming the crown, but when too many powerful members of the non-ruling family started dying, the rules changed. Now the heirs picked hybrids to fight for them. Champions.

And I needed one.

"We'll see," I answered Grev's question at long last. "First, we need to know if he bothered to wait for us. Then—it's his game to lose."

"And yer sure ya want a greensider to represent ya?" Rags asked, picking at bits of wax drying on the table from the honey-scented candles.

It was an old discussion, one that started when I proclaimed my intention to join the Trials two years ago, even though I could have taken my freedom and cut myself free of this continent for good. As one of three princes, it wasn't required of me to join. But I wanted to, and I wanted a greensider by my side when we retook this country and molded it into a better version of itself.

"I know it's been two generations since a champion from greenside was selected," I said. Typically, the duchies chose champions from their own blood or employed someone from the military or another great house: insects with finely-honed abilities who also understood the cut-throat nature of court. "But an underbug is what this competition needs, someone no one will see coming."

Grev trailed his spoon across the bottom of his bowl. "Just like you."

Rags shot him a flinty look. "I want t'make sure he's weighed all his options."

"I have," I said, a note of finality in my tone. "We've gone in circles about this for months. The people will not accept change if they aren't won over by one of their own, and you know it. As someone from greenside, I thought you wouldn't be so dismissive of their talents."

She stared at me, unblinking, for a long moment. Long enough to make the delicate spikes on my arms prickle. "It's not their talents I question, but rather yer understanding of the situation. Even with a greensider at yer elbow, whether they be a thief, a murderer, or a farmer, ya know yer goals will take time to achieve, right? Few people are gonna want the world ya dream for them at first."

I shook off her words. "We can get through that. Once they're shown the way, they'll understand what I'm trying to do. I've come too far, seen too much, to let this rest any longer." I slipped a mint leaf between my teeth and peered over my shoulder at the door, pondering if the figure in the burgundy cloak still awaited us beyond the curtain. "But first I need to claim my champion."

3

Wasted Potential

Nim

I huddled deeper into my cloak, the ragged bark of the building digging into my back, the iciness of the earth seeping up through my pants. The crate had splintered shortly after I sat, sending me sprawling into the mud, but at least the rain had stopped. Water splattered the crumpled casings of discarded food parcels as I wrung out my sleeves, plucking at the edges of the pale wraps obscuring the backs of my hands, paying close attention to the sound vibrations playing across them.

With a heavy sigh, I analyzed the hive once more. The trio had been inside for about an hour, and I hoped they were preparing to leave. Even with my seemingly endless patience, the wait was wearing on my nerves. Too much rested on me getting this right.

A hand clamped around my shoulder, sending waves of panic shooting through my limbs. I'd completely missed the feel of their approach. Quickly, I grappled my assailant's elbow with my free arm while simultaneously sweeping sideways, so my foot hooked around the back of theirs. They barely had a chance to gasp before toppling

14

into the mud.

"Nim, it's me."

Those three choked yet playful words stayed my follow-up punch. "Jax?" Sure enough, my best friend scraped grime off his cheeks with a chagrined smirk. Even in the cold months of fret, his skin always glowed red, like a sunburn that wouldn't quit. Most fire ants were that way. "What the hael were you thinking, sneaking up like that?"

He gave up trying to clean his face and leaned forward, still crouching, forearms braced on his thighs, unconcerned about the muddy water soaking his breeches. It smelled a little like urine. "Since when do you let anyone sneak up on you?" Jax tapped his temple, smudging the dirt on his skin. "What happened to that sixth sense of yours?"

Damn him for having a point.

I wasn't particularly concerned about this part of town, but I'd allowed the merchant to consume my thoughts. No one wore obsession well, myself included. I lowered my hood and tightened the ties at the ends of my long braids, forcing my voice to be light, though I seethed inside. "Maybe I wanted to test your skills. See if you'd learned anything the last time we sparred."

His teeth flashed, and he shook out his mop of ragged red hair. "Weren't we fifteen? Sixteen? You seriously thought I'd learned nothing in the last four years?" He shoved his sleeve up, revealing a puckered scar, and scratched it idly. My stomach panged. He'd gotten that scar protecting me years ago when I'd hesitated while carrying out a critical mission on behalf of the Shells—the gang to which Jax belonged and I'd almost sold my soul. "Besides, I'm pretty sure I won that round."

I scoffed, shoving the uglier memory aside. "Only because Devlin pulled me off your scrawny ass. Without him, you would've had two black eyes the next day."

Jax dragged his fingers across his wide mouth, forcing his smile back so he could imitate his father's deeper voice, "'Sixteen is too old for a young lady to be crawling all over a young gentleman, even if you are throwing punches he no doubt deserved. If you have disputes to settle, you're old enough to deal with them properly or, at the very least, in a place where you won't get caught.'" He lost his battle with his humor and clutched his stomach as he laughed. "You were so spitting mad you refused to talk to him for four days."

"And had I waited five, you know he would have caved and begged me to forgive him." I shook my head, recalling the shock on Devlin's long face when I showed up for morningmeal on the fifth day and acted like nothing had happened.

Jax knuckled my shoulder. "You always were Pa's favorite."

How different my life would be if Devlin really were my father and I wasn't some orphan he'd scraped up off the streets. Jax was, in every way but blood, my brother. I fisted my hand over my heart and heaved a sigh. "Why are you here?"

"What's so interesting about Honeycomb?" In typical fashion, he sidestepped my question. "You've glanced at it at least three times since you took me down."

I ran my index finger over the pounded silver bracelet clenched around my wrist—the only jewelry I ever willingly wore. "Waiting."

"Scouting."

"Same difference."

His features fell into uncomfortable grooves, the wrinkles around his mouth and eyes more fit for smiling than frowning. "If you need work, we can find you something. I know you aren't getting enough hours at the bookstore, and there's always plenty to do around the Firestone." He snagged my hand and threaded our fingers together, thumb trailing over the ridges of my knuckles, another old habit. My heart thudded painfully, the sound loud in my ears. "Pa worries about you out here, you know. You don't need to be alone. It's dangerous, not having someone watching your back."

He let the sentence hang in the air between us, and it didn't take much to decipher what he wanted to say but couldn't. The moment I expressed interest, he would pull me back to the colony that lived in the tunnels beneath our feet, give me a roof over my head and four hearty meals a day. I would have steady employment and a regimented system, things I'd always craved. But that life came with its share of demands, ones I couldn't meet. Again, I skittered away from the memory of my fumbled initiation.

I squeezed his hand to dull the edge of what I was about to say next. "You know my thoughts about joining the Shells. I admit there's a comfort to knowing there's a support system out there for people like us, but I refuse to tie myself down."

"You still want to leave Moldona?" Jax turned his head to follow the path of a wagon rattling past. The wagon master pulled the reins before a vegetable stand, causing the zira pulling it to squawk indignantly, azure wings flapping uselessly, its flight feathers clipped.

"Yes." It was an old conversation. "I love you and Devlin for everything you've done for me. You saved my life, but I'm exhausted, Jax. Every day I spend in this blood-sucking city is a trial; the rucks and pearls don't stretch as far as they used to. The trees are rotting, the buildings are crumbling, and morale has never been lower." I sucked in a breath. "I need a new beginning. Outside of our country's borders."

Jax lifted his mahogany-colored eyes. "And you're sure you can't use your talents for good around here? Even with the Shells, there's so much positive impact you could have, and you know Pa would give you room to make it happen." He released my hand and rested his arm on his knee, revealing the slit along his wrist that was the opening of the slender shaft inside his skin, one that released spikes laced with

17

fiery poison, the natural defense of fire ants. "Your potential is wasted out here."

I considered his words, head resting against the bark at my back, gaze trained on the flap of fabric covering the door to the Honeycomb. Devlin and Jax were the only people in this entire cursed world who knew my secrets, what I was, and what I could be. The only people I trusted enough to divulge the information that could one day end my life.

But every day I stayed in this dirt-encrusted city, the greater my paranoia grew. My fears of someone dogging my footsteps, scouring for the mistake they'd made all those years ago when they'd massacred the hybrids I'd once considered family, grew in density. The options available to me were thin, and I just wanted out. To be done. To make my own life without fear of being hunted for the blood in my veins.

"No, Jax. I'm done with this city, and it's done with me." I dragged my hands down my face, rubbing the exhaustion from my eyes. "Three hundred more crowns and I can carve my own future."

The ant's eyes shaded, shoulders falling. "I get it." He didn't speak again, though he stood and scooted closer, so our shoulders and legs brushed, offering companionship as we watched the door to the eatery together.

* * *

The harsh odor of burning oil snapped me from my reverie, and I brought my knees closer to my chest, watching the lamplighters pass by. Most merchants had packed up their wares for the day, their stalls overtaken by those peddling everything from street food to games of cards to kamp liquor to driftash, the latter of which could take users to the highest of highs. Jax and I had tried it once, years ago, and the crash was one I wouldn't wish on my worst enemy.

My best friend had drifted from my side about an hour ago, claiming Devlin was expecting him at eveningmeal. From how he looked at me, hand braced on his hip, head tilted so his wild hair fell at a slant over his eyes, I knew he was asking me to break my vigil and join them. I'd shaken my head and asked him to give his father my best, ignoring the hollow pangs that echoed inside my empty stomach.

Tonight, that would change, I promised myself, as long as my mark left his hideout soon. I hoped he and his friends had spent the last few hours getting smashed on mead, making it easier to slip away with their rucks. Hopefully. Though my cloak was thick and my wraps added an extra layer of protection, I had yet to dry out from the rain, which presented its dangers as the temperatures fell with the last rays of the sun.

With a soft groan, I braced my hands on my knees and stood, needing to stretch my sore muscles. No one looked over as the shadows shifted, as if noticing the creatures who resided in the dark would signal a sense of doom in their own lives, and I tugged my hood back over my head. Thirty more minutes. After that, I needed to figure out a new plan, even if it meant dipping into my carefully acquired savings to pay the rent due at dawn.

Steadily, groups of people emerged, crowds forming as citizens sought their late meals and a chance at cheap entertainment—from visiting the playhouses to underground fighting rings.

Many crawled from labyrinthine tunnels carved below ground where all sorts of hybrids from worms to ants maintained their homes, choosing to wander the streets after the murky sunlight faded. But others, like the cicadas and mosquitoes, launched themselves from the spiraling copper-based towers that mimicked massive trees, sleek wings outstretched and hair fluttering around their antennae.

It never ceased to fascinate me how Moldona transformed after dark. The flickering torches obscured the trash littering the street corners and cracks in the walls of the stalls, metamorphosing dark, drab attire into comfortable, almost fashionable outfits. Hybrids smiled more, and couples held hands with their children cradled in their arms or pulled against their sides.

Sometimes it was almost enough to make me reconsider my decision to leave.

But the days always lasted longer than the nights.

A couple of flies tugged the opening to the Honeycomb aside and entered the warmth it offered. The drizzle had returned, accompanied by flickers of lavender-hued lightning in the distance. It wasn't enough to chase the insects away, but it was a nuisance. The flap almost settled back into place when it fluttered again.

My heart leaped to my throat as a hand batted it aside, and the merchant I'd been waiting for strode into the street, uncaring of the puddles lapping at his boots. His hornet friends trailed behind, leaning heavily against one another, chattering about their plans for the next day while rubbing their bellies with contentment. The tall one offered my mark a cloak, but he waved it off and threw his arms wide instead, tilting his face to stare up at the rain splattering down upon him.

Again, I narrowed my eyes, considering which insect ran through his veins. Typically, I could tell the flavor of a hybrid by glancing at them. Most tells were obvious based on the shape of their eyes, the feathering of their antennae, or the wings they displayed down their backs, but I occasionally encountered someone who baffled me.

He spun in a circle. "I forgot what the rain felt like here, Grev."

"Really? It feels like wet to me," his male companion responded.

My mark stopped spinning and lifted a finger. "Nah. The rain in Moldona is colder, edgier." He paused, lips thinning. "Dangerous."

The female chuckled and shoved his back, encouraging him down the street, ignoring the looks that others shot their way, judging their drunken ambling. "That's the mead talking. Rain isn't a living thing, Seb. Ya can't wound it with a sword."

But I knew what he meant.

I ghosted along the edge of the street, hugging close to the trees and walls, following their stumbling pace. Maybe it was because I'd lived in Moldona my entire life that I marveled at the travelers who stepped onto our soil, curious about their origins. Would I be welcome in the lands they came from? As mysterious as they were, there was something about our city, from the sharp-tongued merchants to the crashing waves of the Caswich Sea to—yes—even the rain—that felt ripe for danger. For change. Like the razor's edge of rebellion.

The trio reached the end of the road where the lamp lights dimmed. The merchant they'd called Seb flicked his fingers at his friends, the light catching the tapered edge of his triangular jawline. "I've got it from here. I'll catch you at the docks tomorrow, bright and early."

Grev's eyes narrowed. "Are you sure that's wise—"

"I'll be fine." My mark hooked his thumbs in his leather belt, fingers brushing the pearl buckle. "It's only a few blocks and then straight to bed."

Rags shrugged. "Come, Grev. The sooner we get back, the sooner I can win back the coin ya stole from me."

"You really think you can beat me this time?" Grev lost interest in his friend, eyes brightening with challenge. "After losing six in a row, I'm not so sure you have what it takes."

"Ah, shove it."

The two wandered down the left fork in the road, but I took the right, trailing the merchant into the bustle of the crowds. A pair of mosquitoes with stringy hair jeered at a group of females from a table just outside a bar that catered to their kind, withdrawing their straw-like tongues from cups that reeked of coppery blood. Across the road, the trilling hum of a cicada band spilled from the open vee of a door

21

at the base of a coppery tree-shaped building, lights flashing in time with the beat, enticing clusters of moths to cough up the cover charge to enjoy the ambiance inside.

This was my chance, the opportunity I'd spent an entire evening building toward. The merchant's toe caught on the edge of a cobblestone, and he wavered, barely catching himself. He was drunk enough for it to dull his senses, comfortable enough to wander alone, and the clusters of hybrids were dense enough to give me escape options.

I latched on to the tail end of a group of locusts heading in the same direction as my mark, clinging close enough that others might think me part of them while far enough back to not raise their antennae. The males and females chattered inanely about the customers they'd encountered, the price gouging they'd witnessed, about larvae and pets and all sorts of things that I kept half an ear on while I edged closer to the merchant who'd slowed his pace, eyes flitting from brightly-lit storefront to another.

That's right, let your intrigue swamp your senses, I silently encouraged. *Take in the changes to the city you used to know. Ignore the person brushing against your side.*

A dip of my fingers, the clutch of a velvet pouch, a twist of my body.

Ignore the simple female in the simple cloak living her simple life who liberated you of your hefty pouch for the night.

The worn soles of my boots were silent on the street as I melted into a group of gossiping crickets, steam rising from their cups of spiked black tea, pace quickening. The alley that would take me south, back to my tiny room above the bookstore, beckoned.

A knot in my chest loosened as soon as I stepped into the dark, leaving the light, conversation, and music behind me. I'd done it. I pulled the pouch from my pocket. It smelled of fresh mint and felt heavy enough to pay my rent with plenty left over. My stomach grumbled, a yawning hole that never seemed to fill.

Maybe enough for a potpie or two tonight.

That thought drove me to open the pouch, something I never did, usually preferring to make it to the safety of the four walls that made up my base before unearthing my gains of the day. But the call of food was too much, a hungry bitch, and The Anthill was on my way home.

I dipped my fingers into the folds and emerged with...

"Beans?" The word dropped from my lips like a stone.

Who carried a bag of black beans in their pocket?

My jaw clenched, cheeks prickling with heat. My vision tunneled.

A mark who knew he was being trailed. That's who.

When had he spotted me? When had he realized he—

A firm hand pressed between my shoulder blades, shoving me into the wall so hard my cheekbone cracked against the metallic siding. The pouch tumbled from my palm, sending beans clattering everywhere. The warmth of a body much broader than mine pressed against me, and from the corner of my eye, something sharp shimmered in the moonlight.

A long dagger—a weapon the king had banned greensiders from possessing.

My breath caught in my chest, mind whirling with possibilities of escape.

"You're good," a masculine voice murmured, slightly muffled through my cloak. "But I'm better."

4

Degree of Necessity

Sebastian

For a thief, I'd never spotted anyone better. I pressed the male harder into the wall with my body, freeing my arm to sweep him for weapons. A thief this good had to bear arms, no matter what the crown decreed.

He didn't respond, face smashed against siding, muscles stiffening when I patted his arms, feeling through the weight of his dark cloak. Judging by his height and frame, he couldn't be older than sixteen, though he hunched a bit, so that could be skewing my perception.

For someone so young, his skill was admirable. He took care to tuck himself among the unsuspecting, his attire neither loud nor soft, artfully flitting from darkened alleys to shadowed doorsteps. Even now, I couldn't tell which type of hybrid he was, a positive for anyone seeking to escape notice. To top it off, his patience superseded even Grev's abilities, something I hadn't thought possible.

And the slip of his hand... I'd barely felt it.

To boot, he'd replaced his catch with one of his own.

The irony of finding that little burlap sack of white beans made me chuckle.

I ran my hand down his side, still not finding anything. I frowned.

I'd expected him to be wiry with speed, but his muscles, ropy as they were, felt firm. I traded the knife from one hand to another and inspected his right side similarly.

He still didn't speak.

"I have to know," I said, breaking the maddening silence. "What made me stand out? You waited all evening for me—" His heel knocked against my instep, and I grinned, gripping his wrists more firmly in my fist. He didn't like being found out, did he?— "So you had to know I carried significant coin. But what gave me away? I dress no differently from the others around here. My accent is Moldonian. What made me your mark?"

Two figures appeared at the mouth of the alley, shadows like toothpicks stretching before them. I risked a glance, recognizing Rags and Grev. We'd separated for the ruse, but they hadn't gone far.

"Your hands." The male's voice grated like sandpaper, though it wasn't entirely unpleasant.

My hand stilled on his shoulder. I gazed at it, baffled. "Explain."

"Your nails are short but not broken. Clearly you don't work the docks or fields." He coughed, body rattling with the force, as if unused to speaking. "Your palms and fingertips bear calluses, so you aren't from blueside, though I bet you have friends you visit there. You understand the importance of hygiene, how appearance can sway a sale. Only the best merchants are like that." He sniffed in what might have been indignation. "They match, but they don't. They never know if they'll be bartering with the likes of me or the keep."

I met Grev's eyes when he leaned against the wall on the other side of the pupa, boots crunching on the spilled beans, his expression of triumph a mirror of mine. Only back one day and I'd found the very hybrid I'd been looking for.

Rags cleared her throat. "Ya could release him now. I doubt it's comfortable having one's cheek jammed against the wall like that."

25

I returned the knife to the sheath I'd hidden under my shirt, but didn't release the thief. If I let him go, I feared he would slip away, like fog in the first heated rays of morning light. "Like I said earlier, you're good." He didn't need to know his reasoning had never occurred to me. I'd taken care with my attire, my haircut, my boots—even checked my body language when we joined the crowded streets.

But my hands...

"Are you curious how I knew I had a tail?" I asked, hungry to find out more about how his mind worked.

"I'm curious what you want with me," he replied. "Since it doesn't appear you're about to kill me over a bag of beans."

Cheeky fellow. Though I supposed when I was his age, I hadn't felt the weight of the world as keenly either. Yes, he would do just fine, barring one thing.

"How's yer knowledge of weapons?" Rags asked, reading me perfectly. "Sword, dagger, the like."

I could all but hear the thief's thoughts racing. "I don't know what you mean."

"Very good. A beautifully diplomatic answer." I couldn't see Grev, but I heard the ring of approval in his voice. Where Rags was my master of weapons, Grev was my master of words. For him to see promise... my chest swelled. My plan was working entirely too well.

"Now give us the real answer. Seb the Merchant here—"

I turned my head, narrowing my eyes at Grev's wryness.

"*Laying it on a bit thick,*" I mouthed. He shook his head and continued— "is carrying a knife despite the king's decree. And we, as his guards, both bear daggers. We aren't here to take you in, not without risking our own heads. Tell us, how is your skill?"

A mastery of weapon craft wasn't a requirement for the job. That could be taught to a degree of necessity. The thief was young enough for the lessons to stick. But if he were skilled with even one weapon, that would lock in the victory that was this evening—a perfect trifecta. The nation would never know what hit it.

The pupa muttered something unintelligible.

"Speak up," I ordered. "What was that?"

"I cook sometimes," he gritted out. "If chopping carrots and dicing potatoes is what you're after, then I hold my own."

My shoulders drooped, but Grev only nodded. He'd expected as much. My father's decade-old decree barring the use of weapons to the lower and middle classes had effectively stifled most whispers of rebellion, but it left me with a population bereft of workers skilled at the tasks I needed.

"No matter." I patted his back before stepping away, releasing him. "We'll train you."

"Train me for what?" he asked, massaging his wrists.

Grev stifled a laugh with the heel of his hand.

"Oh, yeah," I mused. "We'd like to hire you."

The hybrid stood silently, waiting. It irked me, not seeing his face. So many things could be deciphered from facial expressions. And since I was about to stake my legacy on this unknown's abilities, I needed to see those expressions for myself. Then there was the matter of his aether. I couldn't determine what hybrid form he claimed, though I assumed ant or cricket based on his height. "Would you turn around? I need to see you properly."

The thief hesitated, his gloved hands tightening in the cloak's fabric. Amazement tickled my mind again. Even wearing gloves, two layers of extra fabric, I'd almost missed the snatch and grab. A perilous move, yet he'd executed it with practiced ease.

Thunder burbled overhead, warning of another incoming storm. Grev's cutting gaze told me we needed to hurry this up.

The pupa swiveled on his heel, nimbly avoiding the beans littering the cobblestones. His front was as nondescript as his back, and he

27

kept his head bowed, the folds of his hood obscuring his face, exactly as they had earlier. A reaper made flesh.

"And the hood—" I began.

"Hurry, lad," Grev implored, cutting me off. "Before the storm ruins a promising evening of opportunity. Aren't you the least bit curious?"

Again, the thief hesitated. Thunder rumbled, louder than before. The drizzle fell harder, splattering against the leaves fluttering overhead. I understood his reluctance. We were three older, well-armed hybrids who were clearly people of note, even if he hadn't yet placed my face, and he was a child living in greenside who'd learned to steal to survive.

Our worlds couldn't be farther apart.

Flecks of rain dotted my cheeks, icy as the needles of sea spray I'd recently abandoned. I shoved my hand through my hair, sending it every which way. "Listen, I understand your reluctance. But—I need you."

The statement caught even me off guard. Rarely did I feel the need to justify myself to others, but the hybrid's skills spoke to me, impressed me. His patience humbled me, and the lack of fear he showed, even when pinned down, was a trait every champion needed. Not to mention, he was intelligent, if not snarky, and smart people didn't agree to help others without a reason.

I needed to give him that reason—to open the door to trust.

"My name is Sebastian Octavius." Rags' brow lifted, and Grev dragged his hands down his face, stretching his cheeks. The thief's hood twitched. This was not part of our plan. "Third prince of Eritris."

The thief hissed, and I swore I heard my nickname on his lips as he put the pieces together. He'd overheard my guards earlier. Amazing. I'd thought the distance between us was too great.

"I've been away for seven years, but news of my father's death reached my ship, and I returned." My future warrior drew his arms around his chest, anticipating what I was about to say. "I'm back for the Trials, and I'm sorely in need of a champion."

White hot lightning arced across the sky, followed by a snap of thunder that rattled the maple leaf-shaped shutters of the apartments overhead. Grev cursed as rain overfilled the buckets of the clouds and spilled upon us in unrelenting waves.

I swiped a hand across my forehead, leaning into the thief until I found his eyes, big and bright and silver, in the depths of his hood.

"I don't know your name. I haven't seen your face," I said, lifting my voice over the pounding rain. "But based on what I've seen of your abilities, you're exactly the champion I'm looking for." I paused for another roar of thunder. "If you stand as my representative in the arena, if you fight in my name, I promise you I will be the change this country needs. I will right my father's wrongs."

I grabbed the hybrid's hand in mine and jerked it, a handshake barely worthy of its name.

"Consider it." Silver eyes blinked. "I'll be at The Primrose through the remainder of the week."

Two days.

Two precious days in an already limited countdown.

The thief tugged his hand from mine, tipped his head in a mocking bow, and shoved past Grev. I blinked rain from my eyes as I watched his cloak billow behind him, the fluttering banner of a chariot, before he turned a corner and vanished from view.

5

Fight for Me

Nim

Sunlight glinted off the pale blue stone, highlighting the insignia's carefully pressed into the gold that locked the precious gem into place. A signet ring. Though I had never seen one in person before, I understood its value. Even more so: it's proof of my mark's claim.

Of all the hybrids in Moldona, I'd chosen one of the *princes* to steal from.

I muffled a yawn against the back of my hand before resting my cheek on my palm once more, the pages of a dense history book about Eritris' most prominent houses spread wide on the desk before me while I cradled the jewelry in my lap.

All I'd ever wanted was to dissolve into the crowd, and I'd instead targeted one of the most noteworthy people in the entire nation. A member of the Mantis Duchy. A hybrid who had disappeared with the tides of the Caswich Sea years ago, bound for great adventures. A prince who, without seeing my face, had asked me to stand before the eyes of Eritris and fight for him.

His cause.

But why me? A random thief on a random street on a random night.

Anyone could have picked his pocket, could have staked him out for hours on end. But he'd selected me. Did he know who I was? Uneasily, I tightened the wraps around my fingers. He couldn't know my true identity. I'd been too careful, taken too many precautionary steps for him to place a nameless, faceless hybrid who had been but a larva when she'd escaped the clutches of a massacre.

No, my abilities must have surprised him. Given him enough pause to reveal *his* identity, to extend the banner of trust necessary for a true partnership. Warmth uncurled in my belly at the idea of standing out to someone, for them to see beyond my mask and respect *me*.

I dragged my fingers down the page of the text, inhaling the musty scent of old books like these. It was an aroma that had gotten me through some of my darkest nights, tucked in the corners of homes whose occupants had no idea I'd snuck in to steal something of value. The scent of protection, of finding, of disappearing; it was all too easy to get lost in the papery depths of written words.

Against my will, Prince Sebastian's claims plucked at the ragged ends of my heartstrings. He spoke of change, of altering the status quo. It all sounded so grand, especially when spoken in the darkness of the alleyway amid booming thunder and drenching rain. What would carrying out such plans entail?

The door at my back snicked open, and I pressed the ring harder into my thigh, hiding it with my hand. Ms. Whitmere floated by, her muted, feathery wings fluttering lazily, the toes of her shoes barely touching the dusty floor.

"Good morn, Nim," she whispered silkily, brushing the fringe of her thick antennae from her eyes. "I appreciate you opening the shop in my stead."

I shifted on the padded stool, uncomfortable with the praise the moth doled out as frequently as the wind blew.

She peered at me with round, black eyes that saw far too much, her smile as wispy as her long, colorless hair, and shook her head while lifting a pile of books from the stack beside my elbow. "More history books? When will you allow me to entice you into reading a good fantasy?" The moth didn't bother waiting for my response as she slipped silently into the aisles of her bookstore.

Her inquiry stretched as far back as the day she had hired me. She'd caught me in the stacks, a tome propped open on the shelf, worrying my thumbnail with my teeth while devouring the latest account of the rebellion that had freed our neighboring country of Idilea from the grip of Fior. I'd thought myself clever, tucking myself into an alcove to read since I didn't have enough rucks to purchase anything, but nothing slipped by Ms. Whitmere, not even an orphan more spectral than flesh and blood.

"Always stories full of facts and historical significance with you, isn't it?" she'd asked, her thready voice loud as zira talons on cobblestones when it broke the sacred silence. "Why do I never see you in the fantasy section like so many pupae your age?"

I'd been seventeen then and would never forget my answer.

"Because Moldona is too real for me to believe in something as obscure as hope."

The moth had tilted her head, ignoring the fringe of her antenna when it caught in her lashes, appraising. "You truly mean that, don't you?" A rhetorical query that left me with more questions of my own when she'd offered me a job and a key to the spare room over the shop.

She'd offered it rent free, but I'd refused her charity, insisting I would sooner stay on the streets before I accepted her offer. The moth had fought me for weeks before relenting, settling on a price reasonable for the neighborhood. I'd wanted a place of my own, one I paid for with my hard-earned rucks and pearls, a sanctuary from the streets. My wages were enough to cover the cost of the room, but month after month, I forced myself to tuck the coin into the soft, leather pouches hidden beneath my floorboards, saving for my escape, turning instead to odd jobs to make ends meet.

Thievery was reserved as a last resort.

I opened my fist again, staring at the ring worth more than any of the mansions that lined the streets of blueside. It practically glowed against the silk that wound around each of my fingers, across my hands, and up into my sleeves.

Ms. Whitmere had once offered me a glimmer of hope I desperately felt I didn't deserve, and here came a prince appealing not only to my goal of escape but dangling a hint of change on the horizon. Change this city so desperately craved.

I sighed gustily and sprawled flat across the desk, cheek pressed to the cool wood, elbow nestled against the ancient register with keys that clacked loudly.

Everyone knew about the Bloodletting. Unlike most nations surrounding us, whose lines of succession were determined by the bloodlines, Eritris thrived on bloody battle.

When our monarch died, the duchies waged a competition to determine who was worthy of ascending the throne. All children born to the ruling family were allowed to compete, the only true advantage offered for their parental line of service, and the remaining duchies chose one member each who would partake as well. The Trials—as they were formally dubbed—were nothing to sniff at. Though they were touted as tests of supreme skill and intelligence, their true value was derived from violence.

Hundreds of years ago, the princes and princesses, lords and ladies, used to fight in the Bloodletting themselves, brutally slaying one another for a shot at the crown. It was speculated that the families supported the competition because it eliminated threats to the throne by default. However, that changed about three centuries ago when Eritris waged war against the nation of Fior, which sought to claim our lands for themselves. We nearly lost our sovereignty because the latest round of the Trials had just been won, and we lacked skilled, young leadership.

From there on, each participant selected a champion to serve in their stead.

To die in their stead.

It was considered the greatest of honors to be selected for such a role. Traditionally, royals chose their champions from the best and brightest blueside had to offer. Upper-class families fought among themselves to determine who stood the greatest chance of being chosen. Those prodigies were typically well-versed in combat, games of skill, and knew their history.

A few champions were selected from greenside in the early years. Traditionally, they were hybrids who'd won favor with a family or had exhibited great promise in various ways: merchants, ring fighters, the like—but most died quickly. It quickly fell out of fashion to pick anyone from this side of the copper wall.

I leaned my head on my hands, massaging my temples.

And here came this prince, flaunting convention… choosing me as his champion.

A thief he didn't know. Had never seen before last night.

"If you don't sit up straight, the pillbug queen will steal you away in the middle of the night," said Ms. Whitmere breathily, appearing from between the stacks. She referred to a tale told to children who misbehaved. The edge of her wing brushed my cheek before she settled into the plush oatmeal-colored pillows of a bay window to people watch, toying with the bookmark stuck in the pages of a new marketing text in her lap. "No troubles are worth encouraging bad posture."

I flicked my hand at her, sweeping away her casual mention of my deformity. I'd long since made peace with the slight curvature of my spine along the base of my neck, the hunch to my upper back that made my shoulders ache and muscles tense. It wasn't like there was anything I could do about it most days. Not if I wanted to remain among the living, anyway.

"What would you know of troubles?" I countered dryly. "You run the most successful bookstore in the kingdom with one of the most adept apprentices in the city at your elbow." The moth's mouth tipped up at the corner, and she adjusted the gauzy lapel of her long cardigan. "I saw that write-up in *The Daily Buzz* last week. You've achieved fame, which most of us only dream of."

"Oh, hush." The moth wrinkled her button nose, crinkling her round face. "You forgot beautiful. One of the most *beautiful* apprentices in the kingdom."

"Ah, yes." Brazenly, I patted my cheeks and the silk carefully concealing most of my skin, but for hints around my eyes and mouth. I knew what she was doing but never caved to her careful inquiries. It wasn't that I didn't trust her. More that she was too good and wonderful for the darkness that shrouded my personal life to conceal her. "Just you wait until I emerge from my cocoon."

Ms. Whitmere mumbled something that sounded like, "that's what I'm hoping," before opening the magazine in her lap. She dropped hints like these at least once a week. I never took offense. The moth didn't understand why I wrapped myself in long strips of silk from my hairline to my toes, and she never would if I had any say in the matter.

No one would.

The bell above the door signaled our first customer of the morning, and I greeted the beetle with a smile. The hard shells of his jade wings closed with a snap, thin black antennae flicking in my direction, glittering eyes scanning my face before darting away. From her spot at the window, Ms. Whitmere called out to the hybrid by name, and his face rearranged itself into a smile. He removed his silken top hat and bowed to her with a flourish, inquiring about the latest fashion magazines, my presence quickly forgotten.

A typical reaction. One I craved—the perfect picture of anonymity.

Something that wouldn't be anonymous: serving as Prince Sebastian's champion. I gazed down at the ring nestled in my palm. If I accepted his request, everyone would know the name Nim Reed before the end of the Opening Ceremonies. The female whose face they couldn't see, whose surname didn't belong to any prominent circles. The hybrid who'd clawed her way up from nothing to have a chance at something.

The thief who the prince believed to be male.

Wasn't that grand? My disguise worked too well. I imagined his reaction when he unearthed the truth, how his almond-shaped eyes would widen, how his pointed jaw would drop. He'd probably shove his hands through his messy auburn locks, scattering them even more.

That expression alone might make it worth it.

Granted, I risked more than losing my anonymity if I accepted. I put a great deal of value in my life. I'd fought and bartered and stolen for everything I had. I'd refused to go down when everything I'd ever known turned against me. But going head-to-head with the other champions over the course of five challenges would be a risk to all I'd achieved. I'd be putting my life on the line every single day until a victor was crowned.

The beetle scuttled to the counter and set two glossy magazines before me, still avoiding eye contact. I wrote the titles in a ledger at my elbow, rang up the prices, and handed over his change. He skittered out the door before I could wish him a good day. I held up the pixon he'd paid with, tilting the oval bit of iron this way and that in the light.

If I emerged the victor, if my wits and athletic abilities proved to be the best in the kingdom, I would never want for wealth again. I would never need to scrounge for food or beg for shelter.

I could have my pick of permanent positions within the castle, and my greatest desire would finally, painstakingly, be within reach. Freedom. Freedom from this city, this country, and the prying eyes I hid so carefully away from.

The empty space in the pouch tucked beneath the floorboards upstairs called to me. Three hundred crowns would be mine in a blink if I won.

But if I lost...

The edges of the gemstone ground into my hand as I squeezed it tightly. I'd known my answer the moment the prince had asked it of me. It had tumbled to the tip of my tongue when he slipped his hand into mine. It was my first thought upon waking in my too-small cot.

I would fight for him.

But he had to fight for me first.

6

Eager for Change

Sebastian

"All in," I crowed with a lazy brush of my arm. The twin towers of red leaf chips before me toppled over, the resin-coated pieces plinking as they landed on the pile of wagers in the center of the table.

Rags threw her cards face down. "Ya know what's bullshit, Seb? You. I fold like a chair of twigs under a fat cricket's ass."

Grev chuckled, wiping his amusement away with a brush of his thumb over his lips, attention alternating between his cards and the palm-sized book of military tactics open on the table that he was re-reading for the thousandth time. The other hornet pushed back her chair with a screech on the hardwood floors and padded across the open living room to the kitchen, where she rummaged around in the cabinets, no doubt searching for one of the containers of salted honey sticks she hid all over the place.

"That's the last time ya trick me into playing with ya," she called, words muffled through a mouthful of sweet.

I threw my arm over the back of my chair, waiting for Grev to make a decision. "There's always another game."

"Aye, but there aren't always the rucks ta' supplement it, ya' bastard."

Wasn't that the truth? It was also the reason I trusted my friends with our bounty. Coin had a habit of disappearing when left under my watch. I'd picked up the gambling addiction at sea, fascinated by the clinking of shells and rock, the guffaws and roars of laughter that were foreign to the rigid solemnity of my life within the castle. However, while I was enamored by cards and chips and the enticement of odds, locust luck disagreed, and I lost far more than I won.

Grev fanned out his hand, squinting as he peered at the river of cards.

If I concentrated hard enough, the walls of the apartment we'd rented for the week melted away and the gilded, flashy glamour of a casino rose in their stead. I imagined the earthy scent of cigars curling up from the cushions of my chair, practically heard the clicking of the roulette wheel and its tiny glass ball spinning in an endless circle, and all but tasted the thick, rancid laughter of the desperate and the weary.

"I call."

The glittering lights vanished with a blink, replaced by the dying sunlight stretching its yellow fingers across the floor. Grev nudged his towers of red chips into the center of the table, careful to keep them upright. "I've figured out your tell, and I bet you've got nothing."

Rags squealed around the candy she'd shoved between her teeth and peered over his shoulder, hand braced on the chair. Her brow lifted, and her chewing intensified.

Fuck. I knew that expression. It meant nothing good for me.

Grev laid his cards out flat, revealing a straight.

"Well, Seb, let's see 'em," Rags goaded. "Show us what ya got."

I instead reached for my glass of water and drained its contents, masking my annoyance. Every time I overcame one tell, another would pop up. I'd never felt comfortable lying, and bluffing fell along those lines, too close for comfort. The pirates had taken me under their salt-crusted arms after I lost my monthly stipend time and time again, teaching me how to mask the tics that gave me away.

But nothing stuck.

Fortune rarely took my side.

Grev's pinched face tightened, his heel banging against the floor as his knee bobbled rapidly with nerves. Another beat, another breath, and I tossed my cards down, the painted blue backs staring up at me. "Enjoy your victory while it lasts."

Grev peered at the cards, and I knew he was tearing himself apart inside with his desire to see what I'd thrown away, to know if he'd finally called my bluff, but his honorable half warred with his desire, and he shoved to his feet before the siren's call of temptation overtook him.

Rags recognized no such honor and flung herself across the table. Her loud, rattling laughter filled the apartment as she flipped my hand over. "Damn you and your poker face. Riten save me, if I'd known ya' had nothing…" Without finishing her thought, she tweaked my nose playfully and crawled backward, finding her feet and the stash of honey. "Too good."

Concentration broken, I wandered to the wide double doors leading to the balcony and threw them open, inhaling the gust of fresh air that even blocks from the sea still smelled a little of salt.

Here on the top floor of the Primrose, the rest of the city splayed out before me in unrelenting waves of dense foliage, tarnished blue-green copper, and nickel-brushed steel. Copper used to be in vast supply thanks to our previous relations with Idilea to the north and their vast Copper Mountains. The metal mined from their territory had the peculiar ability of strengthening with age, so it worked well when mixed with the salt of our sea.

However, when Fior overtook the land of the dragon shifters, Moldona's supply of copper dried up, and we'd turned to our own mountains, harvesting the relatively inferior steel that used to be exported for our needs instead.

Economics was among the few subjects that had stuck with me as a pupa, which ran contrary to the addiction I'd picked up in my time at sea. My oldest brother proved best at anything he put his mind to: politics, economics, engineering, swordplay, archery, flight patterns. There wasn't a thing Vincent couldn't overcome once he put his mind to it. My middle brother, Micah, preferred the sanctuary of his laboratory, pushing the boundaries of modern science and mechanics. And I proved to be the stereotypical youngest: spending my time sparring with soldiers rather than embracing my studies.

Perhaps that was why it surprised no one that on my sixteenth birthday, I'd asked my father for the freedom to explore the oceans and the lands on the other side of the planet. Many times over the years when I climbed into my hammock at night, before being lulled into slumber by the ship's rocking, I'd pondered my father's easy wave of dismissal. The flick of his graying antenna before he'd returned to his desk and the paperwork spilled across it.

My relationship with my father had always been a stilted thing. He'd never had time for me as his third child, a surprise neither he nor my mother had expected. But his attitude that day spoke to an indifference that stung me more deeply than I cared to admit. It was partially why I'd remained on the pirate king's ship for as long as I had, preferring his course encouragement and the easy camaraderie of the crew to the weight of disapproval that came with my title and my home.

Yet when word had reached me of my father's death, I hadn't hesitated to react, pulling every string to return home as quickly as possible. I massaged my temple and the headache building within my skull. On the one hand, I didn't miss my father as much as I could have—*should* have. But I'd barely known the hybrid. At court, people

41

only spoke of his victories, and outside on the streets of greenside, hybrids only voiced their frustrations. It wasn't like I knew him as a person. On the other hand, anger and frustration warred in my thoughts, the beginnings of grief that I couldn't begin to comprehend, for the loss of someone with whom I might have forged a connection, given enough time.

A trio of larvae clattered down the cobblestone street, whooping and hollering as they kicked a ball of bundled leaves around tourists, picking pockets with ease as they went. My fingers clenched around the edge of the door as I turned from the scene. Too late. The sticky webs of my increasingly negative thoughts snared around the center of my focus.

A tiny thief who had yet to grace my doorstep.

And the day was running short.

"Are you sure turning to a greensider was the wisest decision?" Though he struggled to call my bluffs, Grev had the uncanny ability to follow the sea lane of the ship that was my mind. "I know you prefer a gamble on the best of days, but can a pupa truly grasp—"

"Give the pest a chance, would ya?" Rags ran a short knife along her cuticles, leg bouncing on the rung of the stool upon which she perched in the kitchen. "I like him. He's got spunk. Everyone knows the best champions are the arrogant ones."

Grev's shoulders heaved on a sigh. "He was arrogant."

"He's hiding his abilities," I interjected. "Hybrids who make a living on the street are hardly defenseless. I bet he knows his way around a knife far better than mincing vegetables. Besides, if he can learn to pick a pocket with such skill, he's able to learn on his feet—or he'd be dead by now." I exchanged a look with Rags. "You've trained insects with less capability."

"Sure have," she buzzed happily. "Even if I have ta push him through every last hour of the next ten days to whip him into shape, I'll make

42

sure he's competent enough ta survive the first trial. An' Grev will have even more time to put him through his paces when it comes ta book smarts."

Grev huffed audibly, unwilling to respond to the gauntlet Rags had so cleverly thrown. I knew he still wasn't convinced I was making the right decision. Maybe now was a good time to change gears, keep him on his toes. He would come around eventually.

"Why don't you two grab us supper?" I asked, rubbing my temples. "There's no need for all three of us to wait here." And I desperately needed a moment alone to think. Isolation had been difficult to achieve at sea, but at least the hornets had given me respite, knowing there were few places to go when hundreds of miles of water surrounded us. But here, on land, they remained suffocatingly close.

Rags straightened, sliding her hands in her back pockets. "Food sounds good."

"I suppose." Grev eyed me knowingly. "You want anything in particular?"

I shook my head, slipping a dried mint leaf between my lips. Its sharp tang flooded my mouth. "Whatever hasn't been in the depths of a hold for a year."

"An' since Grev won the pot, he can treat." Rags threw her arm around his waist, shoving a pouch of coins into his hand. The iron and pearl pieces tucked inside clinked merrily. "Hurry up, ya sorry sod. Let's leave this mess of a prince behind to muddle in his own misery for a wink."

Grev scarcely had a moment to snatch up his cloak before Rags pulled him out the door.

Silence had never sounded so sweet.

With them gone, it was possible I might even nap. That was if I could stop my mind from spinning on its endless wheel. I shoved my hands in my hair, raked the strands over my fingers, and pulled it into a loose bun. If the thief didn't show up, I wasn't sure what I would do. Everything that had happened two days ago had felt... right. Rags would have called it fate—Grev: coincidence. But to me it felt like the smooth backs of a winning hand of cards.

"You three form an equilateral triangle."

The raspy voice at my back had me reaching for the sword at my hip before remembering I hadn't attached it to my belt today.

"It's fascinating, the way relationships work like that, isn't it?" the thief added.

Drawing air through my nose, relief cascading through my body, I turned back toward the open doors to the balcony. The white, lacy curtains billowed wide, revealing the thief in his maroon cloak, crouched on the vine-like copper bars of the railing. The burnt-yellow sun backlit his hood, obscuring his face. It was maddening, the awareness he possessed of location and positioning, how he could see every bit of me and me none of him.

"How did you get up here?" I asked. Perhaps he possessed wings underneath that heavy cloak. That would come in handy. "We're on the tenth floor."

The Primrose was among the most decadent hotels in greenside. Seven floors above ground, three below, the facility catered to every kind of insect. The floor upon which we resided was dedicated to one apartment. Four rooms. Two bathrooms, one attached to the master. A kitchen. A congregation area. And a balcony. So different from the ship, where I'd barely claimed a hammock to my name.

Over his shoulders, through alleyways that reminded me of the gaps in our first mate's teeth, shimmered the emerald-gold waves of the sea. The thief dipped his head. "Even a third-rate pickpocket knows how to scale a wall."

No wings, then. Or none he was willing to boast about. I gave up trying to find an angle to give me a better look beneath his hood and

44

settled against the doorjamb. "Is that what you are? Third-rate?"

"If I were third-rate, I wouldn't have gotten my hand in your pocket." He shifted, adjusting so his weight leaned more heavily on one ankle while his other leg splayed down the length of the rail, a cricket-like pose if I'd ever seen one. In doing so, he changed his grip from back to front, revealing white tape wrapped around the fingers of his left hand all the way to the cuticles of his nails.

Perhaps the tape gave him extra grip.

"I wasn't sure you were going to show up."

"It wasn't like I could keep this, could I?" With a flick of his wrist, the thief presented my signet ring. The gold shimmered against the pale linen that coiled around his palms and vanished into his sleeves. "Can't use it, can't sell it, no point hiding it. Figured it belonged with its owner."

"You trust I am who I say I am?"

"I would have known if a signet ring were reported stolen."

With another flick of his wrist, the jewelry arced through the air. I caught it one-handed. He reminded me of the apprentices I'd worked with over the years at sea. Careful. Quiet. Eager.

He was here, wasn't he?

"You could have left it on the balcony." I slipped the ring past the knuckles of my middle finger and nestled it firmly into place. "Why did you really come?"

"It isn't every day someone asks another hybrid to die for them... honorably." He reluctantly released the word, as if it didn't encapsulate the intended flavor. The antennae I preferred to tuck away twitched. He admitted to being a hybrid, at least. "Why me? Why not someone from blueside? You could have your pick of the best and brightest in the kingdom to serve as your champion. Someone who would stand by your side, no questions asked."

He presented a fair question, one I'd expected. I crossed my boots at the ankles, noting the worn heels and scuffed toes of the thief's shoes. I had to be careful here. I already risked treason charges for what I'd said a few nights ago—not that it bothered me, but I had things I needed to do, and I couldn't do them sitting in a murky jail cell.

"Will you tell me your name?"

"If you give me an answer I believe."

I rubbed my chin, suppressing a grin: this kid and his anonymity. I could almost admire him for his doggedness.

"Like I told you before, I left Eritris seven years ago. The reasons why don't matter much—" Lie. "—and while I monitored the state of affairs in my homeland, I chose not to return until now. I've spent my time on the high seas, on board the ship of a pirate king, visiting nations both near and far, learning everything about as many people as I could." Truth. "I was free, and I was happy."

"If you were free, why return?" He shifted his weight again on the inch-thick bar, agile as a mouser. "No law forces you to take part in the Bloodletting. By not participating, you'd forfeit your claim, but you could have stayed abroad forever."

He had no idea how glorious that sounded. "Believe me, I know. However, I recognize there are inherent flaws in the governing system of Eritris as it stands now. Overseas, I encountered a land where the people elected their own officials, and they cast votes on important matters." I leaned over the railing to survey the bustling streets below. "The system shouldn't work given people's propensity for violence and chaos, but it does. Beautifully. Peacefully. It's a form of governance I would enjoy seeing Eritris embrace. We would be the better for it."

Why I was opening up like this, speaking treason to an urchin whose name I *still* didn't know, was beyond me. Maybe it was instinct from my inner mantis forcing me to speak up, to raise my hand, to stake my claim. I risked a lot, speaking this openly. However, who would believe the word of a peasant over that of a prince, if he did choose to spill my secrets?

Regardless, in my experience, with big risk came an even bigger reward.

"That's very noble of you," he murmured. "But you still haven't said why you chose me. A thief. A nobody. A peasant with no education, no history, no future."

Frustration flared. I snagged the thief's shoulder, felt him flinch, and squeezed the bony flesh beneath his cloak. "No one is nothing. Everyone has a future, even if they can't see it clearly." The pupa flinched, and I glared into the depths of that damnable hood, meeting the silver orbs that were his irises.

"I want a lot for my kingdom. I want so much more than you will ever know." I shook him, stepping closer, our bodies mere inches apart. "And I need someone hungry by my side. Someone who knows what it is to face the worst and wishes to realize the triumph of coming out on top. I *want* a champion who isn't afraid to risk it all because the risk *is* the reward."

I released him, crossing my arms, embracing the darkness swelling in my chest. "It wasn't just my hands that lured you to me the other day. Just like it wasn't a coincidence that I happened to be on that street at the same time you were scouting for your perfect mark." I sucked air through my teeth. "I see something in you that reminds me of myself. Something cunning and vibrant and eager for change.

"If you take up my mantle. If you stand in my name. If you fight and claw and think your way through every challenge—Riten knows it won't be easy—if you support me in this, I swear it won't be in vain." I thrust out my hand, chest heaving, veins boiling. "What say you, First-Rate Thief of Greenside? Will you be my champion?"

He stared down at my hand for five seconds. Six. Seven.

So long my arm trembled.

The flicker of hope blooming in my stomach, that feeble little flame, sputtered. But when I pulled back, he grasped my hand with one of his own while peeling away his hood with the other. My body locked, every sinew drawing tight.

"Prince Sebastian Octavius, it will be my honor to serve as your champion for the Fifty-First Trials." There was no mistaking the shape of *her* face, the bow of *her* lips, even beneath a layer of crisscrossing bandages. The thief's grip firmed. "You may call me Nim."

7

Now or Never

Nim

Beneath the silken bindings, my skin prickled. The prince's eyes drifted down the twin braids in which I bound my hair, across the planes of my face, and over the front of my cloak. I had pictured his surprise so many times, imagining the shock that would sweep across his face.

This trumped everything I'd envisioned.

He brought his hand to his jaw, index finger partially obscuring his mouth, pupils dilating, blinking furiously, processing his mistake.

Silently, I slid off the rail and leaned against it, arms flung casually over the top bar. My cloak snagged on the pointed end of a dead vine, dragging the fabric up my arms, revealing more bandages. Though I was the most covered-up creature in all Moldona, I'd never felt more exposed as his gaze trailed across every inch of my body. I rose to my toes, easing the tension on my cloak, and it fell around my knees once more.

Which of the questions flitting across his face would he ask first?

I knew how I looked, the image I presented. I'd been wrapping my skin since I was nine, protecting myself from the cutting gazes that I knew would linger longer if they recognized what scars I concealed.

Let them look.

Let them judge.

I wrote my story, not them.

The prince chuckled against his fingers, skin crinkling around the corners of his eyes, and he raised his hand in a mocking salute. One I knew he meant for himself. "I see I made an error in judgment."

I rubbed my thumb and index finger together. "You made an assumption, prince. How old did you think I was, anyway?" My brow lifted, the bandages carefully pressed to its upper rim lifting with it. "Fifteen? Sixteen?" He flinched. The corner of my lips dragged up. "Awfully old for a pupa whose voice has yet to drop, don't you think?"

"You caught me there," the prince admitted, surprising me again. "Please accept my sincere apology."

I wasn't a stranger to those who resided in blueside, to the way they talked nor the filters through which they watched others wander in and out of their lives. In only one place had I encountered anyone on that side of the wall open to admitting their own faults, and ghosts haunted its hallways these days.

I held his gaze. "Does this change anything?"

"Should it?" He shoved his hands into his pockets and removed a bit of something green. He stuck it under his tongue, and the sharp bite of mint wafted across the space between us.

"I'm aware of what I'm getting into, if that's what you're asking," I replied.

"You're still the intelligent, cautious thief I first figured you were. More so now, even." The prince adjusted the glove on his left arm, one that started at his elbow and covered part of his hand. The fabric draped across the back and palm of his hand, bound in place by a loop around his middle finger. "Females have a relatively successful track record in the Trials. You're what? Eighteen?"

I fought to avoid bristling. "Twenty."

A gull coasted overhead as he considered. "You fit the age range of the competitors far better than I anticipated, too." He paused, gaze catching on something over my shoulder. "Anything else I should know?"

"I won't do this for less than three hundred crowns." I crossed my arms over my chest. "And no promises of swearing fealty and protecting your back when this is all said and done." I straightened to my full four-foot eleven. "When I win, you get your throne, I get my money, and I'm gone."

He fiddled with his cuff link. "Done."

I chewed my bottom lip. He agreed so readily. Had I missed a step? Was there anything else I needed? No. Greed only bore ill fruits.

"Rags will have twenty-five crowns for you tomorrow morning as a show of good faith." He smiled into the sunshine, the hues of orange and gold burnishing his dark tan. "I'm afraid my friends took the purse with them."

"Fair enough." Ms. Whitmere had given me five workdays to pay up. The prince's offer would leave me more than enough time to pay my debt and secure my home for another month. "What burning questions do you have for me?"

"Just one: Can you fight?"

Yeah, he definitely saw through my fib in the alleyway. "I hold my own."

He flashed a quicksilver grin, one that told me he knew what was behind my flippant façade. "Rags will get you up to speed." The prince lifted a finger. "We would like to evaluate your skills before we throw you to the wasps in the arena."

I remembered the poster I'd glimpsed on the way here, the one with spidery ink, the edges torn from the wind. "You think a fortnight is enough time to train?"

That also threw me off about his request, his identity. While the royal families rarely revealed their champions before the Opening Ceremonies, it seemed odd he'd waited so long to lock down his partner. He didn't seem the type prone to impulse.

My head spun. And what if I had been fifteen? What if I hadn't ever handled a blade? Aside from guards and soldiers, the king's ban on weapons in greenside kept many from learning skills necessary to protect ourselves, let alone go on the attack.

Was the prince so confident in his abilities to ferret out a worthy champion and train them that he waited only a fortnight before the start of the competition to get started? The hybrids I would face would have spent their entire lives training for this moment. Realistically, I stood a millipede's leg of a chance at winning, and I, among those living this side of the wall, had a fair amount of training, plus a few advantages integrated into my very blood. Imagine if it were someone else in my shoes, someone—

"Don't worry about it," the prince interrupted my clashing thoughts. "You're worrying about things beyond our control. We'll be fine. Ten days is more than enough time. Besides, the introductory ceremonies are harmless. An opportunity for the people to place bets and the champions to size up the competition." His grin deepened, expression sharpening. "They prefer to save the blood for the first trial, when people have had time to pick their favorites."

My instincts panged with uncertainty. "If you say so."

"I do, and I'm a prince, so it's my word that matters." He winked, softening his words. "So, Nim, are you prepared to begin training?"

I licked my lips. "Now or never."

"First thing tomorrow morning," he decided. "Take tonight to settle your affairs, get some sleep. We meet here at first light."

8

Strength is Supremacy

Sebastian

The sea ingrained two realities into my being: I could only control what I could control, and *home* was less a place and more an idea. Though I'd grown up inside the many walls of Castle Redfern, it would never be home to me. I'd once believed the openness of the sea and my position on the ship might claim that spot in my life, but that still hadn't felt right. No, my home was with my friends. With Grev and Rags and those who supported me, people who comforted me in an uncomfortable world.

With a glance at the long black mourning banners framing the heavy front doors, I tugged on the collar of my freshly laundered navy shirt and squared my shoulders inside my worn, gray jacket, shoving down the feeling of inadequacy.

Before I could find a reason to delay this reunion any longer, I nodded to the pair of hornets bracketing the entrance, resplendent in sheets of shiny black armor and swords I bet my boots had never seen a spit of action. The guards turned the hand cranks drilled into the walls. Those were new. Marveling at the mechanism, I couldn't help but grin when gears ground together and the stones rattled beneath my feet as the doors swiveled wide enough for me to slip through. Micah's work, no doubt.

Though the door had changed, inside it was like I'd never left. The doors thudded closed behind me, and the archway overhead groaned, settling under the weight of the vaulted ceiling. Black beams latticed the ceiling of the Great Hall like the ribs of a giant fish, fanning outward from a central spine that ran the length of the room.

Living trees were integrated into the walls, their trunks woven with thick vines and flowers of every color. Copper basins shaped like leaves hung in regular intervals up and down the lengths of the walls, intended for flying hybrids to perch upon when hearing their monarch address the assembly. A maid hummed as she ran a feather duster over the tulip-shaped lanterns, wings whirring as she dipped from fixture to fixture. Gathering my nerves, I strode down the center of the hall, peering into the long, open-faced tunnels carved into the floors where those who preferred the earth could gain access to the throne room via a series of granite steps.

In my absence, the only thing that had changed was the drapes covering the six narrow windows running the length of the walls. Black now. A stark contrast to the silver and teal of the Octavius Duchy. Stepping deeper into the room, I honed in on the pair of thrones carved directly into the sides of a pair of oak trees, their naked branches brushing the ceiling. The last place I'd glimpsed my father alive with one half-hearted look back as he heard concerns from greensiders while I departed for the merchant ship waiting for me at the docks.

Between the trunks of the thrones hung our crest: A shield divided in half, one side white with two black spades, the other black with one half of a mantis' spread wings. I murmured the words embellished in teal across the bottom.

"Istan de Metero." Strength is supremacy.

The same crest, the same motto, stitched intricately across my back. My jacket was the only possession I had kept from the start of my journey, though my shoulders filled it out properly now. Not that I wore it on the ship like that. When I'd adopted the pirate's life, I'd flipped my jacket inside out, revealing my personal emblem of a compass with its needle pointing east, a pair of splayed mantis wings stitched in gray at its center.

"Your Highness." The words were spoken with the quiet, even tone of one who'd said them several times to garner attention, and I swung to the maid clutching a broom to her side, dragonfly wings spread wide across her back. She dipped into a low curtsy, the emerald shimmer to her skin glittering softly. "How may I be of assistance?"

Awkwardly, unaccustomed to the fanfare that came with my title, I cleared my throat. "My mother. Where might I find her?"

Her translucent antennae twitched. A fire roared in a hearth at her back, throwing heat in rolling waves. "Upstairs, sir. She prefers her chambers most days."

"And my brothers?"

Her antennae twitched again, likely relaying signals to the other staff members through the subtle gestures. "I'm not versed in their current location, sir." She curtseyed again. "Shall I find out for you?"

"No, that's enough for now. Thank you." Typically, I would ask her name, learn something about her to cement her place in my mind. But this wasn't a typical occasion. I'd waited too long for this reunion. My mother deserved better.

With a parting nod, I strode toward the long, sweeping staircase spiraling off the Great Hall and started upward, preferring to take my time walking rather than exercise my wings and swoop up through the open space at the center of the spiraling tower. The castle was full of open spaces and wide hallways like this, accommodating hybrid guests

55

of all kinds, and I knew even more spaces were tucked between the walls, allowing servants easy access to the various levels and rooms.

Every fifth step, a portrait of the rulers who had come before was framed on the wall, their eyes following me as I ascended. From beakish noses to spear-like chins, our country's legacy was represented all around me. Viotto. Sai. Amana. All had tried their hand at keeping the throne, but only Octavius had thrived in the power it awarded.

As their features blurred together, I couldn't help but think of my little champion, her features obscured by clinical rows of bandages from the crest of her hairline, wrapped around her ears, split around her eyes and mouth, and wound into the dark depths of her shirt. The wraps should have muffled her features, but the fine threads were spun so tightly that the material accentuated them instead, shifting with her expressions. I wasn't aware of any religions that called for such absolute covering of one's form, Eritris' own worship of a singular god included. Was it by choice that she obscured her skin? Or did something else drive her to such extremes?

My stomach clenched, twisting and crawling with possibilities.

Every now and again, as I continued higher into the towers, wood smoke from an errant fireplace drifted down the halls, filling them with the warmth and light I remembered as a child. No, this wasn't my home now, but it had been then: a place of magic and wonder. I hesitated outside a door near the top of the staircase and braced my forehead against the wood, my nose rubbing the thick grain. That child had dreamed of making a name for himself, finding his place in the world.

How would he feel about the adult I was now?

Would he approve of the transformation I'd undertaken to return?

Or would he turn away in disgust, seeing me so far from who I thought I would become?

Trepidation crawled down my spine, and I brushed it away. The past was in the past for a reason. I could only look forward now. Straightening, I rapped my knuckles soundly on the door. Three times. Always three. For I was the third of her children.

"Enter," came the chimelike response, one that wrapped around my shoulders like an embrace. The knob turned easily under my hand, and I pushed through the door, smiling broadly when I scanned the room and found my mother curled up on the violet cushions of the bay window, a book in her lap, its yellowed spine cracked.

Her lips unfurled in a smile, one full of amusement and light. "My child, you've returned."

I crossed the room in five leaping steps, forgetting my age and my mission in those four simple words. She rose to her knees to greet me, her arms folding around me as I pulled her close, my chin propped on her fragile shoulder, closing my eyes against the rosy luster of her spread wings. She ran her hand up my back soothingly before pressing a gentle kiss to the side of my head.

When we withdrew, she carded my hair through her fingers, eyeing it critically. "Four days you've been at port, and you couldn't spare a moment to see a barber before coming to visit?"

The wet glisten of her eyes gave away her true feelings.

"You knew I was back, but you didn't send the guards to fetch me?" I teased. Carefully, I slid the leather tie she'd stolen from her bony wrist and tied my hair into a knot at the back of my head again. "I never thought I'd see the day you'd exercise restraint."

Her laughter filled the room, and she pushed her buttery hair over her shoulder, the pale threads like spun wildfire across the black velvet of her dress. She spun me around, trailing her fingers over the embroidery of my crest. "You and this jacket." She traced the patchwork of stitches holding it together, every tear painstakingly mended, clicking her tongue. "Please tell me this isn't still the only

57

thing in your closet."

I grinned, tugging free of her grip. "I have a cloak now."

"And I don't suppose you'll let me summon the tailor?"

"Mother."

"Son." She drifted toward a table propped up beside the bay window and lifted a cup of mint tea, long grown cold. I'd inherited my love of the herb from her. Back to me, she spared a look into the darkness beyond the pane, eyes glassy, and tipped the contents of her cup into her mouth. Her throat bobbed with a swallow. "I assume you'll be partaking in the Trials?"

I shifted. Unsteady. "I would have made it back for the funeral if I'd had the time."

Her shoulders tightened as she straightened to her full height. "You know better than to lie to me, Sebastian." In the glass, her eyes caught mine. Held. Tears clung to her long lashes.

"Mother—"

"I'm aware of the difficulties you and your father shared. You certainly wrote of them often enough." She crossed to another table and flipped open a box, pulling a sheaf of letters from its depths.

A pang of guilt slid through my insides. It was true. My mother and I had exchanged plenty of notes during my time away, and in them I'd confessed to her some of my deepest feelings of inadequacy. However, those letters had fallen silent a year ago when she'd pressed me to return home, to make amends. I still felt she'd put an undue amount of weight on my shoulders to repair my damaged relationship with my father, though I regretted the words I'd put down in ink, the accusations I'd hurled, and the silence that followed.

Swallowing down the acorn-sized lump lodged in my throat, I said, "Fine. I'm not sorry for missing the funeral." Regardless, there hadn't been enough time in the world for our ship to sail across the Palicides Ocean. "But I am sorry for the words I wrote in haste. I regret how I handled things with you, and I wasn't sure how to make amends."

The walls absorbed what I couldn't say.

"It's why I didn't come to see you sooner," I managed, my words barely louder than a whisper. My gaze fell to my feet, the booted toe wearing a groove in the plush, green rug. "I'm sorry, Mama. I'm sorry I shamed you, and that I stayed away. That I couldn't—" The words choked in my throat.

Suddenly my mother was there, one hand clasping mine, the other cupping my face, tracing the moisture that trailed across my cheeks. "Sebastian." Her voice was tender, her love as apparent as always. Her arms drew around me again, pulling my frame tighter against her delicate form. "You have nothing to apologize for. That you've endured such thoughts for so long—it breaks my heart." One long-fingered hand stroked down my spine, absorbing the shuddering of my chest.

"But my words were so cruel," I said. "How can you forgive me so easily?"

"There was nothing to forgive. We are family." Another slow stroke of her hand. "I feared I pushed too far, that you might never return. I believed you needed space. You always were more insulated than your brothers."

She drew back, her thumb sweeping my chin, blue eyes liquid with unshed tears. Bluer than the skies I'd sailed beneath these last few weeks. "Had I known my silence hurt you, I never would have hesitated. I even wrote you letters when I thought of you." My hand still clasped in hers, she spun to the box and pulled out another sheaf of papers. I read my name in calligraphy on the top envelope. She pressed them into my hands. "They're yours now. Please set your fears and worries over this aside. I'm your mother, and mothers are best at understanding their children, even if their children think they don't."

It wouldn't be as easy as all that. Guilt still clung to me like sticky strings, but I forced the trembling in my hands to steady as I pushed the letters into an inner pocket of my jacket, feeling a little lighter at my mother's confession, at the understanding I didn't deserve.

Maybe she was right. Perhaps if I had returned in time for the funeral, I could have faced my fears about my father. But I felt so conflicted being in this castle, smelling the potpourri wafting through the room he and my mother shared, the memories and emotions too hot and thick to bear.

"Seb? I thought I heard your voice." The wheels of Micah's chair barely made a sound as he pushed across the threshold. "I overheard the servants chattering about your return, but I couldn't imagine you staying here for long."

Steady again, a wide grin engulfed my face, and I took the hand he offered, both of us tugging back and forth playfully. His arms were bulkier than before, but everything else about my brother was the same. Same mess of wavy hair tousled as if he'd slept on it, same analytical gaze that saw too much and far too little all at once. A tumble of what appeared to be cogs and gears from a pocket watch was strewn across a metal tray in his lap.

"New project?" I motioned at a tangle of minuscule chain links spilling from the device.

Micah glanced down as if he'd forgotten about his work, one hand curling around the tray while the other scratched the wild scruff along his jaw. "Something like that."

"He's kept busy these past few years." Tea trickled into her cup as our mother poured from a kettle, calm as when I'd entered. "By day, he's taking lessons from our ambassadors, learning everything there is to know about diplomacy, but at night, you should see him; he truly comes alive."

I knelt beside the chair to examine it better. It was a fair cry better than the first one my parents had outfitted him in as a child, little more than a chair on rollers to accommodate the loss of mobility in his legs and wings from a spinal injury. This one had maneuverability, and what looked like lifts and levers allowed even more accessibility.

"You designed this?" I asked, toying with a band pulled taut around a series of pulleys.

I'd asked him once if his interest in mechanics came from a desire to design a way to fly, but he'd told me he was content with his life. The world made the most sense to him on solid ground, and besides, he'd contended his inventions were rarely for personal benefit.

He believed his situation offered a unique look at the world, aiding him in helping create better lives for hybrids across the kingdom.

Micah tapped the wheel, fingers curling around the grip he'd installed in a ring around the middle. "This. The lift that runs between the levels. The front doors. A new mechanism that improves the accuracy of our crossbows." He tapped the tray absently, rattling the contents. "How long are you back for?"

My brother never was one to tout his accomplishments.

I straightened, dusting off my knees. "The Trials."

"Oh?" He took a moment to process that, head angled in consideration. "That makes seven. An odd number. A prime number." He pursed his lips. "I like prime numbers. They lack complication."

"All three of you are taking part," Mother clarified. "In addition to members of the four other duchies. The most participants since your great-grandfather's Trial." She paused, trailing her fingers along the velvet covering her arm. "Sure to be the bloodiest, too."

A sensation like claws skittered down my spine, and I rolled my shoulders, shaking it off. I squeezed Micah's shoulder. He'd already dismissed the conversation in favor of his latest invention. Then I crossed the room and took the cup from my mother's loose grasp. My nostrils curled, and I fought back a cough at the medicinal scent.

My chest ached at the idea of her relying on sedatives to get through her days without my father beside her.

"Where is Vincent lurking, anyway?" Not that I planned to seek him out. If anything, I hoped to avoid his serpentine graces.

"I'll never understand why the two of you don't along," she murmured, accepting my arm around her waist as I guided her to her bedchamber. I glanced back, but Micah remained absorbed in his tinkering.

"My three children who were nothing alike," my mother continued absently, "but more alike than they acknowledge."

Unsure what she meant, I pressed my lips to her forehead, dragging the covers over her slight form. "You should get some sleep, Mother. It's getting late." Scanning the room, I spotted a pitcher of water and a cup, but she snagged my wrist when I went to collect them.

"You won't vanish on me again?"

My heart twisted, greasy guilt washing my insides anew. This was why I hadn't come back. I hadn't meant to be gone for so long, but leaving was such sweet wonder. Returning was nothing but a black, burdensome weight.

"No. I won't stay tonight, but I'll come again soon."

Her rigid lock on my wrist dropped away, her voice drowsy as she burrowed into her pillow. "Good." With the pitcher and freshly poured glass of water within reach, I turned to leave when she murmured, "If you do leave, though, I understand."

My jaw clenched, the guilt sloshing more wildly.

"I know my children," she whispered. "I'm glad you've found your way home again."

Quiet as could be, I closed the door. Micah had already taken his leave, and a maid had appeared in his wake, tidying the sitting room. With a nod in the cricket's direction, I made my own swift exit, hands shoved in my pockets as I took the stairs two at a time.

My mother wasn't entirely right: I would never call this castle my home ever again.

9

Not a Threat

Sebastian

Hands shoved in my pockets, I strode back through the castle doors, barely registering the guards who turned the cranks to pull them closed for the night. Inhaling gulps of the goldenrod-scented air, the tightness in my chest steadily eased now that the confinement of Castle Redfern was behind me. I braced my hands on the stones of the waist-high wall that lined the path weaving down the mountain cliffs. The grit of the slate steadied me.

Below, lights shimmered from the windows of the Viotto and Sai estates, and to the left loomed the tall, round walls of Archer Arena, where Nim would be introduced as my champion in a fortnight. Behind me, the castle shimmered prettily against the mountain backdrop into which half of it was carved. The front half of the castle appeared as any other, elongated walls and spears of towers daring the skies to threaten them, but farther back, the castle was expertly integrated into the shale and granite that made up this branch of the Iron Mountains. Windows exposed slits of life from the rooms tucked within, both a show of might and of practical defense.

The mountains formed a bowl around the city of Moldona, which occupied every inch of available space from the northern barracks of the army to the sandy shores of Coral Cove to the healthy soil of the farmland to our south. Our ancestors had chosen this land for its protection and practicality, and to this day, my breath still caught at seeing the rolling hills of my people scattered beyond the copper wall dividing the rich from the poor.

"Not only has my dark zira of a younger brother returned home, but I hear you're also planning on entering the Trials, too?" Vincent spoke mildly, his voice drifting from behind me, but his tone was as slippery and critical as I remembered. I fought to keep my shoulders from stiffening, knowing from experience my brother missed nothing when it came to weaknesses.

He entered my field of vision from the right, smoothly blocking my exit to blueside, one hand casually braced on the hilt of his iron-black sword. He wore his hair trimmed closely to his skull now, and the strands rippled in the light breeze. The sleeves of his plain green shirt hugged the muscles of his bulging arms, more evidence of how he'd changed these last few years, though I was glad to see we remained around the same height.

"I was under the impression you were otherwise detained," I remarked. I didn't see a way out of this conversation easily, but with the guards at our backs, I felt better about my odds of escaping without a knife being driven into it. "Mother says you're busy playing politics with diplomats. Tell me, has anyone else picked up on the silver edge to your tongue? Or just me?"

"Still holding onto those childish grudges? I thought at three-and-twenty you would have finally grown into an adult." He clicked his tongue, not deigning to look in my direction. "I suppose that was too much to wish for."

Vincent and I were oil and water, the same side of the magnet, constantly pushing each other away. Six years my senior, he had no time nor patience for me when we were children, and his dislike for me had only grown with age. It wasn't as if we spoke often, so I had no idea why he resented me so, and Micah either refused to give me insight or didn't care.

What I did know was how charming Vincent could be when he wanted something. In my youth, he'd frequently gotten me into trouble by laying the blame for something he'd done at my feet. When he figured out things that made me happy, like archery or a specific mutt in the stables, he went out of my way to take them from me. The archers in the training grounds had turned against me almost overnight, and the pup had vanished almost as quickly.

My father saw him as a ruthless regent he could mold into a worthy king. My mother was dazzled by his ability to overcome every obstacle. The court appreciated him for his straightforward conversation, and greensiders reveled in his stature, that of a hybrid who knew in any other kingdom the crown would be his. And I resented him for all of it. I knew all about his vicious scheming. The knowledge that he was the most likely heir to the throne had played another *slight* role in my return.

"What do you want?" I asked. "We both know we are better off speaking to one another as little as possible. The only reason we're talking now is because you have something to say."

Vincent flexed his wings, the pearly red shade was striking against the pale green of his tunic. "I want you to return to the docks, get on a ship, and never return." His fingers closed more tightly around the hilt of his sword, and I casually reset my stance, bracing. "Your presence in this kingdom is not necessary, and you know it, but you seem to have taken ill of your senses. I'm here to rectify that."

My blood heated at the threat. "You know nothing about me and my senses anymore, *brother*. I'm not the pushover I used to be."

The mantis pressed into my space, our noses almost brushing. His gaze was steady, the malice in his eyes obvious.

"You seem to have misunderstood me, so for your sake, I'll be blunt. Do not enter the Trials. Do not choose a champion. Leave Eritris once and for all, and when I'm king, I promise to leave you alone, so long as you stay on your half of the world." Spines speared through the delicate fabric of his shirt, slicing up his forearms. Mine responded in kind, hostility vibrating in my veins. "If you linger, you and everyone dear to you will suffer. You do not want to get in my way, Sebastian. Surely you remember enough of our history to know I'm not bluffing."

I was breathing heavily, my wings poking through my shoulder blades. "What did I do to you, Vincent? Why am I such a threat to you?"

"You're not a threat. Not to me. I'm merely trying to save Mother the agony of another funeral… so close to the first." With a flourish, he released his sword and dipped in a mocking bow. When he straightened, his eyes glinted, hard as onyx. "You don't know what this kingdom needs from its future monarch, nor do you realize the threats bearing down upon us from all sides. Be on your way. Scurry off like you did the last time. No one missed you then, and no one will miss you now."

I wanted to shout at his retreating back, to not allow him the last word in this fight, but I wouldn't give him the pleasure of knowing how deeply he'd gotten to me. Breathing deeply, I considered the threats he spoke of and the plans he may have in place to face them. Regardless of what I wasn't aware of in Eritris, his words had done nothing but strengthen my resolve to remain in this fight.

I refused to allow my barracuda of a brother an easy route to the power he craved.

10

Mediocre

Nim

Sweat beaded on my silken wraps, but I kept my hands around the grip of my jawram, waiting for Rags to make her move. These weapons were designed by ants for street battles in the days before we were banned from using such tools. The u-shaped weapon had twin blades curving out from a central grip, not dissimilar to the appendages of an insect's jaw; its outer edges were razor sharp, the inside serrated like jagged teeth. A curved piece of metal running along the handle protected the user's fingers from being cut to bits. What I loved best, though, was how the handle could twist apart in the middle, forming two separate daggers.

Breathing deeply, I rocked forward, weapon extended, and braced for her attack. The hornet bobbed, boots sliding on the dirt as she shifted sideways, a pair of thin rapiers in her grasp. She gave nothing away.

After having my ass handed to me twenty times in a row, I would know.

But thanks to Grev standing on the circular balcony behind her, I finally had a tell.

"Are you waiting for me to rush you this time?" I asked the hornet, pretending like my legs weren't screaming and the bruises spreading across my ribs didn't ache. "I'm pretty sure the Bloodletting is more about attacking and less about defending."

Rags chuckled, her toned shoulders shaking. "One step at a time, larva. You'll get yer chance at attacking when ya can hold your ground."

Her gaze slid left, and I braced, bearing my weight on my back foot, jawram in motion as she swung for my right side. Twisting, I angled so her rapier landed inside my weapon, balancing dangerously on the jagged teeth. Before she could adjust, I raised my other hand and swiveled the blade, knocking it cleanly from her hand. The sword clanged in the dirt, followed seconds later by the jawram. Sharp things only got in my way.

Anticipating the swing of her second blade, I opted for the fighting style I knew. An uppercut to her jaw and a right hook followed, knocking her into the dust. As she gasped in a breath, I threw myself on top of her, twisting one of my legs around hers in a lock, my forearm finding her throat. "Cede?"

Rags' eyes narrowed, and she shook her head until I applied enough pressure that her too-large, all-black eyes bulged. Finally, she rasped something that sounded like, "Enough," and I released her, massaging my bruised arm.

"She got you there," Grev hooted. He swung himself over the edge of the balcony and dropped to the stone circle of the training center tucked away in this corner of the Octavius estate. Unruly hedges grew high and wide around us, obscuring my view of the mansion and the stables that I knew lurked somewhere to the west. For that, I was glad. What little I'd seen of the campus had already left me seeing stars.

The main family didn't even live here, and it was still the most ornate place I'd seen in my entire life. And that was saying something.

"If she wants ta cheat, she's more than welcome to win one." Rags took his offered hand and stood. She lifted the edge of her tunic, exposing the cut ridges of her abdomen, and swiped sweat from her forehead. "That's the only way she's going ta win this thing, at any rate."

"I resent that," I called without heat. I had zero interest in standing for the rest of the day and rolled on my back, arms splayed wide.

Footsteps vibrated against the dirt, and the hornet stood over me, blocking out the sun. Her long, slender wings twitched. "What did I tell ya about using your fists to fight?"

"That Riten wouldn't have gifted us such fine tools with which to knock out someone's teeth if they hadn't meant for us to use them?"

She dropped a jug of water on my chest. "Don't make me kick you when you're down."

"Fine." I huffed but leaned up on my elbows and took a glug of cool liquid. It sluiced right through me in a chilled wave, eliciting a shiver from my bones. "You said I should only use them as a last resort. Which—I contest—after you bested me two dozen times, felt like an opportune moment to call a last resort."

Her hands landed on her hips, a gesture I was quickly associating with agitation. "And?"

"And bluesiders fight with blades." I flashed a grin, punch-drunk on adrenaline and the aches growing more pronounced by the moment. "Good thing I'm not a bluesider."

"That's the truth," Grev intoned dryly. He tossed my jacket beside me, and I promptly balled it up to shove underneath my head. "Now get dressed. It's my turn to dig around inside that brain of yours. The Trials are more than brute strength, you know." He shook his head at my groan. "Past Trials have entailed everything from resolving court intrigue to unraveling impossible mysteries to unfortunate scavenger hunts. You'll need your wits far more than you'll need your muscles."

His eyes lingered on the silk wrapped around my arms and throat, my lean limbs exposed by my sleeveless black tunic.

The hornet and his stiff mannerisms reminded me so much of Devlin that I couldn't resist needling him, just like I had my mentor. "Tell me, was it the forty-ninth or the forty-seventh Trials where the champions were dropped high in the mountains along the border with Fior and instructed to design a new ship, one capable of crossing the Cove in half a day?" I winked when he closed his eyes in exasperation. "And wasn't it Champion Taburn who solved the irrigation problem presented in the final challenge of the eighteenth Bloodletting?"

Inhaling loudly through his nose, he gritted out, "Forty-ninth and yes, Taburn was gifted, even among those of his class." He spun toward the building that was one of two guest houses located behind the estate. Bluesiders really were another breed. I'd forgotten their habits over the last decade, but they were coming back to me now. "Let's see what else you know of your predecessors. Hurry to it."

I rose and tapped the flat of the jawram against my palm, pleased to have made a dent in his stuffy attitude.

"He's too much of a stick in the mud to ask if those wraps cover yer whole body." Metal clanged as Rags gathered the various weapons she'd brought out this morning: thunder axes favored by beetles; willow whips that danced in the hands of butterflies; clever, leaf-shaped knives recovered from greenside fights; and pellets that encapsulated everything from powdery dust to colorful poisons. She planted the point of the serrated broadsword preferred by mantises into a groove between the stones and braced her weight against it. "An' why ya do it."

I tugged on my jacket and hauled my cloak into my arms. "But you aren't?"

"I prefer beating people into submission with the sticks I find."

A chuckle bubbled up in my chest, warm and unexpected.

"Don't get me wrong, he's the guy ya want on your side when it comes to learning the ins and outs of diplomacy," Rags continued, her sword sinking deeper into the dirt. "He's got strategy down to a tee, an' I imagine he's plotting just how he'll question ya later. But me," she pointed her thumb at her chest, "I'm all attitude."

"No subterfuge to be found here," I murmured, following her across the patio tiles. I couldn't tell if they were green, blue, or some shade in between. "And yes, the bandages cover my entire body. Everything except my eyes, mouth, fingertips, and tips of my toes."

I wiggled my hand at her, though it lacked the humor I'd attempted to infuse into the gesture.

The guard appraised me, her helmet of short hair mussed and speckled with dirt. Somewhere in the direction of the main house, a zira cawed. "An' the why?"

The stopper in the jug proved tougher to remove this time. "That's a long story." Cork free, I tipped the lip into my mouth and swallowed the last of the water.

Rags broke our heavy stare-off first. Acceptance. Not an apology. "I will be asking again, ya know."

"Oh, I know." I handed her the jawram. "You know my skills with this are mediocre at best, right? You're wasting your time."

The hornet twisted the grip, separating the blades, which she spun around in practiced twirls. "Never a waste. Yer good on your feet. I might not like it, but someone trained ya well with yer hands. I doubt you'll ever be ready for a sword, but the jawram is somethin' else. If it's what yer comfortable with..." she trailed off, brow lifting. I kept my mouth closed, knowing she wanted me to confirm my hybrid heritage as an ant. When I didn't snap up the bait, she shook her head. "Ya might not win awards for yer work, but you'll damn well be able to react when a weapon is swung your direction."

Fair.

With a quick nod of appreciation, I rushed to catch up with Grev. It was fun to test how far he was willing to allow me to needle him, but I didn't want to know what happened when the hornet finally snapped.

11

The Under Ant

Nim

Two days passed in a blur of aching muscles, hypothetical problem-solving, and seemingly endless mental exercises. Why I needed to know why the Sai duke had allied himself to the Amana Duchy two hundred years ago, only for their alliance to fracture within the last decade, was beyond me, but Grev had quickly proven that questioning him was a bad decision, so I reserved voicing my thoughts.

The sweet musk of fresh straw seeped through the threadbare blanket covering my bed and I inhaled deeply. With the last of my strength, I'd replaced the old bedding with new material purchased along Merchant's Row. Rags had handed me a pouch jangling with coins that morning, fulfilling the prince's promise.

I'd offered Ms. Whitmere my late payment, interest included, but with her usual lazy disdain, she refused to touch the coins, forcing me to leave them on the coffee tray in her reading nook. Though we'd forged an agreement, she'd long since made it clear she wanted nothing to do with my money.

With my nail, I peeled back the corner of the yellowed waspspaper

I'd painstakingly plastered to the single, dirty window, peering out into the quiet of the moonlit street. The Dusty Wings Bookstore resided on a corner of Merchant's Row, away from the taverns, closer to the run-down homes. The hustle and bustle of busy insects often lulled me to sleep. However, at this late hour, even the cicadas had called it a night, closing their wings and packing up their instruments, returning to their homes deep within the trees.

Carefully smoothing the page back down, I settled back into bed, head propped on my forearm, enjoying the brushes of vibrations that were the cobwebs fluttering across the low ceiling. Every limb hurt. Fresh bruises sprouted across my skin. And yet, I'd discovered a level of peace that I hadn't recovered since leaving the comforts of the Firestone and the clan of Shells.

Yes, the Trials were bloody. Yes, they were brutal and would take every ounce of energy I possessed to survive—mental and physical. And yes, there was the chance my secrets would come to light. But the longer I trained with the prince's guards, the more confident I felt in my abilities. I could do this. I was stronger than I remembered.

Rolling to my side, I trailed my fingers across the smooth floor-boards, cheek pressed to the blanket. My mother had raised me well, and I was surprised at how much I remembered of her teachings. Those, paired with the skills I'd adopted under Devlin's tutelage, worked in my favor.

I didn't mind playing the part of the dark horsefly.

The under ant.

I'd never minded applying myself to things that interested me, and the Bloodletting held the biggest allure of all. Finally, mind humming with thoughts of what I would accomplish tomorrow, I allowed my lids to fall closed. My hand going limp on the floor.

12

Personal Crest

Sebastian

"Will she survive?" I drew up beside Grev, ensconced in the shadows of the balcony, watching the two figures smacking one another with septant swords below—the same design as the blade that hung from my hip. A breath later, Nim collapsed in the dirt, her weapon flying across the yard, hands raised in supplication while Rags berated her mercilessly.

Damn.

"You always were good at asking the complicated questions, boss," Grev replied, resting his chin on his palm. "Just like your abilities of choosing multi-faceted people with whom to surround yourself."

I dropped the stack of packages I'd brought on a table and dusted off my hands. "Oh, good, more riddles. Just what I was hoping for at the break of bloody dawn."

The hornet's wings flared, buzzing in frustration, before flattening against his back. "Her skills with the bow and sword are nonexistent, as you see, and her abilities with a jawram are rudimentary at best, foolhardy at worst." He shot me a dark look over his shoulder. "I suppose we have your father to thank for that."

When Nim won me this competition and I dissolved the crown once and for all, my first proposal would be to abolish the law banning the lower classes access to weapons. They deserved the opportunity to protect themselves. And it wasn't like the law kept the gangs from getting their hands on weapons, anyway. All they had to do was turn to the shadows.

"In a fight of fists, she can hold her own. Someone spent a significant amount of time training her how to punch a hybrid in the face while sweeping his knees out from under him." Grev coughed into his closed fist. "Even better: she isn't afraid to cheat."

Nim jogged to her sword and hefted it, limbs gangly like dead grass. She had little time to recover because Rags was off, zipping across the tile. The thief's sword hit the ground with a clatter. She raised her arms, fists clenched tight, and twisted at the last second. Nim dipped beneath the sweep of Rags' weapon and wound her arms around the hornet's middle, pulling her wings tight around her waist, and swung her over her shoulder. Rags barely missed skewering herself on her own weapon when she landed hard on her back, winded.

Someone had spent more than time with her.

She was a natural.

"Think you can remember that move?" Nim dropped to a crouch beside the guard and poked her side while dangling a water flask over the hornet's head. "It took me four months to master, but I bet you could get it in two."

Rags sputtered, groaned as she rose to sit, and snagged the vessel, speaking between massive gulps. "You. Cheating. Dung beetle."

"Better a dung beetle than a hornet who lost her wings."

...and mean as one, too.

"I can work with that," I murmured with a grin as Rags shot up, geysering curses like the pirate she was at heart. "Anyone who can get under Rags' skin deserves my respect."

Not just that, I wanted to test her skills myself. On the ship, we deckhands would fight to pass the time. Anyone willing to test their skills was welcome to join. It was how the three of us had gotten so good at wielding weapons that were not natural to our aether. It was a vast change from how things had been when my father only *allowed* me to spar with the best of the best. The crown never wanted to risk having a lower-class soldier off one of its sons by accident.

Which was why I often snuck off to the training grounds in disguise...

Until Vincent put a stop to that.

Now that I was back in Moldona, that part of my childhood reared up, and I found the two sides of my world clashing uncomfortably.

Grev shook his head, drawing my attention away from the makeshift training field once more. "Permission to speak freely?"

I shot him a look. "Since when do you ask for permission?"

"Since now."

"What's on your mind?"

"Something about your thief isn't adding up." He ran his thumb across his lower lip in thought, nibbled on the nail. "Are you sure she's a greensider?"

"She moves like a bug and talks like a bug..."

"On that we agree," he acquiesced. "But I've worked with her a lot these past few days, testing her training in the finer arts, and she's far more advanced than any greensider I've ever met."

Grev's observational skills were second to none. Where I trusted Rags to protect my back in the most literal of senses, Grev offered intellectual support and a keen understanding of how the world worked. Sometimes I relied on him more than I relied on myself.

"She can recite the country's history and the succession of kings. Math is more difficult, but she grasps concepts beyond basic arithmetic. If you pushed me to identify her favorite subject, philosophy would be the way to go. You might not guess it from how she hides herself away, but she loves an argument." Grev rested his hip on the railing. "If you asked me, I'd say she's either a long-lost relative of one of the duchies or she's spent most of her life working in one."

Nim and Rags had given up on training and lolled beside the fountain, backs to us, speaking too softly for the wind to carry their words. The thief truly was an enigma. Curious.

"Has she revealed her aether?" I mused, trying to determine which insect dominated her blood.

Grev drew a knife and a willow stick from his pocket and began working on the nub of a new pen. "No. But I agree with your assessment: she's short, strong, stubborn—all characteristics common to ants. As far as hybrids go, ants don't have much to flaunt, aside from the ones with fire in their veins, so many prefer to keep their heritage tucked away." He paused again, considering. "And there's the way she gravitated to the jawram. If that doesn't speak ant dynasty, I don't know what does."

All the reasons why they were sequestered to greenside with the other Eritrian citizens who bore... less desired traits. Flies, worms, aphids—all known for their aptitude for work, but with skills less befitting more noble senses of the word. Roaches probably should have their own residence among the elite based on their propensity for survival, but some political squabble a few generations past had solidified their standing among the lower classes.

The senseless segregation was yet another thing that needed to change.

"Let's see what I can get out of her," I said, straightening. "Maybe she has a more extensive history with blueside like you imagine. Or, perhaps, there's another logical reason for her comprehension. Either way, I'd count ourselves lucky she's shown the aptitude she has."

Grev saluted me with his knife, not bothering to look up from his work as I vaulted over the balcony and landed in the arena below.

"Since when do I pay you to sit around and gossip, Rags?" I demanded.

Without looking at me, the hornet held up her hand, middle finger raised. She leaned around Nim, who twisted on the fountain to watch my approach. "Does this mean yer actually goin' ta start paying me?"

"And ruin the balance of our friendship? Never." As Rags grumbled, I stopped beside the thief, who shielded her eyes to meet my gaze. "How is training going?"

"Well enough." She adjusted the wrap around the knuckle of her index finger.

"You are aware Opening Ceremonies are five days away, right?"

The thief snorted and shoved up to her feet. "There's little else *for* me to think about." She had shed her jacket and cloak and stood before me in a ragged black tunic and loose-fitting gray pants that ended with boots with holes worn in the sides.

Etret would eventually give way to the icy winds of fret, and I bit back a question about how what she planned to do when the snow drifts piled high and the northern winds howled. Like a weed, concern sprouted and quickly grew long roots—too many of our poor lost digits and limbs to frostbite.

"Grev tells me your aptitude for learning is high."

Her brow lifted as she peered up the foot that separated our heights. "Does that mean I'm more well-rounded than you'd anticipated? Forgive me, my native tongue isn't court."

Snarky. "Well?"

A slender shoulder lifted, the muscles of her arms rippling beneath the wraps. "I work in a bookstore. Surrounded by all that knowledge, it would be foolish not to take advantage."

I filed that away to relay to Grev later. A logical, applicable response.

One that worked with her greensider heritage.

She mistook the expression on my face, and the comedy fled her features. "The owner is aware I'm taking part in the Trials. She'll be filling my post in the coming days, I imagine. You don't need to worry about it interfering with my training."

"I wasn't worried, but I am here to discuss your future." I dropped the pouch I'd brought with me onto the ledge of the fountain Rags had vacated. "You were paid upfront already, but here's extra coin. Feel free to cut yourself free of whatever rent you're paying. You'll be staying with us from now on."

Nim's features went stony, her body locked tighter than a caterpillar in a cocoon.

"You've spent the last week on your own, but I prefer to keep my associates close. We'll need to maintain close proximity throughout the Trials," I explained. "Training. Consulting. Tailoring. When we need you, I want you nearby." And I was a selfish bastard who didn't like sharing my friends. Call it youngest child syndrome, but I wasn't a fan of sharing my toys. Whether she liked it or not, the thief was about to become one of my closest allies.

"Is that all?" Her gaze was flat, muted. I'd assumed her irises were silver, but in the daylight, they were actually a shade of green so pale they were almost gray.

"No, it's not. There's the matter of your attire." I waved a hand at her ragged clothing. Rags emerged at my side, a curious lilt to her expression as she offered the additional packages I'd brought with me. I handed them to the thief one at a time. "Shirts. Pants. Boots. Jacket. Cloak. Anything you need, I will provide. I am the one asking you to die on my behalf, after all," I said dryly.

She cut the twine on one package and leafed through the shirts. Then she opened another and shook out the jacket inside. She ran a hand down the compass embroidered on the back, brow furrowed, eyes narrowed. "I thought Octavius' colors were silver and teal. These... aren't?" She said it like a question.

"Blue and light gray are the colors of the sea," I clarified. "And my personal crest is the tool used to navigate wherever you call home."

They were the colors my comrades and I always wore away from the castle. Colors I hoped would be adopted—albeit temporarily—at the castle, should Nim succeed.

Her mouth opened and closed again. She tugged at the bandages encasing her wrists, the material scuffed with dirt and dust. "I don't know what to say."

"'Thanks,' is a solid start," Rags chirped, setting a jawram on top of the mess. "Ya'll want to wear that once the Trials begin. As the competition wears on, we can refine yer equipment as ya get a taste for what works best for ya." She motioned at the wild array of weapons propped up against a rack.

Nim's eyes darted toward the venomous fang dagger on the right before returning to the hornet. Interesting. It was a weapon that hadn't been used since the Arachnae Duchy destroyed itself from the inside out. The spiders had preferred feeding their own venom into the hollow of the small, precise weapon. Had she ever encountered the blade before?

"Ya've been granted a special exemption to openly carry since yer a champion an' all." Rags tucked a piece of clear glass with the necessary notations scripted on one side into the thief's hand. "Not like the whole kingdom won't know who ya are at the week's end, regardless."

Nim remained silent as Rags stalked back to Grev, who stood off to the side, a set of books clasped under his arm. I nudged her. "You alright?"

"I'm fine." She shook herself free of whatever gripped her. "May I have the afternoon off? I'd like to grab some things from my apartment. Settle some affairs."

"You'll meet us at the Primrose tonight." It wasn't a question.

"Yes."

I'd scarcely nodded when she was off.

13

Riddles

Nim

I kept my apartment.

The prince might be a commanding piece of work, but he couldn't order me to get rid of my old life like it was nothing. I'd already lost everything I owned twice, and I was loath to sacrifice what little I had left to my name voluntarily.

The money was more than enough to cover a month's rent up front, and Ms. Whitmere was pleased to keep me around for whatever reason. Though I hadn't lied, she would replace my front desk position. Her wings weren't getting any younger.

"Time's up. What's your answer?" Grev drummed his fingers on the table.

Crap. "What?"

He glowered, hunching over the curled pages of the book open before him. "The riddle? Were you even listening? I know you're intelligent, and you know the Trials are far more than physical tasks, so why won't you apply yourself?" His fingers drummed faster. Steam practically billowed from beneath the folds of his cap.

The more training Grev and Rags demanded of me, the more I was ready for the damned Bloodletting to begin already. I barely recalled the question but managed to say, "A mirror?"

Grev's amber eyes narrowed to slits, but he directed them back to the page. "That took you less than a second to answer."

The legs of my chair creaked as I leaned back, knee propped on the lip of the table, and rocked in place. "I told you these are too easy. Don't you have anything more complicated in your bag of tricks?"

The hornet dragged his hat over his eyes, releasing a shrill tone that sounded like a kettle. "I can't. I can't anymore, Seb." He glowered at the prince, who turned a page in the book he was reading beside the window. "She's either not paying attention or making a mockery of my work. I'm not a teacher. I never wanted to be a teacher." He huffed. "You know what. I'm taking a walk. Need some air."

The hornet slammed the book shut, shoved it under his arm, and strode from the room. I flinched at the sharp patter of his shoes down the stairs.

"You shouldn't bait him," the prince said. "He's only trying to help." He sat close enough for me to notice the edges of his black silhouette were sharp against the harsh light cast through the windowpanes.

The raised legs of my chair hit the ground with a tap. I rubbed my eyes blearily. "I would love nothing more than being an apt student, but I'm more a doer than a thinker. I'd rather delve into the project than be told how to solve it."

"You believe the Trials won't test you? Push you to the brink of your sanity and knock you clean over?" Another page turned. "That your body won't ache so badly you'll want to slit your own throat just to end the pain? That you won't feel your brain throbbing between your ears as you struggle to understand the mind-twisting tricks they'll play on you?"

Chills ran down my arms.

85

"The Trials are not a joke; the people you'll be up against have trained for this role their entire lives. Rest assured; they will not take kindly to a greensider challenging them for a title they believe they were born to seize."

"It shouldn't be this way, though," I griped. "People will die. They will sacrifice themselves in a vain attempt to put someone else on a throne that comes with nothing more than a power trip and ugliness."

Sebastian turned his head, but the light at his back blew out his features. "On that, you and I agree. It's what I'm desperately trying to change. But I need you to buckle down and accept the tests we are throwing your way if you want to stand a chance of surviving the first challenge."

Bracing my elbows on the table, I leaned my forehead into my interlocked hands and stared at the grains in the oak. He was right. I hated to admit it, but he had a point. For most of my life, I'd relied on my wiles to survive, but this might be the first circumstance where keen instincts and a knack for trickery wouldn't get me out of a mess.

"I get it."

The prince didn't respond, but I felt his eyes on me all the same. Seconds stretched into minutes until I finally lifted my head, searching out his gaze in the shadows.

"What is it that given one, you'll have two or none?" he asked.

I tugged on my sleeve. "Another riddle?"

"Answer it correctly and we'll end your training now." The prince turned fully in his chair, back propped against the wall. "But if you fail, Grev will drill you on arithmetic through the night before Rags gets her hands on you in the morning."

"But the Opening Ceremonies begin at nine sharp."

"Then you'd best answer correctly." He stood and circled the table where Grev and I had worked these past few days. "You said you wanted a challenge. So, rise to the occasion."

I draped my arm over the back of the chair, pondering the question. One of something means I have two or none. That wouldn't apply to many physical objects. I could have one scarf and thousands of threads, but never none. Food was also out. So that left things beyond the physical. Clairvoyant? No. If I believed in Riten, I couldn't have two of them. But what about beliefs? One belief, two options? To believe or not to believe?

Floorboards creaked as the prince paced the room, hands laced behind his back. The sharp scent of mint permeated the small space. I'd already determined the mantis had a mild addiction to the herb and kept a pouch of it at the ready.

Squinting, I willed my eyesight to focus, to show me what the vibrations couldn't.

The sunlight streaming through the window carved rectangles across his clothing. Three princes. Five duchies. One kingdom. Seven champions. If one dropped out, that left six. Choices, so many choices.

My leg stopped bobbing.

"A choice. If I have a choice, I choose between two things or I have none."

Sebastian inclined his head, and clapping came from the doorway. I winced at the sudden sound. Rags pushed two fingers between her lips and whistled. At her side, wry grin firmly in place, Grev pressed his hands together.

"Does this mean we're done training for the day?" I murmured.

"Yeah," the prince replied. "Let's get back to the Primrose. It's getting late, and we could all use a healthy night's rest. The Opening Ceremonies begin in the morning."

* * *

Flags of lavender and white fluttered from the corners of the wide front porch of the Kincaid mansion. It boasted four full stories and a carriage house with not one but three covered vehicles and enough zira to pull them all at once. To me, the house was a breath of fresh air on the long road to the gates dividing blue and green sides. I appreciated the large glass panels running the width and length of the front of the house. Thick curtains granted some measure of privacy, and translucent decorations stuck to the panes cast rainbows on the ground below.

The Kincaids, with their bejeweled wings and frothy antennae, were the newcomers to blueside, only granted their duchiship nine years ago following a significant donation to the crown. Construction on the main house had wrapped up recently, but beyond it, the sounds of hammering and sawing indicated the termites were still hard at work on something else on the estate's grounds.

Of the five duchies, their property was the smallest. That was no fault of their own. They had the misfortune of being squeezed between the Amana estate... and what remained of the Arachnae legacy.

As always, when we approached the final property on the block, I averted my eyes, focusing on the road instead.

"It's a shame the Kincaids chose ta build on new ground," Rags said, trailing her fingers along the railing ringing the property, the metal twisted into shapes of butterfly wings. "I get not wanting ta move into the Arachnae estate, but they coulda razed it and built anew."

"And welcome the ghosts of murderous pasts into your lives? No, thank you," replied Grev, tugging his hat further over his eyes.

The pull on my curiosity was too strong, and despite the burning of my skin beneath my wraps, I took in the Arachnae estate for the first time in over a decade. The walls of the foreboding gray mansion were composed of mismatched wood and stone. Few windows overlooked the sprawling lawn and its many weeds. I remembered a time when intricate webs and long strings of silken ropes decorated the outside of those walls, making them glitter in the morning dew. Now, the silk had frayed to cobwebs, and vines snaked up the splintered shutters.

Otherwise, it loomed, as imposing as always. A narrow front porch dissuaded visitors on the most pleasant of days. A single balcony offered shade over the entrance, though the copper railing circling it dangled precariously, as if someone had crashed through the bars. The next story up boasted nothing but long rows of tiny, round windows, portcullises into the outside world. Higher still, the third and fourth floors boasted no windows, and I wondered at the state of the rooftop garden after years of neglect.

"Seb, what were the results of the investigation?" Rags asked. The group stopped outside the gates to the lawn. "Did they figure out what drove tha Arachnaes ta madness?"

I balled the edges of my new jacket sleeves in my fists, pulling the fabric taut while the prince considered the question. "Pride and warring factions, mostly. You couldn't tell from the outside, but Vincent's investigation found evidence of a house divided.

"Duchess Ava wanted to keep the family on the track it always had been, exploring the outer world instead of delving into internal politics. But investigators said that younger generations were bucking old habits, pushing for more. They wanted to take part in the next Trials, claim more power and prestige." The prince scratched the scruff of his goatee like he did when perplexed. "One thing led to another, and rather than resolve their differences, they murdered one another in a single night."

I shuddered and closed my eyes against the images flickering across my mind, imagining the screaming echoing in my ears. What a horrible, terrible night. But knowing how the family of spiders operated, how keen they were about silence and secrecy, it wouldn't have surprised me if no one passing by had heard the cries for help from within.

Rags sighed. "I can't figure out why they never took part in the Trials. Ya'd think they'd have dominated, given their poisons an' other natural abilities."

"The Arachnae Duchy had a longstanding agreement with the king," I said. Grev turned to me with interest. "They wouldn't participate in the Bloodletting as long as the crown gave them freedom to roam." I rolled my shoulders, uncomfortable under the attention. "Most of the trade routes through the mountains are a result of their efforts."

Grev frowned, toying with the brim of his hat. "Were they looking for something?"

"Could have been wanderlust," Sebastian argued, nudging Grev into motion once more. "But it's a good question."

I swallowed hard and knelt to retie the laces of my shiny, new boots.

"Regardless, it's tragic," Rags said with one last glance at the mansion before jogging to catch up with Grev. "Even the children died. Every last one."

"Tragic, but a lesson all the same." Grev kicked a rock into the gutter. "Power is madness. Best to not get too wrapped up in it."

The prince barked out a harsh laugh. "Always the realist." He slung his arm around his friend's shoulders and tugged his hat off. "Don't you ever tire of your dreary outlook?"

As the group squabbled, I nodded to the hornets guarding the gates separating the classes, trailing at a comfortable distance. Grev wasn't wrong. Power had a way of rotting the mind and disintegrating the soul.

But if my companions were that aware of its demands, then how could they be so certain that acquiring more of it wouldn't affect them, too?

90

14

Enter Unarmed

Nim

Ashes pale as the moon's glow dusted the stacked bricks that formed the western wall of Archer Arena. I dragged a finger across a brick that ran level with my face, smearing the substance between my fingers. The celebratory fires marking the eve of the Fifty-First Bloodletting had burned bright into the night, the glow on both sides of the copper wall visible from the window of my room at the Primrose, where I'd perched half the night, listening to the whooping and drunken hollering.

I rubbed my fingers together again, the film darkening as it mixed with the dirt beneath my nails. Rags had assured me for the fourteenth time this morning that the Opening Ceremonies were more pomp than circumstance before abandoning me beside the gate.

I dipped a second finger into the mess, carving another path through the film. The scattered ashes were meant to be an ominous sign for the champions, a signal of their future if they lost.

But they didn't need to be looked at that way. Was it the Illumi who worshiped an elegant bird-like goddess believed to be reborn every other generation from the ashes of her former self? Her name clung to my tongue like syrup, too sticky to drip. Phetra? Phenon? The page upon which I'd read about her legacy spread before me, the sketch of her naked figure rimmed in gleaming oranges and vivid blues. Yet her name...

"Champion? Or servant?" A female voice smoother than my silken wraps interrupted my musing. Shoulders shifting beneath my cloak, I ensured my hood was drawn as far forward as it would go before turning to the female hovering beside me.

"Major Ectya Day." Her name spilled from my lips before I could bottle it up, and she sketched a bow in response, double sets of wings whirring. The major was well-known among greensiders. She was the first dragonfly ever named to leadership in Wing Command, the first of her class, and heavily decorated. Everyone knew when she passed her final exam that she would start her career no lower than captain.

And she was here.

Outside Archer Arena.

That could only mean one thing.

"You're a champion, too?" I asked, thoughts buzzing.

She touched down, the tips of her knee-high boots gracing the paving stones, and slung black hair so shiny it appeared wet over her shoulder. Jewel green eyes analyzed me, peering beneath my hood, but I hunkered back, limiting her vision, and she straightened, using her wings to pull her spine straight.

She tapped the white pin stuck into the fabric bunched at her shoulder with one long finger. "Representing the Kincaids." Her lips pursed. "And since you aren't ready to reveal yourself, be warned: Your accent relays more than you realize. I recognize greensiders when I hear them." Lips painted white quirked in the corners. "And I know better than to underestimate them."

I lowered my head.

Metal clinked as the dragonfly reached for her belt, presumably searching for the pommel of her sword that wasn't at her hip like the prince had a habit of doing. Her antenna twitched, eyes sliding to the gaping entrance of the arena. Distractedly, she murmured, "Interesting, isn't it, that they ordered us to enter unarmed?"

"It is," I managed. Grev had noted the same thing when the missive had arrived. The thick parchment had borne three pieces of information about the Opening Ceremonies: when, where, and not to arrive armed. "I'll see you inside."

The major thumped her clenched fist over her heart in a soldier's salute and slipped into the shadows beneath the arches, heels clicking on the stones. She would be one I needed to watch—and potentially ally with—if her observation about my heritage was meant as a peace offering.

With one last glance at the ashen walls, I shoved my hands into the pockets of my cloak and followed. The punishment for being late hadn't been relayed, but if it was like everything else associated with the Trials, it would likely be bloody.

The din of thousands of insects packed closely together hummed louder as I strode down the tunnel, barely noticing the flickering of the lanterns secured to the walls. The last time I'd visited the arena had been more than a year ago, and amid particularly desperate times. Running my fingers over the red ribbons binding my braids, I remembered the hunger that gnawed at my belly in those first few weeks after leaving Devlin's security, choosing to exit gang life and make it on my own.

Archer Arena called to me on the third weekend, the sheer volume of people it drew in to watch some sporting event involving long reeds and woven baskets of dried grass was too much to resist. Working my way through the crowd, rejoicing in their distraction, I'd liberated more rucks and stained glass from the pockets of spectators than I knew what to do with. My greed had almost gotten me caught, too, I recalled wryly. A guard who noticed my antics had grabbed for me, only missing because he'd misjudged how little meat remained on my bones.

The tunnel's darkness gave way to light, and I paused at the curved edge of the shadow where it met the sunshine, toes resting against the blurry rim. I hadn't paid attention to the arena's layout my last time here, but I had a feeling it had looked nothing like this.

The grounds were contained within twenty-foot walls, forming an oval. Rows and rows of seats, orderly as a honeycomb, stretched high into the sky, filled with insects of all kinds. At one end of the playing field, the end closest to me, an elevated stage overlooked the competition. Two thrones were seated in the middle, a pair of Octavius flags bracketing them. Stools bracketed the overbearing chairs on either side, divided into sections. I assumed the duchy flags would be brought out when the heads of the families crossed the stage to take their seats.

The field itself was broken into sections. They moved in a gradient, with grass on the outer edge where dozens of aphids and termites wearing army uniforms stood. The grass transitioned to a wide swath of dirt, ending with a rocky, raised hill in the middle. The remnants of an old stone pergola rose high in the area, the long columns of granite-like fingers poking up from the earth.

I shoved my braids back into the recesses of my hood and eyed the earth before the stage where five champions stood. From a hundred feet away, the dragonfly's uniform was unmistakable. She stood beside the tall form of a hornet with his wings drawn close to his back, gesturing in casual conversation. A chill ran down my spine. Everyone knew that hornet and his deadly pleasures: Flint Verity, Wing Commander of the Army.

His brutality was legendary.

Gulping, I slipped into the sunlight and strode across the grass. Like me, two competitors kept their hoods up, identities concealed, minding their own business. But the fifth hybrid strode around, raising beefy arms up toward the crowd, drawing cheers. Antonio Viotto. I only knew of one Goliath beetle, and he was as big as they came: seven feet tall with a head like a hatchet, all hard lines and wide planes. Thick, black, armor-like shells covered his back, concealing his wings. The beetle roared and thumped his chest with fists as big as my skull. Before he noticed me, I slipped in beside one of the nameless figures, trying not to consider their identities.

The three champions I recognized were powerhouses: Dragonfly, hornet, and beetle of epic status.

No doubt, the other two would be equally intimidating.

Sweat slipped down my back as I felt for the jawram beneath my cloak. I'd disregarded the instructions because stepping onto a field of would-be killers without protection seemed recklessly foolish, so I'd taken a risk. Unlike the others, it wasn't like I could tap into my aether to save myself.

In an effort to clear my thoughts, I gazed at the upper decks of the bowl. For once, ants sat beside roaches without trying to shank one another, their faces pointed toward the field in rabid excitement. Merchants mixed with maids, laughing and drinking as if they were friends. Surreal didn't come close to the situation. It was as if I were peering through a pane of warped glass, knowing the world on the other side was real despite its irregularities.

A cheer went up from the ants as they jumped to their feet in a wave of red, louder than the cheer Viotto had wrung from his section. I glanced over my shoulder, and my heart tumbled to my stomach as the seventh champion strode from the tunnel, hand raised over his head, waving.

95

Jax.

My best friend in the entire world was moving toward me.

Wearing the brown and red colors of the Sai house.

In a fight to the death.

I couldn't swallow. The saliva in my mouth had dried up. My arms trembled, and I locked them against my sides, mind racing. Should I reveal myself to him? I deliberately hadn't spoken to him or Devlin over the last week and a half, fearful of their judgment and concern when they found out I'd entered this brutal competition.

Little had I known.

My friend stopped beside me, dragged his hand through his hair, and adjusted the red headband, keeping it off his face. He seemed relaxed despite the scrutiny and squared his shoulders as he faced the stage.

Guilt and worry rose like bile in my throat. I couldn't contain the ruse any longer. Decision made, I started to pull my hand from my cloak, reaching for him to reveal myself, when a trio of trumpets trilled. At the back of the stage, a door swung wide.

15

Reward and Risk

Nim

"From House Kincaid, introducing Duke Ferdinand, Duchess Ida, and their daughter, Lady Jezebelle, who has put her name forward to claim the throne."

The crowd's chattering cut off at the proclamation, and I craned my neck, struggling to pinpoint where the voice was coming from. A few champions stood taller, hands clasped behind their backs, facing the throne. I mimicked them, unsure if there was protocol Grev had forgotten to relay.

A pair of aphids bearing the lavender and white banners of House Kincaid appeared at the gate. A trio of butterflies wearing matching colors emerged behind them, wings waving lazily, and followed their escorts to the edge of the stage, where the elder couple primly took their seats. All three had glossy, black hair, though only Lady Jezebelle displayed her fuzzy black antennae. The duke's wings shimmered a deep violet while the two females bore white wings with spots of black. Jezebelle strode to the edge of the stage and scanned the crowd before nodding at her champion.

The trumpets unleashed another blast, and a new pair of soldiers with red and brown banners strode across the stage. "From House Sai, Duke Eldredge, Duchess Antoinette, and their niece, Lady Aurora, who will represent their house in the quest to claim the throne."

This time, the youngest Sai led the way, standing tall and confident in her embroidered tunic and velvet pants. The centipede's two extra sets of arms were clasped against her torso, while her free hands waved at the crowd. Aurora tossed sun-bright hair over her shoulder, threw a smirk at Jax, and took her spot at the end of the stage opposite the Kincaids.

I shifted on my feet, horribly aware of the fire ant standing beside me. Beneath my wraps, my hands felt sweaty, and I balled them up in my pockets, tuning out the next blast of trumpets introducing the Viotto Duchy. How would Jax take it when he realized who he stood beside? I could imagine his shock and concern. The hurt that I'd kept this from him.

Lorenzo Viotto took up his spot and glanced at the hooded figure who stood head and shoulders taller than me at my side. The furrow between my brows deepened. If Antonio *wasn't* fighting for him, then who *was* fighting for the honor of their duchy?

To the crowd's delight, Lord William Amana buzzed into the arena on fat bumblebee wings and looped around mid-air before taking up his spot before his aunt and uncle, seated before of a pair of yellow and black banners. He touched his buzzed head with a hand rife with honey-colored jewels and threw his arms wide for the audience, basking in their cheers, paying little heed to the champions standing rigid before him.

It appeared rumors about his vanity were spot on.

The trumpets blasted again, followed by the loud thumping of a bass drum.

"Her Majesty, Dowager Queen Victoria."

A loud clattering filled the stadium as hybrids hurried to kneel. We, the champions, too, took a knee, heads bowed, as the wife of our late monarch drifted on stage, gliding forward smoothly as her wings whirred. She laced her fingers across the belly of her teal dress and turned to her sons, who trailed behind.

"Princes Vincent, Micah, and Sebastian have all taken the opportunity granted to them by the rules of the Trials and will represent House Octavius."

Sebastian followed his mother first, gait lazy and eyes unfocused. Micah pushed forward next, thick muscles in his arms bulging as he wheeled his chair across the stage, the boards creaking beneath the weight of the contraption. Like Sebastian, he kept his wings tucked away, but the ridges of poisonous spines lined the outer edge of his forearms. Prince Vincent was the last to appear.

The son who, in any other continental monarchy, would be declared king.

The one who, if bettors were to be believed, would win the Trials with little effort.

My eyes darted down the row of champions and latched onto the single hornet and the smug smile on his face. Vincent had to have Verity on his side. Based on what I knew of him, the hornet would have offered his services to nothing but a sure thing.

"Please rise." The head of the Luminesae rose, the bits of colored glass stitched into his clothing twinkling like lights. I squinted at the black button so out of place on his resplendent robes, assuming it was the device amplifying his voice around the arena. No insect could naturally achieve these volumes.

A circlet of gold rested low upon his proud unibrow, and he spread his arms wide as the hybrids hurried to follow his command. A shudder ran through me. Though I prayed to Riten and never hesitated to barter in glass chips, the Church of Luminescence gave me the creeps. Its members were tight-lipped, and hardly anyone beyond the inner circle knew what they were up to.

"Thank you, my family, for joining us on this joyous occasion," he continued. I muffled a snort. Only the church would call impending unnecessary death joyous. "Our period of mourning has ended. King Nicholas has ascended into the light. Now it falls upon us the difficult task of selecting his successor. The Fifty-First Trials commence today."

I felt along my thigh until I found the grip of the jawram. Today. I didn't like how it sounded spilling from the firefly's lips.

"As written in the laws of Eritris, our next king or queen will be selected through a Trial of wits and blood. You heard the names of our competitors just now, one for each house, forgiving our reigning house, which has three." The firefly paused for effect, the bobbles of light tipping his antennae swaying slightly. "Seven competitors and seven champions will fight to the glorious end, praying for the grace of Riten to light upon them and shower them with success."

Too pretty. That was what bothered me most about the church. Everything sounded too pretty coming from their books and mouths. Nothing about our world: not the palace, not the marketplace, not the sea, was as pretty as these vulgar words and the Trials they endorsed.

"Shall we meet your champions?" The head threw his voice louder than before, embracing the cheers and stomps and claps that met his question. The air crackled with energy, electrifying the arena in a burst of noise and sound. Explosions of vibrations blurred my world, and I fought to retain focus on the field. I hoped it wouldn't be like this for every challenge.

"For House Kincaid, introducing Wing Major Ectya Day."

The dragonfly shot off the ground, wings humming at impossible speeds, and executed a perfect pirouette. The crowd ate it up, stamping their feet and screaming wildly as she performed a few more maneuvers while the head of the church rattled off her more extraordinary accomplishments. When she finally touched the earth once more, she bowed low to Jezebelle, whose eyes gleamed with excitement, hands pressed tightly against her chest.

The Bloodletting was starting to feel real, and it took everything inside me not to shudder at the weight of the task thrust upon me. Was I ready for this? Would I ever be ready?

"For House Sai, introducing greensider Jaxon Case."

My best friend stood tall, spinning in a slow circle, drinking in the cheers that echoed loudly across the arena with a lazy grin. His charisma was apparent. He was one of them, after all, a greensider who stood a chance at raking in greatness.

"Though he may be small for a fire ant, Case isn't one to be counted out. He follows in his father's footsteps, managing affairs for the Shells—" The stomping and whistling from the upper rows hit a fever pitch as the gang recognized their own. "—And though he's had several brushes with the law, none have stuck."

Jax was quite proud of that fact, too, his grin turning cocky. He lifted his hand again in a wave, exposing the slit several inches below his wrist from which he could shoot venomous darts. I knew from experience that if the toxin they released entered the bloodstream, it would feel like being burned alive.

A glance down the line and a furious face stood out. Flint Verity glared at my friend, square jaw clenched and steely eyes burning with hatred. I fought the instinct to step between them. It was entirely possible one of the scraps Jax had escaped involved the hornet. Jax stepped back in line when the head of the church unrolled the next sheet of parchment.

"For House Viotto, Meo Viotto, twin of Lazzero Viotto, whom he represents."

With a violent ripping sound, the hybrid beside me tore off his cloak and tossed it to the ground with a roar. He wore a tight shirt and even tighter pants, exposing every bulging muscle in his seven-foot frame.

Though leaner than the Goliath, the rhinoceros beetle was just as deadly. A red, ropy scar, the width of my thumb, ran from the corner of his mouth, over his jaw, and disappeared beneath his shirt. I remembered hearing a story about him being gored by his brother as a child. The earth shook as he thudded toward the center of the arena, snorting as his face transformed, taking on the aether features of his insect: wide, sloped forehead, curved nose that extended far beyond his face, and flat teeth capable of crunching bones. Plate armor split his shirt to ribbons, a move that had everyone shooting to their wings and feet.

There was a reason beetles had risen from the greenside ranks quickly in the early years of our country. They were damn intimidating and nearly impossible to kill.

And two of them were assembled on the playing field.

The head of the church didn't wait for the arena to settle. "For House Amana, Morris Amana, younger brother of William Amana."

The second unidentified form tugged off his hood, rounded wings sliding easily through holes cut in the garment. Where his brother was sunshine and reeked of glittering pomp, Morris was shadow and darkly composed. Unlike the previous competitors, he barely acknowledged the crowd, keeping his gaze trained on the stage.

"Morris is among the most recognizable faces for green and bluesiders alike. When he isn't fine-tuning his fighting skills, he's leading patrols through the streets, keeping the peace among the people." That certainly explained the jeers coming from the crowd. "If you think his wit is sharp, you definitely do not want to be on the other end of his stinger."

Bumblebees were the worst. Even Shells gave them a wide berth, not wanting to clash with their inflated egos. They weren't the only ones with lethal stingers, but they were so touchy that some felt they were more volatile than hornets.

I drew in a deep breath, body strangely cool despite the rising pressure. Only three of us were left. And since they appeared to be moving in ascending order of importance among the duchies, that meant I had to be—

"Fighting on behalf of Prince Sebastian Octavius, third son of our late king, is greensider Nim Reed."

The crowd went silent, hardly expecting a *second* greensider to join the field. Cheeks hot beneath my bandages, I pulled back my hood, eyes darting over Jax, too much of a coward to face him head-on. I turned in a slow circle, hand raised in greeting, the wide sleeve of my cloak slipping down my arm to reveal more of my wraps.

Many greensiders recognized me, of that I was certain.

But no doubt they were wondering what the hael I was doing down here.

In the silence, I locked eyes with Sebastian, who lifted his hand and pressed it to his heart. Though he seemed tense, I acknowledged the gesture. *I'm with you.* For the first time since our meeting, my low bow was not mocking. He was why I stood here today. His vision—and his capital—intrigued me enough to draw me into this fight. Now I had to make it out alive.

"Reed is wrapped in secrets, an insect tucked away from the eyes of high society. She favors the Shells—" I tugged on the ribbon trailing from one of my braids—"though swears no allegiances, choosing to whittle her days away as a thief with more abilities than she lets on."

Cloudy skies, Sebastian. Laying it on a bit thick, weren't you, I thought, glaring at the prince. He lifted his brow, the tension bleeding from his limbs. "Even smaller than her fellow greensider, her abilities are not to be taken lightly."

If only they knew.

103

"What are you doing here?" Jax hissed from my right.

I risked a glance and found his face twisted in fury, but the worry in his eyes dampened the expression. My lips pulled back in a half-grin, half-grimace, barely hearing the head of the church announce Antonio Viotto would be fighting on behalf of Prince Micah.

"The reward is worth the risk," I murmured back. "What did they offer you?"

My best friend seethed. Knowing him, he wanted to knock me upside the head, then swoop me into his arms, cradling me close so the world couldn't touch me. As a child and an orphan, I'd always loved those hugs, believing in him and his family more than I'd believed in anything else before. Though we'd grown older and apart, he never changed, his protective instincts never waning.

Under the crowd's roar, he said, "We'll talk later. Meet me at the Firestone."

I dipped my head, mentally bracing myself for the dual attack I surely faced, as the Wing Commander himself was announced as Prince Vincent's champion. Like his dragonfly subordinate, he shot into the skies, wings humming as he inhaled the praise showered upon him. The hornet was hardly as tall as either of the beetles, but he cut an imposing figure in his military uniform, colorful ribbons of accomplishments adorning his sleeves. His sandy hair was cut short, curling around his ears, framing an egg-shaped face with a crooked nose and pointed chin.

Narrowed eyes flashed my way, and I caught a hint of the fury he'd aimed at Jax just moments ago. I lifted my chin, absorbing the blow. Maybe Jax hadn't targeted him. Maybe the Wing Commander loathed greensiders on principle.

"The rules of the Trials are simple." The head of the Luminesae recaptured my attention, pacing the length of the stage. "Our champions must conquer a series of five challenges. Some require wit and intuition, while others put brute strength front-of-mind. The Church of Luminescence determines the nature of these challenges and will provide the champions with a single hint prior to the task. Challenges will be issued weekly, unless otherwise noted."

He stopped in the center of the stage, an icy grin spread wide. "There are two ways out for our champions, should they decide the brutality they face is beyond their abilities. First is death." This was dubbed the Bloodletting for a reason. "And second is voluntarily withdrawing. However—" he was quick to add when boos echoed around the field— "should anyone withdraw, they will be banished from our borders, their aether stripped from their being, never to return."

His gaze sliced across my face, and I was surprised I didn't bleed from the cut.

As much as I wanted to leave this country and find a new life for myself, I wasn't sure I could ever willingly choose banishment. Those stripped of their aether rarely survived the blood loss that came with it, and those banished were not received well by other countries— having limited abilities and marked as traitors.

I was fine with the rules.

Except for the fact that Jax stood beside me now.

That complicated everything.

"Our first trial is 'Proof.'"

The word bounced around my skull, looking for a place to settle. Proof of what? How would that help us plan for what was to come? Jax appeared equally puzzled, grinding his heel into the earth in thought. Those gathered in the stands also grumbled, not pleased with this pronouncement. I caught Sebastian's eye again, and he nodded slowly. *We'll figure this out.*

"Ah. You aren't satisfied with that, are you?" The lights on the head of the church's antennae glowed brighter. Everything in my body tightened. This would end badly. "We wouldn't want that, would we?

And with everyone gathered here already, what's the use in putting off the inevitable?"

I would kill Sebastian the next time I was near him. He had assured me so many times that nothing happened during the Opening Ceremonies. I should have known they would pull something like this. The major's comment echoed through me. She'd seen this coming, hadn't she? The lack of weapons. The sharp eyes. She'd known we were in for something horrific.

"The first trial is Proof of Ability." The cheering started once more. My stomach sank so low, I wouldn't be surprised if it dropped from me entirely. "A fight to the first death, so to speak. Our champions will fight in an all-out brawl on this field. When one dies, the fighting stops." More cheers. Louder. "To keep things interesting, our carefully curated army members will add to the melee. If one of them takes out a champion, they earn a promotion."

I chewed my lip, eyeing the dozens of soldiers ringing the arena. Some had swords and daggers, while others palmed miniature harpoons, capable of firing multiple deadly darts rapidly in a row.

This was bad.

My palm pressed flat against my jawram, and I met Sebastian's furious gaze, a sprinkle of worry glinting on his face. A plan formed. A half-assed one, but a plan. Even better, I'd need Jax to help.

"You may begin."

16

Proof

Nim

The gates closed with a thunderclap.

I didn't remember my feet leaving the ground. One moment I stood at attention, the next my hand closed around Jax's, and together we sprinted for the circle of rocks elevated at the center of the arena. *Get to the top, get to the top, get to the top*, I chanted in my head, feet flying, lungs heaving, the images of my foes blurring at the edges of my vision.

Take the higher ground and hold it.

At the apex, I released Jax's hand, and our backs slammed together, bony shoulders knocking.

"What did the prince offer you to risk your life like this?" the fire ant hissed, rolling his sleeves up to his elbows, giving him clear access to his darts.

I ripped my jawram from its sheath and split it in two, one blade for each hand, muscles vibrating with anticipation as soldiers in black uniforms and gray helmets charged across the arena. Before the stage, the beetles were already locked in battle, armored backs snapping into place as they flung opponents to and fro.

"Pretty sure I asked you that first," I retorted.

"Pa didn't tell me the prince chose you."

The scarlet hue of his scorpion-shell jawram flashed in my periphery. Seeing that blade, realizing that he, too, hadn't risked his life by arriving empty-handed, settled me. Jax guarded the weapon with his life, fitting since he'd almost lost it in a fight with a dozen roaches that had earned him the right to be blooded into the Shells.

"Your father—left!" I shouted, blocking the thrust of a spear from the first aphid to reach our circle of stones. Jax's warm back left mine, and his arm shot out, snagging the staff of the weapon and ripping it from the soldier's grip. As he spun away, I lifted my arm and brought the base of my hilt down on the solder's helmet. He toppled to the ground, motionless.

"Like I was saying, your father doesn't know as much as he thinks he does." I ripped at the ties around my neck and tossed the cloak from my shoulders. The extra material would only hinder me. "Besides, he needs his spies focused elsewhere in the kingdom."

A gruff laugh slipped from Jax's throat while he fired a trio of darts at a set of soldiers who charged at us. His jawram flashed wickedly before he twisted his arm and fired a dart into a third soldier's neck. The toxin took hold quickly, and the soldier dropped, skin bubbling, green pus oozing from his pores.

My best friend-turned-competitor planted his hand on his hip. "Just because you and Pa don't see eye-to-eye anymore doesn't mean he doesn't watch out for you. You're practically his daughter, you know."

I didn't answer, already in motion as the blades of two swords peeked around the edges of a stone column. Jax zipped left, giving me a straight shot at our attackers. It felt good to fight with him like this, our techniques as familiar as the silk wrapped around my hand.

Our blades sang as one, engaged in combat. I ducked low, evading the thrust of one spear, but the second slashed across my arm, cutting through the wraps, drawing a thick line of blood. Fed up, I lurched to my feet, shoulder angled, and crashed into the second aphid's chest, knocking her against the pillar. When she gasped for air, I punched her in the face and swiveled as she slumped, barely catching the edge of the second sword swinging for my back. Dipping low, I scooped the abandoned spear off the ground and slashed at the termites closest to me, driving them back.

Bluesiders may have been raised on engaging in honorable battle and allowing the soldier to regain his feet, but the streets commanded their own rules. Honor went out the door the moment blades were drawn. An aphid ripped the staff from my hand, and I jerked my knee up, leg snapping out, ramming the next aphid right in the gut. She crashed back, helmet flying. Her skull hit the ground with a crack, and she went limp.

"I always hated that move," Jax called, the bodies of three aphids at his feet, darts sticking from their necks. His eyes glittered as they swept across my handiwork. "Never seemed fair to me."

Swiping sweat off my brow, I risked a glance toward the stage. The beetle cousins had effectively smashed more than three dozen soldiers, not bothering to hold back their killing blows. A high-pitched whine screamed from the skies, and I winced as Morris crashed into the backs of a trio of soldiers, knocking them flat.

"You know what isn't fair? Wings." Where had the commander gone? I couldn't see him in the mess of fighting. "I wouldn't be disappointed if the next monarch banned them."

"Bitter. So very bitter." The clang of metal on metal reminded me of the opponents who'd followed us. I spun on my heel in time to see a flash of blood, and the soldier hit the ground, throat ripped open. I met Jax's unapologetic gaze, insides squirming. He swiped at speckles of blood on his cheeks, smearing them.

"Have you killed yet, Nim?" The sound of my first name on his tongue jolted down my spine. He never used my first name. Well, not never. He'd used it that one time when—silver flashed from the top of a stone spire.

"I need a boost," I yelled. Jax didn't hesitate. His knee hit the ground, hands linking. My foot landed in the cup of his palms perfectly, just like always, and I launched myself into the air. Twisting, one half of my jawram caught the staff of the arrow the archer fired before I crashed into the hybrid himself, knocking him from his clever perch. He screamed as he tumbled ten feet down to where Jax waited. I barely avoided falling from the three-foot-wide pillar myself and found my feet when I flung my blade. The hilt crashed into the helmet of the termite sneaking up on my friend, who promptly spun and slit the soldier's throat.

My gut clenched as blood fountained, drenching them both.

A scream from the battlefield drew my attention, and I rose from my crouch, squinting at the crush of bodies before the stage. The beetles had separated, and one had gone after Major Day. He crushed one of her wings in one hand while trying to break through the armored plates of her armor. Dragonflies weren't inherently vicious, but they were keen on self-preservation. The major shrieked as she slashed at him with a curved dagger stolen from one of the soldiers.

"Reed!" Jax hollered.

I'd already spotted it.

A blur of yellow streaking toward the ground.

It crashed into the rhinoceros beetle as he broke from a clutch of soldiers. The shifter's head cracked to the side as he hit the ground, the long horn on his head snapping clean off. The commander didn't hesitate. The lethal black stinger clutched in his grip lashed out and sank deep into Meo's neck.

The beetle didn't have time to shout before the poison spilled through his body.

A gong sounded, signaling the end of the Task.

The soldiers lowered their weapons, and the champions paused, chests heaving. They stared at the hornet, who faced the dais, stinger held high over his head.

I straightened, fingers hooked behind my back. Below, Jax worried his lip, gaze somber when it met mine. With Meo Viotto out, the third-highest duchy in the kingdom had lost its chance at claiming the throne.

And it was the Wing Commander himself who'd drawn first blood.

17

The Last Word

Sebastian

If I didn't find the infirmary soon, I would murder someone.

"Boss, I'm sure she's fine," Rags said, zipping along behind me. Grev had stayed behind with the other heirs to see what he could glean from the gossip. Royals were worse than mosquitoes when it came to spilling secrets. "She got scratched on the arm. It coulda been worse."

"And if the weapons were laced with poison?"

"Then everyone but Verity is dead, because he's the only one th' soldiers didn't get in one way or another," Rags said dryly. "And the Trials are over. We can get out on the sea an' pretend like this was all one long, bad dream."

My heart pounded too fast in my chest. Worry for the dreams I'd carefully curated warred with my rising worry for the hybrid I'd put in the line of attack. They'd caught me off guard, commanding the champions to draw first blood as part of the ceremonies. It was unheard of. Exactly why I should have suspected it.

I hadn't missed Nim's eyes flash toward the stage when Bryant proudly proclaimed his plan.

If she didn't hate me, even a little, at that moment, then I'd lost all ability to read people.

"At least the Viotto clan is out." Rags chattered away as we turned another corner beneath the winding tunnels of Archer Arena. When my brothers and I were little, we loved hiding in these hallways, trying to find the best places to pop out and scare the servants. I'd once known these tunnels like I knew the ocean currents. But not anymore. "Those beetles are more twisted up than a worm above-ground. If they'd gotten their grubby hands on tha crown, this country woulda descended into madness."

"You really think they're still into worshiping false idols?" I volleyed back. Like it or not, Rags' never-ending unraveling of everything on her mind helped settle my stomach and calm my mind. "I thought they put that aside two generations ago when they installed all those stained-glass windows."

Rags snorted. "Showmanship, nothin' more. Ya need ta listen to the servants more often. They know what's happening underneath the mask."

Tides. I'd never particularly liked the Wing Commander, but if what Rags knew to be true, then I would shake his hand myself. Eritris had enough problems on its plate without dealing with half-insane beetles worshiping a god living beneath our feet, who they believed would one day devour us all. I'd once been told that the only thing keeping him at bay was sacrifices. Lots of them. As in every-greensider-in-Moldona sacrifices.

Rags wasn't done yet. "I'm tryin' ta remember where he hit Viotto with his stinger." She rubbed her forearm where her own stinger resided. "It isn't easy getting between their plate armor. I wonder how he knew..."

I tuned her out as the light ahead grew brighter, voices murmuring louder. A moth in a long green jacket appeared in the doorway of the well-lit room, a bundle of bloody rags clutched to her chest, and darted past without acknowledgment.

Hovering in the doorway, I went still. A trio of moths fluttered around the room, needle and thread in hand, long shells filled with medicines hung on chains draped across their chests. Two champions relaxed on cots in the center of the room, chatting as bandages were applied to their wounds. First up, Will Amana, one of the few bees I'd gotten along with before I'd left. He sat upright, wrist bound in bandages that reminded me of Nim's. Nim, who clearly wasn't here. The bee toppled back onto the cot as I honed in on the other hybrid in the room.

Jaxon Case. A fire ant from greenside with a questionable background. But more importantly, he appeared to be a close friend of Nim's, if her actions in the arena were anything to judge. The ant winced, leaning back on one elbow, when the moth tied off the suture she'd stitched along his ribs, closing a rather nasty-looking cut.

A healer noticed me standing in the doorway and lowered to the ground, wings pulled tight against her back, dust motes sweeping around her feathery antennae. Her deference drew everyone else's attention, but before they could follow her lead, I fully stepped inside. "As you were."

The ant straightened on his cot, face pale, pressing his hand to his side, eyes narrowed as I approached.

"I'm looking for Nim," I snapped. "Since you seem to be on friendly terms with her, where is she?" My tone was hot as the forge.

Rather than melt, the ant drew himself tauter, scanning me boots to hairline and back down again. He retorted, "You're the one who roped her into this ugly mess."

"I'm your prince and as such, you owe me your allegiance."

Who was I and why was I acting like this? Even on the ship when I'd finally earned my status as second mate, I'd never treated my crew like they owed me anything. At my back, Rags had gone quiet.

"You may be a prince," the ant said, an edge to the way he stated my title, "but I swear my allegiance to someone far more powerful than you." He dipped his head, eyes hidden beneath shaggy bangs, and reached for his shirt. "However, you are responsible for my best friend, so as a courtesy: she was here for a few minutes, mostly fussing over me, and then left. Where she went after that…" He shrugged. "She's an adult. She doesn't need a keeper."

My hackles rose at his implication, and it took every ounce of restraint I possessed to keep my teeth from sharpening, the lethal spikes along my arms tingling beneath my skin. "Very well."

The ant slipped from the cot and stood. He was taller than most of his kind, but the crown of his head still only reached my nose. His muscles flexed as he pulled his shirt on, revealing strength more wiry than honed: a male who lived to survive, rather than the other way around, much like the thief I'd taken under my wing.

I followed him into the hall, brushing past Rags, who shot me a confused look. Once in the shadows, the ant swiveled, shoving me against the wall with surprising power. The red tint of his skin flared, and his eyes darkened to almost black, glaring. "Who are you to drag someone like her into this despicable nightmare? She was doing just fine before you came along, and now you've thrust her into an impossible situation. I should gut you now and free her of her shackles, you mindless, senseless excuse of an Eritrian."

Swiping his spit off my cheeks, I lifted my chin, impressed. Members of my crew would have treated me like this for acting like an ass, but few in Moldona had it in them to stand up to a member of the Octavius family. We hadn't dominated the top of the food chain for centuries because we let people walk over us. Like the insect that ran in our veins, we preferred patience over rash reaction because revenge was best served frozen.

Which was why my reaction now confounded me. Never had I thought the pursuit of my dreams would hold such sway over me.

Jaxon wasn't done, and he shoved me again, my ribs groaning when I hit the wall. "Nim has gone through so much, she's survived more than you'll ever know, and then you came along. What did you offer her, anyway? Money? She wouldn't want anything else."

"And if I did?" She hadn't pushed for anything else. Though I had questioned why she wanted so little of it. Champions could command their own household on blueside if they wanted, could claim any title they desired aside from duke, duchess, king, or queen. Once she'd agreed to join my team, I'd offered her more money. A thousand crowns, even, if she desired it. However, she'd insisted on the original agreement, saying something about being greedy and three hundred being all she needed.

"Then you deserve the disdain of every Shell who walks your filthy streets." Jaxon squeezed my jacket tight before releasing it, energy drained. Rags still lingered behind us, arms folded, but resting on her heels, not concerned about my well-being in the least. I shot her a look.

"Your protectiveness of your friend is admirable," I admitted to the champion. I, too, would protect those I cared for with stinger and tooth if necessary. "And yes, I promised her plenty of coin should she win the throne for me, but she makes her own decisions. I may not have known her long, but I know that much."

The ant hung his head, dragging his fingers through his rusty hair. The glow of his skin had diminished, the fire in his blood cooling. "I know. I'm just—never mind. It's none of your concern."

"I want to make sure she's okay," I continued, softening, knowing fear for his friend had charged his anger. "I saw her injury and need to know if she needs any help. Will you tell me where she went?"

He eyed me, scratching his arm. "I already told you what I know.

She has many hiding spots around the city, so many I don't know where most are." Hand returning to his side, fighting back a grimace at his injury, he started toward the exit. "Good luck. If she doesn't want to be found, you never will."

* * *

"Since when do ya throw yer title around, boss?" Rags asked, hands deep in her pockets.

I nudged her with my elbow, long legs eating up the hallway as we neared the exit. "I don't know what came over me. It's like all at once, my dream of changing the establishment came into hyper-focus, and I couldn't see beyond it. If something happened to Nim, those plans all go up in smoke."

I rolled my shoulders, my mind's eye still seeing the Viotto twin dead on the ground, veins black with toxin. One minute, he was alive and thrashing, taking out soldiers left and right. The next, he was on the ground. Void of life.

Death was no stranger to me, but the Trials were brutal in a way I'd only read about. In the heat of battle in the middle of the ocean, you were literally fighting to stay alive. Anything became possible in those desperate moments of survival. But the Trials and the bloodshed that came with them...

Death wasn't necessary.

The Viotto's were threats, but Meo was a brother, a cousin, a nephew, a son. A damned member of Eritrean royalty.

And now he was gone.

Dead because of history's cry for this sick form of entertainment.

Stumbling, I pressed my hand against the wall, wiping sweat off my forehead with the back of my hand. Too much. All I needed to accomplish was too much.

"She can't just go running off like that," I gasped, straining to slow my racing heart. "There's a system. She checks in after every match. We made that clear this morning."

Rags squeezed my shoulder, recognizing the signs of the panic attack I valiantly kept at bay. "Are you sure it's your dreams you're worried about? Or is it more than that?"

What a bizarre question.

Like my anxiety, I attempted to bat it away to examine it another time. I slid a mint leaf onto my tongue and closed my eyes, allowing myself a few moments to absorb the cool, calming taste. Slowly, my muscles relaxed, and I regained my composure. Thoughts finally even, I pulled my collar straight and exited through the gates leading out of the arena and into blueside. Groups of hybrids still clustered around the gate, eyeing those who left with interest.

"Maybe she's at the Primrose." Rags tugged the gate closed with a clang. "I wouldn't blame her for not sticking around in that sick ward. Tides knows we're probably better equipped to deal with injuries back at our rooms."

Could be. I followed her across the street, blissfully empty of the spectators who had packed the stands. Twenty thousand of them. Likely a quarter of the population of Moldona. Thoughts turned inward, I wasn't paying attention to the shadows lining the streets until one of them stepped out.

"Brother."

I drew up short at that cold, hard tone. I'd avoided hearing that voice for the past seven years. And now I'd heard it twice in as many weeks.

"Vincent." Without thinking, my wings slid from their sheaths at my back, pink and black panels framing my arms and making me bigger. Though not as big as him. Never as big. "Did you need something? I thought we cleared our differences the other night."

Rags sucked in a breath. I hadn't relayed that part of my evening to my guards.

My oldest brother leaned against the dark brick of the alley. One corner of his lip curled in an expression that would never be described as a smile. "Quite a champion you picked, there, didn't you?"

I should have known this was coming, but I'd gotten caught up in the days of training her. Foolish of me to set aside his threat, and now that he knew who Nim was to me, the risk she faced grew ever greater.

"You're familiar with Nim?"

"I know she fled when she had an opportunity to fight." Though mild, his tone hinted at condemnation. His arms were folded lightly, and one long index finger tapped the inside of his elbow. Rags nudged me, hand braced on the rapier at her hip. "A rather... unique choice, I'd say. Given the nature of the competition, anyway."

Forcing my rage down until it was nothing but glowing embers, I replied, "She ran to the most opportunistic vantage point on the field. Save your strength, let the others pick themselves off when the only priority is to save your own life. I'd say that's rather intelligent thinking, wouldn't you agree?"

Vincent's boots were silent on the cobblestones as he approached. The navy of his eyes glimmered black with the sun at his back. "What hovel did you say you pulled her from, again?"

Rags bristled.

"I didn't," I said through gritted teeth. "Who Nim is and what she does should not be of interest to you beyond the parameters of the Trial." Stepping into his space, I gripped his shoulder in something that might have seemed brotherly to anyone but the pair of us. My grip was tight, painfully so. "And if you forget that, I won't hesitate to remind you."

He flicked me with a finger, face revealing nothing of his thoughts.

"So aggressive, brother. Calm yourself. I want nothing to do with your little ant friend. Either of them." Silently, I cursed Nim for making her alliance with Jaxon so obvious. It was a fact that could easily be turned against her. "I'm not implying anything. In fact, just the opposite."

Stepping back into the warmth of Rags' furious heat, I motioned at him. "What are you after?"

"Like I would tell you."

"Then this conversation is over." Grabbing Rags' hand, I tugged her behind me. As we turned the corner to the wall, Vincent called out, "You shouldn't be so dismissive of your potential allies, you know."

Damn him.

"He's always gotta get tha last word, doesn't he?" Rags grumbled, tugging out of my grip and saluting the guards manning the wall with a half-hearted tip of her hand. "Pompous prick. I'm glad yer nothing like him, or else I'd have beat it out of ya."

On the other side of the gate, I paused.

"Something wrong?" she asked. Then took a guess, "Ya really should have told Grev an' me about meeting with Vincent before. We can't help ya when ya keep secrets."

I barely heard her. Something Jaxon had said stuck in my throat, a feeling I needed to settle. He'd accused me of not understanding my own city, that I didn't know how things worked. Maybe it was time I got out of my head and did something about it.

"Boss?"

"You still have that coin on you?"

"Seb, ya don't want to do this." The worry in her voice rose.

"No, I think I do." Before she could argue, I threw in a phrase that always got her to cave. "There are some people I need to see, and I'll need it to grease a few hands along the way."

With a sigh, she unclipped the pouch from her hip. It contained only a small portion of our savings, but she was always loath to part with any of our funds. "As long as yer hands don't get too greasy in tha process."

"No promises."

18

Reasons

Nim

Each twist of the wrap unwinding around my forearm revealed more silvery scars, like stripes in a cat's fur. Some were less than a quill's tip apart, each line no thicker than a strand of cotton thread, crisscrossing one another in a wild array. Using my nails, I cut the wrap at my elbow, and when the stained bandages pooled in my lap, I ran my finger over the dozens of tiny, healed scars and the nasty, new wound slashing through them all.

Spools of powerful silk clattered together as I rifled through a wooden box near my knee until I found the tool I was looking for. It didn't hurt anymore, I reminded myself, stabbing the needle into the flesh around the still-weeping injury. This was nothing compared to the lifetime of pain I'd already endured.

It was also why I hadn't stuck around the infirmary, keeping my arm strategically positioned across my chest while the healers fussed over Jax. The scars did not embarrass me. I wasn't ashamed of them. If anything, I found the delicate patterns beautiful. Unique to me. But anyone who saw them was bound to ask questions, which was far more dangerous than any jawram could be.

I bit the pale thread, severing it near my elbow, and ran a finger over my work. Pristine. With any luck, it would heal in a few days. I rose and crossed my small room above the bookshop to the tinier washroom, carefully avoiding the floorboards that squeaked.

I'd climbed in through the window so Ms. Whitmere wouldn't know I was here and come asking questions. Thoroughly, I washed my arm with a few pebbles of soap, the cool water against my bare skin making me shiver, before crossing back to the corner behind the door. Swiftly, I wrapped fresh silk around my arm, careful to tuck the ends away so they wouldn't unravel later.

The headache I'd fought all afternoon pounded dully in my temples. No doubt the prince was furious with me. I'd left before being debriefed. To my credit, though, I needed time before I saw him, still absorbing the surprise of not only facing the first trial on day one, but also surviving it.

Unlike that beetle.

I scrubbed the back of my hand over my closed eyes, trying to wipe the image of red-tinted foam frothing from the champion's lips when the toxin claimed his body. The way I imagined his eyes screamed for help as his muscles locked tight, fighting his brain's commands, stiffening and shriveling until only a husk of a person remained. A long, shuddering breath rattled my form.

It wasn't my first time witnessing death. Nor was it my second or third.

But it was why I'd parted ways with the Shells the week before my initiation. I accepted death as a reality of life, especially among greensiders, but my stomach quaked with the notion of cutting another being's time short. Of seeing the light in their eyes die because of my brutal hands. Jax had prevailed during his initiation, but after seeing the scarlet staining his hands and face when he murdered a roach who'd crossed the wrong path, I knew his life and mine no longer traveled the same route.

However, in the coming weeks I might need to take that ultimate step, and I wasn't sure if I could do it. Selfishly, I knew I would do anything it took to survive. But so would the other champions. Were we really any different at the end of the day?

When fight came to flight, I knew I wasn't equipped to fly.

Perhaps a visit to Devlin was in order. No doubt he'd already heard of my endeavors, and I owed him an explanation for my actions.

Quietly, I returned my kit to its hiding spot away from prying eyes. With a murmur, I bundled up the clothing I'd changed out of earlier and slipped back out the window, pulling it shut behind me.

* * *

The Firestone was little more than a rough-cut door wedged between two buildings a dozen blocks north of the bookstore. The door opened as seamlessly as always, revealing a small desk where a burly fire ant with red strips of fabric tied around his biceps looked me over. With a grunt, he waved his hand, and the wall behind him slid sideways, revealing the opening to a stairwell.

With a nod of appreciation, I started down the spiral staircase, luminescent blue stones mined from the Iron Mountains lighting my way, two stories into the earth. The bar was the unofficial headquarters of the Shells, and the hybrid manning the door would have already alerted the bartender to my descent into their territory by tapping a unique system of pipes hidden behind the desk. The same pipes he used to silently open the hidden door.

It was still early for the regulars, so the two dozen round tables sat vacant, the chairs circling them inviting travelers to sit, grab a drink, and a hot meal. I knew the undersides of most of those tables better than I knew my scars. Jax and I had spent a fair amount of time here as children, entertaining ourselves while Devlin worked.

The hybrid himself stood behind the bar nestled against the left side of the room, a glass in one hand, a towel in the other. Eyes I knew to be grayer than a rainy day were settled on his work. Like always, he waited for me to make the first move, reach out to him for what I needed. As I skirted tables, Devlin put down one glass and picked up another, rubbing away spots left from the wash water.

Leaving my cloak on, I settled into one of the eight backless stools lined up like matchsticks beneath the lip of the bar and leaned against the padding running the length of the railing. Devlin eyed my trembling fingers and reached for a bottle of brown liquor from the shelf behind him. He poured two fingers into a glass and thrust it my direction. It burned on the way down, and I hissed, recognizing the quality of the fire ant whiskey. Muffling my cough, I set the glass down and stared at my fingerprints smudging the otherwise pristine surface.

"You've heard," I stated.

"The whole city's heard."

That came as no surprise, yet my stomach shriveled to the size of a walnut and sweat beaded along my brow. My moral compass was off kilter on the best days, but the one thing I couldn't stand was disappointing someone. Especially someone I loved.

"That said, I figure you've got your reasons." The hand gripping the bottle of booze relaxed. Devlin waited for me to meet his eyes before pouring another finger. It had been months since I'd seen the old ant. The wrinkles at the corners of his lips had deepened, and the purple bands under his eyes had darkened. His blond hair was thinning, but he still looked like the hybrid I'd known since I was nine. The person who'd found me on the streets, cleaned me up, and offered me a home without asking a thing in return.

"I do."

He appraised me and reached for another bottle. "Let's hear it then."

While he ran through his inventory, I filled him in on everything that had happened over the past two weeks. From tailing Sebastian to discovering his identity to training at the Octavius estate to sleeping on the satin sheets of the Primrose. All of it. I left nothing out.

Putting my hand over the glass, refusing the fourth pour, I finished my story. "His ideas about changing the government intrigue me. Even if he does win the crown, I'm not sure he'll be able to pull it off. But it's a start, right?"

"All change starts with something as small as an idea." Devlin closed the worn leather of his ledger, satisfied with the numbers he'd recorded over the past hour. "It's grand, I'll give him that, but I like the sound of his ideas."

"Really?" I sat up straight, elbows hooked on the edge of the counter. Though a male of few words, Devlin never closed his mind to new ideas. It was what made him such a powerful leader among the Shells and within the community. He'd single-handedly transformed a rag-tag gang into a fully functioning protection unit. One that didn't rely on intimidation to get its way, though it was a weapon its members never hesitated to wield.

He adjusted the glasses perched on his nose, thick lenses spotless. "The government is decaying, and the people of Moldona grow restless. They're fed up with the overt taxation, the laws that stretch into the privacy of their homes. And now the crown is vulnerable. Hybrids are whispering about change." He ran a rag over the already clean counter top. "This idea of your prince's is about as radical as it gets, but it isn't outlandish. Many may find the idea of having their own say in governance appealing. Remember, I may have fought my way into my position, but I'm voted into the job every other year." He scratched his cheek. "And I always welcome competition without retaliation."

It was true. Unlike the roaches, who operated under a classic system of familial dynasty, the Shells kept the option of new leadership open. Devlin had just never given his people reason to doubt his leadership.

The ant peered over my shoulder and slid another glass out from under the counter. I resisted the urge to look. The heat of the newcomer's gaze already bored into my back.

"I don't like you putting your neck on the line like this, but you're an adult. You make your own decisions." A small smile quirked Devlin's lips. "I'll let my son put you in your place for me."

I barely had time to wink back when hands bracketed my waist and spun me around. Jax glowered, his skin scarlet as I'd ever seen it, furious energy buzzing from every muscle. "Just what in the hael do you think you're doing?" he ground out. "Are you out of your eversaken mind?"

"I was enjoying a drink and catching up with Dev…"

The hands gripping my body moved upward, around my rib cage, squeezing ever tighter. "Seriously, Nim? Seriously?"

Eye to eye, I seized his shoulders, shrugging off the shame that attempted to settle. I hadn't told him my plans, but neither had he. "My decision to represent the prince wasn't one made in haste. It wasn't reckless. I—"

"Wasn't reckless?" His voice hit a high note I'd never heard before. He yanked me forward, my nose buried in his shoulder, inhaling the spice of the gingersnaps he was fond of snacking on, his hand cupping the back of my head. "You entered the Trials. You vowed to either win, die, or face banishment, Nim. Death." He lightly tugged me back by my hair, our foreheads touching. "You could die."

"And so could you." My soft rebuke caught him off guard, his eyes growing wide. I swallowed down the pebble in my throat. "We could even be forced to take each other's lives."

Jax shook his head fiercely. "It wouldn't come to that. If it did—"

"—If it did," I heaved a huge sigh, eyes falling from the intensity of his, before sliding back up once again, "I would bow out." The truth of the statement felt right. An afternoon of thinking had led me to one resolute statement: I never, ever would hurt my best friend. Not even for the prince's ideas, no matter how grand they were.

When Jax opened his mouth, I shook my head slightly, "Your home is here. I'm the one who wants to leave. Banishment is just more... permanent."

And more painful. But, as I'd rationalized to myself earlier while stitching myself up, pain was fleeting. I'd already survived the worst.

The fire ant shook me roughly, though I detected the slight tremble in his limbs. "It's not going to come to that," he promised. "Not every trial ends with death—just... most of them. And if it does come to that, we'll figure something out. We always do."

His faith in our abilities made me grin, and I banded my arms around his shoulders in an embrace. When I pulled back once more, tears glimmered on the lower rims of his eyes, catching on his lashes.

"But you could still die," he whispered, voice hoarse. "After everything you've survived, why would you put yourself in that situation?"

"I could die in the Arena or on the streets or anywhere, anytime."

"That's morose."

I sniffed back a chuckle. "*But* I finally have an opportunity to take my future into my two hands and make what I can of it." I weighed my words. "The prince offered me enough money to make it to the border and then some. I can finally be free of these Eritrean shackles."

Jax sniffed noisily and pulled me into another embrace. My head found the comfortable crook in his shoulder, the familiarity of his affection calming the last of my nerves. Glasses clinked as Devlin worked beside us. Liquid splashed against the bottom of a glass, which he pushed across the bar. The sounds of his footsteps faded, and a chair squeaked. No doubt Devlin was at his desk, his head in another ledger.

Where Devlin was ice, his son was fire. And I loved them equally.

Jax trailed his hand over my braids. "I was so scared when you took off your hood. I nearly vomited all over my boots."

I smiled tightly. "How do you think I felt when you walked onto that field?" I pulled away, though I gripped his wrist, not ready to let go completely. He settled onto the stool beside me, his thumb working circles over the bump of my wrist. "You didn't tell me you were competing, either, remember?"

He scuffed his jaw with the heel of his hand. "You would have tried to talk me out of it."

"Seems our reasons for keeping secrets align."

Jax rolled his eyes and snagged the glass Devlin had poured. After taking a sip, he made a face. "Winning would give me an opportunity to influence change. I've been in talks with the Sai's for weeks, and they made it evident they aren't happy with the direction the country is going in." He took another sip as hope fluttered its soft wings in my chest.

"By winning the Trials, we both elevate our status. Aurora wants to influence change within the upper classes, shift a few laws that aren't beneficial for anyone, and I can take those to greenside." Jax cradled the cup against his chest, staring into the distance at a future I couldn't see. "They also promised me a seat at the negotiating table. Me." A smile cracked his handsome face. "A Shell. A greensider. I would have an opportunity to spread some good into the world. Isn't that enough?"

Yeah. Yeah, it was more than enough. I took a sip of water from a fresh pint glass. "That sounds beautiful."

The motion drew back the sleeve of my tunic, and Jax stared at the fresh bandages. "How are you feeling? It didn't look like they caught you too badly."

With a shrug, I scrubbed at the wound. "The spear didn't go too deep, and it wasn't poisoned. What's another scar?" I couldn't meet his gaze, not prepared to deal with the empathy I would find in it. "I think you got the worst of it." I motioned to his ribs. "You crack any of them?"

He stretched, making a show of flexing his muscles before tapping the spot where I knew he was patched up. "They can try to take me out, but they won't succeed."

Reflexes quick as ever, I jabbed him in the side, right below his ribs, and he flinched with a squeak of protest. "That's because they don't know your soft spots." I tried to jab him a few more times, but he blocked me, laughter growing. When the cheer died off, we both drank what remained in our glasses. Devlin had surreptitiously left the bottle of fire whiskey within reach.

"We good?" Jax asked, voice rough.

"Yeah, we're good."

For the moment, anyway. Despite the ant's fervent insistence he and I wouldn't come to blows, I wasn't so optimistic. My stomach churned dangerously, recognizing the hard truth that both of us couldn't survive the Trials—unless one of us walked away.

And I didn't know how if I would survive if my best friend perished.

"You need to train in the morning?" Jax asked.

I shrugged, the movement rolling back my unease. "Probably. But I'm already in trouble with the prince, so what's a few more hours?"

With a sly grin I knew all too well, Jax poured us another round. "Then let's make it worth it."

Our glasses clinked.

The laughter flowed as easily as the alcohol. Gradually, more Shell members filtered inside, many raising their glasses in congratulations to their "pair of champions." Several joined Jax and me at the bar, breaking out decks of cards and cups of dice, gossiping while they tried to swindle us of the little glass and coin in our pockets. I smiled more than I had in months, uncaring when the clock on the wall signaled night had fallen. Eveningmeal was simple, potato soup with soft bread, but it tasted of memories from my childhood, warming my soul.

When I'd walked away from the Shells, incapable of taking the life of the female they'd tasked me with dispatching, I had left behind more than shelter. I'd parted ways with my home, with people who loved me, people who never treated me any differently, regardless of my past.

I was just finishing my third cup of water, because despite what I'd told Jax, I didn't want to die during training, when a hand prodded my shoulder. Bracing my feet on the rungs, I swiveled to face the Shell, smile fading at the stoic expression on his gruff face.

"Yer Nim, right?"

I didn't recognize him, but the group took on new members all the time. "What of it?"

He fiddled with the buttons on his shirt. "I got a message for ye, about yer charge."

My charge? Knowing how this game was played, I dipped my hands into my sleeves, withdrew a sliver of blue glass, and dropped it into his waiting palm. "What's the message?"

"That princely fellow of yers was spotted going into the Den of Wings hours ago. Word 'as it, he's fallen deep into the well." My lingering buzz vaporized. The casino was one of three operated by the Steel gang, nestled deep within roach territory. Few who entered left with what they'd walked in with, and if the prince was losing as badly as this news made it seem, he needed to get out of there. Now.

"How much time do I have?" I asked, shrugging on my cloak.

131

The Shell lifted his shoulder again. "Didn't say."

So very little, if any.

Jax snagged my sleeve as I tugged my collar up. "You need backup? It'll be dangerous."

It would be. But the lax lilt of his lips and the haze in his eyes wouldn't help me now. "This won't take long. We'll be in and out before they know it."

19

Core of Diamond

Sebastian

The few green-leaf chips I had left to my name clinked warmly as I rolled them in my fingers, then tilted the edges of my cards on the table so I could peek at the numbers. Beetlejuice was hardly for the faint of heart, and though I'd lost nearly everything in my purse, I had a good feeling about this round.

Card counting was hardly beneath me, and the river of four cards rippled in my favor. The pair of mosquitoes at our table had already tapped out, and the only player left was a grim-looking roach with an amber-colored patch over his eye. His remaining orb glowed yellow, jaundiced and shot with red.

His intensity gave me pause, reminiscent of the pirate king when he'd spotted a ship to plunder on the horizon.

"Call." I tossed my remaining chips into the pot.

The roach grinned around the cigar resting in the corner of his mouth; what teeth he had left were chipped and stained. "You're a few hundred shy, friend."

As if I would be friends with these fiends. "Maybe I was about to make things interesting." Knowing I had nothing in my pockets, I dipped my fingers inside all the same. A set of lock picks, a bent copper piece from the Villa Isles, and my handy bundle of dried mint. Tides, what a time to run dry.

"Interesting how?" The roach tapped ash into a golden bowl desperately in need of scrubbing.

I opened my mouth to say who knew what, when a hush fell over the casino floor. The roach peered past me toward the door and slowly snuffed out his cigar. A handful of termites at the bar cringed, hunkering closely together, and the dealer beckoned forward a trio of burly bugs who'd lurked in the corner all night, yellow bandannas tied around their foreheads. Intrigued, I turned in my chair, arm resting over the back, to see what the fuss was about, and almost fell from my seat.

Nim crossed the threshold, hood down, chin up, braids slung over her shoulders, their red ribbons draped across her chest like a warning flag. Her head swiveled, taking in the entire floor at once, before zeroing in on me. The thief's familiar maroon cloak swirled around her boots as she pushed past the cricket manning the entrance and maneuvered through the tables like a shark through currents. No one said a word, and she didn't acknowledge anyone until the three bouncers stepped into her path.

She said in a voice so icy I was surprised the words didn't freeze, "Let me through before you regret it."

The roaches rose on their toes, leaning in, muscles bulging, when my "friend" at the table cleared his throat loudly and ordered them to stand down. "Let's see what the lovely lady wants."

"Not what. Who." Nim stopped beside my chair. "I've come to collect my comrade, Rand."

These two knew each other? I was under the impression ants and roaches didn't mix.

The roach, whom I now realized was more important than I'd given him credit, lit a fresh cigar, inhaled, and blew a stream of smoke out the side of his mouth. He leaned back in his chair, tapping the arm with one gnarled fingernail. "Unfortunately, he's gotten himself in a bit of a bind." Spiny fingers twitched in the direction of the violet cloth blanketing the table. "Before you so graciously arrived, you see, he called our wager and was getting to a rather interesting bartering point."

Had she not been standing right beside me, so close her cloak brushed my cheek, I wouldn't have noticed the tension tightening her form. She twisted another strip of red fabric tied in a knot around her wrist. "What kind of wager?"

I put my hand on her arm. "You don't have to—"

She shot me a single glance that relayed one simple command: *Shut up.* For the first time since leaving Rags outside Archer Arena, a queasy curl of anxiety rippled through my chest. The other games on the floor had yet to resume, all eyes fixed on us. Several more roaches had emerged from the shadows, leaning on birchwood canes and fisting objects hidden deep in their pockets. One particularly nasty-looking fellow with a cleft lip sneered while slipping his fingers into a set of iron knuckles.

"What kind of wager?" Nim repeated steadily.

Rand tapped ash into the bowl, the fine powder drifting down the hill that had formed in the center. "He called, but didn't have enough coin to cover his bet. I imagine he was about to place a favor on the table." The air squeezed from my lungs. "And a favor from a... prince has a certain value, don't you agree, *Shell*?"

Shell? The word sounded familiar, but I couldn't place it.

Nim gripped my shoulder, fingers like talons digging into my skin. Her gaze was fixed, breathing steady, but I knew she was calculating the odds. Rand eyed her grip with interest, the tiger's eye gem set in a golden band on his middle finger flashing in the dull light.

"Let me guess. Beetlejuice?" She flicked her thumb at the cards.

Rand spread his hands wide, cigar wedged between his middle and ring fingers. "What else?"

The curl of smoky angst billowed into a full-blown fire in my stomach. Everyone knew what happened if you went out without meeting the quota in Beetlejuice. Not only was the loser out the coin they'd spent on the game, but they owed double the pot the next day. A wicked little game it was. Simple, but unforgiving. My favorite types of gamble.

And the type that had cost me everything time and time again.

Nim met my gaze. "How much do you need to call for?"

"Two hundred rucks."

She didn't ask if I had a winning hand, if I could beat the system. Rand was right, a favor from a prince was immense, and though I'd changed clothing and obscured my hair, I'd thought my disguise had worked. Until now. I had foolishly forgotten the notoriety of the royal family this close to home.

With a nod, Nim reached beneath her sleeve. The tension in the room ratcheted higher, roaches adjusting their grips on their chosen weapons. Nim cast a wan smile at those watching and withdrew a bracelet. The only piece of jewelry I'd seen her wear. She dangled it from one finger.

"Silver with a core of diamond. The impressions you see are nettles, my mother's favorite plant because they are so wonderfully prickly." Her poker face was immaculate, stone cold and weathered as the rocks that took their daily beating from the waves. The cockroach reached for the jewelry, but she drew it back before his fingers smudged the polish. "It's easily worth twice what he owes. More than enough to cover his bet."

Another puff of smoke. Another stroke of his mustache. Rand

136

peered into her eyes like he was staring into her soul. "And? What's it to me?"

"Nothing. I only ask that regardless of the outcome, I experience no interference in my return to my territory." She tugged again on the strip of fabric bound to her wrist. The color meant something. Shame swallowed my anxiety whole. Jaxon had called me out on my ignorance of this city, and in an attempt to prove him wrong, I'd stepped into the middle of what I now recognized as a gang war. "With my friend in tow."

Rand didn't need to think about it. He snapped his fingers. "Done." He snatched the bracelet from her fingers, casually tossing it onto the pile of gold and copper coins with a clatter. My heart panged seeing it there like discarded trash. "Reveal your cards, larva."

Nim's energy vibrated beside me. Tides. She'd put something of hers on the line. Something of her mother's. The weight of her personal effects on the table brought the moment into sharp focus. Casually, I flipped over my cards, revealing the straight I'd kept under wraps. Several roaches hissed, pointed teeth bared in snarls. "It will take a lot for you to trump those cards."

Rand nodded, inhaling more smoke. "A lot. But enough."

My heart shriveled to the size of a walnut when he flipped over his cards. Two pairs, aces over kings. It shouldn't have been possible. It *couldn't* have been possible. I reached for the deck. The kings had already been played. There wasn't...

Nim's hands folded over mine, pressing them to the singed purple felt, a silent plea to keep my cool. "A pleasure as always, Rand. Enjoy your winnings."

The roach surveyed us, sharp as a winter morning. "You best scurry back to your side of the line, Reed. Champion or not, you're not welcome over here. Not wearing those colors."

With one last defiant tug on her ribbon, Nim hauled me up by an arm, pressed a hand between my shoulder blades, and shoved me out the door. What was happening? What had I missed?

"You shouldn't have done that for me," I mumbled. "I would have—"

"There are no 'would haves' with those types, understand? Had you offered it, they'd have taken your favor and shoved it right up where the sun don't shine on some day you need it least." She pushed me forward again, splashing through the puddles from a recent cloud burst. "Keep your face forward, don't look back, and for Riten's sake, hurry."

"I thought you wagered for us to keep our lives."

Her next shove was even harder. "The Steel are notorious for breaking their promises."

That shut me right up. This time, when she snagged my wrist in one claw-like hand, I didn't resist. After about a block of tripping over my own feet, I adjusted to her pace and stopped trying to dodge the puddles, barely heeding the water soaking my socks and squishing between my toes. Every now and again, she would slow, head cocked, lingering at the edge of a corner, critically eyeing the streets illuminated by lanterns lit by fireflies every night.

"I could fly us out of here," I offered. Though I didn't display my wings, I never hesitated to use them.

She shook her head. "Too risky. They'll see us."

I wasn't sure where we were going. We weren't following any specific route my brain could follow, but I trusted her instincts to guide us out of this mess of my making. Instead, I couldn't help but stare at her wrist, the one now bare of the silver she'd sacrificed to keep me out of deeper trouble. It was on the same arm she'd wounded earlier, not that I could identify the injury based on her wrappings.

Just when I started to get winded, she stopped, releasing her cool grip, and pressed her hand to her chest, breathing hard. "That should confuse them well enough," she whispered, lips barely moving, "but just in case, keep quiet. I need to listen."

Rubbing away the weird electricity that had built up on my skin, I attempted to slow my own breathing. "Why are they chasing us, anyway? They got their money."

She lowered her hands to her sides, fingers splayed, dragged in a deep breath, held it and released it, appearing to settle. Silver eyes met mine. "Sometimes the call of fresh blood is too intense—especially enemy blood."

It was the most revealing statement she'd made since our talk on the balcony, when I was half convinced she was about to call our deal a sham and drop to the street below, never to be seen again. "You never said you were a Shell."

The thief leaned against the rough bark of an apartment building carved into the middle of a thick oak tree, the fibers of her cloak catching in the grooves. She flexed her fingers again, as if feeling for something in the air. "Would it have changed anything?"

"No."

"Well, I'm not a member. Now hush."

A few minutes passed. Nim's eyes darted from side to side, head cocking when she heard a snippet of something that evaded my ears. When the tension that gathered between us became too much, I gestured at the fabric tied around her wrists. "Your cloak is maroon, and you wear red around your arms and hair, yet you aren't a Shell? Why would they be after you then?"

"I said I wasn't a member, not that the Shells aren't my family." She hesitated, then dug her nails into the knot in the fabric around her arm, undoing it in a few quick tugs. Our fingers brushed when she passed the band to me. Swallowing back the heat that brushed my cheeks, I pulled the scarlet material through my hands, slowing when I reached the ragged shreds of one end.

"Jaxon, the ant from the arena, and his father raised me as one of their own," she continued. "Devlin also happens to be the head of the organization." Her grin was wry, a little sad, and a little twisted.

It finally clicked, where I'd heard the gang's name before. When Jaxon was announced at the arena. This snippet of information also explained their closeness on the field and the fiery defense the ant had thrown up against me to protect her following the fight.

A small part of my brain considered the status of their relationship, how deep their loyalties truly ran, and only partially how that might impact my goals.

"About two years ago, I went my own way." She tugged on the white bandage wrapped around her elbow, her nails trimmed nearly to the quick. "Couldn't go through with initiation."

I wanted to ask what initiation entailed, what about it was so fearsome that she would rather risk her life alone on the streets than commit herself to the family who had taken her in. Before I could wrap my lips around a response, her head tilted again, alarm flashing across her face.

"They found us." In two steps, she swung onto the lowest branch of the oak and began climbing the makeshift fire escape with fluid efficiency, barely wincing when she slipped and tore a chunk of bark away from the tree.

Her face appeared around the edge of a limb, a good dozen feet over my head. "Hurry. I thought we could lose them in the streets, but they're more persistent than I gave them credit for. Best we take the direct route out of here."

With a heaving sigh, wondering why she wouldn't just let me fly us out of here, though grateful to avoid the strain it would put on my wings, I shoved the fabric into my pocket and followed. About a minute later, when I'd caught up with her, panting, we crouched together on a branch thick enough to hold both our weight. Below, footsteps pounded. I could make out the low mutters of the roach minions, but they spoke too low for me to understand their words.

Nim gestured to the north. The trees sprouted more sparsely for the next few blocks, and the inhabitants of these homes preferred to encase themselves within walls of wax or chewed paper—designs made popular more than a century earlier when the Amana family gained respect for their architectural designs.

"We aren't far from the border," she said, eyeing me critically. I narrowed my eyes at her scrutiny. "Might be time to get your wings out. I have a feeling you'll need them." The grin she flashed was full of mischief, but it was the first smile I'd seen on her face, and lightning sparked in my blood.

I started to ask what she meant, but she was off again, sprinting for the end of the thick limb. My heart launched up my throat when I realized her intentions. She wasn't going to—no. She definitely was. With a grunt, she launched herself into the space between the apartments and the nearest hive, legs moving as if running through the skies, and landed with a roll, nimble as could be.

Imagining her urging me to hurry up, I followed on silent wings. From rooftop to tree branch, she raced along, picking her way across the city with ease. I'd already offered to carry her and knew now why she'd dismissed me so easily. She was a natural. An acrobat. A hybrid who understood this city in a way I would never fathom, and I found myself humbled.

Finally, when I thought her knees might finally give out, she stopped and motioned to the street we'd just passed. "This is the line. Don't cross it without arming yourself to the teeth again."

Pulling my wings back in, I examined the road. On one side, the ramshackle homes bore yellow shutters and doors. On the other, red paint peeled from the bark of businesses. "Shells are red. Steel are yellow."

"The line doesn't fluctuate?" In several countries I'd visited, warfare between gangs constantly shifted the lines. Interesting that here, the lines were as neat as the cart tracks embedded in the streets.

Nim crouched, gaze far away. "Rarely. They care more about maintaining their way of life than claiming more territory. Devlin tells me it used to be worse generations ago, when three or four groups were vying for power. But he and Rand have an agreement. The Steel operate the south side of town with their casinos and whorehouses, and we manage the consumption districts. Vice for vice."

That certainly explained a few things, starting with my long trek across town from the Primrose.

"Listen." Nim's expression became pained, her hands clasped, thumbs rubbing the sides of her palms. "I know you have a propensity for gambling, but you need to be more careful. Greensiders know more than you think, especially the smart ones. And you don't get much smarter than Rand."

If only she knew how frequently Rags made the same request. No wonder the two were so friendly: they were similar souls, bleeding hearts though they fought to internalize their concern. I dipped my head in a nod, sensing her relax. What she didn't know was that I'd added the feud to my growing list of concerns to address once I was in a position to do something about it.

For now, it meant I'd have to give up my favorite addiction—in part. My fingers flexed involuntarily, and my molars ground together. This wouldn't be easy, but I understood what was at stake. And the cost at which my escape had come.

"I will get your bracelet back," I vowed. The black links of her braids shimmered in the pale light cast by the lanterns. "I'm sorry for putting you in a position to lose something important to you. To set it right is the least I can do."

Even as she rolled her shoulders in dismissal, her fingers slipped up her sleeve, wrapping around where her jewelry had once rested.

"Don't worry yourself over it. Anyone worth their salt would make a sacrifice for someone in need."

No, they wouldn't, a truth I knew all too well.

"You should also know that my chronic issue with placing bets isn't reserved solely for monetary ventures." Why I was telling her this, I couldn't say. Something about the quiet of the night, the taste of ocean salt in the breeze, the gray clouds hanging low in the skies. It all put me at ease, a sensation I'd thought I would never feel in the city of my birth. "I don't always know when to quit, but I do know when to go all in, to make my biggest bets." A pause. "That game was rigged. I should have won. The kings had already been cast in an earlier hand."

Her voice was so soft I had to strain to hear it. "I see."

"But the biggest bet I've made in my life is still in play." Hesitantly, I reached for her hand and waited for her to decide if she would consent to my touch. A beat later, her fingers rested gingerly against my palm, and I squeezed the tips lightly, a silent wave of understanding washing between us. "You survived the first trial, and I'll do everything in my power to see you through the rest."

Steam puffed from her mouth as she exhaled deeply. "We'll see."

One tug and her fingers were free. I squeezed my hand more tightly around the space where they'd been, feeling their absence like a blow to my chest.

With a look that spoke volumes, including a clear message that she needed some time to herself, Nim dropped to the cobblestones and took off toward the Primrose with a deceptively casual gait. I watched her until she rounded the corner of a tailor's shop and disappeared from view. Incrementally, I relaxed, shifting where I stood.

Over my shoulder, the castle stood, stark and proud against the mountain. The windows glowed yellow and orange, a reminder of what I'd lost and the future I stood to gain.

Still peering to the east, I tugged the strip of Nim's red fabric from

143

my pocket and wrapped it around my own wrist, knotting it firmly into place.

20

No More Running

Nim

The mattress enveloped my form like a hug, and I fisted the comforter, staring straight up at the latticework of the ceiling. Two weeks into this stint, and I'd finally worked up the ability to stay in the softness of my bed at the Primrose all night. My old cot offered nowhere near the back support. I allowed myself one more tremulous moment to soak in the luxuriousness of my private room before sitting upright, feet dangling over the edge of the bed.

One room. Three pieces of furniture. Four walls. A dozen articles of clothing tucked away in the walnut dresser drawers. Sliding off the bed, I slipped my feet into my boots, leaving the laces undone, the hem of my pants catching on the leather. Yawning, I ambled to the mirror, avoiding my eyes as I surveyed the silvery slivers cut out of my flesh. Occasionally, my skin needed to breathe, and I'd unbound most of my upper body after the prince and I had returned the night before, sweat-streaked and disturbingly melancholy.

We'd come to an unspoken agreement, the two of us. A newfound understanding, one as beautiful and strong as a spider's web. He would take fewer risks with his life, and I would open myself up when necessary. No more running. For now.

My nails dipped into the grooves cut into my arms, examining the marks more carefully.

I was proud of the scars. They symbolized life and perseverance. No one had fought as hard as I had for what I'd made for myself. I'd carved out this life for myself, and I would do whatever I needed to ensure I lived as long as I could. But, as I reached for a fresh roll of silk, I had to make concessions. Though the bandages drew attention to my features, especially in the dense heat of sient when I was forced to abandon my cloak in favor of loose-fitting shirts, they were preferable to the ethereal glow of my scarred flesh.

In no time at all, nearly every inch of skin was bound, the loose ends tucked into place. I shrugged on a fresh shirt, taking advantage of a dresser full of extra clothing for the first time in my life, and prodded the bowl of liquid resting on the furniture's surface. The used and dirty silk had dissolved overnight in the acidic concoction I'd created myself. Only cloudy liquid remained, scented lightly with lavender.

Without thinking, I reached for my bracelet only to come up short. Sorrow speared through my chest, quick and sharp. It was the only thing I had left of my mother, the only possession that was truly hers. My father had gifted it to her on their fifth anniversary, when her belly was round with me. Back when their lives had been promising, their future well-assured. When they used to laugh, and our cottage was filled with sunshine and the warm scent of wheat from the fields on the outskirts of Moldona.

Before the accident.

Before the wasting disease.

Before I was cast out by the only family I had left, dumped in the streets, and left for dead.

Squeezing my eyes shut, I forced myself to walk away from the empty spot on my dresser. Things were just that. Things. Replaceable or not, they were far less costly than lives, and I knew without a doubt I'd saved Sebastian by intervening with Rand's plans. For as stupid as his drones could be, the head of the Steel gang was as cunning as they came.

The sunshine streaming through the window beside my bed slanted across the floor, revealing the time to be far later than I'd anticipated. Only rarely did I sleep later than dawn. Hurriedly, I bound my hair in a single plait before exiting my room. Murmurs came from the end of the hallway, and I padded toward the noise.

The prince and Grev sat across from each other at the circular table, plates and bowls abandoned by their elbows while they pored over a piece of parchment. Rags hummed softly to herself as she lay on the couch, a paperback book held open over her head. It seemed so... homey—a group of friends who'd created this little family for themselves.

It reminded me of my relationship with Jax and Devlin.

Though I hadn't made a sound, Sebastian's attention shifted. "Nim. You're awake." His smile was fresh and bright. "We are discussing options for midmeal."

"Correction," called Rags, "*They* are discussing midmeal. I was minding my own business. An' now that yer awake, they can pester *you* to break their ridiculous tie."

Grev thrust his middle finger in her direction. "You realize we aren't on a ship anymore, right? We can eat more than white fish and rice."

Rags turned a page in her book—a romance novel, judging by the cover. "No pain, no gain."

"That doesn't make a lick of sense." Grev turned on me. "Does it?"

Rolling my eyes, I dropped into the only open seat not laden with books, parchment, and rolls of maps. "I'm not dumb enough to wade into this argument."

"Smart female, jus' like another female in this residence." Rags flipped me a thumbs-up over the back of the couch. "An' Grev, I stay plenty trim an' ready for battle. Perhaps ya should reexamine yer interest in richer cuisines, else ya grow too large for yer armor."

Grev's eyes rounded, and he shot upright, wings twitching. "Are you calling me fat?"

"If the tunic fits…"

The larger hornet zipped around the couch, intent on destroying his comrade, and Sebastian lightly nudged my hand where it rested on the table. Thank Riten, he was not going to bring up yesterday.

"Ignore them. If they don't act like larvae for at least thirty minutes each day, they turn into sad, sullen grubs." Sebastian waved off a pair of guffaws as their heads popped up over the couch. "Seriously, though, I've been dying for seafood stew and heard of this place by the docks that serves up the best."

"Marley's." I drew a nail file from my pocket and pressed the steel to my thumbnail with a rasp. They were certainly listening to the right people. "You won't get much better sea fare anywhere else in the city. What is the other option?"

"Sandwiches," said Grev, returning to his seat. "There's a bakery on the corner that smells heavenly, and Sebastian makes us walk past it at least twice a day for training." He pouted, and I swore tears formed along the waterline of his eyes. "If I don't try their vegetable spread today, I might die."

Nail worn to the quick, I switched to my index finger. Quite the quandary. And establishments on opposite sides of town, to boot. Pondering the options, keenly aware of the two sets of eyes boring holes in the sides of my head, I scanned the table. To the side, partially tucked under a sheaf of paperwork outlining the redistricting of the red and yellow sides from a decade ago, an envelope with golden lettering sparkled in a pool of sunshine. "What's that?"

Sebastian sobered, teasing it out, and handed it to me. The cream-colored card stock was of fine quality, scraped perfectly smooth. The cursive lettering spelled out one word: Protect. The back of the sheet didn't offer any additional details.

"It was delivered just before you woke up," Sebastian said, lacing his fingers together. "From the keep. That's our clue to the second trial."

Putting the page down, I returned to my nails. That's right, we were on the second trial already. After the stunt they'd pulled at the Opening Ceremonies, I reminded myself again not to take anything at face value, to consider all the trappings and to expect the worst. Major Ectya Day was correct when she'd warned against underestimating anyone.

"I wonder what they'll have you protect," Grev said.

"Or who." Rags came up behind me and took the card herself. "The vagueness is perplexing, isn't it?"

"Whatever it is, it sounds defensive," I murmured, switching to my other hand. "I can handle that." I only wished I felt as confident as I sounded.

"What does your aether offer you, anyway?" Grev asked. I kept my face carefully blank. "Even as an ant, you should have some extras. Strength. Perseverance. An extra set of arms. Any of that could help."

I flicked my eyes up and caught Sebastian's mahogany gaze. He'd leaned forward slightly, his interest in Grev's question apparent. Keeping my attention on the prince, I said, "I don't wish to discuss my aether. We ought to act like I don't have it at all."

Grev's lips pursed, his expression darkening, but before he could fire another shot, Rags gripped my shoulders, her nails digging into my sore muscles, making them ache. "Exactly what I'm thinkin'. Defensive training. Lots of it. We have six days. That gives us plenty of time ta drill the basics into that tiny brain of yers."

Sebastian looked like he wanted to protest, but mercifully let it go. "Training it is. Though I'd prefer to stay here, there's no place better equipped than the estate."

I offered him a half-hearted smile and tilted my head toward Grev. "I guess that means sandwiches."

The hornet's foul mood vanished and he jumped to his feet with a whoop, rushing to pull together his supplies while Rags reminded him it would take twice the amount of exercise to work off one carbohydrate. I got to my feet under the mantis' watchful gaze. He eyed the file, then the bandages looping around my knuckles, and nodded, remaining mute as he, too, gathered his belongings.

* * *

The next days passed in a blur. True to her word, Rags threw every defensive measure she knew at me: a blend of hand-to-hand combat, knife fighting, even dancing, which, she explained, would help me learn the rhythm of battle. I woke before dawn and returned to the Primrose when Sebastian fetched us well past dusk. As soon as my head hit the pillow, it felt like I was back up again moments later, shoving food prepared by Grev in my mouth as we raced back to the Octavius estate.

Not once did I ask why the prince was opposed to staying at his ancestral home.

And no one asked me to draw upon my aether, regardless of whatever edge it might give me.

Sometimes, on our way back to the Primrose, drenched in sweat, I asked Sebastian for more details about his plans. He was aware the steps he took toward equal representation by the people would still be in their infancy by the time he died. He called the transition a slow process, usually wrought with war, triggered by a turning point. That said, the prince hoped to avoid the war and fix things before they got too desperate.

He planned to spread votes to key players first: heads of the duchies and representatives from greenside. They would focus solely on policy, reforming what was broken. Debate would be critical and likely a terse affair, one he readily encouraged. Once Eritris became accustomed to not having one head of state, he intended to branch out, vote on the head of state and then expand downward.

While sparring with the hornets, for even Grev got dragged into training, I peppered them with questions about their lives away from Moldona, badgering them between punches for details of their adventures. I soaked up their descriptions of worlds I never had, and likely never would, see: nations ripe with vibrant tropical trees and colorful animals, countries that prided themselves on heavily spiced foods and desert conditions.

People from all kinds of backgrounds who lived all kinds of lives.

They also surprised me with stories about Moldona.

One weary night while dragging our aching feet on our way back to the Primrose, Sebastian entertained us with a tale about a long-forgotten cave tucked into the northern curve of Coral Cove that once produced the finest black pearls. Many a watery battle was fought there. For years, pirates and thieves and representatives of the king ransacked its many crevices, fighting for every last square inch of the plunder. Eventually, their fighting destroyed the oysters that produced the beautiful pearls, and the cave was abandoned.

A haunting tale, but one that lingered in my thoughts.

When I laid my head on the pillow at night, my dreams, though all too brief, tangled with the words spoken by the trio of hybrids, weaving new worlds in my mind. Ones I imagined I could touch and smell and taste. Places that made me ache deep in my belly, a gnawing sensation that felt an awful lot like jealousy.

In turn, they asked me about my time spent with the Shells, pried me open for good places to eat and hidden treasure troves to explore. They were also careful not to push too hard or probe the wounds deep down. Though our friendship deepened, we remained cautious. Recognizing the tenuous position we were in thanks to the Trials.

On the sixth day, as we returned from training, Sebastian halted us at the doorway. When Grev complained loudly, the prince knelt and picked up a piece of pale card stock shoved under the door. It bore the golden script of the first letter, but with greater detail. Grev hushed, and Rags crossed her arms, the three of us following Sebastian inside as he scanned its contents.

The prince dropped into his chair and rubbed his mouth, dipping his head toward the letter, which Grev promptly picked up. "The second trial is a twenty-four-hour challenge. Champions are tasked with protecting their charges from getting hurt in any way. One injury, you're out of the running. If the prospect dies, the champion is not only out, but faces execution."

Rags dropped into her familiar place on the couch, pensive. "Nim isn't fully trained but could easily hold down this place."

Grev shook his head, hair stuck to his forehead with sweat. "We must make two public appearances, and there's a ballroom event. On top of that, champions who not only successfully protect their charges but also take down the 'assassin,'" he emphasized the last word sarcastically, "earn an additional favor going into the third trial. Isn't that sweet of them?"

"How will we ever repay them?" Rags groaned.

I picked at my nails, contemplating whether to trim them. They could be helpful if things got tricky or I wound up in a bind. But I wasn't ready to risk my secrets. Not yet.

"When do the twenty-four hours begin?" I asked.

Sebastian tapped the table. "Midnight."

Two hours from now. Great. Not only was I exhausted from training, but I wouldn't have an opportunity to re-energize myself either. Thankfully, I didn't need much. The guards had already made this place as secure as possible, and Rags had a habit of bringing home weapons and odds and ends she thought she needed, so I wouldn't have to venture out and beg supplies from vendors at this late hour.

"Nim's room is the most secure," Rags argued with Grev. "She has just the one window and no balcony. That limits the possibilities for an attacker immensely."

"I agree," said Sebastian. "We'll trade rooms for the night, then."

I shook my head, fingers curling around the lip of the table. "Think again. You're not leaving my side until this thing is done."

21

Protect

Nim

Gentle hands shook me awake. Grumbling and eyes gritty with sleep sand, I found Grev crouching beside me. "It's five minutes till midnight."

Ah, yes. Brain fuzzy and vision nearly nonexistent from lack of focus, I waved him off and lay there for a few seconds. If I were an assassin, would I choose to strike straight away? Or would I milk the moment and bait my target? If this were anything but a competition, I would have thrown my weight wholeheartedly with the former. However, I assumed the 'assassins' picked for the job would be rewarded heftily if they succeeded on their mission, and given the theatrics of the first trial, the flashier the attack, the better.

Glass clinked as Grev returned to whatever he was up to with Sebastian and Rags. Their low murmurings filled the room with warmth. Occasionally, one of them would scoff, and cards would smack the table. It was easy to get sucked into their realm, to believe I could be embraced as one of them someday. They might be a prince and two guards, but they were more than that. They were family. I

154

respected nothing more than I did family.

Given I'd lost mine.

Massaging the drowsiness from the muscles in my face, I wondered what Jax was up to and if he had a plan to deal with the challenge today presented. Knowing him, he'd happily take his risks, confident in his abilities through and through.

"Dare I ask what game you're playing?" I asked, joints achy as I entered the common room. Yeah, today would not be much fun.

"Miracle of Miracles," Grev growled. I was vaguely familiar with how it was played. The hybrids at the Firestone preferred Hive and Hex.

Sebastian clucked his tongue and slung his arm over his chair. His cards were scattered face-up on the table. A moment later, Grev tossed his cards face down, index finger pointed accusingly at Rags before draining the amber liquid in his cup. "You mite. I should bury you for this."

The hornet in question crowed and dragged the entire pot into her arms, the colorful pieces of glass clinking together as she whooped her victory. "And I'm keeping it all, too, ya losers."

I ran a hand over my hair and scanned the vibrations, checking the security of our little apartment. Doors, windows, vents—nothing escaped notice. The simplicity of the work called to me. This was a task I could do, had done my entire life. Lingered in the background and noticed what others didn't. Exiting the main space, I fiddled with a lantern burning in the corner of Grev's room, not finding anything suspicious.

Methodically, I secured each room, listening to the trio who had given up on their game, content with recounting stories from countries of which I'd never heard. Finally, I locked Sebastian's room as an extra precaution because I didn't want to add the threat of a second balcony open to the elements and returned to the kitchen to grab something to eat. Rags and Grev bowed out not long after that, stifling yawns with the backs of their hands. Neither wished me well, but their eyes were sharp as they passed by while I crunched on an apple.

"Don't mind them," Sebastian said from the doorway of my room, the tips of his fingers gripping the doorjamb above his head. "On the ocean, it's considered bad luck to wish anyone luck ahead of a particularly trying journey or challenge."

I blew out the lantern at my elbow and licked my fingers. "Sailors and their superstitions. The only ones more paranoid work in the fields."

"Too true." He angled his head over his shoulder toward my bed against the wall and wiggled his eyebrows suggestively. "Were you serious about watching me sleep?"

His tone was mild, but it was impossible to ignore the way my chest tightened at the implication. The way my heart flickered a little more quickly and sweat slickened my palms. *Nerves*, I told myself. Nerves and lack of sleep. Nothing more.

I couldn't afford for it to be anything more.

"Absolutely," I replied, and, giving myself a mental shake, joined the prince just inside the room. By my measure, we were only about twenty minutes into the Trial. "In fact, if I could somehow breathe the air before you could, I would. Just to be extra safe."

"Sounds kinky." He toed off his boots, drew back the covers I'd painstakingly folded into place, and slipped beneath the sheets. His eyes were already drooping when he said, "I trust you won't let me down."

Talk about pressure.

Ignoring the twisting of my stomach, I settled against the leg of the bed, a pillow cushioning my back. It was far from comfortable, but that would help keep me awake. In contrast to the tension lacing my form, the room itself was calm, peaceful. The prince barely made a sound in his sleep, his breathing low and steady. More than once, I caught myself staring at his relaxed face, eyes tracing the long track of his nose, the curve of his jaw, the thin set of his lips.

Up close like this, with no need for vibrations to shape the world around me, I couldn't imagine how I'd ever mistaken him for anything but royalty. The confident swagger, the measured gaze, the stiff set of his shoulders, all features of a male who knew his station in life. And that station wasn't any mere merchant, no matter who he traded with.

The third time I caught myself staring, I switched from keeping vigil inside the room to wandering the dark apartment. Once away from the soft scent of mint, I settled again. The thoughts buzzing through my mind quieted, and I focused once more on the Trial, on keeping my charge safe from harm.

How peculiar, that less than two weeks ago, the farthest ahead I could see was my next mark. The next coin. My only drive was the incessant need to *leave* and forge a pocket of the world where I could tuck myself away. Now, here I was, watching over a *prince*, thinking about the present, while also looking more upon my past than I had in the last decade.

A past that included Jax. Riten, what if it came down to him and me? There were still so many steps between now and the final trial, anything could happen at anytime. And though I'd said I would bow out if forced to face him head-on... what if they somehow forced me to take part? Shoved a blade in my hand and said him or me, blood would be spilled regardless of the rules.

They'd already changed the game by forcing the first trial on day one.

I wouldn't back down if forced into a fight with my best friend, but I couldn't imagine his death. Being the one to cause it. It would absolutely destroy Devlin—and very possibly eviscerate what remained of my blackened soul.

Maybe there was some other way out, some other avenue to take if forced into such a predicament. There were ways to make someone appear to be dead. Tricky ways, especially under the intensity of being watched. Something to ponder.

On my third pass around the apartment, something subtle tap-tap-tapped from the living space. Dipping my hand to my waist and clasping my jawram, I exited the hallway and darted to the couch, keeping low to the floor. Vibrations echoed around the large room, bouncing off the table, chairs, and discarded plates and bowls the guards had left behind.

On the other side of the wide doors upon the balcony, a figure crouched, knee braced on the chilled stones. Their hand moved in a circle around the windowpane beside the doorknob, the scratch coming from a knife clasped in their gloved hand. The Luminesae possessed several glass cutters, but last I'd heard, they kept them tightly locked away.

If I retreated, I surely would be seen. There wasn't time to check on the prince and ensure no one was trying something similar from my room. It was bad enough having someone outside the hotel. If they got inside, I would be in real trouble.

Suddenly, the scratching stopped. Something popped, and I risked a peek around the edge of the couch again, eyes widening when the intruder peeled back the piece of glass and set it on the ground beside their feet. Muscles tensed, I braced for the moment of attack. If I timed it right, I might be able to take them out here and now. Save myself the troublesome tasks later.

The figure adjusted the mask obscuring the lower half of their face and reached through the hole they'd created, fingers twisting upward toward the lock.

Now.

I shot from around the furniture, barely registering the widening of their eyes when I slammed the jawram through the back of their hand, pinning it to the door frame. The assassin howled, hand jerking against the weapon.

"Who are you?" I demanded, stomach clenching as I twisted the blade, wringing another scream from their lips. "Drop it!"

Too late, I realized their shouting had obscured their true intentions. Smoke exploded around their feet in a burst of light, and I crashed backward, eyes clouding with tears, my momentum knocking my blade away in the same motion. I struggled upright, closing my eyes against the pain. Something loud thudded outside. Vibrations rippled across my wraps even as I pressed my hands to my eyes, and I knew the assassin had escaped.

"What the tides—" Grev gasped, and hands gripped my shoulders. I was ripped backward, hands touching my jaw, tilting it up. "What—"

Instinct gripped me by the throat, and I shoved the hornet back, forcing him to release me. "An assassin tried to cut through the window." I swiped again at the tears trickling from my eyes angrily. "They dropped tear gas." The balcony doors flew wide, wings whirred, and the toxin cleared, the vibrations rippling through the air revealed it was Rags who had acted so quickly. Rags. Adrenaline surged, and I whipped toward my room. "Is Sebastian—"

"I'm fine." His voice was lethal. Footsteps pounded against the floor. "Are *you* alright?"

I released a long breath, forcing my body to relax and my mind to calm despite the alarm lancing through my skin. The prince was safe. The assassin was too far gone for me to track down. And now I'd have to rely on my aether more than I had in years to see.

The others were talking around me, a constant hum of energy. Grev pressed a cool, wet cloth into my hand, and I brought it to my burning eyes, wiping away the remnants of the gas. Riten, I'd heard of such gas but had never heard of it being used in Eritris before.

"I'll be alright," I groaned, sliding down the wall, elbows resting against my knees. "Just stings."

"Yer room is clear," Rags called out. I assumed she'd done a full scan after I'd gone down. The world around me began to settle as I adjusted to the visual blindness, the nausea churning in my stomach stilling. "They cut a hole in the glass. Looks like Nim stabbed 'em pretty good."

I nodded, sniffling wetly. "They still got away."

"You still injured them before they did," Sebastian consoled. Cool fingers caressed my knee before sliding up my arm, tugging lightly on the cloth. I repressed a shiver at the intimacy of the slight gesture. He didn't know the intensity with which I felt physical touch. "Let me see."

With a wince, I pulled the cloth from my eyes, lids narrowed to a squint. The world blurred into indistinct forms of gray and black. I couldn't make out his form like I usually could: a swatch of ragged black hair, dark dots for eyes, a pale blue shirt tucked into a pair of sleep pants. My next blink did nothing to help the situation.

"Visibility is limited," I murmured. Rags stepped around the prince and handed over a fresh towel, which I dabbed at my face. "Sticks, I've never felt anything like that before."

Someone shuffled behind me. Grev, by the feel of it. "Rags, remember that time we were tear-gassed during training?"

The female's slight form bustled around, peeling open various cabinet doors in search of honey sticks. "Yeah. I jus' about killed Sergeant Billing for that, too. Couldn' see straight for a week."

"A week?" I managed. Sebastian's hand tightened around the cap of my knee, preventing me from stumbling to my feet. I'd be able to manage the lack of sight easily enough. Dev had drilled me countless times over the years, encouraging me to master navigating the world on vibrations alone. But it would make things trickier, especially as I sought to conceal my aether.

Mistaking my silence for worry, Rags hurried to reassure me, "We had prolonged exposure. The point was ta show us the damage that could be inflicted by various drugs an' gasses; they wanted us t' understand what it would be like if someone dropped a smoke bomb into a crowd. You were only exposed for what, a few seconds? At the most?"

"Something like that." I removed the cloth, but the visible world hadn't improved much. My proximity to the source of the explosion might have played a role.

"Then there ya go." The guard dropped onto a stool, sucking on her sweet, feigning a lack of concern. "Ya'll be fine in an hour or so. Though I recommend moving ta the couch. It's bound to be more comfortable than the floor."

Though her advice was sound, I couldn't muster the energy to move. "Maybe in a bit." I rested the back of my head against the wall, the cloth dangling between my knees from loose fingers. My eyes were drying out. "I'm pretty content right here."

Sebastian chuckled, and he brushed the backs of my knuckles with his fingers when he stood up. A trail of goosebumps shivered down my spine. "Tough as copper, what did I tell you?" I wasn't sure who he was talking to, but his words trickled through me like hot cider. "How about I keep watch? Right here?" The air shifted, and he settled against the wall beside me, the warmth of his body radiating along the line of my arm. He groaned. "See. Perfectly comfortable."

"Ya both are weird," Rags said.

Grev added with a heavy sigh, "I might as well get some morning-meal going. Who needs sleep anyway?"

Pots and pans clanked a few minutes later, and the guards murmured nonsense to one another. Sebastian, however, remained quiet, only the sound of his breathing keeping me company. Bit by bit, I allowed myself to relax, occasionally dabbing at my eyes. I forced myself to open them when the pain abated. The brightness of the light changed as I turned my head—brighter where the doorway was, darker against the floor. Gradually, my body adjusted to the frequencies, and I let out a sigh of relief.

The prince nudged my arm with his elbow. "What did I say? Nothing to worry about."

Except how I was going to pull off the rest of this trial.

* * *

"You don't have to taste *everything* I eat," Sebastian groaned as I pushed the half-finished plate in front of him. He held up a hunk of toast with pieces torn from several sides and the middle. "This is excessive, even for a taster."

"Good thing I'm not signing on to that job then, isn't it?" I replied, scanning the empty tables of the restaurant for the hundredth time. The motion was for form's sake rather than an actual gathering of information. I'd told the guards and the prince that my vision had returned to about half-strength, when in truth the world remained shaded in black. However, I had adjusted, so here I was, sitting at the Drunken Spoon, making my first mandatory appearance with Sebastian.

It was so late after midmeal that only a few stragglers remained, most hunched over cups of coffee and copies of *The Daily Buzz*. Grev and Rags were back at The Primrose, working on some correspondence to distract them from their responsibilities. While not explicitly banned from our outings, I wasn't about to risk violating some rule by having the guards stop an attack that should have been my responsibility to thwart.

That said, our walk to the docks had nearly given me a heart attack. Slipping into shadows and monitoring the world for nuances might be in my wheelhouse, but actively working to prevent a threat while doing that was a whole other ask.

The prince dunked his spoon into the bowl of cheddar soup and dripped it back into the pool, lips twisted sourly. "It's gone cold. Like, the cream is separating from the cheese cold."

"At least it isn't poisoned." I leaned back in my chair. The waitress washing glasses at the bar glanced over, but didn't seem inclined to move. "Even if the poison were slow-acting, I would have felt something by now."

"I don't want to know how you know that." Sebastian shoved his tray out of the way. "I'm not hungry, anyway."

"Any chance you'll decide to skip eveningmeal, too? Make my life that much easier?" Though he'd saved Grev's omelets from burning at morningmeal, Sebastian opted against eating his once I picked it apart and sampled every few bites.

His stomach growled loudly, and he shot me a look. "Might as well."

"Come now, what's one day without food?" I pinched his arm and ducked away from his responding swat. "You've got plenty of meat on your bones. A few more hours won't kill you."

"But it might kill you." He turned around in his chair and caught the waitress' eye. She tossed her tresses over her shoulder, feathery antennae twitching, and sauntered over with the check. Not about to let good food go to waste, I wolfed down what remained of Sebastian's meal—the soup was, in fact, colder than the stones I used to sleep on in the alley—while he paid.

"There must be something wrong with your chemical make-up," he grumbled, rising. The temperature had dropped again, the last vestiges of etret breathing its dying breaths, but the prince declined the use of a cloak, preferring his ratty jacket.

"Food is food." I shrugged, shoving the last bite of toast between my teeth. "Energy will keep my senses sharp."

The mantis held the door open for me to exit first. I scanned the streets and rooftops before snagging his arm and pulling him after me. Matching my pace at my side, Sebastian asked, "You were on the streets for a few years, right? What was that like?"

"One year," I corrected automatically. "I spent one year wandering from alley to alley. I was fortunate to find solid employment and an affordable apartment after that. If I hadn't..." I sucked my lower lip between my teeth, nibbling the cracked skin. "I probably would have gone back to the Firestone, figured out a way to help the Shells without signing away what remains of my morals."

A figure behind one of the stalls snared my attention, and I shifted to Sebastian's other side. We passed the vendor, and I heaved a sigh. It was just a rack of tunics. I didn't know how Grev and Rags did this day after day. The job of bodyguard was stressful enough to kill me without a direct attack.

"To answer your question, though, it was lonely." I tugged my cloak more tightly around my shoulders. "Hot or cold, rainy or sunny, that doesn't matter when you can feel bits of your soul chipping away with each set of eyes that pass over you indifferently."

The prince stopped beside a stall, examining a wide array of fruits. He pointed at a bundle of citrus pods. "Three, please. And toss in a few apples." The vendor hunkered in her shawl and hurried to fulfill his request.

"I can understand that." It took me a beat to realize he was replying to my comment. "When I left Moldona, Grev and Rags were by my side, but sometimes it was easy to feel alone and lost, surrounded by nothing but water for weeks on end."

I tried to imagine his perspective. This close to the docks, the salt hung thick in the air, but I'd only been on a boat twice in my life. Neither time had I lost sight of the shore, let alone the mountains that shielded Moldona.

"Weren't you part of a team, though?" I asked, reflecting on the parts of my soul that gaped wide in the years after I left the Shells, the part of me that craved the feeling of belonging. Of having a place and people who needed me.

Sebastian tossed a citrus pod from hand to hand. "Yes. There wasn't a shortage of work, and we all had a place and role to play." He gripped the fruit tightly. "But there were also long stretches of quiet, where the sun beat down on your skin and the shimmer of the sea glimmered endlessly into the horizon. I felt so small then." He paused, inhaling deeply. "And at night, I'd sometimes go on deck when nearly everyone was asleep and stare up at the stars. The black was almost thick enough to suffocate. That's when I felt the most alone."

I steered the prince away from a group of rambunctious maggots, hand resting on the jawram sheathed at my side. The wind blowing from the north quickly snatched away the warmth of the sun on my face. "How are you feeling now that you're back?"

There. I'd dared to ask what I felt was the most forbidden question.

I, myself, had wondered how I would react if I were thrust back into my old life, surrounded by people whom I no longer knew. The idea sent a nasty shiver through my veins.

"That's a difficult one to answer." Sebastian slowed to examine an array of kitchen knives crafted from shells displayed on a vendor's table. I circled his back, sweeping the crowd for anyone who stood out, and came up empty. "I suppose I feel many things: curiosity, frustration, anger, dread." He paused. "Hopeful. Is this whittled from scallop?" The last was directed at the vendor who dipped her head low and offered the paring knife. Sebastian accepted it, bringing the edge to his face. I gave the vendor a curt once-over, and she bowed under my scrutiny, shuffling back a few steps.

"Returning to Moldona is messy. That's the best way I can put it. I've seen a lot, and I'm sacrificing a lot by being back here, but I think it's worth the risk," the prince concluded. "The less I have to see of some hybrids, the better. But that can be said no matter where you are."

Down the street, a bell chimed. Sebastian moved suddenly, spinning around and catching me by surprise. A wide smile stretched across his face. "Is that the Honey Cream Bee? I've searched everywhere, but I couldn't find his stall."

That grin was pure distraction, an expression so radiant I wished I could see it in full. Instead, I basked in its warmth, its joy.

That's all it took.

A moment of relaxed candor.

The vendor snatched a long knife from the table and lunged toward the prince. I reacted without thought, yanking the prince away from the threat and shifting into the blade's path to block it with my body. Pain lanced up my side, but I barely felt it. I surged forward, the tabletop toppling, spilling knives everywhere as I jumped on top of it, reaching for the would-be assassin.

In her hurry to escape my grasp, the scarf around her head unraveled, revealing the narrow face of a mosquito. She snatched another knife off the table behind her and slashed, nicking my forearm. My hand closed around her cloak, which ripped from her form easily, exposing her wings.

I cursed myself as those wings whirred into motion. She tossed her knife at me as she launched into the air. I caught it nimbly with one hand, and in desperation, I flung it back at her, quick as an arrow loosed from a bow. The knife clipped the vibration of her wings, sending her spiraling. With her remaining power, the assassin dropped to the ground a few streets over, where I lost her in the crowd.

I would have given chase had it not been for Sebastian rasping my name.

The prince was pulling himself to his feet, a small crowd of onlookers gawking at the mess we'd made of the quiet street. I rushed to him, all sense of decorum forgotten as I patted him over, searching for injuries. But aside from some bruises from being tossed to the ground, he was unhurt.

"You're alright," I breathed, throwing my arms around him in relief without thinking. Once my embrace locked around him, we both froze. My face pressed to his shoulder. His cheek rested against the side of my head. This was inappropriate on so many levels, yet I couldn't pull away. His solid warmth anchored me in the storm of adrenaline. He didn't seem inclined to pull back, either.

It wasn't until he drew a hand down my side that we jerked apart. He'd touched my wound, making me flinch. "You're bleeding," he said, shock trailing over his face. "You said nothing."

"I'll be fine. It's a scratch."

"Doesn't look like a scratch." He gripped my hand and pulled me down the street, leaving the mess of the stall in our wake. "Let's get back to the Primrose where Grev can get a look at it. We've had enough of an outing for one day."

A part of me I was loath to hope he would never let go.

22

Pomp and Circumstance

Nim

Nim's injury was far more than a scratch.

The knife had sliced open a gash in her side, right beneath her rib cage. Grev had attempted to treat the injury, but Nim got agitated when he tried to separate her wraps and disappeared into her room muttering about taking care of injuries worse than this before.

I was getting used to her sudden moods and relayed what had happened in the marketplace to my guards while we waited for her to reemerge. Ten minutes later, she joined us in the kitchen wearing a fresh shirt and tunic. Rags needled the thief about her unfortunate luck, which Nim took in stride. Eventually, we settled around the table and started a game of Hive and Hex, chatting about inane things until it was time to prepare for the ball.

Nim refused to let me change in a room by myself, and planted herself beside the window, her back to me while I donned fresh attire. As I pulled on the shirt Grev had set out for me, I considered the tension that had built between me and the ant, tension that hadn't existed before Nim embraced me. Her actions were innocent, but my heart had thudded uncomfortably in my chest, leaving a strange ache behind when we split apart.

When it came her turn to change, she maintained the same order as before, only it was my back turned on her. Clothing rustled and I forced myself to swallow down the acorn that rose in my throat. Earlier, I'd seen the evidence that her wraps covered more than her exposed skin, and questioned just how far down the coverings went. How they might hug her slender form.

My cheeks grew hot, and I ran a shaking hand over my hair, trying to dispel the image that flitted about my mind. It was only normal, I tried to reassure myself, to think about her wrappings. They were an oddity. It wasn't *her* I wanted to see... but her mannerisms. I desperately wanted to know what made her tick. And maybe if she unraveled a little in the process...

"You can turn around."

My spine snapped straight, and I patted my cheeks, hoping they weren't as red as I imagined them to be. I shouldn't have worried, because when I turned around, there she was. The same thief as always. Her clothing was freshly laundered, the ironing lines in the jacket and slacks rigid, but it was the same outfit I'd presented her with that day on the training grounds: black boots that she'd now broken in, black pants, white tunic, gray jacket with my compass embroidered across the back.

"I feel stuffy compared to you," I said, holding back a chuckle.

"Clothing is clothing," Nim huffed, strapping her jawram to her thigh holster. "I prefer mobility to shiny buckles when I'm protecting precious cargo."

"You could have at least traded out the jacket," Grev huffed. The hornet stepped in front of her, and, like he used to do with me when we were younger, tugged her collar straight. "Presentation means everything at the keep, and you are most definitely not dressed appropriately." His frown deepened, brows a vee on his face. "They'll eat you alive."

Nim stepped out of his grip, tightening the red strip of fabric that tied off one of her braids. "And I care... why?"

Grev's scowl deepened and Rags chortled.

"Blood will show up quite nicely on this shirt," Nim continued, tugging the fabric tight against the front of her torso. "That's the whole point of this façade, isn't it? To see who bleeds? Who dies? Who loses their dreams?"

In a snap, the uneasy feeling we'd worked all afternoon to eliminate flicked back into place. Nim reached for the bracelet she'd bartered away and retreated just as quickly. Shame soaked my skin, heavy as a drenched sponge.

Rags cleared her throat, shooting me a glance. "Both of ya oughtta get outside. The carriage will be here any moment."

Nim didn't wait for me before jerking open the door and striding into the hallway. From the doorway, I pointed back at my eldest guard. "It will be fine. Stop stressing out."

Knowing Grev was scowling, I jogged after my champion, who waited at the top of the stairs, peering down the carpeted floor. Shaking herself, she led me downstairs, silent as a spider tracking a fly, eyes darting into the corners warily. The bodyguards I'd worked with in the past were far more subtle regarding their observations, but I found her naivety refreshing. The earnestness with which she tackled her job was apparent.

She balked at the sight of the carriage outside. The gray zira with speckled white wings strapped to the carriage sensed her nerves and tossed its head. The footman, whom I recognized from the castle, swept into a low bow and pulled the door wide. "Your Highness."

He didn't seem surprised when Nim darted up the three stairs first, the carriage swaying as she ran through whatever checks she felt necessary to secure passage. When she appeared in the doorway again, she gave a single nod and disappeared into the depths once more. I offered the footman a smile and patted his shoulder as I entered, unhooking my sword from my belt before settling comfortably on a teal cushion opposite Nim.

We sat in comfortable silence while the footman clambered back into position, but Nim's attempts at nonchalance shattered when the carriage jerked. I imagined her knuckles going white with the force with which she gripped her kneecaps, body braced as if resisting shattering into a million pieces.

"First carriage ride?" I offered.

She cleared her throat, making a show of relaxing her arms. "First in a long time." It was said in a tone that made it clear further questions on the matter would not be taken well.

I traced the vines chiseled into the sheath of my sword, wondering for the hundredth time about her history. For a child of greenside, her accent left much to be desired. The rounded vowels were there, but subtle. The fire ant she respected greatly, Devlin, had cared for her enough to ensure her education, but she was more learned than I had anticipated from someone without duchy tutors.

Sure, she worked in a bookstore, but books were easy to read without absorbing the nuances. And tides did she pin down the nuances: understanding the various heights of bows, automatically adjusting her silverware into the proper order, even picking up the steps to the dances Rags showed her with relative ease. The thief tried to hide, but not well enough.

Too soon, the carriage jolted to a stop. Nim was already on her feet when the footman pried open the door, her shoulders stiff as she clattered to the pavement. Her head didn't stop moving, flitting from the shadows surrounding a tangle of bushes beside the carriage to the well-lit entry where a pair of female guards stood, waiting to open the doors for guests.

The carriage pulled away, and Nim made for the entry, her focus admirable, but I snagged her elbow before she got too far. Her brow lifted as she glanced back at me in question. I offered my elbow with a bit of a waggle. "Remember? Decorum?"

The sound that escaped her was somewhere between a sigh and a groan, but she reached out anyway, fingers curling loosely around my biceps, and we fell into step.

"Is this what it's always like for you?" she asked when the guards bowed and opened the doors.

I flexed a little around her fingers, deciding I liked the feel of them. She exuded an incredible amount of energy for someone so reserved and likely exhausted from a long day of watching the shadows. Our shoes squeaked on the corridor floor leading toward the violins and muted conversation.

"You mean guards watching me all the time? Fixing a mask on my face when I wake and not taking it off until I fall asleep? The pomp and circumstance that never quits?" I waited for her silver gaze to tip toward mine, willing her to hear the bite behind the humor laced in my voice. "Why do you think I boarded a ship and left?"

Her grin was quick, lightning over a black, black sky. "If you weren't a prince, I'd say we could be friends."

The bark of laughter ripped from my throat surprised me. "We'll have to see what we can do about that, won't we?" I squeezed her fingers with my free hand before motioning to the room spread out before us. "Ready to put on the biggest act of your life?"

"As if I have a choice." Her hand fell from my elbow, settling on the jawram Rags had gifted her. Together, we stepped into the immaculate ballroom. A chandelier older than my family name hung from the center of the ceiling, its one hundred and two candles strategically placed around the petal-shaped crystals, dancing with soft flames.

From the high walls hung banners of teal and silver, the colors alternating around the glowing sconces. A balcony overlooked the right side of the room, packed with hybrids, some leaning on the white railing strung with green milkweed. A large table laden with finger food was on the other end of the room, where a trio of servers helped guests fill their plates. Over their heads hung the brassy emblem of my family, the one stitched on the ratty jacket that I wore even now.

Nim had settled into pace about half a step behind me, giving me the lead. Hybrids of all blueside backgrounds swarmed the floor. The beetles with their metallic shells hugged the walls, arms crossed and faces set in grim lines. Bees claimed the dance floor, the vibrant hues of their clothing brightening the space as they spun and swirled both on the ground and in the air. Hornets in starched blue uniforms mingled with cicadas garbed in their traditional green, debating military tactics.

Vincent stood with them, smirking, his champion by his side, a glass of something lilac-colored and bubbly in his hand. I made a mental note to stay away from him as much as possible. That said, where had my mother and Micah wandered off to?

A butterfly with coral pink wings shot with swirls of black drifted by, peering at Nim and me from the corner of her eye. I went stiff. Lady Maria toyed with the curl of her antenna, painted lips curved with invitation. My chest tightened, knowing she was about to approach. The relationship we'd fostered as teenagers was intense but harmless, and I had no desire to rekindle those memories.

Nim brushed the jut of my elbow, inclining her head toward a group of centipedes in dress attire, their many arms balancing various plates and glasses. Grateful for her intervention, I nodded to the female who scowled at Nim and veered away.

"Thank you," I murmured. "But you know I'll have to talk to others at some point, right?"

173

The thief scanned the room, settling on a group of hybrids adorned in jewels and various house colors, including a few of my cousins. "Grev made it clear I'm to protect you from *all* threats. She reeked of trouble." The thief motioned vaguely around the space. "How about you find someone you actually want to talk to before I'm forced to take drastic action?"

"Intriguing." I wanted to know what that entailed.

A pair of bees bustled around us, not deigning to hide their stares as they took Nim in. As one of only a handful of greensiders in the room, and one of two ant champions, she was a commodity, not that she seemed bothered by it. Given her preference for slathering herself in linen, I imagined she was more than aware of the attention she drew.

It was all too easy to slip into quiet conversations. Everyone in attendance understood the game we were playing, the push and pull for information, weaknesses, scandals. Though I hadn't boasted many friends as a child, those I had entertained welcomed me back with open arms. It wasn't long before I found myself *enjoying* catching up.

Every now and again, when my throat got too dry, Nim would snag a flute of chilled water from a waiter's tray, down a quarter of it, then hand it to me with a nod. My associates watched our interaction with wide eyes, enthralled and a little wary of what they knew was coming. The undercurrents of anticipation ran thick through the room, impossible to ignore. From what I gleaned, all champions had staved off at least one attack and remained in play.

"When do you think they'll strike?" The quiet voice was not directed at me, but it snagged my attention all the same. I turned slightly, recognizing the low, somber tone. Jaxon leaned his head close to Nim, their shoulders practically brushing. His charge stood behind him, chatting with a butterfly. Nim's expression was relaxed, free. Something feathery and light shifted through my chest, followed shortly by a flare of discontent. What had he said that put her at such ease?

She rubbed the spot where she'd been stabbed earlier. "Soon. I'm picking up weird vibes."

He nodded and glared at a beetle who passed too close to his Sai heir. The beetle turned up his nose and tipped his glass into his mouth in dismissal, though he veered away from Aurora. Message received.

"How did they come at you earlier?" Jaxon asked. I had to strain to hear their conversation. Thankfully, the Amana siblings I'd been conversing with didn't appear to notice my lapse in the discussion.

"Early. It was still dark. Mine tried to get in through a door and hurled tear gas when she couldn't." Nim's eyes were still a little bloodshot from the ordeal. Wait. She? The thief hadn't mentioned recognizing the gender of her attacker. Stung, I struggled to keep quiet. Sure, she didn't owe me explanations of everything going on inside her head, but I thought we'd come to a better understanding than that.

Jaxon peered at her, jaw clenching. "Bet that hurt like a bitch."

"I wouldn't recommend trying it out anytime soon. I still can't see very well."

That couldn't be right. Earlier, she had claimed to have recovered. And she moved with relative ease: springing after assassins, hurrying downstairs, snatching food out of my damn hands. Those weren't easy to do blind. Was she trying to one-up her friend? That didn't fit her character. So, what was I missing?

She shifted her weight on her feet. "What about you? I assume you didn't take yours out, or you wouldn't be here right now."

The ant grimaced, rubbing a hand along his collarbone. "They came at us while we were grabbing something to eat. I got in the way of their dagger."

Nim reached for the wound, her face twisted with concern. "Are you alright?"

"I'll be fine." He carefully peeled her hand from his tunic, threading his fingers between hers to soften the blow. "Just a graze. The Sai's fixed me right up." His lips curled in a half-grin. "I wish you could try their healing elixir. You'd love it—tastes like raspberries." He chuckled. "Which reminds me of the time we stole those boxes from the caravan—"

"—and found the motherload of blackberry mead inside? How could I forget?" Nim beamed, squeezing his hand, apparently forgetting all about her responsibilities. It was stunning, that smile. Even though it wasn't directed at me, it morphed her entire being. Would that be how she always looked if she weren't dealt the hand she currently played?

"I think it took us a week to recover from those hangovers. Worst. Decision. Ever."

"Nah. Our worst decision was when—"

A female shrieked, the tone shrill enough to rattle the windows. Wood splintered. People scattered as two figures plummeted from the balcony. Light flashed off metal. A knife. Major Ectya Day's uniform was unmistakable as she flipped over, wings flattened against her back, using the assailant to stop her fall. They hit the floor with an ugly crunch.

Nim stepped in front of me, the length of her body pressed against mine so hard I could feel her trembling. Our hands touched, and despite the alarm zipping through my veins, part of me wanted to twine my fingers with hers, offer her the same measure of comfort her friend had. With a groan, the dragonfly peeled herself off the ground, rising to one knee in the middle of a growing pool of crimson blood. She reached beneath the attacker's body and lifted the dagger high, strong face blank as she raised it over her head.

Several cheers went up. A few hands clapped, applauding her resolve. With one last look at the black cloak of the dead assassin,

Day rose to her feet and strode away, leaving a trail of blood behind her. Now that the danger had passed, the morbidity of the scene drew the onlookers closer, hands covering their mouths as they murmured to one another excitedly.

"We should get out of here," Nim said under her breath, snagging my wrist.

I didn't disagree with her assessment. As we turned toward the door, hoping to slink away among the distraction, a male shout rose from the hallway to our left. "Oh, no you don't."

William Amana's pale face was stark in the circle of candlelight as his brother grappled with a cloaked figure. The bee's face twisted in concentration as he shoved the bigger person back, fists raised.

More commotion came from behind us, a series of screams that ripped through my thoughts, but I couldn't look away as Nim dragged on my arm. Morris shoved his sleeve up, the skin on the underside of his forearm raised with the staff of his lethal stinger. A body came between us and I lost sight of the bee.

We made it to the wall after ducking and dodging the crush of bodies hurrying from the threats that seemed to be popping up all around. Nim slammed my back against the brick and placed herself in front of me once more. She muttered to herself, jawram clutched in her hand as she tried to look everywhere at once.

It rankled, twisting my insides ugly and black. I hated having someone protecting me when I could fight off a threat myself. But her orders were to not let me get hurt in any way. Even a scratch was grounds for disqualification. All I could do was watch the chaos unfold as champions sparred against those handpicked to take them out.

Morris stumbled from the hallway, face splattered with blood, poison dripping from the foot-long stinger he clutched in one hand. Given he'd left his brother's side, I had a fairly good idea of what had become of his assassin. Across the room, Jaxon held his own in hand-to-hand combat, aiming a well-timed punch that caught his opponent in the kidney. Commander Verity had his sword out, my brother at his back, a slight smirk on his face as he watched females tripping over hemlines and males sliding through the blood.

"Is there a way out of here?" my champion hissed. "Somewhere people don't know about?"

The tunnels. My brothers and I had spent long hours memorizing the routes through the castle during our childhoods. Another scream broke my concentration as I tried to remember which panel of fabric concealed the doorways cut into the walls themselves.

"Behind the banners," I said, lifting the teal panel of fabric beside me, running my fingers over the cool stones, cursing when I came up empty. "I know a hidden doorway is around here somewhere."

Nim shoved me. "Keep going until we find one."

Two more panels yielded no results, and a clock had started ticking in my head, one warning me that our reprieve from attack was drawing to a close. Nim had twisted her jawram in two, the blades clutched in her fists, anxiety apparent in the way she looked around.

Near the corner, I ripped up a silver panel and dragged my nails across the wall in desperation, almost missing the catch between painted stones. Breath caged in my lungs, I backtracked and found the groove again. With a mighty thud of my heart, I slammed my hand into the stone that opened the panel, one set at about eye level. It caved inward, and the stones groaned, rough and urgent.

Spinning, I reached for Nim just as she shoved me to the ground. I blinked. An arrow sprouted from her thigh. My blood froze. Arrows didn't sprout. They were shot. The assassin paired against Nim had finally found her. The thief stumbled, nearly dropping her blades. She reached for the injury, then thought better of it.

Eyes blazing, she ordered me to get the door open. To get us out of here. I moved not a moment too soon, as an arrow exploded against the wall where my arm would have been.

The door finally swung wide, revealing a dark passage within. Nim grunted again, and I yanked her back into the space as she stumbled, a second arrow protruding from her thigh. The door closed with a slam. Darkness enveloped us.

"Are you—"

"No time," she gritted through clenched teeth. Relief and worry threaded through me. I knew the sound of holding back pain.

She leaned around me, squinting. "Do you know the way out?"

"It would be easier with a torch, but yes."

She hummed and, with what might have been a whimper, threw herself down the hall. Her foot dragged on the floor as she hobbled. "Then let's go before she figures out how to follow."

To her credit, she gave it everything she had, but after a few steps, sagged against the wall.

"You need to let me help you," I murmured.

"I'm fine." She batted away my suggestion. "Just need to catch my breath."

For tides' sake. "You have a damned arrow in your leg, of course you're not fine." I hoped she forgave me for what I was about to say, but her pride needed to hear it. "They'll catch us with you slowing us down."

She didn't reply for a long moment. A sniffle. And she reached for me, winding her arm around my neck. "Alright. Just this once."

"Thank the seas." I wrapped my arm around her middle, mindful of the arrow, her injured thigh wedged between us, and we lurched forward. We finally found our rhythm a few steps later, hopping and bobbing through the darkened hallway as I guided us from memory. The thief was as slight as she appeared. Good food and plenty of rest had filled out her form, but recovering from years of malnutrition took time to repair. I hoisted more of her weight against me when we finally hit a wall that I prayed led us outside the castle.

"Ready?" I asked, hoping she could hear me over her pained panting.

She sniffed wetly, voice strained. "You better be right about where we are."

At least her sense of humor hadn't fled with her mobility. The smile that broke across my lips lightened everything inside me. I found the latch tucked into the wall and pulled. The door swung wide with a groan, revealing a row of carriages.

"Looks like I'm right."

She gulped, shifting against my side. "Is your driver nearby? Your assassin has a bow and knows how to use it."

Luck had us again. "He's the closest carriage to us." I peered down at her. Sweat mingled with the blood on her face, dripping from her chin. Her shirt was damp. "Think you can run thirty paces? Once we're inside, we can get out of here."

She dragged her sleeve over her forehead. "I'll do what needs to be done."

"On the count of three." Better not to give her time to rethink her options. Sheer resolve and my upbeat attitude were the only things keeping her going. "You go first."

Wild strands of hair that had slipped loose from her braid clung to her cheeks, and she shook her head. "You first. I'll keep my hand on your shoulder."

Stubborn female. "One. Two. Three."

We bolted, her body awkwardly pressed against mine, bobbing and weaving. An arrow slammed into the carriage door as I reached for it. Nim's hand vanished from my side. I ripped open the door, relieved to find it empty. Another arrow flashed in the lamplight outside the castle, and to my amazement, Nim caught it one-handed and flung it to the ground. She flipped a vulgar gesture at a figure I couldn't see before collapsing inside the carriage. With the door still open, I shouted for the driver to haul us out of there.

Nim leaned against the cushions sideways, sprawled across the floor. Blood smudged the wooden slats, the puddle growing thicker around her thigh. She peered down at the shaft, fingers curled around the chunk of wood, and grimaced, sucking her bottom lip between her teeth. With a sigh, she propped her head on the velvet. "Remind me never to get shot again."

"Not fun, is it?" I asked.

Intrigued, she lifted her head. "You've been shot?"

I nodded. "Years ago, during a pirate raid. I wasn't paying enough attention." As if willed into existence, the puckered pink scar left by the bolt twinged, and I rubbed my hand over the wound. "But they fixed me up. Rags watched them, so she'll be able to help you, since I assume you won't want to visit a healer."

The ant braced the heel of her hand against her temple, eyes closed. "Not the Primrose." She sucked a gasp of pain through clenched teeth. "Take me to the Firestone."

"The bar by the docks?" My brows furrowed. "We should get home. It's secure there. I promise Grev and Rags know what they're doing."

She shook her head and writhed against the cushions. "If you don't. Redirect us to the Firestone now," she managed between pants, "I'll pull myself out of that door. And tell the driver myself."

"But why—"

Silver eyes opened, burning with a raw heat I didn't understand. "You suggested a healer, and I'm going to a healer. The assassin will also expect us to go back to our rooms. This will throw them off." She collapsed against the seat. Those few sentences had sapped her energy. "Trust me."

If she was going to be stubborn about it, who was I to tell her where to seek help? I drew back the board situated behind the driver's seat and relayed her instructions, leaning as the carriage swayed when we turned a corner a bit too sharply. Nim didn't offer anything else, and I would have sworn she'd passed out if not for the tiny grimaces of pain that curled her brow.

What seemed like hours but was likely only a few minutes later, the carriage rocked to a stop. Nim accepted my hand up and leaned against me as we made our way outside. Even injured and in great pain, her eyes were alert, eyeing the rooftops. Warm yellow light spilled from the crack under the door before us. I wrapped my arm more securely around her waist as I pushed it open.

Behind a small desk a fire ant jumped to his feet. He started to protest, but Nim snarled at him to shut up and let her through. Without further protest, he fiddled with something behind the desk and the wall slid back. Nim pointed to the spiral staircase it revealed and I cursed. It would be impossible to make it down with her like this. No way was she walking.

Without asking, I hauled her up into my arms, ignoring her snarl of protest, and darted down the stairs. When we appeared at the base, all conversation stopped, eyes peering at us in the doorway. Nim's blood dripped from the toe of her boot.

"Anyone seen Devlin?" she asked through gritted teeth. She pushed against me, but I gripped her harder against my chest. Pride and appearances be damned. She was two seconds away from passing out. No way was I releasing her now.

A larva of about twelve shot up from a bench and dipped around the bar, disappearing through a door at the back. Nim tilted her head. "If you won't put me down, would you help me inside?"

I edged her closer to the bar, muscles tensed as the silence lingered. We were well within Shells territory. Nim was far too in her element for it to be anything but, however I now understood her wired behavior when she'd pulled me from the casino. I wasn't too drunk on adrenaline to sense the danger that washed across us in waves.

"What is this place?" I asked, mouth nearly pressed to her ear.

Her answering grin spoke of brain-deep exhaustion. Sweat stained the fabric obscuring her face. "Shell headquarters. Devlin is in charge. He's the one who took me in."

That simple explanation opened far more doors than it closed, but before I could voice any of the questions that came to mind, a fire ant with sloped shoulders and a ragged red beard strode up behind the bar, rubbing his hands on a white rag. The confusion on his face morphed into concern when he spotted us. The rag hit the counter, and he rounded the open end, pulling Nim from my hold with a firm yet insistent grip.

She whimpered, tears filming her eyes like gloss. "I need some help, Dev."

He glanced toward her leg. Nausea churned in my gut. "I see that, darling child. Let's get you in the back where I can get a closer look." The look he shot me was filled with warning. "Stay at the bar."

"He needs—"

The gruff male silenced her with a squeeze. "Aye. I'm aware of the Trial. No one would dare harm him in here. Now let's see how bad this is."

Words fled me as the ants disappeared into the back, the curtain draped over the door falling closed when Devlin tugged on a braided black cord. *Trust me*, she'd said. And I'd been helpless to her request. It floored me how, even in her weakest moment, she not only sought help for herself but protection for me. No wonder she'd wanted to come here.

Gradually, the volume inside the establishment picked up, though more than a few hybrids rested hands inside vests and against waists where surely illicit weapons were hidden. A barmaid approached once, offering to bring something on the menu, but I refused, remembering Nim's insistence on taste testing everything before it touched my lips.

Not for the first time since I'd started this whole ordeal, guilt twinged in my gut.

My dreams were important. They were the best course for the nation if we hoped to save ourselves from destruction. But I was dragging innocent people into my schemes. Nim was not the first person to be wounded by my actions, but she was the most obvious.

From flying across rooftops to slinking through alleyways, she'd always moved with precise intention, not a foot out of place. The arrow through her thigh would impact her abilities—a detriment when she wasn't as skilled with weapons as most of her opponents. We'd also met because of her pick-pocketing skills, skills that the injury to her arm would now impair.

And she would have to face another trial in a week, assuming we escaped tonight.

My head dropped to my hands, and I heaved a sigh, wishing I could be by her side as Devlin treated her. Out here, I couldn't hear their conversation, see how bad her wound was. I already felt like a stranger in the place of my birth, but here, when no one dared approach after my rejection of food, I was a complete foreigner.

Now that I had to think, her insistence about heading here made sense. Part of me was dying to know what she concealed beneath those bandages, but whatever secrets she guarded would remain under literal wraps for now. She wouldn't want just anyone peeling away the stained fabric, like she'd prickled beneath Grev's touch earlier, and she trusted the ant who had raised her as a child.

Jealously prickled irrationally. Devlin was a father to her. She'd said as much—multiple times. But I couldn't reconcile my emotions, not as twisted as they were.

When she limped into the doorway more than an hour later, her face was tight, but the stained bandages were gone. The arrows had been removed, and she'd wrapped herself in a fresh set of baggy clothing and new bandages. Devlin helped her around the end of the bar, easing her onto a stool beside me.

"How are you feeling?" I asked, repressing the baffling urge to pull her against me and breathe in the scent of her hair.

Her hand shook when she drank from the glass of water Devlin placed before her. "I've been worse."

"Any word from the keep?" Devlin asked gruffly.

My shoulders sagged when the dots connected. If he was the male who had raised Nim, he was Jaxon's father. He worried about the fate of his son. "Nothing yet, but your son had the upper hand against his opponent when we escaped."

Devlin pressed the backs of his fingers to his lips, eyes filled with worry that I imagined was uncharacteristic for a hybrid of his stature. Then it was gone, and the rough-around-the-edges barkeep was back, making the rounds, inviting light conversation, and refilling the glasses of the patrons who'd waited patiently for his return.

"How much time till midnight?" Nim croaked.

I glanced at the clock on the wall beside the exit. "Half an hour, give or take a few minutes."

"Good. That's good." She rubbed the fabric of her pants over her injury. "I know Rags and Grev will be worried, but would you mind if we stayed here until time's up?"

The answer was an easy one. "We can stay as long as you like." Whatever she needed, I would give. She'd protected me so many times today, it was the least I could do. After all, I was helpless to actually defend her in the way I craved. Not until this blasted trial was over.

"Would you mind doing something for me?" I asked. It was high time for me to release my preconceived notions. To get to know this

185

female, understand her mind, as much of a maze as I was sure it was.

Her eyes danced, turning up at the corners. "Does it require blocking any more arrows?"

"Not at all." I scratched my arm. "Would you share some stories of what it was like growing up here with Jaxon? I want to know everything about this found family of yours."

With an amused sigh, Nim took another sip from her glass before passing it to me. I took a long gulp, finally able to stomach something knowing she was safe. My thief pondered the request for a beat, nodded to herself, and launched into the first of many tales woven from her childhood, spilling stories of what it was like to grow up in the danger and security the Shells had to offer long after the clock ticked the time of safety.

23

Better Off

Sebastian

Our harrowing journey through the tunnels that wound around Castle Redfern and Nim's seemingly endless list of stories had drudged up old memories of my own, and I picked my way through the tunnels once again with Grev at my side, torch in hand this time, gradually making my way down to the underground levels of the keep.

I understood Nim's love for Jax better now. He was the constant in her life, the person she could turn to for anything at any time. The thief had been careful to avoid discussing her life prior to meeting him, but it was clear her teenage years were filled with companionship and laughter.

Those were two things I didn't expect to encounter tonight as I sought out my brother. Antonio Viotto had succumbed to his injuries mere hours ago, the only champion mortally wounded in the trial. Even the healers couldn't fix a knife dragged through the belly.

The news had come by raven while Nim slept, curled up in her own bed. She'd collapsed shortly after we'd returned to the Primrose, and I envied her ability to easily escape the inquisition at the hands of Rags and Grev. Both had been worried sick about us, but they'd stayed behind as promised, pacing the floors while waiting for our safe return.

"If you ever pull a stunt like that again, I'll wring your neck myself," Grev growled as I pulled a lever to open a door carved in the wall. It wasn't the first threat he'd dropped over the last half hour, and I doubted it would be the last. "Next time, find a way to let me know what's going on."

Despite his bluster, he poked his head out the entry and peered around. "Clear."

Following him out, I said, "Sure, the next time my champion's bleeding out in my hands, I'll make it my priority to send a raven."

My friend huffed. "That's not what I meant, and you know it. At least send the driver."

"They could be sabotaged on the way back." I waggled my finger at him playfully. Grev had the unique ability to see the worst possible outcomes for everything, and he used to make a game of quizzing me about all the ways my plans could go awry. "Then where would we be?"

"Then I'll just have to glue myself to your side."

Much like he had today, while Rags kept watch over Nim, a new paperback book in hand. It was the only solution our small group was comfortable with.

Here in the underbelly of the keep, the halls were eerily quiet. Though we knew every nook and crevice that would conceal us if any of the many servants under my mother's care slipped by, none appeared.

Sorrow tugged at my heartstrings. Even now, years after my departure, people were still wary of Micah and his obsession with science. If they would only speak with him for a few minutes, they would bask in the brilliance of his mind.

The door to his workshop was open, a hint of smoke wafting from inside, and Grev ushered me in. After dropping the torch in one of the many sconces carved into the stones, he planted his shoulders against the wall beside the door, arms crossed over his broad chest. "I'll keep watch. You see how he's doing."

The room itself was vast, the architecture Gothic. More than a dozen wide arches framed the walls, holding up the stone ceiling. Bookshelves and long tables were crammed into the spaces beneath the arches, their wooden surfaces charred and stained. Yellowed pages torn from stray books crinkled beneath my feet as I slipped around a series of bookcases blocking Micah's primary workspace from prying eyes in the hall. In the center of the room, beneath the wide dragon's jaws of a ventilation shaft, my brother poured a neon red liquid from a beaker into a test tube. Thick, scarred gloves covered his hands, and a pair of goggles replaced his square set of glasses.

He shook the beaker, dislodging the drops clinging to the lip, and stoppered the tube with a cork. It was then placed in a wooden structure alongside other vials bearing brightly colored substances. With a sigh, he pulled off his goggles and tossed them onto the table, exchanging them for his glasses. Hands braced on the large wheels of his chair, he swiveled. "I wondered if you would visit."

I clasped his raised hand, our forearms touching as I squeezed it hard. He returned the pressure with a cockeyed grin.

"How are you?" I asked, dragging a spare chair to his workbench and settling down so we were eye-to-eye. "I heard about your champion."

Micah scrubbed a hand down the rubber of his wheels and shrugged, the smile bleeding from his eyes. "I feel poorly for the male's family. He didn't deserve to die, especially in defense of someone who knew they weren't going to win."

I traced a scorch mark on the table in the shape of a ring. "What do you mean?"

"I only joined the Trials at the insistence of Vincent." Metal rattled and glass clinked as he fiddled with a few instruments. "He said it wouldn't be right if only one of the princes took part in fighting for our lineage."

His lips tightened, and he gave me a knowing look, one with a hint of sorrow. "Sorry, Seb."

Vincent hadn't believed I would return for the Trials. I knew it. The bastard had bristled like a cat with its fur rubbed the wrong way when I'd visited Mother. I was a complication my oldest brother hadn't anticipated.

Squeezing the arms of my chair, I pushed past the flare of annoyance. "Why did you believe you weren't going to win?"

"Come on. You've seen who he recruited to fight his battles for him." Micah poured a tangerine substance that smelled like vinegar into a brass container. "He's the one who wants the crown. He's the one who stood by Father's side, learning everything to do with our country and its connections over the last ten years. They made me learn diplomacy." His face scrunched with distaste. "But I never got the feel for it. I'm better off down here, in a world I understand, applying my skills to tasks that will actually help people."

He paused, and I knew better than to interrupt his chain of thought. Calmly, I laced my fingers across my stomach and waited, giving him time to piece together his thoughts.

"I didn't want to be king," he said at last. "I don't even need to be in this castle. The estate has a fine enough workspace to accommodate my whims, no matter how big or twisted." Smoke rose from the beaker when he tapped a teaspoon of blue powder into the liquid. "And look at you. You fled the country to divest yourself of royal responsibility. Not that I blame you."

A heavy weight in my stomach that had lodged itself since my arrival at port eased. Mother may be relying on medications to sleep, her sharp and clever edges worn soft with grief. Vincent may have revealed his true colors as a power-hungry weasel with little interest in anyone beyond himself, but Micah was the same as always: intuitive, persistent, blunt.

"I'm glad you're back," he added, almost as an afterthought.

I pressed a hand to my chest in mock shock. "You? Missed me?" I dodged the tweezers he chucked at my head with a laugh. "I thought about you often. You wouldn't believe the advances other nations have made in their sciences."

In fact, I'd written him a few times about my discoveries. However, my brother wasn't one for responding to messages, and when I wasn't sure he was receiving my notes, I ended my efforts.

Micah's brows twisted with curiosity. "I'd appreciate hearing those stories sometime. Maybe there's something worth replicating here."

"There most surely is." If only I could tell him how deeply I believed in that fundamental value. How much I sought to change the world.

"But Seb, you need to be careful." Micah set down his tools, directing his attention toward me in a rare show of absolute focus on something outside of his work. "You and Vincent were always at odds, a pair of chemicals that should never mix, but he's gotten worse. He's changed, and not in a way that I appreciate." He twisted his hands in his lap. "What I'm saying is, the Vincent you left behind is not the same male you'll face today."

Unsettling. It wasn't often my brother took familial struggles into account. That he sought to warn me against Vincent was concerning. I couldn't help but wonder what had transpired between them during my absence, and if it had anything to do with our mother's attitude of late. Anyone who knew Vincent as a child recognized his strong will and desire to grow into someone with infinitely more power. However, something told me his bullying surpassed picking on the staff and lower-class nobles, whom he knew he could poke at without risk of repercussion.

Something to mull over with my friends later.

For now, though, spending time with my brother was nice. Unlike certain members of our family and most of the staff, I felt at home among his things. There was always something interesting to spend hours reading among his many stacks of books. Depending on what he was working on, amazing and sometimes disgusting scents would envelop the room before they were whisked out through the vent. He'd gone through an osteologic stage before I left, and the skeletons of a dozen animals, both large and small, peered down from alcoves in the walls.

The way his brain worked fascinated me, and I wanted to know more.

He'd returned to his work when it was clear my attention had scattered, and I waited for him to finish measuring a spill of black glitter before asking, "What are you working on now?"

He tapped the spoon on the jar, dislodging a scattering of dust. "The healers are looking for a paste that can cauterize wounds in an emergency where they can't rush the victim straight into surgery." I leaned back in my seat as he pointed at his supplies, explaining his thoughts, embracing this rare opportunity to enjoy his company and nothing more.

24

Black Widows

Nim

The door groaned under my weight as I slid down its flat surface, curling cross-legged at its base. Of all the hiding spots in my room above the bookstore, this one in the corner was my favorite. From here, with the lamp extinguished, passersby couldn't even see my silhouette through the covered window. As always, the door was locked. Ms. Whitmere didn't bother me up here, but if anyone tried to force it open, the wood would hit my back, giving me time to react.

Perfect.

I trailed the nubs of my nails down the length of a floorboard. My middle finger caught on a groove in the grain, and I applied pressure until the board popped up with a snick. With a superstitious glance around, I peeled up the panel and set it carefully beside it, revealing a foot-long hole. Thankfully, my eyesight had recovered.

"Did you miss me, my beauties?" I murmured, reaching into the gauzy webs that reminded me of the spun colored sugars sold in the market.

At my beckoning, a trio of black widows emerged from the depths of the hole, seeking attention. I trailed the pads of my fingers over their backs, marveling over their sleek, simple beauty.

Widows were among my favorites of the arachnid family. Typically content, though largely misunderstood, they reminded me of myself, a creature who lurked in the shadows, seeking to avoid the discomfort my mere presence created in the world around me. These arachnids were beautiful in their own way, and they understood the chain of command, submitting to me in a way they would no one else.

Their poison was strong, but mine was stronger.

Murmuring apologies for disturbing their nest, I returned the spiders and parted the delicate webbing. I removed a leather pouch the size and weight of a thick hardcover book. This was the perfect hiding place for one of my greatest secrets. The hole was practically invisible in the floorboards, and anyone who found the spiders' nest would immediately be deterred. Black widow poison might not be lethal, but its effects were excruciating and often left lasting impacts on the nervous system.

From a different pouch I'd brought, I shook a handful of crickets into the hole. "Eat up," I whispered, covering the space again.

I rested the back of my head against the door and hefted the bag I'd recovered. It had once belonged to a bluesider, a simple purse the color of mink with a strap that had snapped. I'd discovered it during one of my few trips close to the castle and recognized the luxury of the leather for what it was. I fished it out of the trash, cleaned it up, and it now held my prized possessions.

The material was soft from use, and the button pinning down the flap slid easily through the hole. With a frown, I removed the rolled bandages tucked inside and carefully lined them up beside my hip. My supply was the lowest it had been in years. Even Devlin was out of wraps after my visit with him during the second trial. Thoughtfully, I applied pressure to my thigh where the muscle ached.

With any luck, the third trial wouldn't involve doing anything overtly physical. That said, the parchment revealing the hint regarding the next trial had arrived this morning, three days following the end of the second task. It was partially burned, with only the letters P and O legible. Rags claimed sabotage and Grev agreed.

We'd gone our separate ways not long after its arrival, hoping to find an ally willing to reveal the true hint, but hadn't had any luck so far. Even Jax, who had fortunately fought off his opponent without serious injury, was mysteriously difficult to locate.

Maybe the advantage given to those who killed their opponents was the hint itself.

I slid my pants down to my knees, revealing the pink tinge of bandages wrapped around my thigh. They desperately needed to be replaced. Slicing through the material with my freshly elongated nails, I quickly unraveled the silk until it fell in a heap at my side. I would dissolve it in acid later.

The injury from the arrow was deep, and Devlin had done a fabulous job stitching it up, but I treated it with an antibacterial pad to be safe. I didn't mind if it scarred, for what was one more scar among thousands, but dying from an infection was not high on my list.

Finally satisfied, I wrapped fresh, clean bandages around my leg, my movements smooth and practiced. It hadn't always been like this. As a child, I'd fumbled in my efforts to hide my damaged skin from the world, but now it was second nature.

A record player sputtered to life in the room below, the soft melody of violins filling my small space. Ms. Whitmere preferred to listen to music when she checked inventory. For my sake, it ensured two things: the shop was closed, and she wouldn't stop to check on me anytime soon, not that she suspected I was here, anyway.

Still huddled in the corner of the room, I unlaced the ties at the top of my shirt and released the tight grip I constantly maintained on my shifter abilities. The skin along my spine parted seamlessly, and I breathed out a long sigh of relief when four narrow limbs sprouted from between my shoulder blades. For the first time in months, I straightened my spinal column to its full length, the vertebrae popping as they slipped fully into place. My fingers, arms, and legs lengthened, their extreme slenderness appearing unnatural, and my nails sprouted into metallic claws. My jaw cracked as my face shifted, and I ran my tongue over the sharpened points of my teeth. A third eye opened on my forehead, one that enabled me to sense heat signatures, and I parted the bandages to allow the lid to open.

If I kept a mirror in my room, I knew what I would see staring back at me: a creature many would call a monster, an abhorrent vision of long limbs and twisted facial features. But I adored my Arachnae side and the freedom my extra limbs allowed me. From the tiny hairs that sprouted the lengths of my multi-jointed legs to the narrow veins embedded in my nails, ready to release poison at a moment's notice, I truly felt what it was to be powerful.

My father had been an ant, lending to my short stature that led everyone to assume I'd gained my abilities from him. I was more than happy to leave them to their assumptions. It protected me against prying eyes. Everything else came from my mother.

She'd painstakingly taught me every detail she could recall about my Arachnae heritage before she died. After that, the rest of my family refused to train me: deeming my long limbs too slender and fragile, a far cry from their inbred, monstrous tarantulas. I wished I could stretch my legs now and rise to my full height of nine feet, but the room was too small, and I didn't dare risk my silhouette being visible from the outside.

With a groan, I reached for the slit at the base of my neck and peeled a trio of threads from it. My spider limbs quickly took over, tugging the parallel lengths before me.

Sebastian and his friends thought my bandages were cotton or linen, opting against asking for more details out of politeness. But I wished I could tell them I spun the wraps from thread I produced myself. It was what made them so reliable and malleable. They naturally stuck to my skin because I chose for them to, urging them to hug my features so they blended in while also enhancing my ability to feel out vibrations. However, if I chose to, I could also weave stronger fibers, ones intended to protect myself against an attack, a feature I had yet to utilize during the Trials for fear people would ask questions, delving into secrets that never should come to light.

It's your silk, you command it. My mother's voice echoed in my head, her advice as sound as ever, and I refocused on my task. Starting from the top, I spun the third thread around the other two, my longer limbs easily accommodating the movement as I wound the bandages longer and longer. The simplicity of the task settled me.

It would be a long night, but I needed more rolls of these to survive the Trials.

25

Only the Beginning

Nim

Someone would pay for this.

Paper crinkled in my fist, and I threw the balled-up note onto the kitchen table, fury burbling in my belly. The spidery handwriting on the high-quality page mocked me, like slashes of claws dug into some hapless victim. Rags smoothed the parchment and peered down at it as if that would change what was written there.

"This is fucked," Grev snapped, stiff in his chair. "How do we prepare you for a Trial of Poison in less than two hours?"

"I wish the church had relayed the original clue. I'm sure that's what the other champions were up to this week, preparing for something like this." Sebastian stopped his furtive pacing, knuckles stretched taut, gripping the back of the chair, pale as the killing frost. "But when I went to the head of the Luminesae and asked him if he could repeat the task, I was told we only get one hint. What happens to it once it leaves their offices is beyond their control."

"It's sabotage. You know that, right?" Grev jabbed his index finger into the table. "Someone wants you and Nim to fail, so they set us up.

If I find out who is behind this, I'll—"

Rags interrupted his rant by putting her hand on his shoulder. "I hate ta be the voice of reason here, but we don't have much time. We're better off focusing on th' trial than encouraging conspiracy theories."

Sebastian roughly dragged his hands through his hair, but dropped into his chair all the same. Grev glared at the note but didn't argue. Rags was right. It didn't help the nausea working its way up the back of my throat, but taking action gave me something to focus on other than the acid.

"The missive doesn't give us much to go off of," I began, relieved that my voice didn't crack. "There's a lot that can be done with poison. Ingesting, creating, and identifying are only the beginning."

"Not to mention inflicting it upon someone else," Grev muttered. "Let's be real here, you're gathering at Archer Arena. That means they want a spectacle of some kind, or why call the entire city together to watch?"

Rags leaned her chair back on two legs. "They'll want somethin' messy. If there isn't someone spewing blood before the end of the trial, it'll be considered a failure."

"It isn't dubbed the Bloodletting without reason," I added darkly. I didn't disagree with my associates. But it wasn't the poison itself that had me fighting tremors rushing down my arms; it was the truth that poison might reveal.

While the Arachnae Duchy held many secrets, they'd made their immunity to poisons widely known, a blatant threat warning other families away from attacking them or trying something sneaky. They were also very proud of the fact that the most potent poison known to mortals ran through our veins, so poisonous that it could counter the effects of queenkiller's lace, a plant that produced the second strongest poison.

199

Assuming it came up today, my immunity would be a dead giveaway to my identity, which had always been a risk I'd assumed when taking this job, but not one I was ready to cope with the fallout for just yet.

"Are there any wide-ranging antidotes you might be able to use?" Sebastian asked. "It's probably safe to assume the poisons they'll use will be fast-acting. They wouldn't want someone perishing after the crowds dispersed. So that must limit our options."

Grev opened his mouth, but I beat him to the punch. "Assuming you're correct, that still leaves us with two dozen poisons to choose from, and there's only one antidote that works remotely well against half."

The hornet eyed me curiously, but didn't object to the information I'd offered. I swallowed hard. Had he finally put together the pieces? Of the trio, I believed he would unravel my identity first.

"Then let's use that." Rags latched onto that revelation like a beacon. She didn't question how I knew what I did. "Where do we get it?"

Sebastian was back on his feet, and all eyes were on me like I had the answers to the universe. In some ways, I guessed I did. I shook my head tiredly. "On such short notice, I doubt we'd be able to secure it outside of the duchies or the church. Then it's a question of whether you trust it. Grev already pointed out the likelihood of sabotage. I'm not beyond extending that to passing along a fake antidote."

The prince peered at me cautiously. "How do you know all this?"

There was the question I'd been bracing for. How does a thief from the wrong side of town know anything about poisons? Thankfully, I had an answer prepared. "I might be terrible with swords—" Rags snorted and I kindly ignored her, "—but I work in a bookstore, remember? I have a lot of time to read on my hands."

Sebastian traced his lower lip. "That's handy." He didn't sound convinced.

It was Grev's turn to pace, circling the room like a prowling feline

I'd only read about in books. After several achingly long minutes, he asked, "Do you know how to brew it?"

I hummed. Though my grandparents and cousins had largely shunned me at the estate, they bore far too much pride when it came to silks and poisons. They didn't need antidotes, but they had several on hand to limit its effects in emergencies. This particular antidote, though effective— "It will take too long. We would need..." I paused, a wry smile curling my lips as I mentally counted off the days.

"Need what?" Rags probed, leaning forward on her forearms.

"We would need five days," I finished.

Grev's fist collided with the wall, his rare show of violence startling the shakes right out of me. A soft plume of dust fell from the rafters, spotting the shoulders of his otherwise pristine shirt. "Well, isn't that convenient? The amount of time we would have had if our clue hadn't been mucked up."

"I bet anything that's the advantage the champions who defeated their assassins gained," the prince mused. He snagged a glass and filled it with water, giving us time to absorb the idea. "Maybe we're wasting our time considering antidotes when they would just take them from Nim when she entered the arena anyway."

"Then what do we do?" Rags scrubbed the table with her thumb, gaze lowered. "Are we really just waiting for this ta happen an' see if Nim survives?"

The sheen of wetness along her lower lids when she glanced up at me floored me. Sure, I considered this group as friends to a certain degree, but I had no idea they had grown attached to me, as well. That was what had me reaching across the table and taking her hand in mine. "Not nothing. Remember all that reading I mentioned? I know a little about the tells of certain poisons. If we hurry, I might be able to get a little more research done before we return to blueside."

"Then what are we waiting for?" The prince was already pulling on his cloak. "Time isn't on our side."

26

Poison

Nim

There wasn't a reason to look at the message sent by the church again; my sweat had smudged the ink beyond recognition, but it was something to do other than listen to the buzz of the crowd finding their seats in the stands.

Even if something new were to occur to me suddenly, it would be too late to implement.

Drawing a deep breath, I abandoned the page in my pocket and smoothed the front of my jacket. A new stage was erected in the middle of the field, over top the pillars Jax and I had fought among in the first trial.

Along one length, a series of identical chairs with teal cushions were positioned facing inward, likely set up for the heirs and any other important persons interested in watching the proceedings up close. My fellow champions and I stood behind hip-high tables on the other side of the stage. They were empty now, but I could already imagine what would be placed on their surfaces in a few minutes.

To my left, Major Day picked at her nails, bluntly ignoring those who shouted her name. Her uniform was pressed and clean as always, her pin denoting herself to the Kincaid cause still fastened on her lapel. She'd drawn her hair back in a sleek spill of a tail, exposing a purple birthmark on her neck. A buzzing of wings drew my attention to the left, where Morris Amana tapped his table impatiently. He caught me looking and threw me one of his infamously wicked smiles. Beneath my bandages, I flushed, not immune to his ridiculous charm.

I would have liked to talk to the bee, but upon entering the arena, guards had told us not to converse with one another. That said, the directive hadn't stopped the commander from chatting merrily with the servant at the end of the row. Jax was stationed between Morris and Verity, his skin paler than I'd ever seen it, and he dodged my attempts at catching his eye.

Worry curdled in my gut. Thanks to his history as my friend, he knew more than the average hybrid did about poison. I knew he used it once or twice in his dealings with the Shells, but he had not killed his assassin, so he was like me, left blowing in the wind.

And despite his extra knowledge, he could still die.

Unlike me, the fire ant wasn't impervious to poisons. One small mistake and he would be ripped from this world forever. I sucked in a breath, battering back the dizziness swirling at the edges of my vision. If I lost him like this... I feared what I would do.

Who I might hurt.

If only he would look at me. That might offer both of us a smidgen of relief.

"Welcome, one and all, citizens of Eritris, to the Fifty-First Trials of our great nation." A dragonfly wearing a glittering blue vest, tight black pants, and leather shoes polished to a shine swooped into the arena from above, speaking into a device that amplified his voice. He touched down on the stage and bowed low, to the delight of the crowd that clapped and cheered its approval. "Thank you all for assembling on such short notice to bear witness to the third of five tasks your champions will undertake."

More cheering. The dragonfly strutted across the stage and stopped close to Viotto, who leaned casually against his table.

"I am Skylar Anders, spokesperson for Castle Redfern and the Octavius Duchy, and I have the distinct honor of being your host for today's event." I thought I'd recognized his too-shiny bowl of hair, but I figured I'd seen him as one of the many faceless guests who wandered into the bookstore, not someone strutting around the castle. "Many of you were with us for that highly invigorating first trial, were you not?"

My blood shivered watching the front row of centipedes clapping their many hands with wild enthusiasm, a banner proclaiming their support for Aurora and the Sai lineage flapping between them. Though I knew not everyone supported the Bloodletting, the sheer volume of citizens who weren't bothered by people dying for their entertainment sickened me.

"You were here when our vivacious Wing Commander cut down the first of the champions." Sticks, Anders was drinking in the applause, wasn't he? A glance down the line of my fellow champions and Jax finally caught my eye, face stiff and stony. He shook his head, hands twisting in the silent language of the Shells; his wide sleeves partially obscured the movements, while the dragonfly launched into a diatribe outlining the highlights from the first trial.

I only just got back into town, he signed. *Father said you were looking for me. Is everything alright?*

I didn't hesitate to jump at the opportunity. *As fine as I will be until the Bloodletting is over. Where were you?*

Flouris. He named a smaller town to the south of Moldona, one surrounded by farms, known for its wealth of thriving greenery. *Aurora wanted me to prepare there this week.*

205

Ah. That made sense. They had known the nature of the trial, and the Sai heir wanted him well-versed in antidotes and ways to diminish the effects of various poisons. Smart, going to a city with a far greater array of herbs and plants on hand than Moldona.

Relief flooded my veins like a cool tidal wave. Maybe he would get through this.

Before my fingers could form a response, I caught Verity peering at us curiously, brow cocked, eyes steely, and I thrust my hands into my pockets as if that had been my intention all along. The timing worked out because Anders was just finishing his recap of the bloody finale to the second trial, where, to no one's surprise, Day and Verity were the only ones to dispatch their assassins before midnight.

"—so shall we bring out our heirs to bear witness to today's trial?" Anders shouted, leaping into the air, one leg straight, the other knee slightly bent. The thousands of hybrids were on their feet or in the air, their cheering mulling together into one continuous buzz. Lightning danced along my nerve endings.

One by one, the remaining heirs mounted the stage, stopping before their champions. About ten feet of empty space separated me from Sebastian, who hesitated before sliding onto his chair. Black eyes locked with mine, a world of comprehension flowing between us. This pained him, putting someone in this position. His knee bounced with nerves, and he dropped his hand onto his thigh, stilling the movement.

The floor shuddered as Anders strutted up the aisle once again. "And now for the third trial: Poison." He spun his hand in a flourish, as if that made this any more acceptable. The crowd quieted, but I imagined them leaning forward in their seats, hungry to hear the rules. "Each of your champions will be presented with five seemingly innocent glasses of water. However, four of those glasses will be laced with some variation of fast-acting poison. Only one will be safe to drink. Your champions are tasked with drinking one glass in its entirety. Assuming they are still alive after five minutes, they will have succeeded in advancing to the fourth trial."

Which meant if any of us picked wrong, we would die.

Servants bearing trays weighted down with glasses marched onto the stage. The sweat soaking the bandages at my back dried as a servant placed five clear pint glasses before me. So Grev was right, they chose to poison us themselves. And they'd chosen quality poisons, if the lack of color to the liquid was any indication.

"We didn't want to leave your champions completely helpless, so we've provided them with a small array of medicinal herbs to help them subdue the effects of various poisons, assuming they are able to correctly identify which poison they are about to consume." The servant slid the box from his tray toward me and exited. It was quite lovely, delicately painted with various insects who called greenside home: ants and cicadas and moths and more.

At my side, Morris had already opened his box and peered at its contents. I followed his lead. Not much would be helpful in this game of death. Turmeric, thyme, a dusting of willowweed, a small packet of what looked like pepper kernels, and a few other leafy herbs I couldn't name upon sight alone. They could dilute some minor poisons, but it wouldn't be very helpful. Judging by the look on Jax's face, he was equally unimpressed with his offering.

I didn't dare look at the prince.

"And that's not all, my wonderful guests. We presented our champions with an opportunity to gain an advantage in today's task during our last event. If they successfully killed the assassin hunting for their blood, they are allowed to bring one antidote with them on stage." The excitement vibrating through the air was palpable. "If you recall, that means Major Day and Commander Viotto may now present us with their potion of choice."

207

The major wrinkled her nose as if our host's choice of words offended her, but she removed a vial of purple liquid from her sleeve all the same. Ashresin. The antidote I would have concocted had I the time or, apparently, the permission. Sebastian eyed the vial with fascination, head tilted to the side. I lifted a brow in affirmation when he returned to me, understanding the question written across his face. The commander's vial was filled with an orange substance.

"Champions." For the first time all afternoon, Anders addressed us directly. "You will have twenty minutes to complete the challenge."

My eyelid twitched. Twenty minutes to identify, fix, and pretend to modify a poison, or poisons, so no one suspected who or what I was. Got it. No problem.

"As stated at the first trial, you may leave at any time, but should you choose that option, you will be stripped of your aether and banished from the kingdom for the remainder of your life." Anders stared at us as if daring us to counter him. "Do you have any questions?"

Morris and Jax shook their heads, the only ones of us to respond to his belittling.

"Then let the Trial by Poison commence."

A wall slammed up in my mind, barring me from the arena's noise. I brought the first glass to my nose and inhaled, fighting back a smile. It was slight, but the scent of caramel was definitely there. Queenkiller's lace. The most lethal poison on the market, known not only for its dangers, but also for its sweet fragrances that attracted its prey. I'd once heard it smelled different to everyone.

Setting the glass down, I reached for the second. Then the third. My amusement faded. All three bore hints of caramel. Was my nose failing me? I sniffed the first one again. No. Definitely there. Anders hadn't said the four glasses would contain different poisons, I supposed. The fourth came as no surprise. queenkiller's lace. Unmistakable. So that meant the fifth would be safe. It had to be.

But when I brought it to my face, everything in my body, my soul, went silent. I couldn't hear, couldn't see. Could only smell. And that smell was death. Death and rot and all the ugly things.

First, the note with our vital hint had arrived damaged. Now all five of my glasses were laced with a poison that would kill anyone but me.

The trial was rigged.

Was it rigged for all of us?

What would this mean for my best friend? Fear surged, hot and wild.

Jax was in the middle of mashing two different herbs together, a glass pulled close to his body. He must have identified something he could remedy. Not queenkiller's lace. A breath shuddered out of me, the tension in my limbs easing.

Morris was impossible to read on, but he appeared torn between two glasses, dipping his fingers into them and pressing droplets to his tongue to better understand what he faced. Also not queenkiller's lace.

Down the line, Viotto dumped the entirety of his orange concoction into his middle glass and chugged it down like a male dying from dehydration, grin wide and slightly manic. A smattering of cheers erupted when he didn't fall to the ground, clutching his throat. The major took a little longer, the furrow between her brows deepening as she scented the various glasses. Finally, she settled on the one closest to me and downed it without adding her antidote. The water. The cheers grew louder when she, too, didn't keel over, frothing at the mouth.

So that meant me. I was the only one given no way out.

My pulse pounded in my ears. Someone knew who I was, *what* I was.

Either that, or they viewed me as a big enough threat to take out under no uncertain terms. But who? Who would know or, at the very least, suspect my aether?

Sebastian was half out of his chair, hands wrapped around the ends of his armrests, expression strained, a sharp contrast to Jezebelle Kincaid, who looked almost bored. Hael, even William Amana didn't seem particularly perplexed by his brother's predicament, though he had yet to choose which glass to ingest. Or—

The pounding stopped.

Everything stopped.

Unlike the other heirs focused either on themselves or their champions, Prince Vincent leaned on the arm of his chair, chin propped on his hand, staring at me, eyelids half lowered. I might have mistaken it for interest in what another champion was up to when facing death, now that his own spot in the fourth round was secured.

Except for the malice that glared back at me.

Just a moment, then he caught me watching, and it vanished. A cloud on a windy day. He knew. Or, at least, he thought he knew. Did that mean that Sebastian also knew? If he did, surely, he wouldn't look half as worried as he did now.

"Ten minutes remaining."

Shit. Moving quickly, I pushed two glasses aside as if dismissing them for something I couldn't deal with and dipped the tips of my fingers into the remaining three glasses, waiting for them to dry before touching them to my tongue, a small enough amount that wouldn't kill a normal being unless it was queenkiller's lace. I needed to throw off the judges and anyone else watching me too closely, maybe give them a reason to doubt what had been put on my plate.

Nodding thoughtfully as if they didn't all taste exactly like caramel-tinted water, I shifted a third glass to join the other two. The trembling in my arms had slowed, but my heart still raced at a gallop. I dumped

POISON

the packets of willowweed and turmeric into the mortar provided on my station and used the pestle to mash them together into a thick, yellow paste. Into the second glass it went, turning it a cloudy yellow.

Cheers erupted in the crowd. In my periphery, Jax threw up his arms in triumph, spinning in a slow circle before the audience. I sent a small word of thanks to our god and tapped the glass with my concoction spinning in it. The bits of yellow drifted to the bottom of the glass, and I nodded with satisfaction as if having expected the outcome. Queenkiller and addermet shared similar properties. I was hoping this would make anyone think I'd identified addermet instead of the former.

"One minute."

Morris dropped whatever antidote he was working on into both glasses, sweat shining bright on his cheeks. I lifted the fifth glass to my lips and tipped it back, barely tasting the liquid as it passed over my tongue. Sticks, this would hurt later. I only hoped I'd done enough to throw off the scent of anyone watching me.

The bee set his glass down at the same time I did, the very moment our illustrious host called time. Morris's lips were tight, pale as ash, expression shaky as he stared down at the tray, arms rigid where they braced the table on either side. In a rare outward expression of reassurance, I held out my hand to him. He hesitated and took it, squeezing it like a lifeline, aware of the audience keenly waiting for one or both of us to keel over.

The seconds ticked by with agonizing slowness, and I struggled to hold back a shudder when the poison sliced through my veins. My heart slammed twice against my ribs, hard as a zira's jab, before its beat slowed considerably. The poison dulled my senses, numbing my skin. I could barely feel the vibrations in the air and almost swayed on my feet, but Sebastian's worried gaze kept me steady, straight. I would do this for him. It wouldn't be easy, but I would secure this

211

victory for him.

And hopefully myself.

After a few moments that felt more like hours, the dragonfly host strutted back on stage in his jewel-toned clothing, which now hurt my eyes. Yes, there were two of him now, and I had to look away, forcing the nausea churning in my stomach to still. I kept my breathing nice and slow. Too much oxygen would overload my system too early, creating a negative interaction with the poison that had bound itself to my blood cells.

"Would you look at that. All five of our champions remain on their feet. It's absolutely outstanding." The dragonfly looked anything but pleased as he brought his hands together in a clap that spread through the crowd like wildfire. In my hand, Morris' palm had grown sticky with sweat. Too much sweat. Wide, yellow-tinted eyes caught mine as he swayed on his feet, swiping at his upper lip. Fear, confusion, and a heavy dose of betrayal stared back at me as the host rambled on about something I couldn't nor wanted to hear.

The bee's head twitched toward his brother, the words "I'm sorry" touched his lips breathily as his knees folded. I caught him before he hit the ground, the weakness in my knees bringing me to the ground with him. His face tightened. Sweat streamed from his pores in rivers. Panic flooded me.

"No." I brought his hand up, pressed the backs of his knuckles to my lips. "Stay with me, Morris. It will be alright. Just hang in there." Tears rimmed my eyes, stinging like nettles. "You can fight this off. I know you can. Remember? The Amanas are stronger than they let anyone believe."

Green bile frothed on his lips, and I was faintly aware of the other heirs and champions crowding around us. Blood vessels burst in his yellowing eyes as he struggled to breathe. Those eyes focused and unfocused on my face. He shuddered violently, big vibrations shaking his whole form, and I pulled him ever closer, folding him into my arms, tears streaming down my cheeks and dripping onto his face.

He was dying a horrible, ugly, painful death.

The bee and I had barely addressed one another directly. We hadn't known each other in a personal or professional sense. Yet a bond snapped firmly into place between us, one only forged between the dying and the living. My heart shuddered, wishing I could do something, anything, to mute his pain.

In a moment of near-clarity, he surged up and pressed his lips to my ear. "I don't—want—to die." Then the life seemed to drain from him, his form falling limp in my arms while he coughed weakly.

Jax was there, on his knees in front of me, helping support the champion's increasingly heavy weight, feverishly watching the bee who swallowed with painful slowness, red flecking the green foam crusting his lips.

"I'm sorry," I said repeatedly, not sure what I was sorry for, but unable to stop the flow of words. I had nothing to do with his death. Morris' blood was on the hands of those who forced us into this sick, perverted game. But my heart broke, agony cutting deep, witnessing a light as bright as his dim.

When he finally went limp, bloody eyes clouding over in a haze of unseeing death, I couldn't hold back the sobs that had threatened.

I didn't know him very well. Only knew the mask he presented to the world.

And I never would.

He didn't deserve this.

None of us did.

And it was time someone paid for this devastation they wrought.

27

Be Serious

Sebastian

Worry curdled like sour milk in my gut as I paced before Nim's closed door, chewing furiously on a fresh sprig of mint. For the hundredth time in the last hour, I almost rapped my knuckles against the surface, demanding she open up, or, at the very least, respond.

She hadn't spoken on the carriage ride back to The Primrose and barely acknowledged my presence, peering instead out the small window at her shoulder with bloodshot eyes, hands fisted in her lap. Sweat and spittle from the bee's dying moments had dried on her clothing, crusty and green, but she seemed oblivious to it. Back at the hotel, she'd marched straight across the common room, shedding her cloak and boots on the way to her room, where she shut the door with too-calm restraint.

"Seb, come on. She just held a male in her arms as he died, of course she's upset." Grev stood over the stove in the kitchen, stirring a wooden spoon in a pot of what smelled like vegetable stew. "Give her a little time. That's a lot to absorb, even if she didn't know him that well."

Slumped over the kitchen table, Rags picked at her nails. She neither nodded in agreement nor denied Grev's assessment, but the sorrowful glances she surreptitiously cast toward Nim's door spoke volumes. I made another pass, arms banded tight across my torso to keep myself from infringing where I clearly wasn't wanted. Space was what she desired. It was the least I could give her. Except—

I leaned against the wood and knocked softly. "Nim? Are you there? Can I come in?" I couldn't take the speculation any longer; the nerves dancing along my bones wouldn't let me. If she cast me away, I would heed her desires. But let her tell me she wanted nothing to do with us. Let her—

"Come in."

Rags' spine straightened with interest, and she waved me forward. Grev shook his head, shaking an extra dash of salt into his concoction. "Go on. Eveningmeal will keep."

The knob turned easily under my hand, and I slipped into the dark space. The curtains were drawn across the window, but my enhanced mantis vision cut through the shadows, spotting the form spread across the small bed. It saddened me how little she had by means of personal effects. No portraits on her bedside table. No trinkets spread across her dresser. Even the floor was meticulously clean, her clothing all shut away.

Closing the door at my back, I toed off my boots and crossed the room. Nim lay on her stomach on top of the covers, an occasional shiver wracking her body. She did not acknowledge my presence, her face pointed toward the wall, but I sensed her eyes were open, alert. I rubbed my hands together, unaccustomed to the sensation of ineptitude that settled over me.

"Is there anything I can do?" I asked helplessly.

A beat. She shook her head, fraying braid shifting across her pillow. That wouldn't do. I had to do something. Help in some way. She

215

was clearly cold. Or in shock. Scanning the room until I found what I needed, I shook out the blanket folded at the foot of the bed. Carefully, I draped it over her, tucking it in around the edges. I might have imagined it, but her shaking rattling the frame lessened a touch.

I looked back at the closed door, considering whether to leave her be, not sure if she was sick or in shock or grieving, when her soft voice whispered, "Stay. Please."

Good enough for me.

Furniture was a sparse commodity in her room, so I folded up on the floor, legs crossed, back pressed to a leg of the bed, shoulders resting against her mattress, and listened to her breathing level out.

I must have drifted off, because when I blinked my eyes open, it took me a moment to figure out what had pulled me from my sleep. The bed was rattling harder than before, its legs quaking, sending shockwaves up my spine. The room also smelled strange. Sickly sweet, like fruit left too long to rot. Wrinkling my nose, I rose and peered over Nim, who clutched the blanket to her like a lifeline. She wasn't asleep, and though her head didn't turn, her eyes slid toward me, her jawline clenched so hard I feared it might shatter.

"Are you sick?" She didn't stop me when I reached for her forehead. A curse flew from my lips. She was scalding, the air around her practically rippling with the heat she emitted. "We need to get you into an ice bath. You're burning up."

But when I went to hook my arms under her shuddering form, she released a sharp hiss of air from between her teeth and batted my efforts away. The pale blue sleeves of her shirt were dark with sweat, and the odor emanating through the room got stronger. "Leave me be."

"Nim, you're sick. You need help."

Silver eyes flashed, a clashing war of thoughts vying for attention behind them. Another brutally painful shudder shook her frame, and when she finally got her panting under control, she shook her head, hair matted to her skin. "Not sick. Poison. My body is clearing it from my blood."

A sliver of ice dropped straight into my stomach. I sank onto the mattress, and she shuffled closer to the wall to give me more space to press up against her back. "Poison? But you tested the glasses. You dismissed them one by one." And she'd looked so confident with her analysis, too. Not a moment of hesitation before she'd lifted the final cup to her lips and spilled it down her throat. "I don't understand."

She squeezed her eyes shut as if closing herself off from the reality she was about to voice. "They all. Were poisoned."

Despite the heat of her skin, I gripped her shoulder through her damp shirt, rolling her slightly, forcing her to look at me. That didn't make sense. The rules were clear: Four poisoned glasses, one safe option. Surely, they wouldn't have messed up. But then again...

Someone had burned the note warning us about the trial, and Nim had seemed on edge when we'd stepped out on the stage. I'd attributed it to nerves or the crowd's shrieks, but now...

"Does someone want you dead?"

Her snort was condescending, but her attitude fractured when another vicious wave rippled through her body, forcing her to curl inward, spine bowing. "Aside from the Trials?"

"Be serious."

She licked dry, cracked lips, focusing on a crack reaching from a corner of the window down the length of the wall. "Maybe. I'm not sure why, though."

Frustration settled like a veil over my flesh, itchy and confining. Political maneuvering was nothing new to me. I'd grown up around two-faced courtesans and sailed the seas with ruthless people who frequently fought to the death for what they wanted. And now, back here, I felt more lost than I had before. I'd returned to Moldona riding a wave of self-assured understanding, a solution to my country's bitterest problems firmly in hand, yet the closer I got to achieving that dream, the more it slipped through my fingers like dry sand.

Nim must have shifted while I sat there, contemplating my thoughts, my very existence, because her silvery eyes that saw far too much were glued to my expressions. Joints snapped and crackled as another shudder racked her. My thoughts dissipated like smoke in the wind.

"What can I do?" I pleaded. The sweat soaking her clothing was even worse from the front, her shirt visible through a gap in the blanket practically black with moisture. "You said it's poison. Do you know what kind? Is there an antidote we can get you?"

Fathomless eyes found my own, her thoughts swirling behind that curtained gaze. She remained silent for so long I feared she might not speak, when she came to a decision. "They were all dosed with queenkiller's lace."

I swore my heart stilled in my chest, a handful of beats that suddenly vanished into the world. "How—I don't—"

She shouldn't be alive right now.

This wisp of a female shouldn't have been able to finish her glass, let alone exit the stage.

How was she here?

Yet the thought of her collapsing, bloodied foam speckling her lips, eyes wide and blank staring into the Beyond jarred me. Rattled me far more than it rightfully should. I'd willfully spun her into my trap, pulled her into a web of deceit that I knew could very well end with her death.

But the idea of Riten calling her home now, when I'd only started to understand how her thoughts clicked together, sent a pulse of dread and fear like none I'd ever felt before through me.

"I'm freezing." Her teeth clicked, exhaustion darkening the skin beneath her eyes. "Like I'll never be warm again."

218

That I could fix. "Let me help you." I shrugged off my jacket and unthreaded a few laces at my neck to get more comfortable before drawing back the blanket, ignoring the putrid odor, and slipping beneath it. She hesitated, eyes glued to the vee of skin exposed by my shirt, before pressing her hand firmly against my sternum. Her eyes closed, and the tension in her skeletal frame relaxed marginally.

"Body heat will help, even if mantises don't run particularly hot." I drew her closer, pressing more of me against her. Tides, she was soaked, as if every pore in her body was expelling the toxin in her veins. Another shiver wracked her, and I tightened my hold. How well she fit against me, her head filling the hollow perfectly between my chin and chest.

We lingered like that for many long minutes, her arms scrunched between our bodies, my hand running down her back, but still she remained tense. Drawn. Muscles seized.

"How are you still among the living?" I asked, incapable of holding back the question any longer. Maybe it would distract her from her obvious pain.

She pressed harder against me, the fronts of our thighs smashed together. "It's a. Natural immunity. A painful one. But poisons won't kill me."

Curious. She'd said she read books, examined all her possibilities, but she hadn't said she'd ingested any poisons as a precaution, building up immunity. But hadn't my tutor mentioned something in our history lessons? Something about—

"I'm still cold."

She knew exactly how to distract me. "You won't like my suggestion."

"I'm all ears if it helps."

I tugged gently on the front of her shirt. "I swear it on my life, I'm not trying anything. But you are soaked through. That chill, even

219

through your bandages, is sapping your warmth. If we—"

She was already shrugging out of her shirt, and I scrambled to put space between us, nearly tumbling off the edge of the bed as she reached for her pants. Nim fought through another shiver and cast me a wry look that caused my heart to seize uncomfortably.

"It's not like I'll be naked," she said. "And you suggested this, did you not?"

"I wasn't expecting you to take your clothes off just like that." Though she had a point. The bandages wrapped up every inch of her skin, leaving only a few select surfaces exposed. They enthralled me, and I reached for her arm, sliding my fingers down it, shoulder to wrist, pads of my fingers rising and falling with the grooves of the fabric. I'd assumed it was linen, but it was so much silkier than that, almost like skin. The wraps held together seamlessly, leaving no gaps. Even when I slipped my thumbnail under an edge, it wouldn't give.

She shivered under my touch.

"What is this made of?" I asked, my breath stirring the wisps of hair that had dried around her temples. "I've never felt anything like it."

No response, though I felt her body relax, sagging against my arm still curled around her back, pressed into the mattress. Swallowing hard, I tried again, stroking the bandages in long, slow motions. "Why do you do this to yourself?"

She held still and silent for so long I thought she'd finally drifted off when she rolled to face me. Eyes heavy, she stroked the back of her wrist before sliding a thumbnail between the bandages. When she found the end of the tape—that I could have sworn was seamless— Nim pulled, unraveling row after row, revealing several inches of skin. But not just skin. I cupped her hand and raised it to my face, convinced the dark was playing tricks on me.

"Scars." Nim's confirmation made my heart ache. "Thousands of them."

The silvery-white cuts scraped in uneven patterns across her flesh, crisscrossing and weaving, as if she'd been bound in thread. Bile rose in my throat. There was no question as to what this evidence revealed. To hide such abuse from the world, to prefer wrapping herself up—her pain must have been excruciating.

My arms ached with the restraint it cost me to hold back from pulling her against me and making her forget about the evils of the world for one hopeless moment. Given her reticence about being touched in general, I doubted she would appreciate such a gesture. However, my fingers itched to stroke her hair, to press her face against my shoulder, to offer her a shield against whoever or whatever had cost her this piece of herself.

As if she read my mind, she explained, voice soft as the blankets swaddling us. "They're about ten years old and don't hurt anymore. And frankly, it isn't that I'm ashamed of how they look. I don't hide them for my benefit, but for the benefit of others." She ran a nail along one smooth line. "Believe it or not, they stare less when I choose my wraps over bare skin. The full reveal..." Nim trailed off, picking over her words. "It's a lot to take in."

I wanted to call bullshit, but I wedged my tongue between my teeth and bit down instead. Who was I to challenge her perceptions of herself and the world around her? She was finally, *finally* opening up, and I would not cut off her stream of consciousness. I was dying to ask who had done this to her. Where her family had been at the time. And surely her friend Jaxon and his father knew.

It clicked then. Why she'd ordered me to take her to the Firestone the night of her injury, refusing to let me see the wound, let alone treat it. They were her family. They knew about her past and all the haunting awfulness that came with it.

I recalled her words to Jax at the ball when she'd spoken about her lack of sight. Yet she'd moved so seamlessly through the world, as

221

if vision were but a small hurdle to jump. Some hybrids had a keen sense of the world and the vibrations that echoed through it: cicadas, termites, bees, and yes – ants were among them.

But at the top of the list that came to mind were the hybrids believed to be dead.

The Arachnae.

It fit. Her reluctance to reveal her aether. The silk wrapped around her limbs. The limited impact that loss of vision had on her dexterity…

Her immunity to poison.

My stomach churned. Something bad had happened, but I didn't know what.

The words burned my throat like acid, questions about her lineage and what had happened in her past that put her in such a precarious position, but still, I bit them back. Now was not the time. Especially when I wasn't quite sure if my guesses were correct, no matter how conveniently the pieces fit together.

"Say it." Nim touched my chest, drawing my attention back to her. The gesture was slight, barely a brush of a fingernail, but heat seared through my breast. "Your questions. What are they?"

Careful now. The last thing I wanted was to scare her away. I had to find the most tactful way to state my question. "Were you an orphan before or after this happened?"

It was the only thing I dared ask, hoping she might show me a glimmer of the truth.

Nim pulled her lower lip between her teeth, rewinding her bandage into place. A tremble went through her, reminding me of her earlier torment, of how much pain she must be in still now as she recovered from the poison. "That's not the question you wanted to ask."

I ran my hand over her shoulder, the calming motion and her quiet acceptance of the touch settling the coals of my rage. But I didn't answer. Let her make of my question what she would.

With a sigh, she scrubbed at her tired eyes, settling her head on the pillow once more. "My mother had just died." Her tone was tired. Beaten down. An acceptance only crafted as the sandy reach of time wore away the sharpened edges. My guard remained high, braced for whatever was about to come out of her mouth, knowing relief was far from sight. "But that doesn't mean those who shared my blood weren't responsible."

Tides. Her family had done this to her. People she'd likely trusted, grown up with, *lived* with. They'd scarred her for life, and for what? What possible reason would they have to do this to a child?

"I'll kill them."

My promise was barely a whisper on my lips, but Nim heard and shook her head, her words slurred with sleep when she replied, "It's no use. They're already gone."

There was a god.

And those pieces of the puzzle fit even more firmly together.

Her admission did nothing to settle the beast raging inside, flexing its claws, demanding blood for the price already paid, but I would accept it for what it was.

Nim's eyes were closed, her breathing even, her muscles lax for the first time since I'd entered the room. I figured she'd fallen asleep when I brushed hair back from her forehead. "Why now?" I asked, my desperation keen. I pressed my lips to the top of her head, the act more comforting than intimate, a balm on my bruised soul. "Why tell me this now?"

She gripped my shirt ever so slightly when I made to pull away. "Because the weight of the lies grows too heavy."

And then she was out. Truly out.

Her entire weight sagged against my arm, still pinned under her side, cradling her close to my chest. The position was intimate but hardly sexual. Instead, a raging desire to protect had the ridges of spines rising along my arms, my insect instincts sharpening. It was my fault she was here, locked in a contract that may kill her. But that didn't mean I was helpless in keeping her safe.

Heeding her unspoken request, I remained there, in that bed, lying next to a female whose depths I was only beginning to explore. So much I'd learned, but her revelations had only created more questions than they answered.

Like why she was so keen to escape Moldona...

And why I had a sinking feeling she was hardly more ant than I was lion...

And who was targeting her specifically in the Trials—

What they might know—and the danger it presented to her.

28

Something Precious

Nim

Years ago, I would have found the weight of Seb's arm slung over my back oppressive and fought tooth and nail to free myself from his hold, but today, I closed my eyes, enjoying the sensation of waking up in someone else's arms. To my relief, my body felt cool, my head clear. The poison had successfully washed from my system.

Beneath my head, the pillow was crackly with sweat and dried mucus. The sheets draped across us smelled sickly-sweet, but I couldn't find it within myself to move. Not yet. It was too nice being here, beside Seb, recalling the rage that had stricken his face when I'd laid the first few of my many secrets bare before him.

He hadn't judged me. Nor had he pushed me away. Rather, he'd taken my sorrows and pulled their weight upon his own shoulders. Even now, pressed to the mattress, the burdens holding me down felt lighter. Peaceful.

I bore no regrets for what I'd revealed. Even in my fever-addled state, I'd been careful with what I said and how I phrased it, and I was more confident than before that he could handle more of my truths.

Truths I had no doubt he was starting to understand. I'd given him enough information, and the prince was hardly stupid.

When I settled deeper into my pillow, my movement must have shaken him, because a low murmuring noise hummed in Seb's throat. The arm slung across me tightened. His eyelids slid to half-mast, revealing brown irises speckled with hints of gold near the center. The visible corner of his lips lifted, skin around his eyes crinkling, seemingly unbothered by our proximity, and bits of spider's thread knotted deliciously in my stomach. I would need to be careful with this one.

"You didn't die." He spoke low and slow, like honey dripping from a spoon.

Those knots pulled even tighter. "So it appears."

"I'm glad." His big hand spanned wide across my back, his middle three fingers caressing the bumps of my spine. "How are you feeling?"

Taking stock, I allowed the comfortable quiet between us to stretch. "Sore. Thirsty. And I could sleep for a week, but that's nothing new." My stomach chose that moment to rumble, and my cheeks heated. "I could probably eat, too."

Eyes crinkled with mirth, Seb drew me closer. The rough edges of his voice smoothed as he woke up. "We should fix that." That said, neither of us indicated we intended to rise anytime soon. Speckles of dust danced lazily in the sunlight streaming in through the window.

A bark of laughter sounded from the living area. Seb's lips flattened, and he levered himself off the pillow, cheek propped on the heel of his hand. "Do you remember what you told me yesterday? Are you alright with what you said?"

He sought my honesty. Warmth pooled in my belly, and I traced a circle on the sheets that had opened between us, breaking the intensity of our eye contact. My nails had lengthened considerably during the night. I would need to file them down. "I remember. And no, I don't

226

have any regrets."

Another slow circle, this time accompanied by a delicious swirl of the prince's fingers over my back. Riten help me, but I actually trusted him. Despite my innate distrust of people I didn't know, he'd successfully shattered a few of the many walls I'd erected between us.

I was glad for it.

We'd started this journey as less than allies, people out for our own goals, working together to accomplish a task. But the more I'd grown to know him and his friends, the deeper I found myself tangled in their web of easy conversation, constructive training, and warm support. If I'd had any doubts about the prince returning my feelings, those had collapsed last night when he'd stayed with me, offering comfort where none was required, empathizing with me in a way I'd always craved.

"I'm glad." Sebastian dragged his hand up, over the hunch in my back, cupping my neck. He drew me forward until our foreheads touched. "Tides help me, little thief. I've never wanted to have anyone rely on me for anything besides leadership, but whatever is happening between us now... I kind of like it."

Now he'd done it. The warmth that pooled like lava in my belly expanded outward, melting my muscles and strengthening them in the same breath. Suddenly shy, I dropped my gaze, concentrating on the rapid throbbing of my heart. My fingers curled into his shirt, index finger catching in the vee he'd loosened last night.

He squeezed my neck lightly, drawing my focus back up. "May I kiss you?"

Cheeks flaming, stomach a mishmash of sparkling, delicious emotions, I nodded. "Yes."

A contented hum reverberated from his chest, vibrating against my palm, and he levered us both upright. Soft touches trailed down my arms, across the back of my neck, along the edges of my jawline. He took his time learning the shape of my body, his eyes tracing the paths his fingers sought. I quaked under the intensity of his expression, like I was something precious, someone to be worshiped.

He traced the edges of the bandages where they rimmed my eyes, hesitating at the corner near my eyebrow. "You're like a present waiting to be unwrapped." His eyes danced with mirth when I snorted at his corniness. "You don't laugh enough. It's a beautiful sound."

I could scarcely breathe. Wasn't sure if my lungs were expanding and contracting. He had me so tangled up inside, a ball of lightning searching for an outlet, and it was I who reached for him next, delving my fingers deep into his thick, dark hair, scraping his scalp. He closed his eyes with a shudder, arms locked around me. One hand still buried in his hair, I returned his languid examination, delighting in the scruff that dotted his chin and cheeks, stroking the taut muscles of his neck and shoulders. Gasps transformed to pants. And finally, when we could no longer put off the inevitable, our lips touched.

Lightning exploded, shards of its violent light fragmenting from my chest through my limbs and back again. His hand fisted in my hair, lightly tugging my face back for better access, a rumble rattling his chest. Helpless against the onslaught, I leaned fully against him, lips touching again and again, bruising with their intensity.

Until we stopped.

Rib cage heaving, I tucked my head beneath his chin, pressing my ear to his chest and the responding thunder of his heart. His hand found my back and dragged long, slow pathways from the base of my neck to my tailbone and back again. I snuggled harder against him, and he laughed, widening his arms and legs so I fit more easily.

Though Jax was loose and free with his hugs and physical touches, I'd gone too long without the embrace of another person. I didn't know how I could ever return to isolation after feeling the dormant parts of my soul rattle free from their chains.

At long last, when our breathing evened and the sunlight streamed bright white through the slats in the window coverings, we parted. To my immense joy, his hand lingered on my knee, thumb rubbing the bump of bone he found there.

"Ready for morningmeal?"

Never was I more thankful for the wraps that hid my flush from his eyes. "You don't think—"

His eyes danced merrily. "Oh, they'll know. Rags will love it, Grev won't. But don't mind them. They don't have lives of their own to burden their time with, so they live vicariously through me."

He spoke so easily, his tone relaxed and bright. But I couldn't help but feel unsettled. Like he was hiding something from me that hadn't been there before. Shaken, I slid off the bed and went to the dresser, desperately needing time alone to think. "Do you mind if I bathe first?"

"Please. Do your thing."

Without looking back, trying to ignore the yawning hole in my chest that grew bigger with every tick of the clock, I slipped out the door. Mercifully, I didn't encounter anyone on the way to the bath.

My thoughts tumbled like the hot water flowing from the faucet, crashing into the white porcelain of the tub. Still wrapped in my silken coverings, I slipped into the water and reached for the soap. The wraps would clean as easily as my skin and wouldn't need to be replaced for another few days at least. As I scrubbed, I thought.

Had our kiss changed anything? Was that the peculiar sense of awareness I felt emanating from him? Did the prince see me differently? Would this affect our working relationship? Would he be a distraction during the Trials? Would he regret his decision the next time he saw me in the center of a ring fighting for him?

Had he understood my confession about my family and guessed who I was?

And if he hadn't figured it out... why did that thought make my stomach sink?

It was too much, too fast. I couldn't think, could barely breathe.

When I leaned against the tub, it was cool against my forehead, and bubbles frothed on the water's surface. I inhaled and exhaled deeply, attempting to ward off an anxiety attack.

On top of the earth-shattering realization that my identity was compromised—willingly, at that—I'd kissed a prince. *A prince.* He was so far above my greensider status it wasn't even funny. And as someone who may eventually lead Eritris someday, the difference in our rank felt like the peak of the mountain surrounding our city. Insurmountable. He had status and wealth and responsibilities far beyond my comprehension. I was an orphan. A child cast away from her home and left for dead. A hybrid determined to leave this cursed city when he was bent on staying.

That was still what I wanted...

Right?

With a groan, I swiped the soap from my arms and drew several deeper, cleansing breaths, reaffirming my convictions. I was leaving. Moldona had done me few favors, and I was through living in the shadows it cast over me. Somewhere else, anywhere else, I could start a new life. Discover a new family. Maybe find a way to bring Jax with me eventually. Kisses with princes changed nothing. My plan was still *the* plan, even if it made me ache in ways I didn't like.

Finally grounded again, I toweled off and slipped back into my room. Someone had opened the window and removed the sheets from my bed, for which I was thankful. The evidence of my torturous night and blissfully beautiful morning was gone. If only it were so easy to do the same with my memories.

Dressed and calm, I padded down the hallway where I found Grev, Rags, and Seb poring over a pristine piece of parchment on the table, expressions grim. The solace I'd only just reacquainted myself with dissipated like old cobwebs. I recognized the handwriting, even across the room. But it was too soon for our next Trials summons, wasn't it? Traditionally, they gave us a week between tasks.

"What does it say?" I ventured.

Rags heaved a sigh, eyes worried. "It's a summons."

"And the clue?"

She deferred to the prince, who ran a finger up the bridge of his nose before holding out the page to me. "Not a trial summons. We've been invited to a royal eveningmeal being thrown for the champions. The best and the brightest of our society will be there, giving you all an opportunity to mingle freely."

I scanned the page myself, my frown deepening as I confirmed its contents for myself. Eveningmeal tonight at Castle Redfern. Wear our best attire. Don't be late. "This—this isn't normal, right? I'm not mistaken, am I?"

Grev shook his head. "Like with the Opening Ceremonies, this is highly unusual."

Steeling myself, remembering the convictions I'd reestablished within myself just a few minutes ago, I squared my shoulders, deftly avoiding the prince's concerned gaze when he tried to catch my eye. "Then we'll go. But we should be prepared for anything."

29

Make it Stop

Sebastian

Silence descended upon the dining room, so quiet it was chilling, before the first of the nobility staring at me with eyes wide as crowns brought their hands together in a clap. It grew, and the more boisterous members of the Sai family whistled. I lifted my cup in acknowledgment and drank. The red wine went down easily, and my head buzzed warmly.

"I can't believe you made it out of that alive," cried a daughter of the Amana powerhouse, hands pressed to her mouth, delight dazzling her violet eyes as I recounted one of my many tales. "I would have been too scared to move, let alone fight."

Her twin sister at her side, plump cheeks rosy with elation, elbowed her. "Pirates don't scare me. I would have pulled out my sword and then—" she mimicked an artful swish and flick with an imaginary blade over the table. Her eyes slid slyly to her parents. "Maybe someday you'll let me sail on the high seas, Father."

The head of the Amana household took a sip of his wine rather than answer, the gleam in his eyes not exactly expressing he was against the idea.

I'd forgotten how much I enjoyed events like this, mingling with the people I someday hoped to rule. It was easy to forget they were people amid the power struggles, but they enjoyed a good story as much as anyone, and I had a plethora to tell.

My mother reached over from her spot at the head of the table and squeezed my elbow, a subtle smile quirking her mouth. "Maybe hold back on the stories that make me want to stab your father for sending you out in the first place, dear."

Lacing my fingers through hers, I shook my head. "Like I could hide anything from you."

She heaved a sigh and turned to Vincent, who sat across from me, seated on her right. He hadn't touched his wine but fiddled with the stem. When he spoke with my mother, he tucked away his smirk, softening his face so much it reminded me of when we were pupae, playing dress-up in our wing of the castle, unknowing of the roles we would play and airs we would adopt in the years to come.

When he turned to me, his expression flattened, barely-restrained malice in his eyes.

"Something bothering you, *Brother*?" I asked, needling him despite myself.

His lips thinned. "Not a thing. I'm simply marveling that we are among the top four. I never would have guessed."

I grinned lazily, lifting my glass for another sip of wine.

My mother interjected before I responded to his subtle jab, oblivious of the undercurrents running between us. "Indeed. I can't remember the last time the Octavius family boasted not one but two heirs in the top half of the competition..."

Conversation around the table picked up as servants appeared, plates of artfully decorated salads loaded with colorful vegetables balanced on their fingertips. I accepted mine with thanks and picked up my fork. A hint of lemon flavored the vinaigrette, and I had to restrain myself from wolfing it down. I would almost say I was enjoying myself, if not for my neighbor sitting stiffly beside me, uncomfortable in the starched uniform Grev had shoved her into.

"Are you alright?" I asked Nim between bites. "You haven't eaten anything. And I know you love eating green things." I stabbed some leaves with my fork, hoping to draw out her smile, disappointed when her expression didn't change.

"I'm not hungry," she replied, hands wedged in her lap, spine straight as the pillars holding up the ceiling. I followed her gaze around the table where the nobles laughed and bantered, sipping from water goblets and wine glasses, chatting between bites of food. She wasn't alone in her lack of interest in the meal. Jaxon and Day also eyed their plates with distrust.

The lettuce turned to ash on my tongue. Of course it would be difficult to consume anything prepared by the very castle that had poisoned them less than 24 hours ago. Though that didn't seem to bother Verity much. His plate was already cleared and shoved toward the center of the table as he asked my mother a question about the newest batch of recruits.

"I'm sorry." I set down my fork and reached for her hand under the table, relieved when she didn't brush away my comforting grip. "I wasn't thinking."

"I'll never understand how people can just… go on. Act like nothing ever happened." Her gaze was fixed on the Amana family, laughing at one of the Viotto cousins who mimed some outrageous joke, if the wide gesturing of his arms meant anything. "Their son died yesterday. Painfully. And here they are…" A shudder ran down her arm, her grip tightening.

She must be recalling holding him in her lap, his head pressed to her belly, tears streaming down her face when he went limp. Her

234

breathing hitched, darkness sizzling in her eyes. She caught herself and secured her blank façade once again. "Morris should be here. That's all I'm saying."

"You're right. He should be here," I agreed, not arguing when she released my hand and scooted ever so slightly away. Together, she and I were going to change this system and its endless cycles of needless death. However, I hoped the process of getting there wouldn't break her.

Especially having glimpsed the very real hybrid beneath her wraps, and realizing how much I enjoyed her company. And then there was her smell, the spice of her taste, how she melted in my arms, surrendering in a way that made me want to pull her to me again and see how quickly I could make her drop her defenses a second time. I wanted to know what sounds she would make when I finally peeled those wraps off her form, scars or no, I wanted to see more of her curves.

A servant collecting our plates interrupted my thought process. I sucked in a deep breath, looking anywhere but her, willing the blood settled in my lap back into my limbs. Fuck. I could still smell her, though.

Before I got caught in the tangle of my mind again, I caught Vincent eyeing us, a divot between his brows. His chin lifted when he realized I was watching him back, a challenge in his stare. And something... more. An expression I couldn't quite place.

The next two courses passed quickly, though, regardless of how delicious it smelled and tasted, I moved my food around on my plate more than I consumed it. Eveningmeal itself would have normally delighted me: spiced bell peppers stuffed with finely diced carrots and cheese; fingerling potatoes seasoned with a mixture of herbs that smelled like thyme and rosemary; and an array of sweetened nuts in a bowl off to the side. Dishes from my childhood.

My mother had just finished regaling me with a story of a servant saving my father when he toppled down the steps after a night of drinking, when Nim brushed my elbow. Twice. Touches so soft I scarcely felt them. Alarm shot through me when I found her pressing her hand against the side of her head, middle finger digging into her temple, eyes shimmering with pain.

"What is it?" I asked, and she flinched as if I'd shouted in her ear. Thankfully, most everyone else was absorbed in their food, drunk on wine, and the company. But Jax watched her like a dragonfly, his entire being attuned to her, arm twitching as if he sought to reach across the table and help her himself.

"Do you hear that?" she murmured.

I tried to shut out all my other senses. "What am I listening for?"

"The music."

In the corner, a cricket perched behind a grand piano, fingers waltzing across the keys, drawing a crooning serenade from their black and white panels. He'd been there all night. No pages. No accompanying instruments. No singers. Just him, his hands, and an occasional sip of water. I relaxed, puzzled by her consternation. "You mean the pianist?"

She shook her head, drawing her hand away from her head and across her chest in a defensive gesture. "It's like strings. Violins. But they're off-key. It—it's hurting my head."

No. I wasn't picking up any violins among the conversations and the rhythmic lull of the piano, and my hearing was as sharp as any among our kind. There wasn't much I could do short of making a scene to get her out of here. But if that was what it took...

"There are two more courses," I whispered, scanning the room. No one, aside from my mother, was paying us the slightest attention. Even Vincent was focused on his potatoes, speaking quietly with his champion out of the corner of his mouth. "Do you need to leave now, or do you think you can manage?"

She stared at her untouched plate as if it bore the answer she sought. "I'll manage."

"Are you sure?"

Her elbow jerked. "Yes. I'll be fine."

Across the table, I met Jax's eyes. He shook his head faintly, but I wasn't sure if he was unhappy with her decision to stick around or agreeing that leaving now would create more of a scene than was truly necessary.

The stress lines around her eyes deepened before the next course was brought out: a small plate of fruit saturated in various liquors, intended to cleanse the palate before dessert. She'd started twitching, just little jerks, an elbow here, a knee there. My mother asked if she was alright when her head gave a particularly violent twitch, and I covered for her with a smooth lie about how she was tired and feeling the pressure of so many eyes focused on her.

I didn't like how Vincent monitored my thief with a distinct level of interest. He barely touched his fruit, he was so enamored by her pain. Dread thrummed, a heavy note vibrating in my chest, a sensation of wrongness settling over me.

"We should go." I barely moved my lips, not acknowledging the servant who placed a chilled bowl of custard at my elbow.

Her breath hitched. "It's getting louder." She clutched her stomach. Could this be the poison catching up to her? I wasn't aware of queenkiller having side effects like this, but I also didn't know anyone who had survived its effects before. "Seb. It hurts."

It was the first time she'd called me by my nickname.

Alarm chimed loudly in my skull. Nim never admitted to pain. Never. It was a point of pride for her in the same way it was for Rags. And here she was, hunched over the table, twitching, practically whimpering for me to do something. Anything. The room had gone eerily quiet. Everyone was watching us. Watching her. Some with concern. Others with intrigue. And still a few, like Verity, with fascination.

Enough.

Slipping my arm around her waist, I levered her out of her chair. "Up you go." To the rest of the table, I nodded. "It appears my champion is not yet recovered from yesterday's trial. We—"

I never finished my sentence.

Nim ripped out of my grip with a shriek, hands flying to her head as if holding her skull together. She lurched, aiming for the door, but collapsed on her knees, another horrifying scream wrenched from her lungs as she bent over, forehead pressed flat to the floor.

"Make it stop," she screamed, braids fraying as she twisted her shaking fingers in her hair. "Make it stop. Make it stop. Make it stop."

The guards were as stunned as the rest of the room. Three stepped forward to put themselves between my champion and the other guests, the rest edging backwards, knuckles white around their weapons. Several members of the various houses stood, leaning over the table to watch Nim as she released another scream so filled with anguish I felt it wrack my body.

I'd taken half a step forward when her flesh rippled. Her spine snapped and cracked, morphing beneath her vest and tunic as if some parasite were crawling up her back. The hunch in her back straightened, the bulge wriggling. Fabric split with a rip. Stumbling in surprise, I caught the back of the chair, supporting myself as four long legs spliced from between her shoulders. Several hybrids screamed, racing for the halls on the other side of the room. But most were like me, fixated on those slender, multi-digited appendages that flexed from her back and hoisted her upright.

The spit dried in my mouth. I couldn't feel my legs.

Arachnae.

I'd guessed correctly.

Her aether wasn't an ant. She was a spider.

Nim shrieked again, still clutching her skull with claw-like hands, black nails digging into her scalp. One of her newly emerged legs buckled, spilling her onto the colorfully patterned tiles. A guard stepped too close, and she hissed, swiping at him with an elongated arm. The sleeve of her shirt, which had fit perfectly earlier, now barely reached her elbow. Her other hand remained pressed to her ear, a dribble of blood dripping from her lobe and staining her shirt.

That sound. Something about the sound she'd heard was causing her pain.

But what sound? What could possibly do this to a hybrid?

Again, she heaved, body curling in on itself. So much pain. Whatever was going on with her was beyond her control. Beyond what I'd ever seen another shifter experience before.

Nausea roiled in my stomach watching her go limp, legs splayed, head lolling as if the energy had sapped from her soul. Movement beyond her caught my attention, and Jax edged closer to his friend slumped on the floor, hands raised in submission. Her head lifted the closer he got, tracking the motion.

"Nim, it's me. Jax. Your best friend, remember?" he murmured, voice calm as a snake charmer I'd met overseas. "I'm going to get you out of here. Just stay still. Like that."

Whispers started, the sound like skittering claws on the floor. Some of them I heard, people claiming she was as mad as her family when they'd butchered themselves that fateful night a decade ago. Others spewed vitriol, more afraid of her than they dared let on.

Jax got within two paces when Nim jerked away, the long limbs from her back finding their strength and hoisting her several feet into the air. A third eye appeared on her forehead, parting the wraps, its iris flattened like a lamb's and ever-moving. Claws on the ends of her legs clicked on the tile, and she hissed and spat curses between the sharp teeth that filled her mouth. The guards edged closer, and she skittered again, spinning wildly.

Fear. The emotion came off her in waves.

She was terrified.

I had to help.

With a sudden burst of energy, I dove around her legs, barely registering the rasp of the hairs scraping across my pants, and came between her and the guards, who stopped, spears extended, helmets down. My mother screamed my name, but I didn't answer.

"Get out of here," I shouted over my shoulder, motioning to the doorway at her back. "I'll make sure they don't follow."

Her wide eyes drank me in, glazed with agony and terror, and then she was gone, skittering and sliding into the shadows. I turned my attention back to the room, hands held out to suppress the guards, wide wings flared. One face stood out among the rest. Where most seemed fearful, shocked, astounded, even a little impressed...

Vincent's face beamed with triumph.

He exchanged a glance with his hornet champion as he slipped something weighted and round into his jacket pocket. I didn't have time to consider that now, let alone confront him.

Without another word, I darted after the hybrid I'd set free, slipping in my haste to follow her through the doors, the array of shocked servants slumped against the walls the only marker I had to use. Feet pounded behind me, and I spun, hand braced on the hilt of my sword, coming up short when I found Jax on my heels.

"I'm coming with you," he said. "You're going after her, aren't you?"

"I am, but—"

"I know her better than she knows herself." Eyes bright as jade and equally fierce bored into me. "You won't find her without my help."

It wasn't even a question at that point. "Lead the way."

30

Sharpened Silk

Nim

Life would never be the same.

I thought I'd made peace with that concept when I returned Seb's signet ring. Every second of every day I'd worked in his employ, I'd known that someone would learn my secret. Secrets were harder to keep in the limelight, after all. But somehow, I'd clung to the idea that revealing myself would come on my terms. Hael. I'd come so close to revealing my true self to the prince just this morning.

And now it was ruined.

Fury and frustration had fled, leaving a hollow void. I felt drained and broken. The tears that had flowed down my cheeks, a mixture of pain and fear, were now stemmed, leaving only salty trails. I hadn't bothered to wipe them away or obscure them with my hood.

It felt far too much like accepting my failures to do so.

Legs swinging in the swirling mists between the dock and the sea, I leaned forward, my elbow bumping the wax bottle of rum I'd lifted from a male at one of the pubs I'd raced past in my hurry to escape the castle. I wasn't convinced the guards weren't scouring the city for the abomination that was me, and the abandoned docks on the northern part of the coast felt safe. The cork in the bottle was still firmly in place, but there was no telling how long it would remain that way.

Tracing chilled fingers over my temples, I closed my eyes, recalling the pain that had rendered me blind and deaf. Never had I lost control of my spider before. I couldn't explain what had triggered my aether. The music. Something about it. It had started soft, violins harmonizing a tune that sounded familiar, yet not. But it had grown in intensity, the music swelling, louder and louder, until the tune changed. Gone was the haunting beauty, and in its place: violence. The bow ripped at the strings with unrelenting viciousness, drawing horrible screeching noises from the instrument. And the pain. It set fire to my limbs, nestled deep in my brain until I couldn't discern right from left, vision from vibration.

I'd regained control over myself midway down the path leaving the keep, and that control was tenuous. Barely enough for me to recognize the need to pull in my legs or risk inciting a mob. The farther I'd stumbled out of blueside and deeper into green, the more aware I'd become. And now I was here. Alone. Not sure what to do next.

My nails trailed down my cheeks before my arms slid into my lap. The claws were gone, but the length of the nails remained. Lethal. I would have to file them down before I hurt someone with the poison flutes embedded in the keratin.

Feet pounded on the dock, and I braced, head tilted toward my lap, keenly aware of my peripheries. From the mists emerged a slight figure, and my heart lurched. Jax. He was panting, gasping for air, his shoulders slumped. Our eyes met. Of course he'd come. He knew me better than anyone. He would know how much I needed him now. But still. I'd hoped that—

Behind him, a taller figure emerged, one that had the knots in my stomach tightening uncomfortably, my heart thudding a faster tempo. I'd never seen Sebastian use his aether, and his second form was impressive. Taller, thinner, skin shiny with armor, eyes bigger, spread farther from his nose. He reminded me of myself when I shifted, the unique form of beauty that emerged with the magic. Wings that nearly brushed the earth when closed against his back twitched, and with a shake of his head, he slipped back into his human form.

"You came."

I wasn't sure I'd said the words out loud, but when Jax dropped to my left, his side pressed against mine, he replied, wounded, "Did you think so little of me? My best friend is hurting. There's nothing that could have kept me away."

"I didn't mean it like that. I'm glad you came." I leaned my head on his shoulder, pressing against him in apology. He kissed my tangled hair, and I peered up at the prince who loomed over us, a dark specter who asked questions with his eyes rather than his mouth. Closing my eyes, I dipped my head tiredly at the spot to my left.

He accepted my offer soundlessly, keeping a careful centimeter of dew and shadow between us.

"What happened?" Jax asked, winding his arm around my back. It had always been like this between us. Easy. Accepting. Rooted in truth and the unconditional love I'd craved so desperately as a child. His mere presence had the tension leaking from my muscles, exhaustion settling in its place.

If pressed, I would admit it wasn't his arm I wanted around me, but rather one with more muscles, a hand firm with sea-hardened calluses trailing circles across my skin.

"I don't know," I admitted. "I've never lost control like that before. Didn't know that was possible."

Sebastian tugged on the collar of his jacket. "Could it have been the poison?"

Jax stiffened, his grip hardening, then he seemed to remember everything I'd told him about my history, and he relaxed again. "What did they poison you with?"

"Queenkiller's lace." Never had I held back from the fire ant, and I wouldn't start now, even knowing his antennae were humming with worry and concern. "They set me up. All five glasses were tainted with it. I think someone either knew who I was or suspected and used that opportunity to test their theory."

It was the only thing that made sense.

And damn them, they'd succeeded.

Jax's arm dropped away, palms pressing together in his lap in thought. "You think they tested you yesterday and, when you survived, which anyone else wouldn't have, they exposed you today?"

"Yes," I answered.

Jax shook his head. "How did they do that? What caused you to lose control?"

Pressing a hand to my ear, I shuddered deeply. "All I could hear was this awful, ugly sound. It felt like it was tearing me apart from the inside out, like worms writhing in my stomach, nibbling away at what made me... me." Gritting my teeth, I fought back a third wave of tears. "It hurt so much and my body just... reacted."

It felt intentional, what had happened to me. An obscene violation. And I couldn't explain how anyone would have done it or why I was the only one in the room affected. Were they able to target Arachnae aether specifically?

A lonely foghorn sounded out at sea, and the lighthouse cut a dazzling beam across the water, sending our shadows dancing raggedly across the dock.

"Why would they be so keen to take you out?" Seb inserted himself in the conversation after remaining conspicuously silent. "I get that we're in the middle of the Trials, and anyone can be removed from the competition at any time. But even though you're in the final four, you're hardly the biggest threat to the field. Or you weren't anyway."

I licked salt from my chapped lips, toying with the frayed edges of the bandages around my hands. My transformation had split a number of the wraps open. Jax butted his shoulder against mine in solidarity. Together, we'd crafted conspiracy theories so outlandish no one would listen to them, but ones we believed to our cores. Beliefs that had guided every step I took for the last ten years of my life. And ones that felt more tangible than ever before.

"I don't think the Arachnae family murdered themselves in a fit of rage on one wild night." I gripped the back of my neck. "I believe someone took them out and made it look like they'd massacred one another."

The prince didn't utter a word; his expression didn't shift. Casually, he lifted a hand and gestured for me to continue. That was all the encouragement I needed.

"I lived in that household for three years after my father died. My mother was Arachnae, and shortly after he died, she was forced to move back to the estate because she was diagnosed with a disease that consumed her from the inside out. Slowly." I tugged on the loops of my rattiest braid, releasing it from its confines. "None of the Arachnae liked me much, especially the duke and duchess. They called me half-breed and other ugly names whenever my mother wasn't around. Because my father was an ant, you know, and I was half their size because of it." Seb's knee jerked, knocking into mine. "Not that I cared." Or tried not to, anyway. The acid coating the back of my throat spoke differently. "I held my own. I didn't care what they called me; I only cared about my mother."

I sighed heavily, squeezing Jax's hand in reassurance.

"I don't care what the rumors say. That family was not insane.

246

Far from it. Never in my life have I interacted with people more cunning than they were. Not your family, Seb, not Devlin, not any of the merchants I've traded with. No one." Braid unraveled, I began the tedious process of winding it back up. "Nothing they did was without purpose; everything they said was with intent. They were as manipulative as they were cruel, and they knew exactly how much power they held, the fear they would command should they exercise their abilities."

Did Seb believe I was rambling insane theories based on a rotten childhood that few should have been forced to endure? Or maybe, against the odds, he believed I was telling the truth. Jax rubbed my back, shoulder resting firmly against mine.

"They certainly weren't insane. Not a person in that house was anything less than exactly what they were born to be. Predators." I tied off the end of the braid and shifted to face the prince more fully.

"The Arachnae have always gotten what they wanted from the crown. Your parents understood that if they ever chose to enter the Trials, the Arachnae would sweep the floor with them. No doubt about it. You aren't born with poison in your veins as deadly as ours without a certain... threat coming with it." I rubbed my face. "They used that tool to their advantage every, single, day. Every generation. But it takes control to maintain that kind of manipulation, that hard edge of power. They didn't win every battle they waged out of sheer luck. No." My braids smacked my back when I shook my head. "They won out of spite and by planning the shit out of every action they took."

I gave the prince a moment to drink that in. Desperately, I craved to know what he thought of my tales.

"That I believe," he acquiesced, scratching an itch on his thigh. "But that doesn't explain how they go from being a powerhouse one day and dead the next. Or why you're so afraid to show your true self."

I traded another look with Jax, who squeezed my shoulder. "Tell him," he murmured.

"The day before they shunned me from the household and left me for dead, the heads of the duchy held a meeting." Even now, the details of that meeting were hazy. I'd lost so many memories of that time because of the trauma I'd endured in the hours afterward. But I remembered the pieces that mattered. "They didn't know I was inside the passageways hidden in the walls. My mother loved to explore them with me on her better days. I think she hoped it would give me something to connect with my cousins." I waved my hand, dismissing that line of thought.

"Anyway, I watched from behind the wall as they met with someone who I knew wasn't part of the family." I remembered the dagger that person wore on their hip, the gems embedded on the hilt that flashed with warning. Emerald and sapphire—stones as big as my thumb. "I don't know who, only that the front door opened and I didn't recognize their voice. I never saw their face. They threatened that individual, announcing intentions to participate in the next Trials if they didn't get what they wanted. I don't remember what it is they wanted, but—"

"But you think that pushed whoever they spoke with to murder them all." The prince's voice was rough as the burlap sacks I'd wrapped myself in after cutting myself wide open from the threads my former family had bound me in. "I follow you. But it doesn't explain how they pulled it off so convincingly that everyone believes the Arachnae took themselves out. Or what they would have used to pull off such a job."

Jax leaned forward, peering at Sebastian over my lap. "Haven't you made the connection yet, dumbass? Think about what happened tonight. Are you really that daft?"

I loved Jax so much in that moment.

Seb's eyes burned black. "Unlike you, I haven't had the last decade to percolate over this. I understand Nim's control over her abilities was stripped away tonight. What I don't get is how that affected Nim and what we need to do to stop it from happening again."

Slightly more settled, Seb's hand sought out mine, the rough pad of his thumb rubbing the back of my hand. Jax zeroed in on the gesture. I shook my head and mouthed the word, "Later." His eyes narrowed, but he leaned back on his palms all the same.

"I think it's safe to say that whatever weapon that person used against me tonight, they won't hesitate to use again." I waded back into the discussion with the care of a water strider casting a line into the lake.

Sebastian sighed. "We start with taking a hard look at everyone in that room. I'm not saying any of them are behind this treachery, but one or more of them are playing a hand in this." He scrubbed his free hand through his hair. "All of them would have a motive to cut your family down."

"Least of all your own," imputed Jax.

Rather than take offense, Sebastian dipped his head in a low, pensive nod of understanding. "You're not wrong." He stared out into the milky hue of the fog. Was he visualizing the freedom that came with the open ocean? The easy escape a ship offered? Because whatever he saw wasn't the same thing Jax and I did. "Nim, would you... would you tell me what really happened the night you were cast out?"

My shoulders locked, spine stiffening. "Why?"

"Because I loathe the Arachnae with all my being for what they did." His hand locked tight around my own, voice soft and dark and haunted. "And I want to know if I need to drag them up from the depths of Hael and destroy what remains of their souls."

Something soft and warm glowed in my belly, an ember of hope. He wasn't disgusted by me or mortified by my lie of omission.

249

OF MONSTERS AND MADNESS

He accepted me. Enough to crave revenge.

I glanced at Jax, whose throat bobbed in a hard swallow. "It's your story, Nim. I'm here for you regardless."

Skin itching, I released Sebastian's hand and rubbed at my arms, seeking warmth that wouldn't come. I'd hoped opening up would rattle loose more details of those days, but they hadn't. So I vowed to keep it quick. The details short.

"Two days after my mother died, they made it clear I was a plague upon their family name. They wanted nothing to do with—" I swallowed back the slur my cousins had flung at me every day for years—"someone like me. Someone they didn't think deserved their blood running through their veins.

"The duchess came for me in my sleep." If I hadn't already hurled up everything in my stomach, it would have risen now. I remembered the gleam in her pale eyes so clearly, her arms too strong for me to fight. "She dragged me downstairs where the whole family assembled."

Such ugly things she'd shouted over my sobbing and pleading. How I would serve as an example of what happened if anyone dared go against the duchy's wishes. So keenly I could recall the sympathy on the faces of my two uncles, my mother's brothers, and the hatred burning on the rest. A leech. A plague. A creature unbefitting of their incestuous name.

With a shudder, I reminded myself to push through. "They stripped me down and wrapped me in a cocoon of sharpened silk." I touched the back of my neck and the slit that ran along my hairline. Sticky residue clung to my fingers, and I pulled a strand out. Easier to remove myself from the memories, focus on the facts. I would be alright. I'd survived, after all. "Arachnae manipulate their threads in many ways. It can be strong and unbreakable as wire." I held it out to Jax who, understanding my intent, tried to slash it with his jawram, but couldn't. "As malleable as cloth." I motioned to my bandages.

"Even sticky or sharp, whatever you need.

"That night, they wrapped me in sharpened threads and dumped me in an alley. They said only a true spider would be able to escape its clutches. If I could escape and find my way back, then I could be one of them." My breath shuddered in my lungs. Jaxon wrapped himself around my back. The muscles in Sebastian's arms bunched as if restraining himself from hitting something. "I slashed my way out with my claws eventually. But I didn't go back. I refused to." I cocked a crooked grin that strained the muscles in my face. "Jax found me. He brought his father, who took me home and raised me like his own daughter. I never tried to go back."

A muscle in Seb's cheek jumped ferociously. His eyes were obsidian chips when he finally met my gaze, hatred burning in their depths. Hatred unmatched by those who'd cast me from their home. "If they weren't already dead, I would rip them apart and scatter their remains for the sharks to enjoy." His voice was hollow, haunted. "Those aren't people. They aren't Eritrean. If I could pull them up from the depths of Hael—"

He broke off with a choke, face shadowed and bent over his lap. I'd never felt more sensitive in my life, as if emotion had gained tactile strength and I could feel and taste it. Jax nudged me. Hesitantly, I wrapped an arm around Seb's back, barely touching him. It was as if that motion set off a chain reaction, because one moment I was on the dock, uncomfortable in my skin and the next I was in the mantis' lap, his face pressed to my throat, wetness trickling down the line of my pulse, wrapped in a grip so hard and so warm I felt I might explode with the acceptance I absorbed from him.

Gradually, I relaxed in his hold until my arms, too, came around him, cheek pressed to his hair, embracing him as he battled back tears, his chest quaking with the weight of his pain, pain he'd pulled from me and taken as his own. Finally, after who knew how long had passed,

Sebastian pulled back, eyes rimmed with red, cupping my face.

"I'm so sorry you went through that," he murmured, tracing the paths of tears. "No one should have gone through what you did at the hands of those monsters. If I—"

I shushed him with a finger to his lips. "There's nothing you could have done. Now or then. I suffered, but I also triumphed where they expected me to curl up and die." I reached behind me, relieved when Jax took my hand. "If they hadn't cast me out, I never would have met my best friend."

"Damn straight," Jax said, voice tight as he, too, warred with his emotions. "No better best friend in all the world than me."

It relieved the bubble of tension that had built in my chest, and I settled deeper into Seb's lap. "I never would have been embraced by the Shells. Never would have explored the majesty of greenside. Never would have found my bookstore and all my favorite haunts." My nose brushed his, and I closed my eyes, resting my forehead against his, arms wound around the mantis's neck. "Never would have tried to steal from you."

The tightness in his shoulders relaxed, his grip less painful, and he exhaled. Hard. "You said the massacre came that night, after they threw you out."

"That's right."

"So you would have died with them had you been there."

So thankful I was for the darkness behind my eyelids. It was a thought that had occurred to me more times than I dared to admit. "Most likely."

"Then I suppose we have them to thank for not recognizing what a wonderful creature you are—"

I felt him searching. Searching for the name that eluded him still. "Nimmarah."

He breathed it back to me, like breathing life into my lungs, stars shining in his eyes.

And never had I felt more complete.

31

Perception of Power

Nim

"Do ya poison people through yer bite? Or…" Rags jumped up and down, gripping the back of the chair, vibrating with energy. She and Grev had been at it all morning, peppering me with questions about my bloodline and all its peculiarities. Swallowing down my amusement, I begged for patience.

"Ducts run through the centers of my nails." I held out a bandaged hand to Rags, who took it with the radiance of accepting the crown jewels. "Our nails naturally form extremely sharp edges, so if we cut anyone or dig our nails into them, the poison is injected."

Grev reclined in his chair, feet propped on the table. He'd initially feigned disinterest when Seb and I had slipped through the door several hours ago, but when Rags started in on her questioning, he'd gravitated toward the conversation, eyes gleaming with curiosity.

"That explains the constant nail filing."

I tapped said steel file on the back of my hand before pressing it to my thumbnail. Still too long. "Can't be too careful. They grow quickly."

Across the room, the prince shook his head as he dunked a plate into the sink filled with soapy water. He'd urged his friends to give me space when we'd returned to the hotel, but Rags had shoved a missive in his hands and dragged me to the couch, muttering something about getting her turn with me. Though her comment entertained me, I'd refused to answer her questions until Seb read the letter out loud.

The Trials were on hold. The council, head of the church, and the dowager queen were meeting to discuss my *status* and whether I would be allowed to continue in the competition. Seb hadn't seemed too worried about the whole situation, saying the rules didn't exclude anyone from competing, nor did they state anything against champions withholding information about their lineage.

Finally satisfied with how my nail looked, I scrubbed the keratin dust off on my thigh and shifted to another nail.

Grev cleared his throat. "Your hunch is because of your extra legs?"

Ignoring the tightening of my shoulders, I replied, "I think it's my ant heritage. I'm small for my kind, and my legs are stupidly long." Similar to a daddy long-legs. Too long for someone with my limited height. "When I retract my limbs, they fold into the top of my spine. I don't think there's enough room for them."

The spindliness of my legs had been yet another thing that set me apart from the rest of the Arachnae clan. They believed so strongly in maintaining the purity of their bloodlines, only mating between themselves and the occasional hornet, because they were so mean, that it twisted their aether. My mother told me early pictures of the Arachnae depicted the slender legs I bore, but over time they'd thickened with extra muscle, becoming more compact, the hair running their lengths thick and furry.

"I can't imagine not having room in my body for my wings ta fit properly." Rags fluttered her translucent set. "Does it hurt?" She motioned at my spine.

That gave me pause, trying to recall the last time someone had asked me such a question. Perhaps Jax? When we were small? "It doesn't hurt, but I'm more comfortable when my legs are out."

"Alright, Rags." Seb nudged the hornet out of the way, apparently finished scrubbing the dishes. "That's enough for one morning. Answering one hundred thirteen questions would make even you crazy."

The hornet pouted but shrugged gamely. "Fine." And she tossed herself over the side of the couch, landing on the cushions with a thump. Her hand shot into the air over the back. "Can't help I think she's the coolest thing ta grace our kingdom since the Chain of Pearls."

She referred to the series of underwater caves that produced most of our precious pearls, which also happened to form a line the length of the shore.

"'Cool' is one word for it." Grev leaned forward on his elbows, chin resting on his clasped hands. "But 'advantageous' is far more suitable for our purposes."

The prince took the spot Rags had vacated beside me, and I realized I hadn't asked about the nature of our relationship. He'd made no secret of his attraction to me, had proven he stood by my side by chasing after me when I'd fled, and hadn't expressed disgust at my true form. But he was a mantis, a prince, a future king. I was... an outcast. Even more so with my identity revealed to the whole of Moldona.

The Daily Buzz hadn't concealed a single detail of what happened at the exclusive eveningmeal, its splashy front page headline screaming for all to read: *Lost Heir to Arachnae Duchy Exposed as Trial Champion*. I doubted it had taken much effort to get the story out of the bluesiders in attendance last night. They all wanted to spin my topple from relative grace to their advantage.

Rags groaned, and a pillow soared over the couch, beaning Grev in the side of the head. "Jus' spit it out ya stupid hornet. What are ya really tryin' ta say?"

"Exactly that: we should use the Arachnae name to our advantage." He held up his hands when I rolled my eyes. "I know you don't claim the name as yours, and I empathize with your feelings. However, many think the Trials are about power, when, in reality, it's about the *perception* of power." He raised his fingers as he ticked off the most important rulers in the history of Eritris. "Gregory. Riccardo. Cleo. Trinity. Xander. All of them made controversial decisions. However, they were revered by the people. Even those who came between them played their roles to a key; and not one of them didn't have the support, or very least fear, of both blue and greensides at their backs."

I tipped my head back into the cup of my hands, fingers linked, staring at the ceiling. I felt several pairs of eyes on me, obviously waiting for a more explosive reaction.

Grev cleared his throat again, acutely aware of the finely strung tension collecting between us. "The Arachnae name carries weight. I'm not saying a bluesider and a greensider can't rule the nation, but Seb, you have been gone for the past seven years. The people don't know you anymore. They certainly don't know who you've become, and it's difficult to say how that will be interpreted.

"And Nim, as a greensider, you face discrimination from both ends of the spectrum. I'm not saying that without your added status, you wouldn't be well-received. I have every faith that Seb's plan of revolution through politicking will work." He nodded to the prince, somber as ever. "However, that jar of ideas is smashed and scattered across the floor. There's no picking up that mess. But we have been handed a new jar. One that's shiny and new and full of possibility."

Incapable of sitting still any longer, I stood, heels of my boots clicking on the wooden slats of the floor. "You want me to wield my family's name as a weapon."

I didn't like it. I'd never claimed the Arachnae name, never intended to. The spiders were such a horrific part of my past, yet I promised myself I would hear the hornet out. No matter what misgivings churned in my stomach.

"Bluntly put, but yes." Grev flexed his wings, like he did when he was stressed. "Let's look at this from a purely scholastic level. As a greensider, you already had the sympathies of those on this side of the wall. In fact, we got lucky because you're so recognizable—" he motioned at the wraps around my arms— "and you are associated with the heads of one of the ranking gangs. That gives you weight no one else but Jax boasts. Adding in the fact that you're one of them *and* have the blood of one of the most powerful families in our country's history running through your veins, plus abilities that everyone can't help but respect, that shifts even more support to your side."

I didn't want to hear this. All I'd ever craved was anonymity and escape. Hael, I'd made it through three trials without anyone being the wiser to my true identity. If only I could have made it two more. Then I could have taken the prince's crowns and hurried to the border.

That was what I'd agreed to when I'd taken this ridiculous role of champion.

And now I felt like those dreams were slipping through my fingers.

Ever keen to my thoughts, Seb picked up where Grev left off. "You'll win the respect of the duchies. They never will appreciate having a greensider as their champion, even if you leave like you plan to do. It helps, you leaving, but it's always there. That a greensider bested the bluest of bloods. But since you're Arachnae, you're now one of them. You're deadly. You're powerful. And you're a mystery they can't unravel."

"It will also make 'em nervous." Rags chimed in, cheek resting on the back of the couch. "Nerves are easily turned against yer enemies."

Sticks, they knew which buttons to press. Seb himself had still outlined the option of my leaving. If something happened to Jax before the final challenge and I won... I could still exit the country *with* my aether. And if it came down to a battle between him and me, then I'd deal with the loss all the same.

This new and improved plan meant I'd have to adopt a persona that made my stomach knot a million different ways, but I might come out of this thing alive. Maybe they'd even be keener for my departure, the last-known spider taking her leave of Eritris.

Wielding the weapon of my ancestry might make victory easier.

"I hear you." I heaved a long sigh, leaning against the table. "And I agree, we need to use every advantage we have. But what would you have me do? A name is just name, no matter what word the letters form."

"You own it."

I turned to face Grev. The steely determination in his eyes helped me breathe more easily.

He continued, "You take that name and become entrenched in it: exude confidence, express your opinions, prove yourself to be—if not lethal—someone *capable* of taking such action." He shrugged as if this wouldn't be the biggest feat for me to conquer to date. "The Arachnae historically stayed out of most fights unless it benefited them, speaking only when they felt it pertinent or advantageous to their position. That already suits your personality. But you need to take that name and use it against your enemies. Make them remember your history and realize you are an extension of that powerful brand."

Hip braced against the kitchen table, I folded my arms over my chest, trying to make sense of the storm raging in my mind. My identity was out. Nothing in any of the kingdoms would stuff that secret back in the shadows. Maybe I could use this to my advantage. It meant getting what I wanted in the short term. And in the long term...

"Alright. It won't be easy for me to do this, but I see the merit." I straightened, strengthening my voice. "I'll adopt the Arachnae name until the conclusion of the Trials. And then I'm out."

Grev heaved a sigh of relief.

But it was Seb's expression I sought. The softness of empathy in his face, and the nod of approval that made my chest squeeze with a semblance of what might have been pride.

32

Subtle Offerings

Sebastian

Sapphire glass sparkled like shattered teardrops across the threshold. I hesitated, peering into the gloom beyond the door, so unlike the last time I'd ventured into my brother's workspace. Dozens of clocks ticked on the wall. Dusty shelves bore hundreds, if not thousands, of forgotten bits of metal and stone and nick-knacks, yet I'd never encountered anything truly broken in here before.

"Your thoughts are deafening, Seb." Micah's voice drifted from between the bookcases. "You might as well come in before your brain overheats from working overtime."

Alright then. Highly cognizant of the crunching beneath the soles of my boots, I stepped into his office. It reeked of sulfur and smoke. An experiment gone wrong? A door had been drawn mostly closed across the vent above my brother's workspace, one that also eliminated most of the light. Yet, it remained murky enough that I could make out his ratty hair falling about his shoulders as he peered over his work.

Or what I thought was his work, until I realized his table was empty. His bare arms were limp where they rested on the wood.

"What happened?" I asked, hovering on the edge of the half-circle of light, shoulder braced against one rickety bookshelf.

Micah had yet to raise his head. His shoulders lifted in a sigh. "What makes you think something is wrong?"

Worry fluttered its grasshopper wings, but I tamped it down and picked up a tool with a sharp, curved bit of metal on one end and a hollowed hole in the other, holding it up to the light. "The only time I don't see you tinkering with a device is during formal eveningmeals." I reconsidered. "Or on stage during the Trials. Aside from that, you're always fussing with something."

Micah snorted, fingers curving around the rubber grips of the wheels on his chair. "I'm between projects."

Yeah. Like I believed that nonsense. The brother I'd grown up with always had fifty different ideas swirling through his head at any given time. I doubted the adult he'd become was any different.

Wood creaked, and he shoved away from the desk, moving into the dusky ray of light. One of his eyes was swollen shut, the skin purpled with bruising. A cut beneath his eyelid still wept. He didn't flinch under my scrutiny. "What can I help you with?"

My jaw clenched, molars grinding together. "You can start by telling me who punched you in the face."

"You shouldn't worry about me."

"That's bullshit and you know it." I forced my jaw to relax. "You're the keeper of a million secrets, I know, but you've never hidden something like this."

"Seb. Drop it." His good eye fixed me in a flat stare. "What did you come for? I know you'd never voluntarily enter the castle unless you were desperate for something."

I wasn't going to get anywhere with this line of questioning. Things had changed in my time away, and though my brother and I had always been cordial, we'd never enjoyed the relationship he shared with Vincent. Those two were thick as thieves, while I lingered on the outskirts, watching their antics from afar.

Micah twitched when I lifted a vial of black, metallic flakes and shook it. The flecks clung to the glass like static before settling. I had come here for a reason. Nim's comments from the other night bothered me. The sound she had heard. It had done something to her, caused some switch to flip inside her. Not for a moment did I believe her to be unstable or out of control. If anything, she was more in control than any of us.

No. Something was wrong.

And there was only one person who could help me solve the mystery.

"Would it be possible for someone else to control another person's aether?" I rolled the vial between my palms, the heat of my skin warming the glass. "Hypothetically or realistically?"

Micah snagged the tube and settled it back into the case beside the rest, hands trembling. "This have anything to do with that Arachnae champion of yours, by chance?"

I didn't answer, and he braced his shaking palms on the rims of his wheels, rocking back and forth, refusing to look me in the face. "There is research that suggests sound vibrations could impact the flow of magic through an individual's body." He stilled. Risked a glance up at me as if realizing something, then pulled a box out from beneath his desk and rooted through it. Eventually, he emerged with a bit of string and a chunk of amber glass. With a few deft twists of his fingers, he dangled the glass from the string, holding it before him. "You're familiar with hypnosis, correct?"

I eyed the colorful bit of clear glass. "The rhythmic pattern can put a subject into an almost meditative state, allowing them to access different areas of their brain. Even uncover forgotten memories." I shoved my hands in my pockets. "One of the countries we visited overseas uses it to treat those who have experienced extreme trauma."

Micah nodded. "You're half right. The rhythm of the motion does some of the work, but an even bigger part of the trick is the words that accompany them, the tone of them, how they're spaced out. That sound and the vibrations that make that sound have a far greater impact on how our brain works than you would think." With a jolt, he dropped the glass to the desk, covering it with his hand, making me jump. "That's the same research that believes someone else could, hypothetically, manipulate the aether of another. The vibrations unlock something inside of them."

I slipped my fingers into the corners of my pockets, thinking about how Nim had seen the world when tear gas impacted her eyes. I hadn't asked about her abilities to view the world clearly, but I remembered reading somewhere that spiders were highly susceptible to vibrations. "Could those vibrations impact some types of hybrids more than others?"

"Undoubtedly." Micah peered at me through the swollen skin around his orbital bones, silently imploring me to understand something he refused to voice. "It would take some experimentation, but I don't see why different frequencies couldn't be used to influence insects in varying degrees. We know there are very simple insects, like worms and cicadas, who operate on a much different level than more complex insects like mantises or crickets."

Or spiders.

Micah did know something, I was sure of it. He was involved in this twisted scenario, but something restrained him. *Someone.*

Awareness prickled the back of my neck.

"If it isn't my brothers reunited. How wonderful." The sneer in Vincent's voice shattered my train of thought. Micah hunched over the table, fiddling with a finger-length tool, avoiding eye contact, and I forced my fists to unclench. Shadows shifted along the shelves of a bookcase I'd passed on my way in. My brother took much less care stepping on the glass shattered on the ground, his boots. No, *two* sets of boots crunching through the mess without care.

Vincent emerged first, the planes of his thin face twisted in a mocking smile. He wore green today, a tunic the shade of the pines that sprawled across the Iron Mountains. At his back, broad shoulders straight in his uniform, appeared an even less pleasant character.

"Vincent. Verity," I greeted, face blank. "Such a surprise to catch you down here."

It was. Before I left, despite his tight-knit relationship with Micah, Vincent avoided his workshop as if it was cursed. Once, after too many glasses of chilled wine, he revealed the controlled chaos Micah surrounded himself with gave him hives. He had no interest in the science of how or what or when, only in the results. And what they meant on a grander scale.

"I could say the same, Seb," Vincent replied, propping a hip on the table beside us, wings slightly flared. The position put him well above us seated in our chairs, the way he preferred. Always had. The male was born for sitting on a throne, and he knew it. "I wasn't aware you frequented the keep. I assumed you preferred the estate and its more... subtle offerings."

Mentally, I rolled my eyes. The Octavius estate was as well-equipped as the castle, and he knew it. It wasn't like I didn't know he had spies relaying my every move to him; I'd just never known him to be so forward with it. "Just catching up with Micah since he's been eliminated from the Trials, that's all."

Metal clanked, drawing my attention to Verity, who poured over a sheet of chain mail, its links threaded with an ivory substance that might have been silk. His hands were clasped behind his back, nails neat and clean, exposing the slits on his forearms where he could produce stingers at a moment's notice. At my side, Micah put down one tool and reached for another, one that conveniently presented

265

more of his back to us. The feeling of unease spread across my skin like hot oil.

"Ah, yes, the Trials. Were you aware your champion was keeping such a delicious secret?" Vincent asked, the table creaking when he rested more of his weight against it. "I, for one, was caught *completely* by surprise when she exposed herself to be that monster of a creature over eveningmeal. Losing control of her aether like that." He clicked his tongue. "Highly irresponsible. Imagine how much destruction she could have caused if you hadn't been there to usher her out."

I swallowed. Hard. If my antennae had been extended, they would have vibrated with awareness. Vincent knew something. He had to. And so did Micah, not that he was about to tell me anything. Verity returned to our small group, face cast in shadow. He reached into his jacket and produced a letter, which he handed to Vincent with a nod.

"Despite the danger, or perhaps because of it, the Trials will continue as planned," Vincent proclaimed. He held out the letter, its golden wax seal broken. "A little gnat told me you were here, so I offered to bring this to you directly."

I accepted it, thumb sweeping across the cracked seal. Biting back the response resting on my tongue, I replied, "How thoughtful of you." A pause when I shoved it into my own jacket without reading its contents. "There was never a doubt in my mind that the Trials would be allowed to proceed unimpeded. Even before my champion was exposed—" I paused again, eyeing the two males who knew more than they were letting on, letting them know I'd copped to what they'd so thinly revealed—"I knew Nim was a nightmare to be reckoned with."

The keen grin slipped from Vincent's face, leaving behind an expression of pure, puckered bitterness. After patting Micah's shoulder in farewell, I pushed away from the table and stood. Vincent may walk like he stood a foot taller than everyone else around him, but when that haughtiness was put to the test, like it was now, he remembered he and I were the same height.

With a tiny, mocking bow that had his entire frame stiffening, I said, "May the Trials reveal our true leader."

And without a backward glance, I strode from the room, a whistle on my lips.

* * *

So rattled was I by the encounter that I forgot to escape the castle through the tunnels. Instead, I found myself navigating the winding basement tunnels, slipping up the staircases until I emerged outside a familiar door. The music room. My mother's favorite room in the entire keep.

The soft strain of violins carried through the closed door, and I carefully turned the knob, stepping inside. Plush velvet curtains hung from the walls, creating a soft barrier between the room and the stone walls, allowing the music to breathe. In the center, her hand sweeping across the strings of her instrument with a long, grass bow, stood my mother, eyes closed and expression fierce as the music pouring from her fingers.

My grandfather, her father, was a well-known craftsman. His hobby was designing instruments from bits of forgotten wood, preserved leaves, and other spare items commonly found around Moldona. He'd taught my mother how to wield those instruments, though to her chagrin, none of her children possessed even an ounce of her skill.

Her bow stilled on the strings, bringing the song to an abrupt halt. Her eyes flew open, and she pulled the violin from the crook of her neck. "Sebastian. I didn't hear you come in."

"You still play beautifully," I remarked, tucking my hands in my pockets. "I'm glad to find this space unchanged."

With care, she nestled the instrument back into its case and returned it to a shelf against the wall to display. Her back to me, she fussed unnecessarily with several other cases. My antenna twitched again when she failed to respond, her silence stretching like taffy.

Unable to stand her disregard any longer, I broached the quiet. "Is something wrong?"

Her shoulders stiffened, the line between them horizontal to the floor. When she turned, I almost stepped back, recognizing the face of the queen, not the female who was my mother. "Something wrong, you ask? Sebastian, are you truly so dense as to ask me such a question?"

I flinched at the sharpness of her tone, effective as a willow switch.

"You knew, didn't you? That *she* was one of *them*?" Her words were tinged with disgust, and I knew without a doubt who she was referencing.

"Mother—"

"Have you forgotten everything your father told you about the Arachnae Duchy? Every warning he uttered?" She stalked to the wide window flung open on the other side of the room and peered out over her city. "That family was nothing but poison. The problems they created for your father—the vicious politicking they pulled. You have no idea how glad I was when I learned of their demise. When their threats died with them."

This was the cold side of my mother that I rarely saw. The side that made her a good queen and a master at manipulating the duchies to the will of the king, because she understood the world in a critical, analytical way.

But she was wrong about one thing.

My father had never discussed the Arachnae with me. It was Vincent to whom he turned when it came to matters of state. Whatever political maneuvering the duke and duchess had planned was above my head and beyond my care.

"Nim's family threw her out on the streets," I spat, striding to the center of the room. "She was a child, barely older than ten. Her mother was dead. Her father long-gone. And they threw her out with the trash. Whatever her family threatened, whatever they held above your head, had *nothing* to do with her."

My mother spun, her mouth pressed into a thin line. She'd begun to morph, her wings splaying wide in anger. "She is an Arachnae. That's all I need to know."

"She's an orphan who's done nothing but denounce the people who *failed* her," I seethed. My own aether sparked, and the spikes along my forearms lifted. My wings slid out from the slits along the backs of my shoulders, their dragon fruit and onyx colors flaring in my periphery.

"I know you're grieving the death of Father, but I thought better of you. I thought you were understanding. But you—you refuse to see beyond your own bias. That hybrid—that *female*—knows more of honor than you ever will." I could barely see through the haze in my eyes. To hael with her discrimination, her condescension. This conversation highlighted everything that was wrong with this city. Everything I'd vowed to change. "If you knew how much of a struggle it's been for her to accept that everyone in the city knows exactly who she is and where she came from, you would change your tune."

"I will never change my view of her," my mother—no, the *queen* snarled. "And if you ever want to be welcomed back inside this castle again, you would do well to cut your ties with her and her kind. No son of mine would disgrace me in such a fashion. Such disrespect for your father."

There was so much more to say, but none was worth uttering. Her mind was closed.

Wings flared, I strode past her to the window and flung myself out into the sky. It had been a mistake coming here, thinking I might find answers, comfort, acceptance.

This was why I hadn't wanted to return.

It was almost enough to make me retreat, to reclaim my freedom.

Almost.

33

Worthy of Trust

Nim

Prowl.

No matter how much I squinted or scratched at my knuckles, the gilded letters remained in that simple, infuriating order. Unmistakable. Just like the head of the Luminesae's signature, written in graceful calligraphy at the bottom of the page.

Rags flipped the sheet of paper over as if that would reveal some new tidbit of information. She huffed through her nose when only the golden seal appeared, bits of the wax scattered across the table. It was the third time she'd done this, flipping the letter over and back. "I don't like it."

"You don't like anything cryptic," replied Grev, sipping on a cup of black tea that smelled of fennel and lemon. My nose wrinkled, and I took a small step away. Though a beloved drink in Moldona, I'd never acquired a taste for the stuff.

"At least the other clues hinted what was to come," Rags replied. "Even ya must admit this is vague ta the point of meaningless. Prowl." She scoffed, chomping down on a honeystick, chewing like mad.

"What I wouldn' give ta prowl up to the Luminesae and shove this up their—"

"Enough." Seb intervened with a long-suffering glance at his guard, who ripped a peeler from a drawer with unnecessary force and tackled a mountain of potatoes beside the kitchen sink, the skins striking the bottom of her pail with dull thuds. We'd already dined for eveningmeal, so I had no idea what she meant to do with her pile of pale root vegetables.

"Arguing about the cryptic element of the clue isn't helping us," the prince continued. "We need to be more productive with what little time we have. I need ideas. Go."

Grev scratched the scruff thickly layered across one cheek. "'Prowl' reminds me of slinking around, avoiding notice. Like a spy. Maybe you need to spy on someone? Collect clues?"

"Not bad. Keep going." Seb snapped his fingers and pointed at me.

My fingers itched to find my file. "It has to be bloodier than that. We're down to four champions and two trials. The executors of this demented system will want to whittle us away quickly now." I tapped my nails against the table. "I like Grev's thoughts about spying. Maybe we need to spy on someone to get a weapon and use that on one another?"

Rags' peeling had lost its frenetic energy. "Prowling reminds me of big animals, the kinds with lots of sleek muscles an' sharp, white teeth." She pitched an idea of sneaking around, launching quiet attacks at one another, seeking to make it to the final round.

Around and around we went, spinning theories deep enough into the night. Eventually, around five the next morning, we stopped to enjoy a hearty bowl of potato stew that Rags whipped up. Nothing we came up with felt right, and the tension of not knowing knotted my shoulders, the muscles in my arms and legs twitching with the need to do something. Go somewhere. Anywhere.

"I can't keep sitting here." Shoving my bowl into the center of the table, I shot to my feet and crossed to the doors propped open to the balcony. Tall stacks of storm clouds billowed along the horizon, speckles of pink and blue lightning flickering in their depths, silhouetted by the sun rising behind them. "We're spinning ourselves in circles, and nothing fits quite right. But there is one commonality in every idea we've thrown out there."

"Which is?" Sebastian leaned against the railing at my side, arms crossed over the black bars.

"This trial won't be contained to Archer Arena." A low burble of thunder snaked through the alleyways. Beneath my wraps, the tiny hairs on my arms twitched, sensing the electricity in the skies. "We'll be in the city. Among the people."

Sebastian didn't bother asking me to continue, didn't glance over his shoulder, dark brows knitted in question. He knew me well enough to know I would get to my point when I was good and ready. The idea of someone besides Jax and Dev knowing me well enough to anticipate my behaviors used to make me nauseous with anxiety.

But now, I felt… differently. Like the idea held appeal, even pride.

Something to unravel later.

"The more I know the layout of the city, the better prepared I'll be for whatever test they throw my way." I rubbed at my tired eyes. Sleep would have to wait. "I've navigated the streets of blue and greensides my entire life. I think I know them well, but it can't hurt to add to that knowledge, see if there are any shortcuts I've missed. Any hideaways I'm not aware of."

Grev hoisted himself up onto the railing, legs dangling, wings spread to keep him seated against the increasing intensity of the wind. "Sounds like you need maps."

"And I know just where to get them."

* * *

I'd never been a particularly extroverted pupa, preferring the worlds I read about in books and those spun by my mother on our long walks through greenside. After being tossed from the duchy, I'd drawn even tighter inside my shell, embracing the solitude I found beneath the hood of my cloak.

Sensing dozens of eyes watching me pass, the crowd notably quieting when they noticed me striding down Merchant's Row, made me want to crawl into the nearest hole and not emerge for a millennium or two. I'd promised Seb I would follow his orders and assume the confidence and power fitting a monster bearing my mother's last name, but it was more challenging to keep my hood down and my shoulders straight than I'd anticipated.

The bandages that had always shrouded me in mystery, accepted and dismissed as a peculiar vagrant who largely minded her own business, now acted like a white flag, attracting all kinds of unwanted attention. Some eyed me with undisguised wariness. Others, hatred. Some with awe. Many with fear. Where moths drew closer, worms slunk back. Members of the king's guard patrolling the streets gave me a wide berth, hands tight around their swords and spears.

No matter how much my instincts screamed for me to dip into the shadows, pull my hood over my hair, and vanish into the alleyways, I fought back. My stride remained unhurried under the intensity of the scrutiny. I'd filed my nails before leaving the apartment, and I fought the urge to click them together. With my extra legs drawn in, I couldn't straighten entirely, but I forced my shoulders square, my spine rigid, holding the gaze of anyone who dared meet my eye.

I'm one of you, I wanted to shout.

You've accepted me as one of your own, before, I felt like crying.

But I was an Arachnae. They'd taken me under their metaphorical wings under false pretenses, and I doubted they would soon forgive me for that offense.

Finally, after what felt like the longest walk of my entire life, I pushed open the door to The Dusty Wings Bookstore. An acorn bell rattled, alerting those inside to my entry. The musty scent of old books filled my lungs, contrasting with the jewel tones of freshly printed tomes. A mosquito perched in my old chair behind the desk, idly running her fingers down the long bridge of her nose, a bob the color of straw obscuring her eyes. She greeted me without looking up from her novel, curvaceous form curled over the pages with rapt attention, cheeks flushed. Must be a romance.

I made it two more steps before Ms. Whitmere emerged from the side door, dusting cloths in hand. "Annamarie, would you be a dear and—" Her feathery antennae quivered, rendering her mute. A smile cracked and reformed the wrinkles etched into her face.

"Nimmarah," she exclaimed, the three syllables humming from her lips. I flinched.

Of course, she would use my given name over my preferred one now that she knew it.

The word sent a jolt through the clerk who snapped to attention, black eyes fixed upon my bandaged face, nostrils flaring, likely scenting my blood for abnormalities, hungry to spread gossip now that my secret was out. The moth patted her new apprentice on the shoulder, keeping her from rising. "Please dust the front, my dear. Nimmarah and I will be in the back, should you require anything."

The mosquito didn't bother hiding her disappointment, muttering beneath her breath as she grabbed a handful of gray rags and slouched to the wide panes of the front windows, shooting glares over her shoulder.

True to form, once tucked away in the stacks, the moth folded me in a warm embrace that I, for once, didn't try to pull away from. Pressing my face into the soft fabric of her gray-blue sweater, I hugged her hard, allowing her familiar, motherly presence to drain the tension from my bones. To my surprise, tears formed in my eyes, rimmed my lids, and I sniffled them back, caught up in the storm of my swirling emotions. She ran a hand down my braid, brown and gray wings swaying lightly, sending small waves of her subtle, flowery perfume wafting over me.

I'd only worked here for a year.

But it felt like I'd known her my entire life.

I imagined, if they were still alive, my parents would hold me like this, take my stress on their shoulders, if only to make me feel momentarily better. I wished I could remember their faces. Recall the cadence of their voices. But time had left me with meager impressions and outlines of memories.

"Honeycake?" the moth asked, gesturing toward her office.

Swiping the moisture from the corners of my eyes, I huffed a soft laugh. "Sure."

The sweetness of the treats settled my stomach, and Ms. Whitmere refused to entertain serious conversation until our fingers were sticky and our bellies full. Laughter filled the small room, rebounding off its many windows, creating a wall of sound between the quiet store and the roaring of the storm thrashing outside.

"I'm glad you finally came to see me," the moth said, leaning back in her chair.

I tipped my half-drunk glass of water in her direction in question.

"I hear you upstairs, you know, prowling about like a thief in the night."

Her use of that particular verb snagged my attention, and I fought to remain lazily sprawled in my seat. Refused to let the Trials ruin this one moment of peace I'd felt in Riten knew how long.

"But you never come to see me, no matter what hour. Fortunately for you, I respect your reclusive behavior and desire for privacy." The bookkeeper flared her fingers wide in dismay, expression drooping. "I always knew you harbored secrets, but I'd wished you might one day share them with me. See me as someone worthy of your trust."

My throat clicked when I swallowed, a hollow pit forming in my gut. "I wanted to. You have no idea how much I wanted to. But..." I cast my gaze around the room and its many bookshelves crammed with novels and sketches and pens and spare bits of parchment. The words I desperately wanted to say wouldn't come, like extracting moisture from a decades-dry lake.

"I never told you I was raised a Reed, did I?" I straightened at the moth's quiet confession. Reed. Moldona's common name for bastards. The unwanted. The lost and the broken. The last name I'd adopted. "My mother died before I breathed my first, and my father caught a knife in his gut when I barely knew how to read." The moth smoothed one long, frilled antenna. "I spent five years at the orphanage down the way. You know the one."

I did. Everyone knew of Wings of Refuge and its ten-story building, built square on the line separating the fire ants and the roaches. The Luminesae granted it a yearly stipend to keep its doors open, but everyone knew the priests who monitored the charges housed there did their best to maintain order, but there were far too few of them and far too many mouths to feed.

I was one of the few lucky Reeds to avoid stepping foot inside its dark and grim halls.

"The year the hurricanes swept away the docks, all of us Reeds were pressed into service with the reconstruction teams." She flexed her long fingers again, the nails painted a pretty pink, as if recalling the days she'd held a hammer and saw. "Hard work. Long hours. Some of us never made it back. But I'll forever be thankful for those days, because I worked alongside seasoned craftsmen and caught the attention of a moth—one who had a son my age. When our work wrapped up, he petitioned to bring me to stay in his home. I grew up and eventually married that male." A vibrant smile flashed across her pale lips. "That's a story for another time, though."

I cleared my throat. "I had no idea."

Those four words hit me hard—a sickly realization of how I viewed the world and my place in it. I hadn't seen beyond my own misery, failed to recognize this hybrid who shared my history and wanted nothing more than to offer her assistance.

How selfish I was, refusing to see beyond my own problems.

"We all have our secrets, Nimmarah," the moth said gently, casting me a long look that I understood all too well. "It's why I have a habit of taking Reeds under my wings." She flicked an antenna toward the door. "Your replacement out there? She shares your surname. A lost little mite in need of a place to find herself."

"You must adore that she reads romance."

The moth's laugh was like dandelion seeds in the breeze. "Fantasy actually. But spicy fantasy. I never could convince you the best worlds are those we'll never experience for ourselves." She paused. "But she's far less attentive at her work than you, I'll admit."

I drained my glass of water, listening to the rain patter the windows.

"Now. You're in the middle of the Trials, so as much as I wish you came to see me of your own volition, I have a feeling you're here with a purpose in mind."

Like the snap of fingers, the quiet reminiscing shattered. "I need maps of Moldona. All kinds of maps. Of the streets, the castle, the Church of Luminescence, the sewers, if you have them. I'll take whatever you have." I pulled a pouch of coins Rags had handed over before I'd left. "And I can pay."

The moth dismissed the sack with an idle wave of her hand. "No need for that. Just bring them back when you're done."

278

With one last shared look, she snagged an oiled case treated against water and ambled into the stacks in search of what I needed.

34

Frequencies

Sebastian

Rain splattered the sill of the open window, its clean scent immediately wiped away by the harsh colognes preferred by my brother. I checked the lock on the door, making sure it was bolted, and wandered deeper into the room, closer to the fire roaring in the hearth. My heart palpitated in my chest. I hadn't been in here since I was a child. Ironically, Vincent hated it when his space was disrupted; little changed with time.

A wide bed with tangled black sheets took up most of the space in the middle of the room, its many pillows haphazardly tossed about, speaking to a night of little sleep. Tunics and shirts and robes and pants were scattered across the floor and draped across chairs and the settee, abandoned where they fell. I knew his bathing chambers were through one door to my left, the closet beside it. But my focus lay on the desk and the tumble of paperwork scattered across its surface.

My fingers shook when I drew a tin of leaves from my pocket. The taste of mint on my tongue brought me back into the present. Settled. Secure. Intent.

I hoped Nim was still asleep. After two days of poring over maps recovered from the bookstore, she needed as much rest as she could before tackling today's trial. The champions were due at Archer Arena in five hours' time. I'd arrived far earlier, hoping to connect some dots to the mystery that shrouded my champion and her aether.

Carefully, I rifled through pages stacked haphazardly on one side of Vincent's wide desk. I wasn't sure what I was looking for, but I knew Micah had evaded me when I'd spoken with him earlier, before Vincent had shown up with his leech of a champion.

If anyone could create a device to screw with another hybrid, it was Micah. He had to be involved. And for him to hide something from me, even after my long disappearance, Vincent had to have coerced him. Besides, I couldn't forget his expression when he'd watched Nim writhe at the party, the grin that touched his mouth when extra limbs burst from her back. Where most were afraid, Vincent was fascinated.

Discarding the paperwork, I pulled open one drawer and then another, finding bits of metal and rubber, blocks of wax, and extra writing utensils. The third drawer took some finagling; it stuck a bit on its sliders. Inside, I discovered a box about the size and width of my palm. "What are you?"

Cupping it in my palm, I brought it to my face. The square of wood had been carefully constructed, heavy as a full mug of tea. It appeared to have a lid, but no matter how I dug my nails into the tiny rim separating the sections, I couldn't get it to budge. I imagined a tiny key inserted into the minute keyhole would make it work, though. When I shook it, I detected movement inside, the subtle shifting of gears and metal. A safe of some sort? Maybe a toy?

Setting the box aside on the desk, I dug through the remaining drawers, emerging with nothing else for my effort. No key. No clues. No incriminating evidence.

Again, my attention settled on the box. Why would Vincent have a child's plaything in his room? I couldn't recall him having this contraption as a larva. He was always so proud to show off his toys, especially the ones I couldn't have. And this one was carefully maintained, smelling of linseed oil.

I popped another leaf in my mouth, working it between my molars.

Micah said sound frequencies could impact aether.

Nim recalled hearing music that no one else could.

She'd lost control when she claimed she'd never wavered before.

And Vincent and Micah knew something.

But what might that be?

Armored boots pounded down the hallway outside, and I shoved the box back into its drawer, careful to set it back exactly as I found it. It wasn't like I could take it with me. I couldn't get into it, and I couldn't risk angering Vincent at this stage of the Trials. Better he thought me oblivious to his plotting.

The jangle of keys on a ring came right outside the door.

Without a word, I slipped out the window, ducking my head under the fall of rain, pulling my jacket and its compass tighter around myself. Carefully, I crossed the narrow roof into the pre-dawn darkness. I couldn't help but feel I was on the cusp of something extraordinary. I just needed the final pieces to fall together.

35

Prowl

Nim

Archer Arena felt distinctly spooky without the shouting of crowds, the scents of cured meats and sweets, and the rumble of anticipation that threaded through the air. Bereft. I fought the urge to shift on my feet beside Jax. We had arrived at the arena together but entered separately, tight-lipped and shadow-eyed.

A reality was spreading its roots, one we'd pushed to the backs of our minds and knew we would have to face after this trial. A reality we'd acknowledge at the dusk of this nightmare.

There could only be one champion.

And there were two of us.

Would I bow out like I'd insisted so many weeks ago? Would I even make it to the next trial? What would that mean for Sebastian and the future he so clearly believed in? Or did Jax have something up his wing? Some way for both of us to survive?

Too much uncertainty to focus on now.

The major had beaten both of us to the arena. The fire and candor I'd admired in her at the onset of the competition had all but vanished from her quiet demeanor. Her shoulders hunched under her military jacket, eyes glassy and moist, like a creature hiding from a predator stalking its steps. Her brilliant wings that cast rainbows were tucked away.

Stress impacted all of us differently, but what had her so on edge? She was the prize of our newest recruiting class, a hybrid with a point to prove, whether at the point of a sword or in a verbal spar. Unlike Jax and me, she'd gone through intense military training. Surely that was more stressful than a handful of challenges.

Before the bells tolled, wings whirred overhead, and a figure dropped beside me. I stiffened but didn't bother looking. The commander had a flair for the dramatic. Only he would have waited until the final moments to make his grand appearance. In my periphery, I watched him pluck at his uniform, straightening his knife-like collar, scrubbing his clean-shaven jaw.

"Would you look at that, the abomination emerged from her hole, after all," he drawled.

Jax cracked the knuckles of one hand, eyes narrowed. I rolled my shoulders, shedding the tension that gathered in the line of my spine. To reply or not to reply. I rolled my eyes and opted for silence. That didn't prevent him from continuing.

"I figured someone would have driven you from this country by now, *Arachnae*." He stepped fully into my line of sight, the badges on his sleeves flashing brightly. "You and your kind have proven yourselves to be monsters in every interpretation of the word. There's no place for you here. Not in this city. Not under this crown. Not on this continent." He spat. Greenish muck landed on the toe of my boot. "How about you do us all a favor and abdicate your position now? Save yourself a lot of unnecessary pain."

Cocking my head, I allowed a smile to slip through my demeanor. A sly one I normally preferred to keep hidden. Bullies shared many faces, but their attitude never differed. "Not on your life, Verity."

The commander tipped his head back and laughed. Day stepped away, hand braced on her rapier.

"She'll show you who the real monster is," Jax stated when the ugly sound faded, sleeves shoved up, giving him access to the painful barbs buried under his flesh. "And we'll see who's laughing then."

"You really think you can beat me?" The commander slicked a thumb across the ribbons and medals gracing his sleeves. The silver hilt of his sword glittered from his hip. "You greensiders are more delusional than I thought."

My retort died on my lips at the sound of footsteps on the stage.

"Thank you all for your punctuality," crowed the dragonfly who'd hosted our Trial by Poison. Skylar Anders. Mentally, I rolled my eyes when he stopped at the edge of the stage in a spray of glitter. Thousands of bright blue sequins were painstakingly threaded together, forming his sleeveless shirt. His trousers were made of a panel of pure silver that glimmered like a lake on a calm day. Four armored aphids stood at his back, helmets down and spears in hand. "I'm sure you're all wondering what the fourth trial will entail."

"Sure. 'Prowl' doesn't offer much of a hint," Jax intoned dryly. Day made a sound in her throat that might have been agreement.

If the esteemed dragonfly was bothered by his snark, he didn't show it. "Your trial today is a scavenger hunt through the city. A prowling task, if you will." His dazzling white smile expanded. "You will have four hours to locate three objects, items, or people by following a series of prompts. At each station, you'll find a bowl of colored glass. The colors indicate different locations. You'll need to collect a piece of glass from each bowl. The first to return to the Arena will get an advantage in the final trial. The last to arrive faces an additional trial."

"What if we don't make it back in four hours?" Day asked.

Anders smoothed a nonexistent wrinkle in his shirt. "I wouldn't recommend returning."

I fought a shudder. Death or exile. Thank Riten I'd scoured those maps until my eyes burned and itched, incapable of scanning the ink a moment longer.

The aphids who accompanied the dragonfly marched down a set of stairs and stopped before us, one guard for each champion. As one, they drew familiar pieces of smooth parchment from their cloaks and presented them, gold ink shimmering. My fingers barely brushed the black wax seal when Anders added in his grating, high-pitched voice, "Four hours starts now."

Ignoring the itch to slit his throat for being an annoying prick, I cracked the seal, allowing bits of wax to crumble into the dirt. The top half of the page reiterated the rules of the trial. Midway down, things finally got interesting:

Seek glass tokens at the:
Sundial swathed in shadow...
The home of the woman in red...
And the place of wonder once known now lost.

Day had already taken to the skies, with Verity hot on her scuffed heels, before I could shove the document into my jacket. No matter. Let them use their wings. It wasn't like I didn't know where I was going. The woman in red could only be the specter Himnatae, whose wax likeness lived inside the compounds of the Navy barracks, a prize stolen from pirates who attacked and nearly sacked our harbor several decades ago.

Jax appeared lost in thought, fingers curling around the parchment. I didn't dare meet his gaze, slinking past him and into the belly of the arena. The tunnels winding beneath the city were easy enough to access, and the run to the barracks would give me time to consider the remaining two clues.

* * *

With a grunt, I planted my hands on the edges of the manhole and hefted my weight from the dark and dank tunnel. Only after the steel cover was back in place did I dare lower the scarf obscuring my mouth and nose. Though the wool was thick, it only barely took the edge off the stench of the river of dung and piss that snaked beneath the belly of the city. I would have to burn my calf-high boots after this. There was no coming back from the disgusting mess that rotted down there.

But it had its advantages.

This clue posed its own set of issues. Both barracks were difficult to breach, even on a good day. Heavily guarded at the gates and along the walled compound, it was nearly impossible to sneak in without authorization. And I was under no illusions that the masters behind these Trials would do us the favor of setting the bowl of glass tokens outside the walls.

No. They would want us to get past the soldiers to accomplish our mission.

The more danger we faced, the better.

This particular vent opened inside the main offices of the Navy. Or I hoped it did, anyway, if the maps I'd memorized meant anything. The door released a quiet squeak when I edged it open to peer down the hallway. The light offered by the rounded window cut into the stone walls revealed the inside of a custodian's closet, complete with mops and cleaning salves and other implements. Briefly, I considered donning the janitor's uniform to disguise myself, but I just as quickly dismissed it. I didn't have the luxury of time at my disposal, and I couldn't afford for someone to take such a disguise seriously and send me off on some useless task. I would just have to make it quick.

Leaving the door open a crack, not wanting to risk it locking at my back just in case I needed an extra way out, I slipped into the hallway, my dark leathers standing out in sharp relief against the pale walls. The blueprints I'd examined of these barracks were out of date by a good fifty or so years. Ms. Whitmere had apologized, her antennae drooping when we'd spotted the date on the documents. I'd dismissed her concerns. I highly doubted the military wanted accurate drawings of its highly classified areas scattered throughout the city.

At the very least, the sewer system had brought me to the building I sought. Now it was just a matter of finding the correct balcony. And if memory served, the figure was on the eighth floor, propped up for incoming ships to see above our walls.

I made it up the first three flights of stairs before being forced to vacate the stairwell when I heard the clatter of steps above me. The hallway was also mercifully empty, but I dove into an office anyway, taking a moment to separate the bandages on my forehead. Concentrating hard, I released a sliver of my tight control on my aether, opening my third eye. This one was sightless, its iris milky. But that wasn't its intended use, anyway. This one could detect heat signatures. Another handy tool those of my ilk had hidden, another secret they hadn't wanted revealed. It could see through stone and steel, uncaring of light or dark. Perfect for sleuthing.

With its help, I wound my way up four more flights of stairs before I found my way barred. Huffing, I considered the locked door. It appeared they required specialized keys to access this level. It was where the commander of the Navy kept his offices. There wasn't time to pick the locks, especially since I wasn't sure what extra contraptions I might find within this device without proper research. So, I backtracked, emerging on the seventh floor instead.

Voices trailed from an adjacent hallway, low murmurs impossible to understand at such a distance, but I couldn't risk being spotted. Not this close to my prize. The next handle I tried thankfully jiggled, and I darted into yet another office. This one had been recently vacated, if the steam wafting from the cup of tea on the desk was any indication. No matter. The window opened easily, and I trailed my fingers along the sill, hoisting myself up and out. Luck held on my side. I'd ended up on the ocean-facing wall of the building, and overhead, a few yards to my west, a hint of red peeked over the edge of a balcony.

Standing, I tapped the pads of my fingers to the lip of skin at the back of my neck, coming away with stickiness. I slid the window closed, the tips of my toes touching the pane of glass, and pressed my hands to the wall, satisfied when they stuck, yet peeled away easily at my muscles' commands. I'd employed similar measures reaching Seb's rooms at The Primrose. A handy skill I didn't get to use anywhere near enough.

Rapidly, I scaled the wall and hoisted myself over the railing surrounding the being in red and took a moment to observe her form.

Tears trailed from Himnatae's eyes. One of her hands was wrapped in the chains connected to an anchor, the other lifted high as if searching for the sunshine. The stories said the woman had loyally served her captain for a decade, only to be shoved from the gangplank when he suspected treason among his crew. As she sank to the depths of the sea, she screamed for her paranoid leader to believe her plea of innocence with her last breath, and when the last of the bubbles broke the water, light flashed in the green-blue depths of the sea. The woman gained her godly powers, proof of her claims. Her captain tried to plead with her, realizing the error in his decision, but she spared him and his ship no mercy, eyes blank as she blasted a hole in the hull, forcing it to the bottom of the sea.

Even now, pirates believed her spirit roamed the seas, searching for treasonous crews to smite. It's why many ships carried her figure as a show of respect, hoping to ward away her wrath.

Dipping low, I plucked a piece of red glass from the iron bowl at her feet. Three pieces remained after I pocketed my prize.

It was pretty for a story. Awful. But pretty. And though I knew it to be just a story, my skin still prickled under the blankness of her gaze. I wanted to leave, but instinct had me turning to face the sea, follow her line of sight out over the blue-green water and the white gulls swooping low, their cries carrying far and wide. No ships rode the horizon today. No white sails billowed in the distance. Instead, the way forward was clear. The saltwater empty. I followed the line of cliffs that rose from the beaches north of our numerous docks, and stilled.

The place of wonder once known, now lost.

I recalled the story Seb had told—the one about the cove that had once produced the finest black pearls in all of Caswich Sea. The one that had fallen to ruin when too many hybrids harvested its wares.

Once well-known, now lost.

That had to be it. The answer to the third clue.

I peered up into Himnatae's face one more time, her expression one of tragic pain and sadness. "I hope you find your peace one day, lady. Story or not, you didn't deserve the wrath of man."

Slipping from the balcony, fingers freshly sticky, I couldn't help but compare our circumstances. How neither of us deserved the stories others doled out for us.

36

Small Sacrifice

Nim

Sand slipped beneath my boots, and I struggled to keep my balance. Despite living in a city beside the ocean, I boasted few sea-faring friends, so I'd taken the long way around to the lost cove, hurrying through the bustling docks and emerging at the outcropping of rocks that marked the end of the pier and the start of the natural terrain.

While I jogged, I reasoned out the first clue. The sundial still gave me issues. It wasn't anywhere in greenside. Something like that would have stuck out. I also couldn't picture it inside the Church of Luminescence and its large stained-glass windows. A copper sundial would stick out like a trout on land, far too modern for such an ancient establishment.

That meant it had to be on blueside. But not somewhere obvious from the street. Inside one of the mansions. My gut knotted, twisting uncomfortably. There was only one mansion I knew well, and that left all the major players, including the Octavius estate. I'd only been allowed in the guest establishment, the main home reserved for the rest of the family.

Soft, pale sand gave way to shale, and I crouched low, maintaining my balance on the surface made slippery by the sea spray. Ahead, the mouth of a cave loomed, tall and wide enough to allow small sailboats entry. Not that any floated nearby. This place truly had been forgotten by treasure-seekers.

Most of them, anyway, I amended, avoiding the burned-out pit of a fire and bits of broken bottles that littered the rocks around it. I would bet all the glass in my pockets that young hybrids visited the cove as dares. Occasionally, I imagined some adventure-seeker went too far inside and got trapped by high tide, left alone to die. Jax and I had never partaken in such games, finding more than enough intrigue on the streets of greenside to entertain our youthful minds.

Hooking my fingers in the grooves of a particularly large boulder, I pulled myself to the top and sat cross-legged, panting, surveying the terrain. Tide was low now, thankfully, though I wasn't sure how far in I would need to go. From the outside, I couldn't see any bits of colorful glass perched on rocks. I could swim, but not well. And being soaked to the bone wouldn't help with finding the final clue.

Maybe someone had left a raft. Shading my eyes from the hazy mists that scattered the sun's rays in every blinding direction, I squinted—and tumbled off the boulder a moment later, barely avoiding the sharpened tip of the arrow that exploded on the rock where I'd perched. I'd only felt the shimmer of something too firm to be anything but metal at the last moment.

My head ached where I had smacked it on the ground, and I slowly pulled myself upright, keeping the boulder between me and the entrance of the cave. Tentatively, I pressed my palm to the ache and hissed between my teeth when my bandages came back red. Adrenaline pumped too hard for me to feel the other bruises and aches I'd endured from my sudden fall.

It had been too much to ask for this scavenger hunt to be straightforward. It only made sense that they'd left obstacles in the way. The barracks had only proven a natural deterrent. The risk of drowning wasn't anywhere near exciting enough for the sick bastards behind this competition. They already had several assassins in their employ. Why not use them for the remaining trials?

Keeping one hand pressed to my skull, fighting a wave of dizziness, I pulled a mirror the size of my palm from my pocket with the other. I toed a lengthy bit of driftwood closer to my hiding spot and fastened the mirror to one end with a bit of webbing. Back pressed to the rock, I edged around, branch held out, angled so I could see around the obstacle. I glimpsed a dark figure crouched on the earth outside the cave before another arrow was loosed, shattering the bit of glass.

Shit.

Even if I'd had a quiver of arrows handy, an expert marksman I was not. And I'd bet good money the bowl of glass rested somewhere behind the bastard protecting the cave. Sealing my injury with a thick gob of webbing was the best I could do for now, and once my injury was taken care of, I patted down my jacket, taking inventory. Lock picks. A deck of cards. A length of rope. Bits of paper and spare tacks. The jawram gifted to me by Rags. Every pocket came up with some useless item or another.

Until my knuckles rapped on the flat, firm disc I'd shoved into my breast pocket. I gnawed the inside of my cheek. A smoke bomb. I'd purchased it more than a year ago, hoping to deploy it against Jax as a prank, and I'd grabbed it off my shelves at the start of the Trials on the off chance it would come in handy. Assuming the damn thing still worked.

I didn't dare attempt peeking around the rock again. An arrow would probably find my eye. For all I knew, the assassin was creeping up on my hiding spot now, ready to fill me full of arrows.

Forcing that nasty thought from my head, I focused instead on the disc. That would give me the cover I needed I get around the boulder as long as I moved quickly. The wind wasn't blowing particularly hard, so the screen it offered should hold for more than a few seconds. I scratched my temple, wincing when I inadvertently brushed my injury, and a gob of webbing that hadn't dried stuck to my finger. Rolling it between my thumb and index fingers, an idea came to me. One inspired by a memory of watching my cousins playing games of tag at the Arachnae Estate.

This might just work.

Concentrating hard, I released my hold on my aether, muscles relaxing and lengthening as my longer legs emerged. They would find much surer purchase on the pebbles and rocks that littered the beach between me and my target. The extra limbs also enabled me to keep my hands free. On top of that, my reflexes were always sharper when in my second state. I'd just learned to adapt without them.

Sucking in a deep breath, I lit the fuse of the bomb and launched it high over the boulder. It clattered against the rocks, and for one heart-stopping moment, I feared it was a dud or too old to be of use. Then something hissed, and gray smoke billowed. I didn't waste a moment, scrambling out from my hiding spot like a cobra from its hole. As anticipated, my spidery legs easily found footholds in the unstable earth, and I dodged the arrows fired through my cover. The assassin was shooting blind, hoping to hit a target out of sheer luck.

Snagging the first of my pre-made balls of webbing, I threw it as far as I could when I emerged from the smoke. It soared over the assassin's shoulder and splattered against the cave wall. The figure flinched and rolled, crossbow still clutched tight in its grip, and managed to fire another shot before dipping behind a rock. The sharp edge scraped my side, but I wasn't about to be deterred. I'd already cleared half the open space. Not much more to go now.

I threw another ball of web over the boulder. It, too, splattered when it hit the ground, followed shortly by a third and fourth ball. The assassin popped up, yet another arrow notched, and we fired at the same time, my ball splattering against the boulder. Their arrow smashed into my shoulder, sucking the wind from my lungs when I toppled sideways. My enemy tried to draw back but couldn't. Their eyes widened. Their sleeves were stuck to the rock. They struggled, managing to slip out of their cloak, crossbow abandoned where the wood was trapped to the surface of stone, but they didn't get far with their boots stuck to the slate. No matter how much clothing they pulled off, it wouldn't be enough. Just as I'd intended.

I threw my last sticky ball, which exploded on the assassin's chest, drenching them in gooey webbing. They toppled over, arms stuck together, trapped in a cocoon of their own making. Remembering the games my cousins played, I knew it would be hours before the webs lost their strength. And then there came the task of peeling off the stuff. It was a nightmare and a half to contend with.

My long legs easily picked out clear spaces in the rocks, and I dipped my hand into the bowl, removing a piece of sea-green glass from its depths. Only one piece remained. How had the other two avoided the arrows?

With a grimace, I jerked the arrow out of my shoulder, sucking in a gasp as the head ripped from the muscle. I tossed it aside without another look. After probing my skin, I produced another ball of webbing and pressed it into the wound. It hurt something fierce, but as with my head, it would help the blood clot.

Stepping back, I hovered over the assassin, her eyes wide as she took in my elongated fangs and claw-like fingers, which flicked the piece of glass back and forth over the backs of my knuckles. She was young. Younger than me. Her slight form giving her an advantage when it came to slipping through tight spaces and hiding in the shadows. I traced the curve of her cheek, appreciating the way her breath hitched in her chest as she stared up at me. With a flick of a nail, I slit a hole in the ooze over her mouth, giving her room to breathe.

Without saying anything, I peeled away. No need to stay any longer.

Besides, the memories from my childhood had given me another idea.

One that might help me find the third clue.

* * *

During my days as an honorary member of the Shells, too young to blood myself into their ranks, I'd preferred to stay on the green side of the wall. I enjoyed pitting my skills against the wiliness of those who'd grown up knowing everything could be taken from them in a moment's notice. The challenge helped me hone my abilities, gave me a sense of accomplishment at the end of the day.

Jax, on the other hand, always chose blueside when given an option. He took great pleasure in stealing from the rich, taking their valuables from under their wings and antennae. My best friend used to bring his trinkets back to the Firestone and share secrets of what he'd discovered inside their homes. Sometimes, it was more than just jewels, stained-glass figures, and pouches filled with crowns. Occasionally, he imparted minor scandals or secrets he overheard while slinking through hallways. Sometimes he talked about strange statues he observed or windows that opened into seemingly empty rooms.

Not too long ago, he told me about a copper sundial he'd come across in the solarium of the Viotto mansion. It had caught his attention because of the diamonds embedded in its surface, jewels the size of his fist. He'd tried to pry them from their brackets, but they'd held fast, leaving him bitter with regret at the end of the night.

The Viotto Duchy had to be the final clue.

Especially when considering that anyone who grew up on blueside would know exactly what the clue meant from the outset.

Well. Bluesiders and greensiders who happened to sneak into places they weren't meant to be.

Once again, I chose to keep my hood bunched around my shoulders, back straight, ignoring the throbbing in my shoulder, as I strode down Merchant's Row. My newfound status opened a pathway I couldn't have accomplished any other way. In my head, the clock ticked down. I'd spent far too long getting around the assassin, and I would need to make this quick if I had any hope of getting back to Archer Arena in time. The guards fisted their spears as I dipped through the opening separating the rich from the poor, but I barely spared them a glance, just glad they hadn't thought to run me through in my haste.

Bluesiders acted much the same as greensiders when they saw me, first noticing my wraps, then the expression of intense focus on my face. Fortunately for me, The Viotto Estate was to the north of the gate, the opposite direction of where I normally turned to get to the Octavius Duchy, and it also happened to be the closest mansion to the Arena. Maybe my luck would hold, and someone would have dispatched the assassin crouching in wait here, making this an impossibly quick in and out.

Far too aware of the time, I sprinted down the road before pulling to a stop outside of the duchy known for its tough-as-copper beetle lineage. The wide front gate was wrought iron, shot through with colorful vines and long strands of ivy. Flowers blossomed along the lengths, even this late in the season, and I traced the petals of a fire lily as I strode through the open gates. Crushed shells in clear polymer formed a long, glittering walkway to the front of the house, which countered only the Octavius estate in sheer size.

Rather than aim for the front door and risk a fight straightaway, I turned the corner. Hardened yellow and red leaves crunched beneath my boots, their ends curled around the wilting prairie grass. The solarium would be around the back and should have a door that opened to the greater yard. In anticipation, I withdrew my set of lock picks and thumbed through them absently, anxiety mounting the longer I went without encountering any members of the duchy or servants on the vast grounds.

My mouth went dry when I spotted the first figure slumped against the trunk of a silver maple, a feathered bolt through his breast pinned him to the bark. Hand resting on the dagger at my thigh, I slunk closer. The blood pooled around his form felt tacky, thick. Cold. He'd been here for some time. I didn't recognize him or the figure of a female who was crumpled on the ground a few steps away, wings crushed beneath her form. Her skin had collapsed around her blackened veins, mouth wide with gaping horror, fingers stretching for the short sword in the grass.

Verity had been here. Only hornet's venom reacted in such a way.

Touching my index and middle fingers first to my forehead, then my mouth in a sign of respect for the dead, I crouched lower in the grass, control over my aether clutched firmly in hand, ready to release it at a moment's notice. The large, clear windows of the solarium shimmered hotly in the afternoon sun, the glare they cast too much for me to look at.

The door was thrown wide, and I ducked inside, immediately wanting to be out. Sprays of dirt and fragments of cracked pottery littered the ground of what I imagined had once been an immaculate space. The leaves of ferns and potted plants were shredded beyond repair. Delicate statues had shattered, their forms indecipherable. Pebbles from the walkway were scattered and rolled underfoot as I advanced deeper into the space, wishing for the first time I had antennae to alert me to movement.

Limbs of a bonsai tree had been ripped from its trunk, and sap oozed from a spiny plant torn down the middle. Across from it, I gasped, free hand flying to my mouth to muffle the sharp sound. Major Ectya Day lay crumpled in a puddle of her own blood, her throat slit so deeply I glimpsed white bone among the shredded muscles. Eyes once vibrant and clever were glassy, glazed over in death. The fingers of her hands bent in awkward angles, and bits of glitter fluttered around her still form. Not glitter. Fragments of her delicate wings crushed and scattered.

I stumbled back, moisture flooding my mouth, and hurled into the broken crockery of a fern. I heaved until there was nothing but bile left, and even then, the impulse returned when I glimpsed her body in my periphery.

This wasn't just murder.

It was an execution.

A humiliation rendered to a female who hadn't deserved her fate.

Too many thoughts filtered through my mind, too quickly for me to analyze. I couldn't. Couldn't stay here. Look at her again. My hands shook so hard I could barely tap my forehead and mouth, and I half sprinted, half stumbled down the ruined pathway, stopping only when the warm form of the copper sundial emerged, isolated in a square of silvery-white sand, soft as a baby's skin. Beside it, cupped in the sand, rested a bowl.

An empty bowl.

My knees thumped into the sand, dismay curling like smoke inside me. It wasn't possible. The other bowls had plenty of glass pieces. Why was this one different? My fingers coiled into fists on my thighs. Someone had taken more than their fair share. Sabotaging anyone who had the misfortune of arriving after them. And I couldn't return to the Arena without the glass.

The dial's surface told me I had a scant fifteen minutes left to figure out a plan.

There wasn't time to search the destroyed foliage to see if the saboteur had thrown the glass bits away in haste. I didn't even know what color the glass was to begin my search. I had no idea where Verity and Jax were or if they'd already made it back to the Arena. But maybe I could return and hope to catch one of them off-guard, stealing their pieces in the process. That said, my stomach rolled at the idea of sabotaging my oldest friend, and something told me if I wanted a hope of surviving the commander's wrath, I needed a better plan than a sneak attack.

But I did know where the fourth champion was.

"No." The word fell from my lips like a stone. My eyes closed, and I swallowed the bile back down. No. No, no, no, no. I couldn't go back there. Couldn't look upon Day's still form, let alone root through her clothing.

Yet, if I didn't, I was a dead hybrid. Or one exiled without her aether.

That was enough to sway me.

The major lay exactly as I'd found her, body crumpled and ruined. Blood squelched around the soles of my boots. Refusing to search her form with her staring at me in the throes of death, I closed her eyes with a hand that shook. A quick look around didn't reveal chips of glass of any color anywhere. Swallowing back another gush of bile, I pulled her jacket open, feeling around the fabric, finding daggers and darts and all sorts of weapons now useless to her. Moving to the pockets of her pants, I found them empty. Shit. Sucking in a breath, I withdrew, fingers brushing her belt and a... button?

A hidden compartment was embedded in the leather. It took a moment to work open, the angle odd from where I crouched, but two pieces of glass tumbled into my palm when I did. One red, the other amber. She'd visited the barracks before coming here, and she'd beaten whoever had killed her to the second location. Shoving the pieces deep into my pocket, I bowed my head over her body, repeating the signs of respect again.

"You didn't deserve this," I murmured out loud, needing to hear the words hang in the air.

Then I was gone.

Never had I run faster in my life. Through the solarium door, across the grounds, into the line of trees separating the Viotto estate from Archer Arena. Ducking and dodging branches, I could hear the clock ticking in my head, the seconds counting down at an impossible speed. The massive walls emerged before me, and I swung right, shooting for the main entrance. Skidding on rocks, I slid through the opening and raced to the stage where two figures already stood.

On my heels, the pounding of other feet, someone who ran with a dragging limp. They were injured. Either enemy or another champion, I didn't know. I pushed all the harder. Halfway across the arena Verily stood before me, hand cocked on his hip. That meant it was Jax behind me.

My best friend.

Who would have to endure another trial if he came in third. Who would be dead if he didn't.

Heart slamming in my chest, breathing hard, I forced myself to slow, to look over my shoulder at the fire ant through a sheen of tears. He had done so much for me: shared his home, his father, his life. No one had forced him to do it, to save me when I was at my worst. But that was the kind of hybrid he was. Pure. And kind.

And he would never make it with that limp. Not in time.

It was time for me to do something for him. A small sacrifice for his sake. I could prevail through another trial. I knew I would, especially with my spider out in the open. But him—I didn't dare allow my mind to wander down that path.

His antennae twisted in confusion when I stormed toward him. But when he opened his mouth to speak, I slung my arm around him, under his armpits, hoisting his bad side against me and propelled us forward, bearing most of his weight. Blood dripped down his mangled limb and dripped on the dirt. Maybe the bone had shattered.

"You put your glass down first," I panted into his ear.

He twisted in my grasp, eyes fiery with protest and pain, but I snapped my head from side to side. "You need to heal. That leg will take time, and we both know time isn't a luxury in this test."

"But Nim—"

"But nothing." I glared at Verity, who regarded us with a half-cocked smile. "Do this for me. And don't you dare look back." With a shove, I pushed him onto the stage. He caught himself from falling by hooking an arm over the platform, and with one small, sad smile, sweat beading down his face, he shoved his hand into his pocket and slammed three bits of glass down in front of Anders.

A breath later, and not a moment too soon as the tower gonged, I followed, eyes hard on my prize. Not the red, sea-green, and amber bits before me. But on my friend. Knowing I was capable of being selfless when it mattered most.

Anders crouched and nodded first at Jax's collection, then mine. At our backs, the commander stood, haughty as ever, arms crossed, not a bead of sweat nor smear of dirt marring his skin or clothing. Just how quickly had he completed the task?

"It appears our fourth champion will not be joining us," Anders said, straightening. "A wise decision. The guards will be searching for her."

My molars gritted together, and I forced my jaw to relax enough to force the words out. "She's dead." Jax shot me a look, but I didn't dare take my eyes off the hornet or the vile smirk curling across his face, confirming my suspicions about who had killed the dragonfly. Mutilated her body.

Anders clapped twice. "Then it appears we have our final three. Ms. Reed, we will be in touch about your additional trial."

I'd expected to feel relief at this stage of the game.
But only hatred and trepidation burned in my bones.

37

Deserve Better

Sebastian

"Who are ya' and what did ya' do with the Seb we know an' love?" Rags teased.

The sound of my name drew me from my stupor, and I twisted my hands in my pockets, the loose change jangling around my fingers. "Pardon?"

Grev snorted and navigated around a pair of crickets standing in the walkway, chattering over a bolt of puke yellow silk, antennae flickering wildly. The evening lamps had already flickered into life, though it was still too early for the evening crowd to emerge.

"Your thief survived another trial. One more challenge and she's in the finals," the more somber of my guards intoned, falling into step beside me. "There once was a time Rags and I would need to drag you from the clutches of whatever dice game you stumbled upon first in celebration." He nodded vaguely at a cluster of roaches gathered around a makeshift table, cards clutched in fists, bits of colorful glass littering its surface. "Yet somehow I get the feeling you haven't registered the last five games we've passed."

I hadn't. That was true. Too deep in my head, I supposed. Too many thoughts fighting for purchase, clamoring for attention. Roughly, I shook my head, agitated.

Hours ago, Nim exited the arena in a foul mood, arms trembling and bandages covered in blood. Rags had gasped and raced forward, patting Nim over in search of the injuries, but the spider had shrugged her off, insisting the blood wasn't hers. Most of it anyway. Jax emerged from the shadows after her, expression drawn and eyes clouded.

"We advanced. Nim gave up her spot in the finals for me," he explained when it became clear Nim had no intention of opening her mouth. "Verity murdered Day, though. Nim found her."

Rags immediately peppered the friends with questions, Grev paying sharp attention. The relief I'd felt loosened what felt like every muscle in my form, holding me back. She'd survived. Against all odds, my little thief, the champion I'd plucked from the darkened alleyways of greenside, still had a chance of making it to the final task.

As quickly as my body relaxed, it drew taut again.

Assuming she passed the next challenge, she would then fight her best friend in a duel to the death.

I understood the dull sheen in her eyes. She knew the reality and already grieved it. I didn't know how she would handle this, the impossibility of the task put before her. However, when I tried to catch her eye to commiserate with her, she avoided my gaze and bumped Jax with her elbow. "Let's get cleaned up and grab a drink." She offered a smile, one we all knew to be fake. "Celebrate."

Jax cracked his knuckles, worry creasing the skin between his eyes. "Sure thing. Mind if we skip the Firestone tonight? Pa has some... *business* he's conducting."

I could only imagine what business a gangster conducted in the middle of the week.

"I haven't been to Cup and Hearth in awhile," Nim mused. "And they prefer payment in coin over glass."

Why that mattered was a question I wasn't about to get answered, though I assumed it wasn't anything good if the mischievous smile that slipped across Jax's face meant anything. "Let's go."

The two had ambled down the street and away from me, Jax limping and Nim's shoulders stiff. Guests were clearly not invited on this outing.

Grev shot me a troubled look, but Rags brushed it off and pointed the way back to the Primrose, chattering all the while about what the extra task Nim faced might be.

And so hours had passed, the light bleeding from the sky like a wound that wouldn't clot. There was so much I wanted to talk to her about, starting with what happened during the latest trial, but I respected her need for space. I hoped she actually celebrated for one night.

Salt-crusted boards creaked beneath my boots, and I finally drew to a halt, surveying the sheet of rippling black that was the Coral Cove. Even as a child, I'd sought the water in my most contemplative moments, and here I was now, returned to the hint of freedom stretched far before me.

"What's going on?" Rags murmured, crouching to run her fingers over the water's surface. Ripples fanned out around the digits. "It's not like ya' to be this quiet."

Running a hand over my hair, I cast a look up and down the piers. "Let's get on the water. Too many ears here." If anyone could make sense of the tangle of my thoughts, the conflict in my head, it was these two.

A pair of rucks and a pat on the shoulder later, Grev secured us a small, serviceable sailboat. Our small group settled easily into the rhythm of managing the sails and ropes. When the shoreline vanished in the distance, the only light sources coming from the lantern on the mast and the stars in the blanket of sky above, we relaxed the rigging.

I opened my mouth and spoke.

It all poured out: my conversations with Micah, Vincent's cryptic nature, the curious box I'd found in my brother's desk, my frustrations about what he was up to, and my concerns about Nim. My worry over her well-being. How, when I'd selected her as my champion, I'd never thought I'd grow to care for her as much as I did, like she was as crucial to holding me upright as my ligaments and bones.

"If she wants me to succeed, she'll have to kill her best friend," I finished, leaning over the side of the boat, arms crossed on the rail. A headache had bloomed midway through my verbal vomit and pounded steadily against my right temple. "How can I ask her to do that?"

"I think you're forgetting Verity remains in play," Grev stated after a beat. "And Nim still needs to beat a task between then and now. It's hard to say how things will go until both those factors are secured.

"As for your brother, I think your concerns are spot-on. I never liked that pissant, and he's always been a power-hungry freak, doting on your father like he could change the course of history by simply existing." The hornet sucked air through his teeth and spat on the deck. "It doesn't surprise me he'd do everything in his power to win the Trials. And I mean *every*thing."

"He has to be stopped," I said, straightening. Had the stars always looked so bright this far out at sea? Like pinpricks of glitter on an ocean of black. "He can't be allowed to come into that much power. To control the minds of others—there's no telling how far he'll go or the cruelty he will be capable of. There's no other option."

Rags hummed low in her throat, drawing my attention to where she perched on a short bench, whittling a wooden block with one of her smaller knives. "There is another option. Ya' just don't want ta see it." I stared at her, silently urging her to go on while simultaneously hoping she wouldn't.

With a sigh, she exchanged a cursory look with Grev and set down her carving. "Seb. Ya' owe Moldona nothing, Eritris even less. This cursed country has plenty of hybrids who will eagerly take the crown an' do what they will with it. Yer birthplace in the castle means nothing. Yer father gave ya leave an' ya took it. You were free. You still can be free." She paused, allowing her words a moment to sink in.

"You, me, Grev, Nim, Jax—whoever else you can think of—all we need to do is board a ship and we're gone. No crown to claim. No more blood ta be spilled. We can head to a country where the people already rule through a system of voting, make a new home. No need ta start from scratch. We just... go." She slashed her knife through the air as if severing a cord. The last one tying me to this godforsaken land.

Stomach roiling, I held Grev's dark gaze and saw he agreed with his counterpart. She spoke a truth I couldn't deny. Sliding to the deck, I leaned against the slats, pushing down the urge to fire off a retort of frustration simmering hot and angry in my belly. Rags deserved to be heard out, for me to consider this option.

Cowardly? Yes. Practical? Also yes. Rags had a point: I had been free. This country had never meant to me what it did to Vincent. Though a prince of royal upbringing, I'd cut my ties to foster the need to breathe that existed in my blood. Fought for my right to freedom rather than remain shackled inside the walls of the keep. I'd only returned because I'd found something I felt could save my struggling, suffering homeland. A government that might change the world.

I'd returned and witnessed the suffering of its people first-hand. Watched them separate behind their pretend walls and artificial barriers classified by colors. I'd interacted with the heads of both gangs, struggled to breathe while in the presence of my older brother, seen the violence in an outdated political system, and what it cost its citizens to maintain.

Maybe Eritris was too broken for me to fix. I could cut my losses and leave. Find a ship and sail into the ocean once more. If she'd come with me, Nim would find a place of her own, too. A place where her scars wouldn't mark her as a demon. By withdrawing from the Trials, she would be an outcast, but maybe she'd want to find her home near me.

With me.

If she felt for me anywhere close to how I felt for her.

I lifted my face from where I'd buried it in the sleeves of my jacket, tipping my chin back to peer up at the expanse of the sky. But there was so much more I'd experienced inside the borders of Moldona, too: the loving relationship Nim shared with her found family, the liveliness of the artisans who enjoyed their work, the pride in Major Day's face when she looked at the nation's flag, the shimmer of hope that ran in an undercurrent beneath the cobblestones.

Those people deserved better.

My country deserved better.

As keen as I was to leave it all behind. My childhood craving of finding freedom had changed. I now wanted to find my place here on land. To embrace the tides of change and usher in waves of a victorious new world. To give credence to all those who'd dared hope for a better future.

No, I didn't want to leave, but the pressure I was exerting on Nim still weighed heavily on my chest. Rags and Grev saw the conflict on my face, in the slump of my shoulders, and both hornets settled on either side of me.

Rags took my hand, squeezed. "Maybe ya' need ta talk to Nim. See what she has ta say before settling on a decision."

That wasn't a terrible idea. I hadn't considered the possibility of her not coming with me if I were to leave, or how I would feel if she still chose to leave, should we win. It carved a gaping hole in my chest, imagining a world where I wouldn't wake up and know she was somewhere nearby.

I had to know her feelings before I could forge my next steps.

"When did you get so wise?" I asked, voice watery. I cleared my throat, but it didn't help. "We'll talk to her in the morning."

38

Feel Things

Nim

"I think—I think I like him more than I should." I threw back the dregs of ale remaining in my glass and set it on the bar top with a heavy thunk. At my side, Jax chuckled and stacked a tower of coins beside our glasses, which the barkeep swept into his palm with a nod and a grunt of dismissal. My friend looped his arm around my waist and led me out the door, weaving, knees wobbly and weak, the result of too much drink and too little food.

"I wondered when you'd admit your feelings for the prince," Jax commented, closing the door at our backs. The air outside was brisk, and I felt myself sobering under the dull yellow lamp illuminating the beetle hefting an ax and a large mug of beer on the Cup and Hearth's sign. "I knew it the moment—the first time I saw you two… together."

He was slurring, a contradiction to the nimbleness of his footwork as he skipped across a handful of cobblestones before sliding, knees bent, and leaping into the air. He flipped a pair of thumbs up my way when he landed. Laughter bubbled up easily from my belly, warm and frothy. Whenever we drank together, he got like this: silly, jittery, a little too cute. A little too bold. Too often, nights like this ended with our hands fishing through drawers of homes that didn't belong to us, eager to beat the other for the best find.

"No, you didn't," I replied, resuming the fragile strand of conversation. It was Jax's fault, anyway, insisting we stay for another two rounds. In contrast with his drunken antics, I turned introspective. Admitting truths I didn't care to examine in the daylight. "We hardly knew one another. And he was such a stick-in-the-mud. I barely tolerated him—"

"Lies." Jax batted at another sign hanging over the street, making the panel swing on its rusted chains. In my dwindling moments of sobriety, I'd requested we not return to the Primrose, and my friend had agreed, overjoyed at the idea of spending a night together in the Firestone like we used to. "You never barely tolerate shit. He intrigues you, challenges you, *believes* in you. Sebastian makes you *feel* things."

The way he said the prince's name while rubbing his hands down his chest and abs suggestively, eyebrows wiggling, wrenched another rare burst of laughter from my lips. A couple across the street glanced our way before hustling down the road faster.

"Hide your feelings from the rest of the world, Nim, but never from me. I *know* you." He jogged to my side and slung an arm over my shoulders, smacking a sloppy kiss to my cheek. I made no move to brush away the lingering wet of his lips. "I know you wish you were dead inside, but you're not. And all it took was one mysterious male on a mission of righteousness to make you remember that."

I snuggled deeper into his side. "Maybe," I acquiesced. When his fingers played over my ribs, nimbly finding my only ticklish spot through my cloak and bandages, I jerked and twisted in his hold, which only relinquished when I shouted he was right. Always right.

"I knew it. I knew I'd get you to crack, you sullen ninny." Panting, cheeks bright with liquor and humor, Jax slicked back his hair, dodging my jab. He jogged forward and turned on his toe, dancing backward. "You admit you like him. Was that so—"

A figure dropped from the dark sky and landed in a crouch behind Jax. I barely had a moment to process the hybrid's crooked smirk, his knowing chuckle of bitter laughter. A shout rose in my throat to warn Jax, to call for help, to do who the hael knew what. But Verity was already gripping Jax's arm in his powerful grip. His dagger slashed, and my best friend dropped, tumbling sideways into the dirt. It all happened so quickly that the laughter in Jax's eyes hadn't succumbed to fear.

Blood gushed from his throat, the injury so deep only his spine held his head onto his body.

"I tire of waiting," the hornet snarled. "The ant was in our way of the true fight. I look forward to finally eliminating the abomination of your kind once and for all."

I wasn't aware I was screaming. Dropping to my knees, body curling in on itself, one hand outstretched to do what, I didn't know, screaming at the top of my lungs. A sound I'd never made in twenty years on this earth. Not when my father failed to return home, when my mother passed in her sleep, when I was thrown from the mansion and bound in razor-sharp silk.

My soul was splitting, shattering, fracturing into a million unmistakable pieces. I was the one bleeding out on the ground, sliced to a hundred pieces. Not my best friend. Not the only being who loved me with his entire heart. It was me, and yet it was him. And over him stood a hybrid—a murderer.

That was all it took. One look at Verity's face and the dark hatred smeared in the blood that flecked his skin, the triumph of his kill reflected in his eyes. That was all it took for a vital piece of my heart to snap and drop into the dark abyss of my soul.

My pain morphed into fury; agony shifted to a bleeding urge for vengeance. I barely felt my body shift, the restraints on my aether vaporizing in the single beat of my heart. One moment I was curled on the ground and the next I was lunging forward, knife-like nails extended, elongated fangs bared as I reached for Verity's throat, intent on ripping his jugular straight from his neck.

The hornet narrowly dodged my reaching grasp, wings flaring wide as he leaped into the air.

No. I wouldn't let him escape, not like this.

Not—the claws of one of my many legs found purchase in Verity's thigh, digging long grooves in his flesh, raining blood upon my face. He screamed, his leg kicking, catching me in the forehead. I dropped like a rock, something metallic clattering on the stones beside me, and I stared, unblinking, as the hornet retreated toward the keep.

39

Light in the Abyss

Nim

Loud and ragged as my screams were, no one came. Not a single door opened. Curtains didn't twitch around the edges of darkened windows. I was alone in my torment. Alone and numb and dead inside, sprawled in a pool of cooling blood, Jax's head in my lap, stroking his hair, his cheeks. Droplets of my tears splattered on his freckled skin, clearing small trails through the gore.

I could count the times I'd cried since being banished from the Arachnae Duchy on two fingers. Two. And this torture had split that dam wide open, the emotions overwhelming me internally and gushing from me on the outside. I didn't sob. Couldn't gasp. Instead, tears flowed down my cheeks, dripped off my chin, a stream of agony that refused to be stemmed.

Jax had saved me. He'd offered me a home and love and happiness. A spot at his side when no one else would. He'd convinced his father to make room for me in their lives. It was laughter that drew me out of my head in the days after I'd cut myself free of the silk. His bright-eyed encouragement that drove me to rejoin the world beyond the front door. Jax's eager need to see me succeed that mended the broken bits of my soul and pushed me to find a place all my own.

He was the light in the abyss of my darkness.

And now his light was snuffed out. One moment laughing that joyful sound that still rang in my ears. The next he was gone, so quickly I wondered if he'd felt the pain. Hoped he hadn't.

Serrated teeth dragged down the naked and abused remnants of my soul, and I smoothed his hair behind his ears, careful to avoid nicking him with my claws. This city was cursed. It had taken everything from me and more. I'd allowed myself to be wooed by a mysterious prince with high-reaching dreams of hope and beauty. I'd allowed myself to be drawn into his delusion, only now realizing his gusto for what it was: a story. A tale fed to children at bedtime, hoping they might forget about all the awfulness that came with a life in Moldona, a city where the powerful always won and the powerless died.

My hand knocked against something when I leaned my weight against my arm. Almost dreamily, I realized it was a dagger. Verity's dagger. I must have knocked it from his grip when he'd launched himself into the air, trying to dislodge my fingers from the meat of his muscles. Riten hear me, I hoped the hornet would bleed out.

Its blade was still wet and red with Jax's blood, and I regarded it with detached interest, spinning the weapon over and over, the jewels on its hilt flashing. The feeble overhead light barely illuminated the whorls and spades etched into the silver surface. I lost myself in the twinkle of the light, the shimmer of the thumb-sized sapphire pressed opposite an equally impressive emerald. Emerald. My head tilted to the side, blurry eyes focusing.

Sapphire and emerald.

Unmistakable stones on a hilt of silver.

I could almost hear the hybrid's voice from my memory as he strode down the hall, oblivious of my hiding spot under the stairs. I was cowering from my cousins, avoiding their hushed whispers and spiteful pinches. My mother had just died, and with her went my protection. To them, I was nothing more than a half-blood, a baby spider who would never amount to much in their estate. A plague that wouldn't leave.

"I've heard you intend to take part in the upcoming Trials, whenever that may be," the stranger said.

"You hear true," Duchess Ava responded in her silky-sweet voice, adding that they had plans, and the Arachnae refused to be threatened by the ruling family, not when it was our power, her power, that gave the Octavius Duchy its legendary might.

"Don't test me," the hybrid snapped. *"You know not of what I'm capable."*

A voice I'd heard multiple times in these past few weeks, yet had never pieced together.

Prince Vincent had been there. It was he who had encroached on the household the very day before I was cast out, raising quiet threats. Less than a day after my eviction, everyone within the walls of the duchy was dead. The sapphire flashed in my gaze once more, and I set the blade on top of Jax's still chest, long fingers curled around the hilt.

It wasn't the city that was cursed.

It was a hybrid. One infected family pulling all the strings.

Wearily, I stood and shoved the dagger into my belt. I didn't know what to do with it or what my plans were for the weapon that had cost my best friend his life, his future, his laughter. But I knew I needed to get Jax to his father. To get him home.

Soundlessly, I hefted his body in my arms, carefully cradling his head. I pushed myself to my full, monstrous height, and, dripping blood, I began my slow and steady way to the Firestone and the fresh round of grief that awaited me there.

40

Want to be Found

Sebastian

Blinking back the fog of slumber, I shifted blearily, seeking a more comfortable spot on the couch but finding none. Giving up, I rolled to my back, gazing at the exposed beams of the ceiling. The living room. I must have fallen asleep waiting for Nim to return. But she hadn't. I was too light of a sleeper for her to have snuck past me.

A series of knocks hammered on the door impatiently. I rose onto my elbows. That's what had woken me—the heavy, urgent banging at the door. Nim wouldn't knock, and if she had, she wouldn't slam the side of her fist against the wood like a battering ram. My boots smacked the floorboards running alongside the couch at the same moment an envelope zipped through the crack beneath the door, spinning to a stop several feet inside the room.

That sent a surge of energy through me, shattering the remnants of sleep clinging to my skin, and I was across the room in a burst, the parchment heavy in my hands.

The summons had never been delivered with a knock before. Typically, we found the envelopes left outside or slipped under the door, the messenger uncaring when or if it was read. It was part of the Trials, an extra measure ensuring champions were truly paying attention enough to keep up with the clues.

The seal of the heavy envelope popped open under the pressure of my nail, and I slipped the card out, tucking the envelope behind it. On it were three sentences dashed in glimmering golden script:

Champion Jaxon Case is dead.
The final trial is to be held in four days hence, when the noon hour strikes
long.
Power.

Though the message was clear, I had difficulty prying my eyes from the first five words. Jax was dead. Nim's best friend was gone? That couldn't be right. They'd spent the evening together. My hands trembled, breath catching in my throat, and I barely heard the door opening behind me.

"What's the message, Seb?" Rags asked with a yawn, slipping past me, intent on the kitchen and its promise of a strong cup of tea.

Jax couldn't be dead. Not with Nim with him. If he was dead, then surely she was, too. But if she were dead, then why was a final trial spelled out clearly here? On the same letter? In three strides, I was across the room, shoving my way into Nim's room, heart slamming against my ribs, eyes frantically scanning the space, knowing what I'd find.

Nothing.

She wasn't there. She hadn't returned last night. Her things were exactly as she'd left them. Her bed as pristine as always, the edges of the sheets knife-like in their precision. But if she hadn't come back and she wasn't dead...

I felt more than heard Grev at my back, and I shoved the letter into his hands without looking at him. I needed to find her. She must have been with him. And if she hadn't been with him, she needed to know. If she didn't already. And if she did…

The thought of her grief stilled my shaking arms while I shoved them through the arms of my jacket. I'd liked the fire ant, and I appreciated his protectiveness and knack for humor when the moment called for it. To Nim, he was everything. Her savior, her best friend, her family. If he was gone…

I felt his loss like a punch to my kidneys. It would be like losing Rags or Grev. Two people as vital to my existence as the very air I breathed.

Rags drew a quick breath, and her cup shattered on the floor. No doubt, Grev had shown her what was written on the parchment, the dreadful message it relayed. "We need ta find her." The urgency in her voice forced me upright again. The mission was there, clearly stated. Unmistakable. I wasn't going crazy. What I'd read on that page was real.

"I'll check blueside." Grev squeezed my shoulder, gloves already in hand. "You and Rags head to the docks. We'll find her. There aren't many places in the city she can hide."

* * *

As it turned out, there were a great many places to hide, even in a city as small in acreage as Moldona. I barely felt the pain as Rags nursed the ragged shreds of my knuckles, the damage inflicted by the brick wall I'd punched in frustration. Dusk was setting, and I had no idea where the thief might be. No clue where she would have squirreled herself away.

The sign of the Dusty Wings Bookstore creaked overhead, and I peered through the window again, catching the somberness in the moth's gaze. She knew Nim. She confirmed Nim rented the room above her shop, yet she hadn't seen her in ages. In fact, she'd gone up to check on her tenant at midday when word spread through the streets of Jax's passing, the shuddering of unrest that came with it.

The loss of the ant sent a rippling effect through the streets of greenside. It was impossible not to feel the tension, to sense the anxiety that gripped like death. Rumor had it Commander Verity had slit the ant's throat in cold blood, right there on the street.

Right in front of Nim, the last of her ancient kind.

Jax had represented much to the residents of greenside: a beacon of hope, an opportunity for change, a fleeting idea that there might be something better for them if they only dared reach for it. And now he was gone. A young hybrid known by so many cut down in his prime, killed in an act not associated with one of the trials.

An act as cowardly as it was ruthless.

And one that was entirely legal. Champions could take out other champions at any time.

All day as I'd raced through the streets, dipping down alleyways and scrambling onto rooftops, I'd sensed the shifting tide. What began as alarm transformed to grief and now, impossibly, a rumble of intent. Vicious, cunning, searing intent. This would not do. These hybrids had so much taken from them by society, the guards, the king, their country. Now I wasn't sure what they would do. How they might react and the force they might have at their backs.

I feared what would happen when their shifty gazes and rumbling murmurs gained strength.

Not that I had time to think of that right now. Not when I had my champion to track down.

"Seb, I don't think she wants ta be found," Rags said, not for the first time. She dogged my steps with quiet assuredness, her calm complexion contrasting with the heavy angst twisting in my breast, threatening to rip my insides to shreds. "I think—"

321

"You think what?" I demanded, rounding on her under the lamp of the street corner. "You think I should give up? Leave her to her own devices? When she's hurting and in pain? I can't do that, Rags. I can't imagine what she's going through." I wanted to shake the hornet with a vicious violence I was unaccustomed to. "He died in front of her. Don't you understand what that might do to a person? How they might not come back from that kind of agony?"

Her palm was cool on my wrist when she touched me. The concern and empathy I found in her all-black gaze banked the fire burning in my belly. "Aye. I do. But running in circles isn't helping her. Maybe it's time we wait for her ta come to us."

Grev was back at the Primrose, pacing grooves in the stones out front of the hotel. If she returned, he would know it. Rags had a point, but I wasn't ready to give up yet. "Just one more place first, please?"

She nodded, eyes sliding past me and down the road to the tavern we both knew lingered only a few blocks away. "We've checked the Firestone already. They said she wasn't there."

Desperation clung to me like sweat. "But maybe she's there now."

"Alright." Gamely, my friend and guard motioned me forward, following my footsteps, keeping a wary eye on the growing shadows stretching from the buildings. My recklessness had shoved aside all forms of caution, but Rags was as unshaken as always, alert and intent, hand resting lightly on the hilt of the dagger on her hip.

The door to the Firestone didn't budge when I tried the handle, so I knocked. Three times. The sound echoed hollowly down the relatively empty street. No sound came from the cracks around the door. My chest heaved, a putrid burn rising in my throat, and I was about to knock again when the door opened, revealing Devlin. His bloodshot eyes were exhausted, the quiet confidence I'd noticed about him before gone, grief a physical weight on his shoulders.

"Like I told ya this morning, she's not here, Prince." Devlin cleared

322

his throat, the knuckles of the hand gripping the edge of the door bone white with pressure. "I can't help you."

"Please." I was begging. I'd drop to my knees if I felt it would gain me traction. "If Nim's not here, where is she? I need to help her. To make sure she's..." My voice trailed off. She wouldn't be alright. No way in hael would she be fine. Whatever sentiment I'd hoped to share stuck like sap to my tongue, thick and impossible to swallow.

To my surprise, Devlin didn't close the door in my face, only gazed at me thoughtfully through a haze of grief. "You'll find her when she wants to be found."

Then he shut the door, followed by a series of clicks that were deadbolts sliding home.

The bitterness roiling inside me stilled, sucked into a void of numbness that shook me to my core. Leaning forward, I pressed my forehead to the door.

"What have I done?" I whispered. I'd drawn the thief into this mess. I'd made her an offer I knew she couldn't afford to turn away. I'd pushed her to her limits, driven her beyond her comforts, and for what? More loss?

Had I finally made a bet too big to cover? One that would cost me and everyone I loved everything? My hands shook and with a sigh I shoved away from the door and beckoned for Rags.

"Let's go home," she said quietly.

Together we made our way back up the street, silent under the sheet of night.

41

Value in Life

Nim

"He's persistent, I'll give him that." Leather squeaked when Devlin took his seat at the bar. I didn't respond.

He didn't sit beside me, but one chair over. I swiveled the full glass of honey tea between the palms of my hands. It had grown warm long ago, and I had yet to take a sip from the amber beverage, a show of solidarity with the full glass of mead set before the stool between us. The place where Jax would have sat, yucking it up with the regulars, trading war stories on the good nights, and sharing sorrows on the bad ones.

Devlin ran an index finger around the rim of his own full glass, forearm propped on the counter. "You'll need to talk to him at some point, you know. It's not his fault what happened."

"I know." I scrubbed at my tired, swollen eyes. I'd run out of tears around noon, but my skin felt stiff from the trails of salt, and I knew if I were to look in the mirrored surfaces of the silver steins that lined the shelves across from me, that red still rimmed my eyelids. "I know it isn't his fault. But I don't want to see him right now."

How could I explain to Devlin that Sebastian didn't fit into my world? He was the piece to another puzzle that had found its way into my box. The prince wasn't part of this family, hadn't grown up in this lifestyle. He knew the sorrows of the seas but little of the troubles here on land. My troubles. And his presence now felt like an insult to Jax's memory.

Devlin leaned across the bar and filled a pair of clean, mismatched pint glasses with a pitcher of water he'd set aside earlier. Members of the Shells had stopped by the Firestone periodically throughout the day. Some said their goodbyes, slapping Dev on the back in solidarity, while others just sat, staring at the glass of mead as if they could will my best friend back into existence. A few brought food and left it in the icebox when it became clear neither Devlin nor I had any appetite. Now that the sun had set, it was just us.

What remained of our little, fractured family.

"Did I ever tell you why I formed the Shells?" Devlin took a pull of water, wetting his raspy throat. "Why I pulled together the misfits left behind by the War and established the community you see today?"

I scratched at the bandages over my wrist. "No. I don't think so." If he had, I couldn't recall the story and wasn't sure what point there was to sharing it now. Devlin's wife had died giving birth to Jax, and now his son was gone, too. How he could think about anything else right now was beyond me.

The fire ant nodded soberly. "I wanted to protect those who mattered to me. The smoke hadn't cleared the streets yet, the king's soldiers still meandered the alleys, and I knew in my bones if someone didn't act quickly, the ash might never settle."

The Gang Wars of twenty-five years ago were the stuff of legends. Four smaller gangs grouped together and took on the biggest gang in the city. What should have been a straightforward takeover turned sideways when the alliance shattered, sending the city into chaos that lasted a fortnight.

"I'd just married Marcela, Riten love her for loving me despite being blooded into the Coppers." The old male shook his head slowly, a wry smile twisting the corners of his lips. "I met her because of the gang. Saw her on the street while collecting tolls from our businesses. Marcela with her heavy basket and thick, blue shawl, her eyes cornflower blue and hair the color of chocolate, and I knew she was meant to be mine."

He smiled fully now, his wrinkles rearranging themselves into a surprisingly handsome face. This was a story Jax and I knew well, one of Dev's favorites to share. He never withheld his love for his wife and encouraged his son to foster love for a mother he'd never met.

Devlin cleared his throat, and I took my first tentative sip of water, drawn in by the trap of his voice. "We Coppers fell first, barely more than children we were, facing off against soldiers built for war. But I escaped the carnage and watched. And waited. And watched some more. And when all that was left but ruin, I knew I had to protect Marcela at all costs. If the city fell, we would fall with it." He squeezed a fist. Released it. "I pulled my neighbors together. Then their neighbors and so on, until we united half the city. The Shells and the Roaches. Enemies, but peaceful ones.

"Don't get me wrong, the Shells cost me a lot. But I don't regret a moment. The Shells helped me protect Marcela until I couldn't anymore. It gave me a home to house my child, and he led me to this scrap of a larva defiant as she was bloody." He turned on his stool, eyes meeting mine. "It was important to me to uphold my duty and responsibility, offering myself and my services for the good of this city. Even though my son is gone, I will continue to do so. Because that's what I'm meant for: offering salvation in a city where little is to be found. I will protect my people because I know nothing else."

Goosebumps skittered down my arms, yet I couldn't look away.

Didn't dare break this moment, the monumental heft of his words wrapped around me like armor. Thick and sure and weighty with responsibility.

"I know you made a commitment to the prince." His jaw firmed. "It's honorable to hold strong to our commitments, but there's also honor in knowing when to back away from a bad decision. There's value in life, and you should never forget that. Ever."

Devlin dug into the worn pocket of his cracked leather jacket and withdrew a pouch. He set it on the table with a jangle, the sound of coins unmistakable. I looked from it to him and back again, a tiny thread of fear twining around my heart.

"Jax told me how much you needed to cross the border." He tapped the table beside the pouch with his index finger. "This is enough to cover your deficit and then some. If you choose to walk away, I'd never blame you. I'd never hold it against you." His jaw quivered, and he cleared his throat again. "I'd respect the hael out of you for it, even if it costs me both my children." He paused, then murmured so quietly I almost missed it, "I would have lost one of you, anyway."

Impulse had me reaching across the table, snagging his wrist and rubbing the rough skin, seeking to offer him comfort as my own arms prickled with unease. He was right. I'd known the truth from the beginning, that the Bloodletting only ended with one victor—and had it been Jax and me in the finals...

Either he would have been forced to kill me...

Or I to kill him.

We'd known the avalanche was coming. The cascading tumble of hurt. No matter what I'd said about backing out, of leaving the spot, I knew I would have stayed.

And that if we both were to survive, one of us would die.

It was a reality that hit me harder than any punch thrown by a Viotto.

Devlin gripped my hand and continued, "But if you choose to stay, to finish out the Trials, I won't think anything less of you either. You'll always be my little larva, my found daughter."

The Trials, where I would now face Verity, were I to remain.

Devlin released my hand. Trickles of moisture slid down my cheeks, and I swatted at them, my chest tight with the love I knew it took for him to say such things. He stood and shoved his hat on his head. "I need to walk. Just for a bit. And while I'm gone, I want you to think. Think about the kind of person you want to be. Where your future lies and how much you're willing to sacrifice for it."

I nodded, incapable of getting a single word past the lump in my throat. By the time I'd scrubbed my face clear of the newest tears, the fire ant was gone, the door to the back swinging slightly in his wake.

* * *

I didn't know how long I sat there, head propped on my hand, staring at that little sack of coins. Long enough for me to drain the glass of water twice over.

He'd left enough money for me to cross the border into Idilea. Everything I'd endeavored for myself before the Trials was now within reach. It didn't matter if I finished the Trials, if I stuck around to collect my gold from Sebastian's tricky fingers. I could leave now. This very minute. I had everything I needed, including the maps... which were tucked in my pack back in the Primrose. Mood souring, I hopped off the chair and opened a door to a private chamber to relieve myself.

Screw the maps. I didn't need them. I could recall the general direction of the trails I needed to take, the areas I needed to avoid. The rest of my coin was tucked away in my rooms. I just had to sneak in like normal, snag it and my black widows, and my reasons to stick around Moldona were gone. Easy as that.

After washing my hands, I splashed chilled water on my face and scrubbed the tear tracks from my skin, the flesh shading pink due to the harshness of the abrasive towel. Tossing it aside, I gripped the sides of the cracked porcelain sink and leaned in, forcing myself to stare myself in the face, meet my own eyes.

My mother had once told me she made decisions based on whether she would be able to look herself in the mirror afterward. It was the reason she left the Arachnae Duchy to marry my father, her basis for having a child outside of the incestuous royal structure. And why she returned when she got sick, her resentment of her childhood home not enough to dissuade her desire to protect me from the harsh reality of the streets.

Yes, I could leave today and be outside the city borders within an hour.

But I was lying to myself if I thought I wouldn't leave anyone behind.

Devlin. Ms. Whitmere. Sebastian, Rags, and Grev. They all were here, counting on me.

Half the city had rallied behind Jax, behind his greensider title. Maybe when they heard Sebastian's plans, when they learned how much change he hoped to instill in our country, they would come to realize a brighter future was closer than they knew.

Maybe I would help them see their potential.

Then there was the matter of Verity. Of the gnawing ache of vengeance that took root in my gut and spread its long, dangerous limbs. My best friend was dead, and his murderer remained. I knew his face. I had his dagger. There was also the matter of my lineage. The massacre I had little doubt he'd partaken in, if his parting words hinted at anything. I may have hated those who shared my blood, but they hadn't deserved their end. Not like that.

If anyone would take the commander down, it was me.

Shoving away from the mirror, I slammed open the door and strode to the bar, where I snagged the sack of coins. Footsteps clattered on the spiral staircase, and Devlin appeared at the base, starting when he saw me advancing. I grabbed the hand he had yet to shove into his jacket pocket and dropped the pouch into his palm.

"Keep your coin," I snarled, curling his fingers around the fabric. "There's still work to do."

I refused to let Jax's death be in vain.

42

New Sort of Freedom

Sebastian

Her dress was new, but she had yet to discard the black mourning garb. A lump rose in my throat, and I choked it down, refusing to cave to the fragility of my emotions as I stepped past the threshold of my mother's rooms. The guards closed the door at my back, and the queen finally looked up from the flowers she was arranging, blinking away the glaze of what I suspected were tears in her eyes.

"Sebastian," she cried, sweeping to her feet, arms spreading wide. "I wasn't expecting you until tomorrow."

I held up a hand, stalling her advance and the embrace that would surely break me. The corners of her lips drooped, and whatever she read on my face had her falling back into her settee. "What's wrong?"

Her tone was so different from our last encounter.

More evidence of the queen's power vying with her motherly responsibilities.

The words still choked me, and I wasn't entirely sure what I wanted to say. In an attempt to organize my thoughts, my *feelings*, I paced over the elaborate rug of blush pink roses on a background of navy sea. My skin felt too tight, my thoughts too chaotic. I couldn't make sense of the tumultuous storm whirling and frothing in my veins. My mother watched me, her eyes tracing my path back and forth and back again, lips pinched with concern.

"May I—" I gripped my fingers tightly behind my back, squaring my shoulders. "Mama—" My voice cracked, and I mashed my lips together in muted horror. Her eyes rounded, and her fingers went white against the table where she forced herself to remain sitting. This was going even worse than I'd anticipated.

Rallying my resolve, I pushed on, looking her square in her pale face. "I need you to be my mother right now. Not the queen. Can I ask that?"

"Oh, my child. That you even have to ask." Her wings fluttered, and she was on her feet, sweeping her arms around me and pulling her tight against her. "Come here."

I stood a head taller than her slight form, but she cupped the back of my head and pressed my face to her shoulder, humming like she used to when I was a child. Tears stung my eyes, and I lost the battle of holding them in. They slipped silently down my nose and soaked the fabric of her dress. Heedless of my weakness, still humming, she flattened her palm against my spine and rubbed slow, reassuring circles. I threw my arms around her, gulping in air between quiet spurts of tears.

I lost myself in her embrace, the familiar scent of her daisy petal perfume. This was my mother, the female who encouraged me to walk, then fly for the first time. The hybrid who taught me my most important lessons about compassion and responsibility, the person who encouraged me to embrace my dreams and *do* something about them. To chase my desires and embrace my freedoms.

Finally, the tears dried, and when I came back to myself, I realized my mother had lowered us to the settee, her arms still tight around me. My skin felt normal again, and I was thankful the buzzing and humming of chaotic thoughts had stilled, leaving a pool of tranquility in their wake.

Sensing the change in my mood, my mother drew back and put her hands on my shoulder, a small smile tilting her lips sadly. "Of my three children, you always were the one who felt things more powerfully. I'll admit, I'm relieved that hasn't changed." She smudged the trails of tears on either side of my nose before passing me a cup, the porcelain chilled to the touch. "I'm afraid the tea's gone cold, but you need the sweet. Drink up."

Obeying blindly, just like I had as a child, I gulped down the minty brew. That, too, smelled familiar. Comforting. And I sniffled, managing a shaky smile. "Thank you."

"No need." She took her own cup of tea in hand, though she didn't drink. "Now. What's got you so wound up?"

I couldn't tell her about my concerns regarding Vincent's ruthless desire for power. Nor could I express my fears that Nim might not return to the Arena—and the relief I was scared to admit I would feel if she chose exile over a battle to the death. Mother had made her thoughts about the Arachnae clear, and I had no desire to stoke that fire once more.

So instead, I settled on the most unsettling issue. "What's freedom?"

Her wings drew tight against her back, the only hint of her surprise at such a question, and she tucked some hair behind her ear, eyes lowered, thinking. Allowing her time to process, I dribbled honey into my cup and tipped the too-sweet concoction into my mouth. She was right. I needed it.

"Where is this coming from?" Her voice was soft.

Balancing my elbows on my knees, I leaned forward, hands still clasped around the delicate cup. "When I was sixteen, you and Father pushed me to pursue my dream of living on the open seas. I loved it. Loved the water, the languages, the people I met, the continents I visited. That was the ultimate freedom, forging my own path, finding my own way. No titles or customs or rules to hold me back." I drew a deep breath, amazed at how clear my thoughts felt.

"But I couldn't get Eritris out of my head. I couldn't stop thinking about what could be, and how I could evoke change. I learned so many things from so many diverse people and cultures that I wondered how I could implement that here. In Moldona." I swiveled in my seat, addressing my mother straight on. "So I came back. I found my champion and entered the Trials. I thought I'd found a new sort of freedom, one in a future that I could shape and people whom I could help."

A sigh shook my body, one still ragged from the onslaught of emotion. "But now things are so jumbled in my head. We're so close to the end. I've seen so much ugliness—from the Trials to how bluesiders treat greensiders, to the strife between rival gangs. It feels suffocating. Too much. And now—" I hesitated, unsure how to bring up Nim, then decided to dive into it. "Now I'm not sure if I have a hope in the Trials because Nim isn't anywhere to be found. Her friend was killed, and I haven't had a chance to ask how she's doing. And I don't know if it's worth sticking around and waiting to find out.

"That's why I'm trying to figure out... what is freedom?"

My mother shifted, though her form was relaxed. "Before I answer your query, I have a confession of my own." Her antennae drooped. "I reacted too swiftly in my condemnation of your champion. History has played an unfair hand in my dealings with the Arachnae in the past, and I'll admit my fears and concerns about her kind flared at an unfortunate time. I sought to protect you and... fear I pushed you away."

Her kohl-lined eyes flicked up to meet mine briefly. "She's served you well and has performed honorably. After doing some of my own research, I've concluded she was but a slip of a child when the worst of the atrocities between our kinds were committed. I will not hold those crimes against her. No matter my dislike of… spiders."

I didn't know what to say, and I hadn't expected this confession.

"That said, she is grieving." Wryly, she swept a hand over the fine fabric of her gown. "I'd like to think I know a thing or two about grief and how it impacts all of us differently." She reached for my hand and swept her thumb over its back. "Give her time. She's likely grappling with her own feelings about her life, her family, and her future. You're both so young, it's unfair to put the weight on your shoulders like we have, though it's necessary all the same."

She peered over my shoulder, eyes unfocused, and I squeezed her hand lightly, drawing her attention back to me. "As for your question, freedom is as much a construct as time. How you perceive it changes with age, and what you want from it also fractures and reforms. It doesn't come without its own shackles, rules, and endless stretches of sea or road.

"Freedom is waking up and knowing you're the person you want to be. Freedom is making mistakes, finding those you love, and making changes for better or worse. It's what you want it to be—and it always comes with its own set of pressures." She paused and took a sip of tea. "Does that answer your question, Sebastian?"

It did. More than she could have imagined.

I nodded, feeling the confounding pieces of the puzzle of my life falling together. Relief swept through me, strong as hurricane-force winds, shoving the stress of the unknown right from my shoulders. My mother had given voice to the thoughts that I couldn't make sense of.

It was right that I came back. My priorities had changed, but I still felt those ideals in my bones. Freedom wasn't the open seas anymore. Freedom was something I found within myself, within the people I surrounded myself with. This was who I was meant to be. And now, I needed to have faith in Nim that she would come through for me in the end.

"Now that's settled, I have a question for you." The sadness in my mother's face had faded, leaving her a decade younger, with pink brushing her cheeks. "I've only ever visited Idilea, and that involved no travel across the sea. Which continent was your favorite and why?"

Tipping my head back in a laugh that felt too good to be true, I leaned back against the chair and began to talk.

43

Last Toll

Sebastian

The arena buzzed and hummed with excitement. Hybrids tripped over one another, crowding into their seats, cups of ale and hard salted pretzels in hand, chattering eagerly. I shifted uneasily on my feet. The former heirs who had claimed champions spanned out between Vincent and me, the remaining successors to the throne. Behind us sat the heads of the duchies and other notable figures from the church. Above them were the dignitaries, including several from foreign lands.

I recognized the patch of the Idilean flag sewn onto the tunic of a woman seated behind my mother. Long, blue-black hair framed her rounded face, her navy eyes a tad too large for her delicate features. She tugged her cloak around her, rustling the feathers stitched onto the fabric. She spoke animatedly with her companion, who caught my eye, one reddish brown brow arching in question.

Viveca Helvig. I'd met her once when we'd stopped to resupply on the western coast of Idilea. At the time, she accompanied her king, who cut an equally impressive figure, though he had seemed distracted through our brief conversation, his gaze settling everywhere but on me. I noted the flash of silver on Helvig's hand, a similar glimmer of silver on the woman beside her. That must be her wife, Telleree Falk. A woman as legendary as the dragons her country worshiped.

I nodded respectfully when our eyes met and redirected my attention to the dirt of the arena. The stages had been stripped away, leaving nothing more than dirt, grass, and the ruins of old columns in the middle. I knew the rumors. Had familiarized myself with them to the best of my ability, thanks to the help of my guards. Widely, most believed Verity and my brother would win this outright without any blood being shed on this day. No one had seen or spoken to my champion since the evening of the fourth trial, myself included.

Not for lack of trying. We'd spent most of the last few days searching for Nim, scouring the city for evidence that she hadn't run away. Devlin refused to speak to me, but I knew he knew something. My champion wouldn't have left him behind without a word. Not her family.

I drew a steadying breath, watching the commander march up and down the stretch of earth below the nobles, sword in hand, sketching bows and offering cocky grins. He probably thought what everyone else did, that he was a given to win. Mere minutes to go, and Nim had yet to show herself.

I couldn't give up my faith.

I'd calculated my cards, watched my brother bluff. I knew I had the winning hand. I just needed her to show the courage and grace I knew she possessed to the world. She had to be here. She had to.

From outside the arena walls, a heavy bronze bell tolled.

Noon.

The crowd went quiet, many rising to their feet, eyes fixed on the main entrance to the arena grounds. The bell tolled again and again. Six. Seven. Eight. Not so much as a flicker of a shadow from the doorway. No hint of life. I forgot how to breathe. Nine. Ten.

Eleven. My tight grip on my aether loosened, and long spines of flesh grooved out from my arms, splitting my jacket sleeves. Anders took flight, megaphone in hand, clearly prepared to announce the victor. I'd never hated anyone more than I did him in that moment.

On the last toll, the doors swung wide.

Through the opening strode Nim, back straight, chin lifted. Outfitted in the uniform I'd gifted her on day one of training, she lifted her hand high into the air, and I registered the cheering, clapping, and shouting. The arena chanted her name as she crossed the center of the grounds, making her way to her competition.

44

Power

Nim

Cold-blooded murderer. Psychopathic killer.

I forced myself to lift my hand, to wave at the crowd of hybrids stomping their feet and shouting at the top of their lungs, hailing my entrance, while inside I seethed, misty rage fogging my view of the hornet who'd stripped my best friend of his life.

Murderer.

Monster.

The wide sleeve of my tunic flopped back to my elbow, revealing more of the bandages I'd painstakingly woven over the last day, scarcely stopping to eat or sleep. The work had almost cost me the time I needed to collect my other weapons, like the short sword I'd swiped from the Octavius estate that jabbed awkwardly into a sheath at my hip. Rags had told me the weapon was too heavy for me, that I wouldn't be able to heft it for long. But I didn't need it for long.

Just long enough.

I drew to a stop several feet from Verity, unable to force myself any closer, no matter how much side-eye Anders shot my direction. His introduction didn't register, and I tuned out the commander when the audio amplifier was passed his way. I didn't need to hear his bowing and scraping, his proclamations and promises of bloodshed.

Instead, I locked eyes with Sebastian, forcing my apologies into my gaze, hoping he would understand. The prince appeared gaunt, his eyes rimmed purple with sleepless nights, his cheeks pale from worry. But there was relief, too.

He was still with me. Still stood beside me.

The cool handle of the amplifier touched my hand, and I took it from the host, who shot me another look of irritation. *Get used to it, buddy.* I was no performer. Never had been. Never would be. I was me, unforgiving and broken as ever.

"Citizens of Eritris, by now you've likely heard of me. You've known me as the thief who lived amongst you on the streets of greenside, scraping every day to get by. I'm also the last living member of the Arachnae Duchy. No doubt, those two versions clash in your minds. I don't blame you, but I'm not here to make you piece them together in some macabre masterpiece."

Dust from the arena coated my throat and I spat, forcing moisture into my mouth. "I don't care if you support me as the thief you knew or hate me for the royalty I once was. All I want is for you to rally with me against this plague on our nation." I raised one long arm, index finger extended toward the commander whose eyes went to slits. I caught his gaze. Held it.

See me now. I dare you.

"This hornet murdered one of your own in greenside, on the streets he knew and *loved* and owned." My voice rose into a shout. "He murdered Jax Case right before me, slit his throat before he knew there was a threat." I squared my shoulders against the commander, conscious of the silence vibrating around us. "Commander Verity stole my best friend from me, cut him from your lives. He desecrated the streets of greenside, of your *home*." The crowd in the upper decks rose to their feet, stomping, jeering, clapping. "He is a con and a coward. For that, he will die. I promise you."

Never had I felt more powerful than I did now with the cheers of thousands at my back.

I was Nimmarah Arachnae. Orphan. Daughter. Greensider. Bluesider.

I didn't wait for the queen to rise, to announce the start of the final trial, the Trial of Power. No. I tossed the amplifier to the dirt and drew my sword with a shriek of metal, barely bringing it up in time to block Verity's downswing. Sparks flew where the metal crashed, and I dropped to a knee beneath the weight, forcing my momentum back up. The commander took a step back, all the room I needed to regain my footing.

Again and again, we drew together. His attacks brutal and heavy. It was all I could do to parry, dancing around and around, dodging the blows I could and blocking the ones I couldn't. Sweat streamed down my back, clotted in my hair, streaked across my face, but I didn't dare lift a sleeve to wipe it away. After a particularly hefty swing that caused vibrations to shake up and down my arms, I knew it was time to push him harder. Farther.

"What's wrong, Verity? I thought you were the Wing Commander." I rolled to avoid his next powerful swing, nearly losing my sword. But I was back on my feet soon enough. Just as I'd hoped, the thoughtful tactician had slipped farther away with every attack I blocked, and the hornet's face contorted with rage.

"I'm just a greensider," I tossed out, blinking sweat from my eyes. "An untrained little pest. A *spider* you should be able to crush with a single step. And you're losing."

The hornet staggered, hatred flickering across his features, eyes black as his soul. With a roar, he threw himself into the sky. He had the upper hand in the air. We both knew it. But he didn't know he'd fallen into my trap.

No sooner had his feet left the earth when I'd dropped my sword, sprinting for the center of the arena. I released my hold on my aether and slipped seamlessly into my secondary form, gaining speed as I went.

The hornet shot toward me, but the vibrations alerted me to his approach. I dodged the attack, zipping to the side so he missed by a maddening margin. A grin stole across my face. Though I'd hidden this side of myself, I was damned proud of my Arachnae blood. Never more so than now.

I reached for the thread at the base of my neck and pulled, slapping the sticky end to the first column I encountered, veering around it and narrowly dodging another dive-bomb attack by the hornet. He'd lost his sword at some point and now hefted dual stingers dripping with green venom in both hands.

Verity slashed out, but I was too quick, dodging around another column. He charged, then thought better of it. It was clear I was too fast on my extra legs. But he could still come at me from the sky. Or try to, anyway. Around and around, we went, my legs pumping, his screams of rage echoing in my ears. Could those in the highest seats see my plan? Understand the intention of my dizzying pattern?

Legs burning, lungs heaving, I dodged yet another of Verity's stingers, one tossed at me with lethal force. The edges of my vision were gray with fatigue, but I pushed past the pain and scrambled up the center column, pulling more thread between my hands, watching for the hornet. Waiting. A glint of metal. A blur of black. And I launched myself at him. One of those deadly spears snagged my tunic, but I twisted, wrapping myself around his body and landing with a bounce on the web I'd woven.

"What the—" the commander tugged at the sticky strings holding him taut, confusion blowing out his earlier fury.

I didn't bother with an explanation, hardly wasting a moment as I bound his arms and legs to the wider web, wrapping him up nice and tight. There was nothing stronger, nothing stickier than Arachnae thread when we willed it to be.

Now I could hear the cheers. The crowd had never been louder. I ripped the dagger from my belt. His dagger. The weapon he'd used to murder my best friend.

The hornet's eyes widened when I held up the hilt, mouth gaping in recognition.

In his ear, I hissed, "This is for Jax."

And drove the dagger toward his chest.

45

Only Way

Sebastian

Nim crumpled, the blade falling from her hands before it punched into the hornet's chest. Her fists flew to her head as if to keep her skull from splitting apart. I shot to my feet alongside a half dozen other royals. Screams ripped from her throat, raw and ragged. Animalistic. The dagger tumbled to the dirt at her side. Snared in her web, Verity stared with wide eyes, bucking his hips, his howls of outrage joining her shrieks of agony, searching for weaknesses in her trap.

I'd seen this before.

My head snapped to the side, eyes snagging on Vincent and the dials of the pocket watch he fiddled with in his lap. Without a doubt, I knew that was the device hidden in that box in his desk.

A sneer twisted my brother's ugly face. "You," I shouted, diving over the legs of a pair of heirs, my foot snagging on an errant ankle. Vincent's head shot up, and he shoved the device into his jacket pocket, shooting to his feet.

Too late.

I snagged his wrist, drawing him up short, and slammed him back into his chair. Females shrieked, and male hands groped at my body, struggling to separate us. But I was loath to be separated and fell into my brother, my hands diving deep into his vest. Nim's screams filled the arena in blind desperation.

My fingers wrapped around the cool metal casing of the contraption, and with a hiss of triumph, I ripped it from his pocket, snapping the chain connecting it to a belt around his narrow hips. Vincent scrambled for it, but I had the better angle, wings whirring as I ripped myself off his form. Two rows up, Rags and Grev shoved through a cluster of tightly-packed bodies, forcing their way toward me.

In my fist, the watch clicked, steady as a heartbeat. I fumbled with the trio of dials gracing the side of the device, frustration slicking my skin with sweat, and my fingers slipped on the steel. Vincent's hand wrapped around my wrist, struggling for purchase, but I ripped myself away. How did I shut the damn thing off?

Someone shouted, "He's free."

In my periphery, Verity flung himself off the webbing, reaching for Nim's dagger while she writhed and contorted, bloody froth flecking her mouth.

No.

With all my might, I threw the watch at the ground. It exploded, sending gears and chunks of metal every which way. Vincent threw himself at me with a snarl, eyes bloodshot and round with fury. The screaming in the arena stopped. I grappled with my brother, struggling to dislodge his grip while frantically looking over his shoulder. Nim threw herself out of the way of Verity's attack, but the weapon sliced open the shoulder of her jacket.

I shoved Vincent aside, grasping for the bars of the railing, heart slamming in my throat. My champion tumbled and caught herself with one arm, chest heaving. With effort, she rose to her knees and wiped the moisture from her mouth. Our eyes snagged for a single heartbeat, long enough for her mouth to open in a shout.

I couldn't hear it but read her lips: "Behind you."

Pain exploded in my shoulder. A dagger sliced through my bicep, and I flung myself to the side, clutching at the injury, panting. Vincent twirled the jawram in his hand, its edge dripping with my blood. A manic expression darkened his eyes, his jaw lengthened, wings snapping out behind him. Spikes drove through the fabric of his jacket, the poisonous ridges of his second form splitting the material.

"You're no brother of mine," he spat, lashing out with the weapon again.

I tripped over the leg of a chair, stumbling back, releasing my own aether. Other insects scrambled to get out of the way, leaving a wide circle around us. In my periphery, Rags threw herself against the barricade formed by soldiers, no doubt in Vincent's employ. Even if anyone *wanted* to help, there was no way through. This fight was between us.

Brother to brother. Heir to heir.

"Can't you see what my plan is, Sebastian?" Vincent ripped off the ruins of his jacket. "Or are you too dense? Too lost in your fanciful dreams? Just like you were as a pupa. Too stuck in your head to see what was right in front of you."

He ducked, missing the poisonous barbs I fired his way.

"You want to control this kingdom," I shouted, uncaring of who heard. "You want to take over their minds, force them to do your will." Several hybrids gasped in our periphery. "That's wrong, brother. It's sick."

"What did I say? Shortsighted. I want to see this kingdom succeed," Vincent shouted, throwing his arms wide. "The discontent will always be that way. Why should they be allowed to undermine our might when I could just harness it myself? For the good of the kingdom."

The flesh of Vincent's arms took on a greenish tinge, the surface sharp as armor. I mimicked him, the barbs sinking back into my skin and allowing the steel-like blades of my forearms to harden.

"How is this possible?" my mother cried, shoving through the arms of the guards. Her dress was ripped in several spots, strands of hair torn from her immaculate twist. Her expression was frantic as she stared at her eldest son. The horror dawning on her face. "Vincent, what—what have you done?"

On the other side of the soldiers, Micah spoke up. "I made the clock for him. It does what Seb claims. Vincent said he wanted to help the lower classes reach their potential, to learn new skills to aid the kingdom. I had no idea he planned anything like this."

"Then I'm surrounded by idiots," Vincent snapped. "The crown is mine. My will is the only way."

"I won't let you," I snarled, holding my arms up, wings flapping, ready to propel myself forward. Ready to attack.

"Then your body will be among the last I step over to make this kingdom see what's right for it." And he flung himself toward me.

Nim

Verity was fast. But I was faster. That narrow margin was the only reason I still stood. That and the reinforced bandages I'd painstakingly woven together. My armor—its fibers weakening under the repeated blows. Already, I bled from a half dozen cuts where the dagger had snuck past my defenses.

But I refused to back down despite being unable to tap into my aether. It was as if the shrill screech of the music had snipped the threads I held to my magic.

I refused to stop.

Not with Jax's laughter in my ears, his face imprinted on the backs of my eyelids.

My fist caught the commander in the jaw. His head snapped back. One eye was already swelling where another solid punch of mine had caught him. He stumbled, then kicked out, his leg knocking mine out from under me. I smacked into the dirt, choking on dust, gasping and writhing. The fall had whipped the wind from my lungs. It hurt so much. Too much.

A shadow fell lengthwise across my chest. Verity regained his footing, stalking forward.

Coughing, I rolled, finding my hands and knees, crawling away from the heavy footfalls. Incapable of catching my breath. Red tinged my vision.

Not like this. It couldn't end like this.

Sebastian

The blades of our arms sang, crashing together again and again. I snapped my jaws, the razor edge of my teeth nearly catching the meat of my brother's shoulder when he tumbled out of the way too slowly. Blood dripped down my side, the injured muscles weak with pain.

I swiped a sleeve at my forehead, blotting the sweat, and used my wings to propel myself at him, my fingers closing around his wrists when he flung them up in defense.

"Don't you see?" Vincent said, "I can usher in a new world. *We* can usher in a new way of thinking. One of our own making. Where we need no more Trials, no more bloodshed. Because they will see us as their rightful rulers. Us."

I tossed him away from me, and he caught himself before his skull cracked on the stone. "There is no more us. No more ruling class. This system is flawed, and it's time someone makes it right."

Vincent tipped his head back and laughed, a harsh sound that rattled my bones. "Oh, Sebastian, how naïve you are. There's only one way to make this right: through power."

A scream punctuated his drawling statement. One I recognized.

Forgetting myself, forgetting the danger of the male who lay sprawled on the ground, I spun toward the arena where Nim stumbled backward, gripping the hilt of the dagger buried in her abdomen.

"Looks like the bitch knows whose world this is now, too," Vincent drawled over my shoulder.

Nim

Agony spiked like lightning through my body, flickering across my vision.

No. It wouldn't end like this.

My aether exploded out of me in a sonic boom. The being that had sliced me from that cocoon of deadly threads as a child emerged now, shoving me backward in my mind.

Verity's gloating laughter stilled. His eyes snared on my face. On whatever inhuman creature he glimpsed there. The me I forced deep down inside. The monster I caged because I refused to lose myself to its wild nature. To rail against all those who'd wronged me.

It—I—was finally free.

In a beat, we planted our four long limbs in the dirt. Our body rose, our human legs dangling over the earth. We skittered forward, overtaking the hornet in the space it took to draw a single breath. He landed on his back, writhing. A bug stuck in a trap. Our trap.

Leaning down, our body horizontal to the ground, we distended our jaw and roared in his face, blood and spittle flecking his skin. His pupils were flecks of black in the center of his irises. The crotch of his pants was wet, a noxious odor rising from the liquid.

The monster drew back, giving me room to speak.

"You took my friend from me. And it will cost you everything."

Our long foreleg drilled forward. Ribs cracked. Blood sprayed. We punched through his chest, ripping ribs and sinewy muscle out of our way. In his chest, his heart throbbed desperately—the blood black where it congealed. And we dove down, teeth sinking into that beating flesh.

And tore it from his chest.

Sebastian

Black blood streamed down her face as Nim rose, a chunk of thick muscle grasped in her fangs, lethal poison dribbling down her chin. With a hiss, she spat out the piece of heart. Her contorted features lengthened further, and she shrieked in triumph. A sound that made my blood run cold.

Her arms lowered again and this time she ripped what remained of the commander's heart from his chest and lifted it high, squeezing the blood so it rained down on her form.

"No." Vincent breathed. He'd drawn up beside me, his fists white where they gripped the bars. He repeated the word again. His champion was dead. Verity was gone. And with it—

"I will not let you take the throne," he snarled.

I glimpsed the slash of his forearm, the lethal edge of the blade tilted my way. But I was prepared. I snagged the sword a guard had dropped, one I'd backed toward with careful intent. Hefted it and slammed it through Vincent's chest.

His eyes rounded. His arms reached. Then he went limp, choking and gasping. I released the sword, still lodged in his chest, and thrust it away from me in disgust. A dark waterfall of blood dribbled over his lips, dripping off his chin. And he went slack.

Brother for brother.

Champion for champion.

Blood for blood.

The arena had gone ominously silent. At some point, the soldiers had dropped their barricade, jaws slack and eyes wide as they stared at their prince, lying unmoving in a pool of his own blood. Their dead commander, his chest flayed open in the center of the arena, a shrieking monster with two feet planted on his corpse.

Limping away from the massacred remains of the hornet, my spider surged forward. The heart of her victim dropped from her grip, splattering on the grass. Gradually, carefully, she wrangled her aether. Her long legs folded into her shoulders once more, the hunch of her back returning. Her extra eye sank back into her flesh. Blood streaked her skin, her wraps shredded and hanging from her limbs. It was so quiet I could hear her every footfall, make out every shudder of her breath. The knife still stuck from her belly, grotesque and ugly. But she ignored the pain.

For one long moment, she stood before me, head arched back, body notched in odd angles. But her eyes were as sharp and all-seeing as always. Jerkily, she folded into a crouch, one knee pressed to the dirt, her hands braced on the cap of the other. Her head arched in subjugation.

"Your highness."

Around us, more knees hit the ground. Hybrids falling in supplication.

That same title dropping from their lips.

Highness.

I'd won.

We'd won.

Eritris had a new king.

46

Enough Incentive

Nim — One week later

I didn't attend the coronation.

I'd agreed to fight for Sebastian, champion his cause, and bring him the victory he deserved. But nothing about our arrangement stated a requirement of attending ceremonies once my responsibility was complete.

Besides, I'd read his speech beforehand.

I think Grev had hoped it would convince me to stay.

I swear to you, citizens of Eritris, change is on the horizon.

My legs stretched out before me, the black of my attire blending in well with the broken tiles of the rooftop. The blue of the ocean glinted off the shuttered windows, and I shuffled my shoulders, seeking a more comfortable spot against the side of the duchy, back braced on the latticed boards between the windows.

The stitches lacing up my stomach wound twinged, but I resisted the maddening urge to itch them. Verity's knife had inflicted significant internal damage. I'd nearly bled out on the battlefield, keeling over moments after the prince realized his new authority. However, thanks to a black-blue paste forced upon me by Seb's surviving brother and the healer moths at the castle, I'd pulled through. The injury still ached and I couldn't move quickly without risk of pulling out the stitches, but the fever had finally broken. I had pulled through.

Two days ago, I'd left the room assigned to me inside the keep, crawled down the many corridors to the exit, and returned to the Firestone. Devlin was a mess of conflicting emotion, as expected, but together we'd propped one another up, sharing our mixed grief and relief.

The loss of Jax in my life cut a massive hole in my heart.

We've endured much loss these last many weeks. Hear me now, the Trials will end with my rule.

Now I was here, in blueside, Moldona unfolded before me in a complex array of colors and patterns. Many people bustling on the other side of the wall couldn't care less about the transition of power. To them, a new king was just another hybrid in a position of power.

They had no idea how much Sebastian meant to change.

During a meeting with advisors that included me, his guards, Prince Micah, mother, and a handful of others whose faces I knew but couldn't name, Sebastian had agreed to don the crown. Too much change at once was a shock to the system. At the same time, he promised to start small and gradually implement his plans of electing officials to speak for the divided factions of the kingdom, diminish his power, and dilute the old ways until they melted into the new.

I vow to lead you with the just and merciful oversight you're due.

The church had protested vehemently, but Sebastian refused to be swayed from that promise. Several dukes and duchesses also raised their voices in protest, arguing the Trials were as much a part of the kingdom's code as insects were in our blood. But Seb cut their arguments down one by one. No one would shed blood for the entertainment of choosing the next sovereign ever again.

Several Sai children ran down the street, sticks clenched in their many tiny hands, chasing one another—a game of knights and robbers. I was familiar with their antics and kept an eye on them until they rounded a corner.

How different things would have been had I grown up like them.

From my pocket, I withdrew a hefty sack of coins that clinked and clanked. I dipped a hand inside the opening, emerging with a pair of crowns, which I lined up on the backs of my hands and danced across my knuckles, the gold flashing in the sunlight.

Together, we will usher in a brighter future.

Sebastian and his ideals. I shook my head at his vision for the country, but I had never met someone I believed in as much as I did him. And I'd grown up under Dev's roof.

A shadow dropped onto the rooftop beside me, and I shaded my eyes. Seb drew his wings back with a snap and straightened first his collar, then his cuffs. Cracked tiles creaked and splintered beneath his feet and he dropped beside me. A circlet of gold nestled atop his auburn hair was the only evidence of his altered status.

"I missed you at the coronation," he murmured lightly.

I dropped the coins back into the bag one at a time. "I'm sure Rags was more than capable of keeping your ego in check in my absence."

"It was a brilliant affair. So much pomp. All the frills, the celebrity. Everyone of note was there. I could see the greed and desire to twist my ear to their fortunes on all their faces." He laced his fingers atop his propped-up knee. "You would have loathed every moment of it."

"Why do you think I'm here and not there?" I enjoyed this. The ease of our conversation. How relaxed I felt in his company. My thoughts listened to, my opinions weighed and considered.

Thinking back to that darkened alley, part of me had known he meant me no harm. I'd never feared him, never resented him. To me, he was just another person.

A person who now wore a crown.

I released a snort of amusement.

"I'll admit, I'm surprised you chose here of all places to spend your first day of freedom." The sunlight slanted across Seb's face, turning his dark brown eyes a milky shade of chocolate. "I assumed you'd want the Arachnae estate razed. I would have complied, you know, called it a token of my appreciation."

Exhaling deeply, something that might have been a sigh, I stroked the surface of the cracked window beside me. "This is just a place. Nothing more, nothing less. My fears were never rooted in the house but the people within its walls." I paused, weighing my thoughts. "I believe there's still plenty of life left in these shoddy bones, so much more good it can bring our country despite its sordid and bloody history."

Sebastian regarded me, then nodded at the bag nestled between our thighs. "You have your freedom and your gold. What are your plans now?" The bump in his throat bobbed. He reached for my hand, then drew back, fingers clenching. "Still heading for the border? The Idilean delegation will depart in the morning if you wish to accompany them. I have it on good faith they'd love to take you under their considerable wings."

He was rambling, a sign of nerves.

I hummed softly, low in my throat, and scratched an itch on my collarbone. Sebastian tracked the movement. Would I leave? Did I *want* to leave? This city had brought me so much pain, so much devastation. But it also bore fruit of promise. My memories of Jax lived on these streets, within these walls. Devlin had only ever shown me compassion. And Ms. Whitmere was a light in the absolute darkness.

Once I'd thought my only place in this world was elsewhere. Now... I wasn't so sure.

Devlin's confession following the death of his son, his insistence that I consider my place and what I stood for had solidified my spine and forced me to think objectively since my life had spiraled out of control along with the prince's—king's—offer.

Sebastian mistook my silence. "I never wanted this power, you know. I never wanted to lead this country, to have tens of thousands of hybrids look to me for the answers."

"I know."

"Hael, I left for Riten's sake." He tried to rake his fingers through his hair, only to catch on the unfamiliar heft of his newly donned crown. "I wanted my freedom. The salt of the sea, the promise of new countries, ambitious and curious people. I had it. It was all in my grasp. But I gave it up. You know why?"

His eyes implored mine. "Why?"

"Because somewhere along the line, my dream changed. My idea of freedom... shifted. This—" He tapped the crown with a sad lilt of his lips— "is my future now."

This time it was I who reached for him, he who stilled when I laced my fingers with his. "It's what makes you the perfect ruler, Sebastian. Maybe someday you'll see that."

His grip firmed around mine. The distance between us closed.

"It never was my dream to fight in the name of this country, either," I mused, staring out over the city, the guards patrolling the wall. "I wanted to leave and start fresh. I never wanted to get sucked into the plans of a pure-hearted prince with a vision of grandeur. A king who needs support to fulfill his worldly desires. Yet here I am, sitting on the rooftop of a home that was never mine, contemplating a situation where I help him. Again."

The king's eyes glimmered brightly, a smile curving his lips. "Are you saying you'll stay?"

My answering grin felt coy. "Maybe. If there's enough incentive."

He clicked his tongue. "You're saying a life spent at court arguing with a bunch of haughty royals bent on maintaining the power structure isn't incentive?"

"Not quite."

"How about a promise of change? Of witnessing Moldona transition into a better version of itself?"

"Still not enough."

"Then what about this?" Sebastian uncurled his other palm, the one not clasped in my tight grasp. I couldn't contain my gasp, taking in the silver bracelet nestled against his tan skin. Delicate nettles were carved into the metal.

"You got it back?" My voice sounded breathy to my ears, and my hand shook when I lifted the gift from his hand, the metal winking in the light as I held it before me.

The king released a laugh. "It wasn't easy, but when I couldn't find you before the final trial, I knew I had to do something. I guess that meant recovering something precious—for someone I consider even more precious."

This time it was I who gulped, who tilted my chin toward him, heart fluttering in my breast in an unfamiliar patter. One that spelled promises and futures and a world in which I had never imagined myself living.

"Will you stay by my side, Nimmarah Arachnae? Daughter of Greenside with a dynasty of ancient blood." His face was so close to mine. I could count his eyelashes, every freckle dusting the rims of his cheekbones. "I can't promise our road will be easy. In fact, I believe it will be quite the opposite, but that's why I want you with me, and me with you. Because somehow in this screwed up realm we found each other, and I want to explore what that means." He leaned in so close I could smell the mint on his breath. "Will you?"

The pressure of our lips touching was light and easy. The second touch, more insistent. How I came to grip the lapels of his jacket, holding him against me, his arms wrapped around my waist in turn, I'll never know. He tasted like freedom and righteousness and visions of a kingdom so sweet. "Let's take it one day at a time, my king."

His lashes lifted, expression imploring. "You'll stay?"

"We'll start with tonight, my king." The full smile stretching the wraps of my face felt foreign and perfectly, wonderfully right.

His answering smile deepened, want flickering in the depths of his eyes. He stroked a hand down my cheek, brushing the curve of my jaw. "I like the sound of that."

I brushed his lips with mine again. "Then let's see what tomorrow brings."

Please consider rating or leaving a review for Of Monsters and Madness on your favorite retailer or book-tracking website. I'd love to find out what you think and grow the community around my novels.

The part of my brain that loves spinning stories never quits, so I'm always tinkering with some project or another. Stay up-to-date with my work by signing up for my newsletter. In those, you'll discover book updates, behind-the-scenes takeaways, and even free, exclusive content.

To find out more, head to www.septemberthomas.com.

Author's Note

This book is such a joy to talk about because of the reactions I get:

"That sounds so cool!" or....

"You wrote a book about... insect-people?"

I'm still not entirely sure how or why I took all the steps necessary to put together a book about an insect-hybrid nation on the cusp of a civil war, but it started with an image:

A girl covered head to foot in long wraps not dissimilar to ace bandages. Wraps she willingly put on every day to disguise part of herself from the world.

What was she hiding and what happened to spur that decision?

Where did she live and how did those around her handle her decision?

And since it's fantasy: what were the rules of the magical system?

Somehow, some way, that led me to a world ruled by insects and spiders. A place where the abnormal is completely normal. A country seeking hope in a government that seemed to give none.

My editing partner-in-crime Fiona McLaren, Riten love her, she heard my pitch and fell in love with the concept. It was her research that pushed me to create a distinct setting, forcing me to consider the complexities of the hybrid manifestation, and bask in the weirdness I'd dreamed up. I wouldn't have wanted to take this journey with anyone else.

To Rebecca Frank, the bold cover designer who's abilities I envy....

To my family, who always asks how my writing is going and

speaking with pride of my accomplishments. Not everyone has such a fantastic support system. To Maureen for listening to my ramblings and quickly throwing your hand up when I asked for ARC readers. To Anna for reading this book despite your disgust for all things arachnid. To Josh, for understanding when I need to hash out a theme or when I just desire silence.

And to Sydney, the beautiful fluff who never leaves my side, my twin in another life. The puppy as special as she is wonderful. Here's to seven books. Let's make it eight.

About the Author

September Thomas is the author of The Three Kingdoms trilogy and The Elemental Gods series. She lives in Nebraska with her boyfriend and rescued Australian Cattle Dog. She also boasts a large collection of owls that some consider amusingly ridiculous.

You can connect with me on:

🌐 https://www.septemberthomas.com

f https://www.facebook.com/SeptemberThomasAuthor

🔗 https://www.instagram.com/september.thomas

🔗 https://www.pinterest.com/september_thomas

Subscribe to my newsletter:

✉ https://www.septemberthomas.com

Also by September Thomas

Of Dragons and Defiance
Seventeen years after hiding from the wolven conquerors who murdered her kingdom's royal family and defeated its dragon shifters, Telleree Falk is thrust into a rebellion alongside two drakken—one a loyal friend, the other a dangerous enigma. As war brews and hearts tangle, Tell must decide if she will fight for her kingdom... or let it burn.

Walk on Water
After 2,000 years, magic is finally back. 17-year-old Zara Ramone wants none of it. Too bad a dark force bent on destruction won't let her stay on the sidelines.

Fan the Flame
My name is Zara Ramone.
I should have died several times now.
But the fates aren't ready to let me go.

Wind and Reign

When the magic turns against its maker, is she ready?

Zara Ramone set out to get stronger.

She didn't expect to uncover a sinister plot to destroy magic forever.

War of Earth

Reincarnated God of Water Zara Ramone finally understands who she is and what she stands for, but will she have the fortitude to overcome her greatest challenge yet?

Rise from Ruin

Zara Ramone sacrificed her magic, body, and soul to save the world from annihilation, only to release a far greater evil.